ALPHAS OF
Danger

PROCEEDS BENEFITING
A PAWS FOR ABILITY · SINCE 1998

Shayla Black
Lexi Blake
Mari Carr
Kris Cook
Anissa Garcia

Kym Grosso
Jenna Jacob
Kennedy Layne
Isabella LaPearl
Carrie Ann Ryan

A Once Upon An Alpha Anthology

Devoted To Wicked
Copyright © 2017 Shayla Black

Countdown
Copyright © 2017 Lexi Blake

Power Struggle
Copyright © 2017 Mari Carr

Cia Covert Team: Rainbow Knights
Copyright © 2017 Kris Cook

With A Vengeance
Copyright © 2017 Anissa Garcia

Hard Asset
Copyright © 2017 Kym Grosso

Revenge On The Rocks
Copyright © 2017 Jenna Jacob

Seducing Danger
Copyright © 2017 Kennedy Layne

Enforce Her
Copyright © 2017 Isabella Lapearl

Executive Ink
Copyright © 2017 Carrie Ann Ryan

DISCLAIMER

All rights reserved. No part of this book may be reproduced or transmitted in any form, including electronic or mechanical, without written permission from the publisher, except in the case of brief quotations embedded in critical articles or reviews.

This is a work of fiction. Names, characters, businesses, places, events, and incidents are either the products of the author's imagination or used in a fictitious manner. Any resemblance to actual persons, living or dead, or actual events is purely coincidental.

This book is licensed for your personal enjoyment only. This book may not be re-sold or given away to other people. If you would like to share this book with another person, please purchase an additional copy for each person you share it with. If you are reading this book and did not purchase it, or it was not purchased for your use only, then you should return it to the seller and purchase your own copy. Thank you for respecting the author's work.

NOTICE

This is an adult erotic romance book with love scenes and mature situations. It is only intended for adult readers over the age of 18.

Published: Once Upon An Alpha 2017
Cover Design: Cover Me Darling – Marisa-rose Shor
Cover Model: Jase Dean
Photographer: Wooden Gate Production
Editor: Blue Otter Editing, LLC
Proof Reader: Fedora Chen
Formatting by: Indie Formatting Services

ISBN-10: 0-9982222-3-2

ISBN-13: 978-0-9982222-3-3

Welcome to *Alphas of Danger*, Once Upon An Alpha's second anthology. We have brought you a collection of stories from authors who we love and admire. Each story features an alpha with a twist in the story, we're bringing suspense to the table! We hope you'll fall in love with them.

All of the proceeds from the sale of this book will go to *4 Paws for Ability*. *4 Paws for Ability* is a worldwide agency that enriches the lives of children and veterans with disabilities by training and placing quality, task-trained service dogs. For more information about this nonprofit organization: http://4pawsforability.org/.

In this anthology you'll read stories from the following authors, who have graciously donated their time and work to this great cause.

A HUGE thank you to all the contributing authors, designers, model, designer and formatter. With out their generous donation of their time and phenomenal talent. This would have never been possible, all because you support the 4 Paws for Ability I stand behind and are as passionate about the cause as I am.

AUTHORS
    SHAYLA BLACK
    LEXI BLAKE
    MARI CARR
    KRIS COOK
    ANISSA GARCIA
    KYM GROSSO
    JENNA JACOB
    KENNEDY LAYNE
    ISABELLA LAPEARL
    CARRIE ANN RYAN

DESIGNER
COVER ME DARLING – MARISA-ROSE SHOR

COVER MODEL
JASE DEAN

PHOTOGRAPHER
WOODEN GATE PRODUCTION

EDITING
BLUE OTTER EDITING, LLC

PROOF READER
FEDORA CHEN

FORMATTING
INDIE FORMATTING SERVICES

To the service dogs that support our children when they feel a little unsteady.

*To the children that show us parents how strong we are
when we are in doubt.*

*To families and the best salt circle of friends.
May the salt circle forever be strong for the times one of us feels uncertain.*

*To my two beautiful girls, Amber and Autumn.
My own strength lies within you and your daddy.*

To you, the reader. Thank you.

*We hope you enjoy our anthology. Read at your own risk.
Overheating can occur thanks to these very steamy stories.*

*With Love,
Shannon Hunt
Once Upon An Alpha*

Devoted to Wicked

SHAYLA BLACK

1

Karis Weston paced the cold tile floor of her hotel room, not really seeing the oceanfront paradise that had lured her to Cancún. It had been twelve hours—a whole night—since she'd sent out a cry for help. She hadn't slept a wink, hadn't stopped shaking, hadn't stopped wondering why someone had targeted *her*.

The phone on the nightstand jangled loudly. She started and gasped, then lunged for the receiver and pressed it to her ear. "Hello?"

"Karis?"

"Yeah." She breathed a sigh of relief at the familiar voice. "Cutter? Thank god. Did Jolie pass you my message? What's going on? I didn't hear from her. Are she and the baby—"

"They're fine. Take a deep breath. Your sister got your message and called me because she and Heath have gone to the hospital to—"

"The hospital?" Alarm pealed through Karis. "So they're not fine? I told Jolie that all those long hours at the office, even if Betti's expansion is going well, was bad for her pregnancy and—"

"Hold up. She's not having a miscarriage. Your mother dropped in unexpectedly after she and Wayne the Pain broke up."

The sarcasm in Cutter's voice mirrored Karis's own opinion. Her mom should never have started dating her soon-to-be ex-husband's brother.

"Is my mom okay?" *Other than not being smart about her love life...*

"Apparently Wayne drove to Dallas early this morning so he could tell Diana face to face that he never had any intention of leaving his wife. Your mom got mad and um...swung a garden hoe at him—don't ask—but caught herself in the leg instead. She's having an x-ray and stitches now." He huffed. "Things are handled here, but Jolie can't come to Mexico, and Heath needs to stay behind to make sure she doesn't overdo it. That's why they called me. Tell me what happened with you, little gypsy."

Karis softened at his nickname for her. Despite getting off to an awkward start, she and Cutter had become fast friends when he'd done his best to bodyguard her through a threat to Jolie and her women's apparel company, Betti. Too bad she couldn't have mustered an iota of chemistry with him. He was a great guy.

Unlike his older brother, Cage, who was a raving jackass.

She knew that...and yet, just like her mother, Karis had let her terrible taste in men tell her hormones that it was a fabulous idea to fall for the older Bryant. In fact, she'd taken one look at him, flashed hot all over, and instantly wondered if he could be her soul mate. After too much tequila and an amazing one-night stand, proof of his assholery had soon cured her of that notion.

If she saw him on her deathbed, it would still be too soon.

"You there?" Cutter prodded. "Did you hear me?"

Focus. "Yeah. Just trying to collect my thoughts. I'm rattled. I haven't slept. I don't feel safe and—"

"You've been through a lot. I'm tied up here in Dallas but don't worry. I sent the cavalry. He should arrive any moment. You're going to be all right."

She froze. "Who did you send?"

A pounding on the door interrupted the conversation, startling Karis. She pressed a hand to her chest.

"That's him now," Cutter said. "You two can call me later."

Cage. Spend time with him. Talk to him. No doubt she would have to resist him, too.

She sighed. "Come in."

Cage strolled inside her hotel room, his tall, rangy body crowding her against the doorway. He peered at her with dark, hungry eyes as he dropped his bag. "You look good."

She glanced down at herself. Her entire vacation wardrobe had consisted of bikinis, cover-ups, an occasional pair of short-shorts, and high-heeled sandals. This morning after tossing and turning sleeplessly, she'd rushed through a shower, wondering if whoever had scared the hell out of her intended to come back and finish the job. Absently, she'd tossed on an off-white, almost-too-small bikini with a rose-and-swirl pattern over her breasts. The contraption was held together by thin, sunny yellow straps. Cage's stare walked all over her top before straying to the lone flower barely covering her down there. Sure, she'd tossed on a lacy cover-up but it was entirely transparent, there for decoration more than actual protection from the sun or prying eyes.

If she'd known she was going to have to deal with Cage, she would have brought turtlenecks and mom jeans or a nun's habit—something to ensure he'd never look at her twice.

Refusing to let his perusal fluster her more, Karis shut the door behind him with a soft snick. This wasn't about them or the night they'd spent together, just about ending this ill-advised vacation and getting home.

"You mean I look good for a girl who's had everything important stolen from her hotel room and currently has no way of getting home? Don't bother with the compliment. I don't need it."

Her reply came out bitchier than she intended. It had been a rough night, and she was always grouchy when she hadn't slept. Coupled with all the uncertainty, the hint of danger, and the feeling that she'd been violated, Karis wasn't at her best.

"You need help." Cage's face softened. "I understand and I'll help you. But just saying...you always look good to me."

The unexpected compliment came out both sincere and serious—

Oh, he better *not* have done what she suspected, not if he wanted to keep his balls. "Who did you freaking send?"

Cutter didn't answer right away. "Relax. You're in good hands. I'll hold down the fort here. I'm sure your sister will update you about your mom when she has news. See you when you get home, little gypsy. Take care."

"Don't you even think—"

But Cutter did more than think about hanging up. She'd only finished half her sentence when he actually did. Damn it. Grumbling, she slammed the phone down.

Maybe she was wrong. Maybe Cage wasn't on the other side of the door, waiting to needle and poke and irritate her with his disreputable good looks and signature tomcat smile. But when she stomped across the room and wrenched the door open, all her wishful thinking went out the window.

"Hi, cupcake." He gave her a wink and a teasing smile.

She knew exactly what sort of man he was and yet he still made her belly flutter. *What is wrong with me?*

The muss of his golden hair hung low on his forehead, flirting with his eyes. He clearly hadn't shaved in a couple of days, and the stubble dusting his jaw made it look even sharper. He'd abandoned his winter coat and draped it over the duffel dangling from his right hand in favor of a faded blue tank top that read TEQUILA AND TACOS.

Karis gritted her teeth and did her best to ignore the broad, bulging muscles of his shoulders, now filling her doorframe. She didn't like Cage here because she didn't like him, period. She didn't want to *feel* anything for him. Been there, done that. She'd burned the T-shirt. He was the kind of man who would never be faithful. After a lifetime of watching her mother fall for that kind of guy repeatedly only to wind up brokenhearted every time, she refused to follow suit.

Sure, she could slam the door in his face or play dumb and ask why he'd come. But her sister and brother-in-law couldn't help her out of this scrape. Neither could Cutter. She'd already tried to solve her problem alone, to no avail. If she wanted to go home, she had to rely on two things she would never have imagined Cage was capable of. She tried not to let his words make her feel marshmallowy inside.

"Thanks." She gave a halfhearted shrug. "I'm sorry your brother sent you to 'rescue' me. I know you have better things to do."

"I don't."

She frowned. "This is awkward."

"Not for me."

Of course not. Everything seemed to roll off his back, even the feelings she'd shared with him that breathtaking night. Whatever. It wasn't as if she cared. Okay, she did…a little. But he didn't need to know that. The best way to convey ambivalence was to simply pretend that he didn't affect her one way or another.

"Great. I appreciate you coming here to help me out. Did your brother have you bring my passport photo so I can get home?"

"Yeah." He made no move to hand it over. "But you still haven't told me what happened."

She sighed. For whatever reason, he wasn't going to just hand over the picture. Did he think that after what happened a few weeks ago she'd be amenable to falling into bed with him once more?

Think again, buster.

"I've been on this vacation with Jolie's receptionist and my friend, Wisteria. She just broke up with her boyfriend." Again, but this time most likely for good. "I came back to the room after dinner and a couple of drinks at the pool bar. The door was wide open. Someone had picked the lock on my suitcase and taken everything—cash, what little jewelry I have, credit card, and my passport. I told Wisteria to go home on the flight we'd originally booked this morning. No sense in her losing a plane ticket and missing work when she couldn't help me. Then I called my sister, who called Cutter, who apparently called you. That's it."

He nodded. "Anybody following you while you've been here?"

Now he was slipping into cop mode. It was his job, and she was glad he had skills, but it probably wasn't going to help this far from Dallas. "Not that I'm aware of."

He scowled. "Anybody been flirting with you?"

Karis refused to answer that question. She'd come here in part to escape the sudden cold that had enveloped the North Texas area as January came to a close...and in part to forget Cage. They'd spent one hell of a New Year's Eve together, and with every kiss and touch, she'd believed they had something special. What she'd discovered the following week had blown that foolish hope to hell.

She lifted her shoulder in an offhanded shrug. "It's not as if I came here to be alone."

Karis hadn't planned to be...but she had somehow ended up by herself. On their first night here, Wisteria had met a hunk from the Hill Country, located a couple of hours south of Dallas. The two of them had hit it off instantly. Hayden seemed completely different from her previous douche of a boyfriend, and they had been inseparable for the seven days and six nights they'd vacationed in Cancún. In truth, she'd barely seen Wisteria after the woman had met him. And as luck would have it, he'd been able to change his flight to travel home with her. She was probably landing in Dallas now and finding something way more interesting to do than dealing with the former lover she wished she'd never taken.

Cage's jaw clenched. "Who have you been spending time with while you've been here?"

He sounded a little bit jealous.

"I'm sure it hardly matters, especially to you."

"Is that what you think?" He cocked his head and sent her a challenging stare. "Enlighten me why."

She had this fantasy of telling him she'd figured out he was a cheater and a liar, but what would it solve? She refused to give him the satisfaction or to care what he did anymore. And if she kept her attitude nonchalant, he would back off sooner or later.

She shrugged. "Well, the night we spent together was pretty meaningless, so—"

"Is that how you'd categorize it?"

Now he sounded downright pissed, so she switched tactics. "Can we talk about that later? Right now, I'd really like to focus on getting my paperwork in order so I can go home. Isn't that the reason you're here?"

He didn't look pleased, and Karis wondered why he wasn't breathing a sigh of relief that she'd let him off the proverbial hook.

"All right," he said finally. "Have you talked to resort security? The *policía*?"

"Yeah. Apparently, there are no security cameras in the hallways, so they can only see people coming off and getting on the elevators, but I was gone during a three-hour window and a lot of people were milling around my floor during that time. So I don't expect anything will come from the police report. I spent part of last night printing out the forms on the State Department's website so I can get a new passport. Thankfully, I still had my driver's license in my pocket, so all I needed was the passport picture. Thanks for bringing it to me. FedEx would have worked, too. But I can take it from here."

"Look at you go, Miss Independent," he quipped, shaking his head. "But that's not how this works. I'll be staying with you until you fly home."

She gaped at him. "It will probably be a couple of days."

"All right."

A terrible thought occurred to her. "Where do you think you're sleeping?"

With a glance around, he took in the room—the unforgiving tile floors, the sofa that was way too short to accommodate his six-three frame, and the king-size bed. He nodded at the mattress. "Next to you. It's not as if we haven't slept together before."

Karis stepped back. It was one thing to resist him for a couple of hours, but he looked good enough to nibble, eat, slurp, suck, and lick. How would she outlast him for a couple of days? Her willpower wasn't that strong, especially because she remembered how mind-blowing he was in the sack.

"No. Absolutely not." She shook her head.

"Your sister made me promise I'd stay with you, get to the bottom of this, and escort you safely to your plane. I'm a man who keeps his word."

She almost snorted at that, but he hadn't actually made her any promises when they'd rung in the new year together buzzed and naked and orgasmic.

With a sigh, she slung her fist on her hip. It was on the tip of her tongue to ask him what the hell he was up to, but she refused to get into this now. She simply wanted to go home.

"Can't you get another room?"

"If this thief broke in once, what's to say he couldn't do it again?" Cage glanced back at the door. "I don't see any sign of forced entry. And since they don't have electronic key cards, I'm guessing he picked the lock with a little finesse. What's to stop him from coming back for seconds?"

Nothing. Which was why Karis hadn't slept a wink last night. "Fine. You can sleep here. Keep your hands and any other roving parts of your body to yourself."

He shrugged and flipped her the kind of annoying half smile that made her want to scream and climb his body all at once. "We'll see, cupcake."

AFTER DICKING AROUND AT THE US EMBASSY FOR MOST OF THE DAY AND getting Karis's paperwork in order, Cage helped her into a taxi and they headed back to the resort. The officials said they would do their best to process her passport in two business days. He was hopeful that would happen, but he wasn't holding his breath.

Once they'd reached the upscale land of palm trees, umbrella drinks, and crystal water, Cage all but carried Karis up to her room. By the time they got through the door, she looked ready to fall over.

"Take a nap. I'll order us some room service."

She shook her head. "I'm going to find a lounger by the pool and some food. You can stay and nap if you want."

A biting quip streaked through his brain, but he swallowed it back. Not for the first time, he wondered what was up her ass. Their New Year's fling had been everything. Ground-shaking. Life-altering. Heart-bending. The next morning, he'd gotten tied up in an unforeseeable situation that had taken a long, sad week to extricate himself from. He'd called Karis the moment he could. She'd wanted absolutely nothing to do with him then—or now. Even repeated calls to his brother hadn't shed any light.

"Wherever you go, I'm going, too."

She looked exasperated but too exhausted to argue. "Suit yourself."

He almost told her that he always did—then she started peeling off her T-shirt and shimmying out of her shorts to reveal the tiny bikini beneath. Yeah, he'd seen it through the short, lacy getup she'd been wearing earlier, but now there was absolutely nothing to disrupt his view of her lean, sun-kissed body. The top barely contained her lush breasts. He didn't mind seeing her cleavage and healthy swells at all… but he didn't want some other guy looking at them.

As she reached for a cover-up and a pair of flip-flops, he grabbed the room key and thrust it in his pocket. "Lead the way."

When he opened the door, she sidled past him, looking over her shoulder. "You don't have to babysit me."

Cage let the door shut and checked the lock behind him. Flimsier than shit. Theft was likely a raging problem here if that was the best defense between the contents of a guest's room and a stranger.

Shaking his head, he hustled to catch up to Karis, who was halfway down the hall, pretty ass swishing with every step. Fuck, he hadn't forgotten brushing the underwear from those cheeks, kissing them during his oral travels across her body, clutching them as he plunged deeper into her with every thrust.

"You been wearing that bathing suit around the resort all week?" He glanced at the round flesh half peeking out from the formfitting fabric.

Her thighs looked sleek, as if she was the sort of girl whose cardio often included a good run. She had a bit of thigh gap, enough to look good in tiny outfits but not so much that he worried she was starving. Her filigree tattoo began mid-back and wound gracefully to the small of her spine with feminine swirls and curved lines, then disappeared into her bikini bottoms. It turned him the fuck on. Everything about her did, from the wispy ringlets curling at her nape in the humidity to her narrow feet.

"I've got a collection of similar ones. Why?" She pressed the button to call the elevator.

Because he was hard-pressed to believe that men at this resort hadn't been tripping all over themselves to get close to her. Instead, it looked as if someone had chosen to take the goodies in her suitcase rather than the goodies in her panties. To him, that didn't make sense.

As the elevator doors opened with a ding, she stepped inside and he followed. "I'm wondering if you might have flirted with or rebuffed someone around here who decided to get your attention in a totally different way."

"I've talked to a lot of people."

Cage didn't want to imagine who.

When it came to one-night stands, Karis was hardly his first rodeo. He had no idea why he was so hung up…except that there was something about her. She'd felt better than good in his arms. She'd been funny and sensitive, sexy and interesting. Different. Vulnerable.

He'd never been that guy who lost his head over a woman. Hell, he'd barely had a romantic relationship that lasted more than a few weeks. One-nighters and friends with benefits were more his speed. But he'd hoped Karis took him more seriously, wanted more from him than sex.

Now, Cage was beginning to think he'd been a dumb ass and that she'd just wanted a good lay after all. It sucked. "Stop dancing around my questions and tell me the truth. Have you slept with anyone since you've been here?"

She reared back at him. "Not that it's any of your business—"

"Well, if you want me to help keep you safe until your paperwork comes through, then I have to figure out who might have gone stalker on you."

"It was a theft," she reminded as the elevator descended.

"Absolutely, but he didn't take anything of Wisteria's?"

Her frown said that puzzled her, too. "No."

"I noticed your iPad was still on your nightstand, so he didn't take that, either. How much was your jewelry worth?"

"Next to nothing."

"How much cash did you have?"

"Forty bucks I stuck back in case of an emergency. The rest of it was in my pocket."

"And has he tried to use your credit cards?"

She paused, then shook her head. "So far, no." And she sounded almost puzzled by that. "When I called to cancel them, the banks said there'd been no activity on the accounts at all."

He nodded. "Normally, that's the first thing a thief would use because they know the numbers will be voided soon. So mostly what this guy took from you was your way out of the country."

The elevator came to a shaking stop. After a long moment, the doors opened. Automatically, Cage fitted a hand at the small of Karis's back and escorted her out. She shivered at his touch. He couldn't miss it, just like he couldn't escape the zip of heat that flooded his blood and settled into his cock.

With a little jerk, she pulled away and looked back at him with a warning not to lay hands on her again.

What the hell? The night they'd met, she hadn't been able to get naked with him fast enough. She hadn't been able to pull him inside her deep enough. She hadn't been able to slake her hunger often enough. In fairness, he hadn't either. From the moment his younger brother had introduced them, she'd reduced him into a puddle of oil, then tossed her flames all over him. The bonfire they generated had been a fucking combustible conflagration.

Now she seemed to have the personality of a glitchy freezer.

"Maybe...you're right," she conceded. "I didn't stop to look at the situation that way."

"You were too rattled. You felt violated."

"Yeah." The glance she gave Cage as she made her way to the pool bar said she was more than surprised he understood.

"And you're mad, too."

"Totally."

She looked even more shocked at his insight. Really, it wasn't that hard to guess. He heard from victims every day on the beat. But it was nice to have found a point of connection with her. Still, it didn't stop him from needing some facts. "So let's try this again. Have you slept with anyone since you've been here? He'll be my first suspect."

"No."

Cage held in his sigh of relief. He didn't have the right to expect that he was the only man in her life—yet. But he couldn't deny that he wanted to be. "Anyone who...I don't know, bought you a drink?"

"It's an all-inclusive resort. The booze is included."

"Or any gesture like that. Someone who shared a meal with you? Invited you to his room?"

"No." She tossed on her sunglasses as they emerged from the brightly colored lobby to the infinity edge pool overlooking the Caribbean Sea.

At the restaurant's entrance, they waited for someone to seat them. A few moments later, a smiling young, dark-eyed woman showed them to a table on the waterfront, tucked under the shade provided by the grassy roof overhead, swaying slightly in the warm tropical wind.

He helped Karis into her chair, then they both grabbed a menu from the table as the sun began to sink to the west. They both did a quick scan before setting the laminated list of foods aside. The moment they did, a Hispanic waiter approached the table with two glasses of water in hand—and eyes only for Karis.

"Hello, señorita. *Buenas noches.* How have you been?" He smiled as he set the water down, a glass in front of each plate.

"I'm all right. Thanks, Miguel."

The twenty-something punk—probably closer to Karis's age—beamed. "Thank you for remembering me, Señorita Karis. You look *muy bonita.*"

When he winked, Cage wanted to hurl. How often did the guy use that line on lonely tourists? He was good-looking enough, so it probably worked more often than it should.

It wouldn't have any impact on Karis, Cage decided. Not while he was here.

"I appreciate that." She gave him a small, slightly dismissive smile, obviously ready to order.

"Were you not supposed to travel home this morning?" Miguel asked.

She nodded, looking glum and agitated. "Yeah. Someone stole my passport last night, so I'll be here another couple of days."

The waiter turned a shocked expression her way. To Cage, it looked awfully staged.

"That is terrible. I'm so sorry someone would mar the Mexican hospitality we have done our best to show you this week with an act so callous. If I can do anything beyond bring you food to be of assistance—"

"I'll take care of her," Cage assured.

The slick Latin lover finally looked at him, expression tightening. "Señor. Hello. Are you a new guest with us, then?"

"Looks like it."

His mouth pursed further as he slid another stolen glance at Karis. No doubt, the little shit was displeased.

"Very good," Miguel said as if having him here were anything but, then turned his attention back to Karis. "What may I bring you today?"

She leaned her elbows on the table, probably not realizing how much cleavage she flashed the waiter. "I'll take a chicken quesadilla and a margarita, heavy on the tequila, light on the salt."

"For you, señorita *bonita*, anything." He clapped a hand to his heart, then flung his arms out to her as if to say he was giving her all his love.

Cage resisted the urge to puke—or throw a punch. Instead, he settled for taking Karis's hand across the table and holding it firmly when she—predictably—tried to pull away. "I'll have the same. And some privacy to talk to my girlfriend."

At his words, Miguel scowled before masking it with a politely bland expression. "Of course. Let me know if you would like anything else."

Then the waiter finally melted away.

"Your girlfriend?" Karis hissed the moment Miguel disappeared from earshot, pulling her hand free. "Let's get one thing straight—"

"We're going to get a lot of things straight," Cage assured her. "But I can almost guarantee he's your suspect."

"What? He's just a guy I ordered meals from this week."

"He knows your name."

"He knew Wisteria's name, too. Being friendly is part of his job."

He snorted. "The guy wasn't so friendly with me."

"Miguel just met you."

"Still, I guarantee he's never going to call me señorita *bonita*."

She stared at him across the table as if he'd lost his mind. Hell, maybe he had. Karis Weston did something to him. He didn't want to argue with her. He just wanted to get deep inside her and stay.

"I thought you'd be happy he didn't call you a pretty lady. But hey, if you want him to, maybe you have a whole private life I don't know anything about."

Cage gritted his teeth. That was it. He was determined to get to the bottom of whatever was eating at her. Sure, she was thrown off by the theft and the abrupt change of her plans. She'd probably wanted the comfort of her sister, not the guy she'd fucked once, then rebuffed. And if she itched to take her frustration out on him, he could deal with that. But her hostility seemed to stem from a different place. He had to understand it if he was going to call a truce and move them past it.

With a deep breath, Cage looked her way. "My point is, Miguel knew your name and when you were leaving. He's a terrible actor, and I don't believe for one second that he was shocked someone had stolen your stuff. Since the moment he opened his mouth, my instincts have been screaming. I think he's your bad guy."

Finally, Karis looked as if she was considering his words. "That would make him a little unhinged. I mean, we've talked some, sure. Wisteria, Hayden, Miguel, another waiter, and I closed down the bar one night and had a ball. But nothing happened between us. I didn't give him any reason to think we were a 'thing,' even temporarily."

"Some guys have been known to assume more intimacy with less encouragement. I'll keep investigating, but I'm just saying…I've got a bad feeling about him."

Karis cocked her head and leaned her elbows on the table. "I can't tell whether you're for real or just being stupidly jealous."

"Both." Why lie?

A little frown settled between her brows, like his assertion confused her. "Wow. That may be the first honest thing you've ever said to me."

What? "I haven't lied to you once, cupcake. I didn't lie to you when we met or when I told you that night I wanted you or when I said the next morning I wasn't sure I'd ever get enough of you."

She dipped her head to cover the flush that rushed up her cheeks. "You're right. But I didn't realize what a player you are. Don't worry, I got the message quick."

Now, he was getting to the crux of her nose being out of joint. "What message was that?"

"New Year's didn't mean anything, and you already had someone in your life." She leaned back in her chair and glanced out at the ocean, as if she couldn't bear to look at him.

As if he'd hurt her.

He mulled that for a minute, along with her words. "I don't have an exclusive relationship with anyone. I never have."

Karis flinched, then tried to shrug off her reaction as if it meant nothing. "So it's normal for you to go from one bed to another. Okay. It's your life."

Suddenly, Cage suspected he knew exactly what had happened. "Look at me, cupcake."

She rolled her eyes and sighed, but she reluctantly complied. "What?"

He wished he could see behind her sunglasses. He had a feeling there was a wealth of info welling in her eyes, along with some tears, too.

Before he could say another word, Miguel dropped off two huge frozen margaritas and two quesadillas, piled high with sour cream and guacamole. He lingered, offering more napkins and fresh pico de gallo and whatever else he could think of until Cage shooed him away.

"You saw me with a blonde shortly after the night we spent together, didn't you?" he challenged the moment the pesky waiter disappeared.

Karis reared back like she was stunned he'd guessed right. Then she schooled her expression and dug into her plate. "Yeah, but like I said, it's your life. Your brother told me you're not into relationships. It's my fault for not listening and—"

"I wasn't into relationships until you. And that's not a line." He raked a hand through his hair, wondering if there was any way to tell her what he was thinking without revealing all the raw places inside him. But he wasn't good at head games. "This is as straight up as I can be: I've had a lot of friends with benefits. They were pretty much the only female friends I had. But the night I spent with you changed something for me I still don't understand and I don't know how to explain. I'm not sharing benefits with anyone right now because I can't stop thinking about you. I can't stop wanting you. And I'm guessing that somehow you saw me with Madison, the blonde, after the night you and I spent together."

"Yes." Her answer sounded curt and crisp.

She was hurt. Cage understood, and he was relieved to finally have the mystery solved.

"Madison called me literally two minutes after I left your house. We've been friends..." He paused and realized there was no point in being less than honest. "Yes, with benefits, since our senior year of high school."

"You've had her at the top of your booty call speed dial list for the last...what, fifteen years? Clearly, you've tapped that a lot."

He tried not to get pissed off that she wanted to cast the worst possible light on his admission. The last twenty-four hours had not been kind to her. And if he'd seen her cozy up to another man right after their amazing night together, he'd be fucking furious and not very gracious about it, either. Besides, she had daddy issues—just like he did. So he had to cut her some slack.

"Yep. Not even going to deny it. We both treated it casually. She's a career woman who doesn't have time for guys and relationships, but she still sometimes wants a man to hold her. Until I got together with you, I didn't see the difference between screwing and making something more meaningful, so Madison and I never turned one another down. That's the unvarnished truth. But the morning I left you, she called to tell me that she'd just rushed her father to the hospital. She's an only child. Her mother died a few years ago. She was all alone, and she couldn't face what was happening without a shoulder to lean on."

"Oh." Karis stared at him with pursed-mouthed contrition before she took a sip of her drink. "So...you stayed with her while he recovered?"

"Yes and no. He died the next day, so I couldn't just leave her. That's the thing about my friendship. It wasn't simply about the benefits. I tried to be truly supportive, lend her my strength until she could bury her dad almost a week later." When Karis chewed on her lip, mulling his words over, he chowed down on a bite of his meal and took another approach. "What would you think of a man who walked out on a person whose last parent was dying?"

She sighed. "You had to stay. I didn't realize... And now I feel really stupid. I came by to bring you cookies, you know. I barely know how to bake, but for you I tried. Yes, I was that gaga about you. So when I saw you with her on your porch, hugging her and kissing her forehead, I assumed..."

"I would have assumed the same thing, cupcake, if the shoe was on the other foot. I would have been mightily pissed off, too. But I swear, Madison and I haven't exchanged benefits since I've been with you."

"It was a traumatic time for her, and sex was probably the last thing on her mind—"

"Well..." He rubbed at the back of his neck, deciding if he was going to be honest, he better be brutally so. "Actually, she...um, hit me up after the funeral. She needed to feel alive, she said. She needed to forget." He shrugged. "Straight up? I got her off with my fingers so she'd have some relief. I ended it there. Hell, she cried the whole time. But the truth is, after you, I didn't want her sexually anymore."

He glanced Karis's way to gauge her reaction, but she looked blank and unreadable. "Then what happened?"

"Well, I told her that I could no longer be *that* guy for her but I'd always be her friend. *Just* her friend. She was disappointed but she understood. Then I set about trying to open the conversation with you again. You put me off for weeks. And no matter how much I begged, my brother wouldn't help. Then you left for vacation. Here we are."

"Do you have any more friends with benefits I should know about?"

"None I won't think twice about ignoring. I'll even delete them from my phone while you watch, if you want. I'm serious."

"Why do you think what you do matters to me?" She tried to appear unaffected, but he saw her uncertainty.

"Cutter told me about your mom, about all the selfish douches who have cheated and strayed and abandoned your family. My dad was the same kind of asshole, so I know how hard coping with that as a kid can be. It sucks to look up one day to find your dad gone."

Karis bit her lip, and behind her sunglasses he could see her emotion. He was getting to her. Reaching her. He didn't know precisely where they were going, but his every instinct as a cop and as a man told him that nothing right now in his life was more vital than winning this woman back.

"It changes you. I was a kid when my dad walked out. Apparently, he had a girlfriend, and one day he decided that being with her was more important than staying with his wife and daughter. I don't think I ever really forgave him. And it definitely changed the way I approached men and relationships. I was always looking for the guy who wouldn't do that to me." She laughed at herself. "I was looking for Prince Charming."

"And I didn't seem like him."

"That night, I believed you were. I really hoped that you were the guy for me, the faithful one my mother never has found. When Jolie got lucky and fell for Heath, I started letting myself believe it was possible for me, too. Then you felt so…I don't know, right is probably the best word. Like we fit together or something. Like we belonged, you know? Or maybe you don't and I'm just babbling."

"No, I get you totally. I was feeling it, too. So when I was sure Madison wasn't going to fall apart anymore and she understood our relationship now, I called you. When you didn't want to talk to me, I won't lie. I was kinda devastated. But I wasn't going to give up. I'm still not. That's why I'm here."

Karis tucked away another forkful of her quesadilla and washed it back with a sip of her drink. "I have to admit, I'm shocked. I didn't see myself ever being this close to you again."

"How did us being apart make you feel?"

"Crappy. Sad." She hesitated, then finally tore off her sunglasses, revealing the tears pooling in her eyes, just about to spill over the rims. "It hurt."

"Me, too. And that's not bullshit. I don't have any experience with making a woman happy out of bed, but I want to try, see where we could take this."

A pretty little smile crept up her face, which she promptly hid behind her napkin as she wiped her mouth. "All right. I'd like that."

"Me, too. Still hungry?" He nodded at her plate.

"Not really. What about you? You've only eaten two bites."

"Fuck food. I'd rather be with you."

She gulped back the last of her half-melted margarita and left her barely touched plate. "Me, too."

As they rose, Cage caught Miguel staring. He narrowed his eyes at the smooth waiter when his prying glance followed Karis retreating.

The guy approached him, adjusting the jacket of his starched uniform. "Would you like your food to go? I will be happy to find you a box so you can have your meal later."

He didn't like Cage any more than Cage liked the waiter, so the sudden desire to be helpful only made him wonder if Miguel had tainted or poisoned his food. The guy was definitely up to something. "No. But here's what you can do for me: back away from Karis. She's not available. I'm pretty sure you know something about the theft of her passport, and I'm telling you now that I'm here for—and with—her. She doesn't need your 'help' and she never will. Fucking get lost."

Miguel pressed his lips together, seeming to hold in his temper. Cage almost heard the gnashing of his teeth, but the guy collected himself, as if suddenly remembering that he was supposed to deny the accusation. "I stole nothing. I would never do such a thing. I was not aware that attempting to be helpful and friendly would be misconstrued as flirting. Of course I respect our guests' lives and privacy."

Every word Miguel said sounded like a preplanned speech, and

Cage wanted to call bullshit. But Karis was waiting at the sliding double doors heading back into the lobby. As much as he'd like to have it out with the waiter until the guy understood that he needed to fuck off, he would ten times rather be with Karis, kissing her, peeling off her clothes, whispering in her ear, making her feel good. Convincing her that he cared about her more than he probably should after one night —and he didn't see that changing anytime soon.

"Great," he growled. "Stay away."

Cage didn't wait around for Miguel's reaction. He also wouldn't underestimate the guy. He'd be willing to bet Karis wasn't the first guest to have her passport and other goodies stolen from her room. He'd also bet the majority of those guests had ended up warming Miguel's bed for a few days.

Racing over to Karis, he hustled her inside the air-conditioned common area, away from the watchful waiter's prying eyes, and took her hand in his. "Can you wait for me by that fountain for two minutes, cupcake?"

She turned to look behind her at the big stone water feature in the middle of the lobby. As evening descended, the place wasn't bursting with people, but enough straggled in with suitcases or hung out with drinks that Cage didn't worry Miguel or some other potential cohort of his could take their anger out on Karis.

"Sure." She looked a little confused but hung back like he'd asked.

He couldn't let her go that simply. Cage gave a gentle tug on her wrist and pulled her against him. After a little sway, her chest collided with his. Her head automatically fell back and she delved into his eyes. Jesus, what was it about her? She was a bit zany, not terribly practical. According to Cutter, she had a free spirit and a gypsy heart. She was his polar opposite.

Maybe that was the attraction. Maybe that was the reason every moment he'd spent with her over New Year's, he'd felt more balanced and more certain that she belonged to him.

Cage didn't dare kiss her now. They might not make it upstairs before his need to feel her again overwhelmed him. Instead, he nuzzled her cheek and pressed his mouth to her ear. "Want to know why I call you cupcake?"

"I've always wondered," she breathed.

"Because from the moment we met, the first thing I thought was how adorable and sweet you were. And just like a cupcake, I could hardly wait to eat you."

He smiled as he left her standing there, looking somewhere between stunned and excited, as he fished his phone from his back pocket and strode across the lobby. Glad he'd picked up an international calling plan before he'd left home, he made his way to the hotel's offices and hit one of the names on his speed dial.

Forest, better known as Trees, was the quietest member of the operative team at EM Security Management, his brother's employer. In fact, Trees was downright scary. All those guys who worked for Hunter and Logan Edgington and Joaquin Muñoz were. All former special operatives, they lived on the edge and craved adrenaline as their drug of choice.

The private security route was all well and good, he supposed. Cutter made good money, and Cage wouldn't sneeze at it, but all he'd ever known was being a cop. It worked for him. These dudes, like Trees, possessed specialized skills that would come in really fucking handy about now.

"Cage?" He sounded surprised.

They didn't talk much and they weren't pals exactly. But they also weren't enemies, so he was hoping the shaved-headed fucker would do him a favor.

"Yeah, look... My girlfriend is down in Mexico..." He filled the guy in on the crap Karis had gone through and whom he suspected was the culprit. "Would you do me a favor and hack into the hotel's employment records, tell me if any of the previous female guests have filed complaints against this guy?"

"On it. Has this Miguel cat threatened her? Do you need backup? Mexico sounds nice. It's really damn cold here, and I can't stand the kind of sniveling asswipe who threatens a woman."

He'd probably offered his assistance more for the vacation than anything, but it was nice all the same.

"I've got it so far, but I'll holler if that changes."

"Roger that."

In the background, Cage heard the guy tapping on a computer at what sounded like lightning speed. He didn't ask how Trees had learned his hacking skills, he just knew from hearing his brother talk that they were mad. He was also both surveillance and navigation on the team. Cutter was in charge of engineering and demolitions, which seemed like an oxymoron to him, so he teased his brother about building something only to blow it up. Josiah and Zyron he didn't know much about. And One-Mile...whatever his current situation with Brea, the guy had still taken advantage of her. In Cage's book, he always be a prick and a half.

But Cage had his own problems right now.

"Can you call me back when you've got something?"

"Yep. They've got some security on this system, and there's the translation problem, but it should only be a couple of hours."

"Thanks, Trees. I owe you big."

"Maybe you can make your brother introduce me to some women in this godforsaken town. I just moved to Lafayette. All the good ones seem to be taken, and my dick is damn tired of my hand."

Cage laughed. "I'll twist my little brother's arm, and we'll work something out."

They ended the call, then Cage strolled to the front desk and asked for the manager. After some backing and forthing, along with a good, old-fashioned bribe, the suit blabbed that Miguel's shift ended in another three hours. Good to know when the pouty little bitch would have free time to make mayhem. He was coming for Karis, no doubt. Cage was determined to be waiting.

STILL STANDING AT THE FOUNTAIN, KARIS WATCHED CAGE STROLL BACK toward her. What the hell was he up to? It was something, given that swagger. He thought he had everything under control. He'd taken charge of the situation because he was the man and he intended to protect her.

It was actually kind of sweet.

"Hey," she murmured as he approached.

He winked. "You ready to head upstairs?"

Though her heart was pounding, she raised a brow at him. "For a rousing game of Charades?"

"That what you want?"

She wrinkled her nose. "Putting this back on me? Okay, I'll be brave. Not really."

"Good." He pulled her close, and she melted against him. "I promise, I won't leave you guessing what I want."

When he all but yanked her toward the elevator, Karis had to suppress a laugh. She felt lighter than she had in…well, since the start of the new year.

She'd begun January first full of hope and lightness—and impatience for Cage to call again. Seeing him with Madison a few days later had been the worst shock. Wondering if only she had felt the earth move between them had filled Karis with pain. After his explanation today, she understood where he'd been coming from. No, she didn't like that he'd touched the blonde again, but weirdly she understood his act of compassion. People wanted comfort in times of loss. Besides, she and Cage hadn't made each other any promises of exclusivity during their one night together.

Sure, he could be lying about the whole thing. Men did that. But Cage was so much like his true-blue brother that Karis didn't think so.

She pressed the call button. "Jolie could have simply overnighted the picture to me, you know."

He shook his head, the mussed tousle of his hair so sexy. "I was with Cutter when Jolie called him for help. My brother was actually going to come to your rescue." Cage grimaced. "I insisted on coming instead. I never told him what happened between us that night…but he's a smart guy. After he warned me that I'd better bring you back in one piece and not to break your heart, he helped me book the next flight out."

Cage had come for her, seemingly to make things right between them. Karis couldn't think of a single time a man had gone so far out of his way simply to make her life better, keep her safe, or give her a reason to smile.

She slanted him a glance, feeling as if she glowed from within—like her happiness. "Thanks."

The elevator opened with a ding. A family stepped out. She and Cage eased in, totally alone.

"Did you miss me?" he asked as they started to ascend. "Because I missed you like hell."

Once given, Karis knew she couldn't take her answer back. She would be exposing her heart. "I thought about you a lot."

"Ditto, cupcake."

He grabbed her hand as the elevator stopped at their floor. Together, they raced to her room. She felt excitement dancing between them. It gripped her stomach. The ache between her legs swelled.

As he inserted the key in the lock, he studied her. "You need anything? Another drink? A shower? A minute to enjoy the sunset?"

She frowned. Was he trying to distract her because he didn't want to have sex with her after all? "No."

"Thank god." He shoved the portal open, nudged her into the room, then slammed the door and locked it behind him.

Karis barely had time to draw in a breath before he urged her back against the wall, covered her body with his own, and slanted his mouth over her lips in a possessive, toe-curling kiss.

Instantly, she looped her arms around his neck and whimpered. She'd missed him so much. That familiar feeling of belonging to him swamped her again, along with desire. He tasted of tequila, just like he had that first night, as well as something spicy and manly. Cage overwhelmed her senses. He fried her resistance.

She loved it.

He tugged at her pool cover-up, and Karis helped him, breaking the kiss only long enough to whip it over her head. He tossed the garment away and attacked the strings of her bikini next. Between one breath and the next, he exposed her breasts, cupping them, dipping down to lick them, suckle their tips one at a time, then sink lower still to yank down her bikini bottoms.

"Step out. I want your pussy. I've been craving my cupcake something fierce."

Her heart fluttered and her ache coiled as he dragged the scrap of fabric down her thighs. She was still stepping out of them when he lifted one of her legs over his shoulder and fastened his mouth over her clit.

Fire burst through her at the contact. She gasped, flattened her hands to the wall, tossed her head back, and groaned. "Cage..."

"Hmm." He didn't let her go, didn't come up for air, just continued to savor her as if she was the sweetest treat to ever cross his lips.

Under his mouth, she unraveled. It was so intimate, so passionate. He held nothing back, unabashedly pursuing her pleasure. Every touch demanded she give it to him. As his tongue laved her clit again and again, concentrating exactly where she needed him, Karis canted her hips to him, opened for him, gave him everything, including her mounting need.

She thrust her hands in his wavy hair and gave a tug. "Oh, god. Please..."

"Come for me," he muttered roughly against her thigh. "Cupcakes have cream frosting, and I want all your sweetness on my tongue."

Cage had a dirty mouth. She remembered that from New Year's Eve. Now, like then, his wicked words unwound her and left her breathless.

Under the lash of his tongue and the nip of his teeth, the burn behind her clit swelled and grew. She felt it filling her veins, flooding her head, drowning her in a well of ecstasy.

When he sucked her into his mouth again, she went under with a long, harsh cry. Cage only took that as his sign to go at her with more gusto, and he wrung out every moment of bliss from her body he could. He left her panting and limp and glowing.

He stood slowly, kissing his way up her body. When his face filled her vision, he was wearing that proud, cocky grin. "Best cupcake ever."

Despite feeling completely spent, she laughed. "You certainly ate it with gusto."

"I have a feeling it will always be my favorite dessert." He dragged his lips up her neck. "In fact, I may never eat another cupcake again."

When he straightened and pressed his forehead against hers, he stared at her with a dark, dead-serious gaze. Something about it seized her insides. In the next instant, she knew why, and her breath caught.

Cage wasn't playing in any way—except for keeps.

"Are you going to take me to bed now?" Her voice shook.

"Absolutely," he murmured as he lifted her rubbery legs and settled them in the crook of his arm, supporting her back with the other. A few steps later, they were on the bed, Cage on top of her. Together, they pushed and tugged and yanked until he was naked. Well, she did more of the work. He seemed orally fixated on her mouth and her nipples… and she wasn't complaining a bit.

Finally, he fished a condom from his pants and rolled it down his length with one hand, opening her to the swollen crest he fitted against her entrance with the other. Karis held her breath, lifted her hips, aching with the wait to feel him deep. No one had ever given her pleasure like Cage Bryant. No man had left his mark on her heart the way this one had. Sure, she'd had silly fairy-tale dreams of meeting Mr. Wonderful…but that had been a fantasy borne of the broken promises of a father to his little girl, of her mother's endless string of terrible boyfriends.

Cage was real.

"Ready?"

"Hurry…" she moaned.

"Yeah. I'm going to lose my fucking mind without you, too. Hold on to me."

That was all the warning he gave her before he braced himself, spread her wider, and filled her with one rough thrust.

He delved deep. Her head fell back. Her nails dug in. Her breath rushed out in a moan. Already, he was everything she remembered and more.

"Oh, fuck," he groaned loud and low. "You feel so damn good, cupcake. Jesus…"

"Amazing." She couldn't quite catch her breath. She definitely couldn't stop wriggling under him. "I need more, Cage."

He breathed harshly against her skin. "I'll always need more from you."

Karis had no time to process his confession before he plunged into her again and again, establishing a hard, slow rhythm that scraped every nerve ending and held her in thrall. Every time he shoved inside her, he wrung a gasp, a whimper, or a kiss from her.

"Faster!"

"Not until I make you come," he gritted out between clenched teeth. "Once you're there..."

Couldn't he feel her tightening around him, clamping down on him? Her folds swelled. The need ratcheted up so hard and fast Karis found herself wrapping her arms and legs around him, pressing her lips across his bulging shoulder when she wasn't panting in his ear.

God, this need felt as if she hadn't had sex in four years instead of four weeks. She rocked under him, lifting and rolling with him, welcoming him deeper than ever. He gave more. Need gripped her. She was going under again. Holy hell, no man had ever driven her to two monumental orgasms in under ten minutes. A few had even spent hours trying to get one from her and left empty-handed. But Cage touched her in every way, even her heart. It swelled and beat and filled as he did the same to her pussy.

As she sat on the precipice of orgasmic bliss, Karis sank her fingers into his shoulders and squeezed hard.

He read her signals. "Oh, cupcake... Yeah. Give it to me."

Then he pistoned into her faster. The ache grew to something that nearly engulfed her, gnawed at the last of her composure, and now threatened to swallow her whole. Her body pulsed and jolted as she cried his name, giving him every bit of her bliss.

And her heart.

Yes, she'd feared this man would steal her heart on New Year's Eve, but now it was official. She loved him. Actually loved him. She'd been infatuated with guys enough to know the difference. She'd seen her mother "fall" enough to know when it wasn't real.

Her heart told her this was love.

As if he felt it too, he groaned as he emptied inside her with short, sharp thrusts and buried his head in the crook of her neck. When he came up for air, he looked right into her eyes. "I love you."

She smiled at him. "I was...um, just thinking the same about you."

His grin overtook his whole face. "Were you now? You sure you don't need round two in order to know for sure?"

Karis loved the way he played in bed. She loved the way she felt cherished when she was with him. Heck, she loved everything about him.

She slapped on an answering smile. "You know, I just might..."

CAN A MAN DIE OF HAPPINESS? THAT QUESTION CIRCLED CAGE'S BRAIN AS he lay beside Karis. She'd tangled her arms and legs up with his, resting her head on his arm. Her lashes swept dark half-moons over her cheeks. Absently, he brushed his fingers through her silky hair as she slept.

The two days of sex, sun, and talk they'd shared had been amazing. Idyllic. Exactly what he'd needed to be sure Karis was his future. They might be opposites, but they had a surprising amount in common. They wanted the same things out of life—marriage, family, happiness. She was still a little skittish, and he understood with her background. But he also wasn't giving up. Cage intended to leave here knowing Karis Weston was his.

What he didn't like was how quiet Miguel had gotten. Maybe the asswipe would just go away since Cage had made it clear the waiter couldn't fly under his radar anymore. But his gut told him Miguel wasn't a quitter. He was even more convinced after Trees called back to say that several past female hotel guests had registered complaints about the wannabe Romeo's forward behavior. And what do you know? Several had reported their passports stolen, too. No one had fired the little shit because the manager of the property, Raul Nabaté, was his uncle. And no one had caught Miguel red-handed.

Cage intended to change that.

With any luck, Karis's new passport would come in today so they could get out of here, go home, and start their future. He was still plotting the best attack plan—besides beating the devil out of the prick—when his cupcake stirred beside him.

"Morning." Karis stretched with a smile. "What should we do today? Yoga class starts at ten. Interested?"

Cage kissed her forehead. He already knew from inquiring that Miguel was due to report to work at the same time. That would be his best opportunity to resolve Karis's Latin-lover problem. If his hunch wasn't right, Cage would have another man-to-pipsqueak chat with Miguel after he filed a formal complaint with hotel management and hoped they did something this time. But he'd rather not leave anything to chance.

"Nope, but you go ahead. I'll check on your passport while you're downward dogging. If it's ready, I'll see about getting us some flights home. If not, we'll grab some beach time."

"Then a sultry siesta?" she suggested with a wink.

"Is there any other kind?"

Karis laughed, and he held her close as they dipped in for a quick shower…that turned into a deep, slow orgasm. Then they grabbed some breakfast from the buffet, and Cage started feeling her out on the subject of a deeper commitment. He was getting green-light vibes when she suddenly looked at her watch.

"Damn. I've got less than ten minutes until class starts. I need to go."

"I'll walk you there and meet you when it's finished."

She stood and kissed him slowly. "I'll thank you properly later."

"I'll definitely look forward to that."

As their embrace ended, he saw Miguel in his peripheral vision. The asshole hadn't missed their exchange. And since he was wearing his starched uniform, he must be on duty. Perfect.

After a glare Miguel's way, Cage escorted Karis to the yoga studio, then dashed through the lobby and exited the hotel, catching a taxi. He had just under an hour to dig up some answers.

Since Trees had hacked the resort's entire file on Miguel Nabaté, including his home address, Cage intended to make full use of the information. No, he wasn't playing by the rules...but neither was Miguel.

Hoping the guy lived alone, he exited the taxi in front of the old, blue-stucco apartment building. "Wait here."

When the driver nodded, Cage sought out apartment 201. It took less than two minutes to find the door, pick the lock, and begin sifting through the cluttered space. Cage thanked his police training. He'd searched hundreds of locations and had a nose for contraband. He'd find whatever Miguel had stashed here. Maybe he should feel bad about the illegal search and seizure. But he didn't—in the least.

What a fucking slob. Cage grimaced at the nasty pad just before he struck gold. Inside the drawer of a dresser, he found a half dozen passports, all reported stolen—including Karis's.

"Gotcha, you motherfucker."

Shoving them all in his pocket, Cage rearranged the apartment exactly as he'd found it, then locked the door behind him. A glance at his phone told him he had thirty minutes before Karis's yoga class ended. She would be safe with the others until then.

Jumping back into the taxi, Cage urged the driver to floor it to the hotel. Everything was going according to plan...

Until he returned to the resort's yoga studio and found Karis gone. With the class in session, he couldn't ask anyone questions.

Cursing, his heart pounding, Cage dashed to their room to see if she'd returned there. Empty. Nor could he find her in the gym, hanging around the lobby, or by the pool...

Don't panic. Don't panic. He repeated the litany over and over. It didn't help.

When he poked his head into the restaurant where Miguel worked, he couldn't find the creeper there, either. That made Cage's gut tighten with worry even more. When he stopped a pair of waitresses to ask around about Miguel, they shrugged, swearing they hadn't seen him in a while.

Son of a bitch. Raking a hand through his hair, Cage forced himself to think. Where would Miguel have taken her? He'd have many options, and the resort was too big to search quickly without help.

Hotel security. Cage sprinted to the guard station and found a strapping guy in a pseudo-police uniform, baton at his side, shiny shoes gracing his feet. His name tag proclaimed him Mateo. Yeah, this guy was mostly for show, but he had a gleam in his eyes like he was itching for real action.

Cage rolled the dice and hoped for the best. "One of your waiters, Miguel Nabaté, has a habit of stealing women's passports so he can strand them at the resort and seduce them. The guy took my girlfriend's passport a few days ago." He tossed the collection of official documents he'd collected at Miguel's apartment on the counter. "And now she's missing. I need help finding her ASAP. He's potentially dangerous."

The guard flipped quickly through all the passports and swore. Face tightening, he barked a few words of Spanish into the walkie-talkie sitting near his elbow. After a few static-filled replies, Mateo regarded Cage with fury.

"Mr. Nabaté has been warned repeatedly that his nephew is a liability. Everyone on property is looking for Miguel now. A scan of the employee parking lot indicates his car is still here. No one has seen him leave the property. Where did you last see your girlfriend?"

When Cage explained, Mateo called to speak with the yoga instructor. The exchange was brief, and when it ended, the guard nodded as he hung up. "Your girlfriend stayed for roughly half the class, then excused herself because she received an urgent note. The instructor did not know what it said. I will access the camera feed in the common areas to see if I can ascertain what happened next."

"Great. Can I help?" Cage flashed his Dallas PD badge.

Mateo was taken aback, but shrugged. "Of course."

After a quick troll through the security footage, they finally spotted Karis leaving the yoga studio. She paced down the hall, then passed through the lobby. She didn't glance twice at the elevators, but dashed through the double door outside, toward the ocean, looking frantic. She paused on the back patio and looked around, glancing at the note in her hand.

Miguel wandered into the shot a moment later, said something in her ear, and patted her on the back. Seconds after, she went limp in his arms. Then the dirtbag dragged her behind a bush and down a little-traveled path, out of the shot of the camera. The time and date stamp said that had happened twenty minutes ago.

Cage's heart stopped. He'd gone out of his way to reconnect with her after their New Year's fling. They'd cleared the air and gotten truly close. It couldn't be too late. "What's down that path?"

The guard shrugged. "A liquor storage shed for the bar."

"Take me there." It wasn't a request.

Mateo didn't hesitate. He bellowed into the walkie-talkie, then strapped it to his belt before leading the charge out the back of the resort.

The crashing waves of the ocean and the sound of his pounding heart were all Cage could hear—until they were mere feet from the shed. Then Karis's scream of terror split the air.

Breaking out in a cold sweat, Cage lunged for the door and tried to rip it off its hinges. Of course, the bastard had locked it.

"Get me in there," he growled at Mateo.

But the tall guard was already shoving the key into the lock and wrenching the door open. Cage shouldered the guy out of the way and found Karis trapped in the corner, holding the strap of her torn bikini with one hand and threatening Miguel with a hefty bottle of booze in the other.

Cage saw red. Karis was his. *No* other man would ever touch her, especially against her will.

Miguel whirled to the sound of the interruption with a snarl. Cage charged him and grabbed the waiter by the back of his stiff jacket, punching him in the jaw. "I warned you. Back away from my girlfriend."

"Cage!" Her voice trembled.

He wanted to go to her, comfort her. First, he had to deal with the threat.

"It was a simple misunderstanding," Miguel backpedaled. "She said she wanted a tour of the private areas. I misinterpreted her request and—"

"Fuck you. I found the passports you've stolen from other women in your apartment. Security knows. Your uncle soon will, too. You're going down. And you're not putting another finger on my woman—or any other—for a long while."

Miguel sputtered and blanched. "No. No, I—"

"Shut up, asshole." Karis swung the bottle and broke it over his head.

The scent of cheap gin doused Miguel as he crumpled to the ground.

It was over. Thank god.

"We apologize profusely, señorita," Mateo said as he motioned to his peers to take Miguel's inert form from the shed.

Karis looked away from the sight, flinging herself against Cage with teary eyes. "Thank you. The note said you were hurt and needed me."

"Miguel tricked you."

She nodded. "I feel so dumb. I didn't think. Thank you for coming after me..."

He cradled her face in his hands. "I always will. I love you, cupcake. You okay?"

"Yes." She hugged him, silently assuring him. "You got to me before..."

Cage knew all too well what Miguel had intended. He'd seen the angry lust in the man's eyes. He'd seen that same look in others he'd arrested, too. He held her as tightly as he dared, grateful she was safe in his arms.

"I'm so damn glad." He caressed her back with a soothing touch. "I found your passport. You want to go home?"

Obviously, there would be a security interview, police reports, and other official stuff first. But Cage was determined to get her on a plane tonight.

She nodded, tears spilling. "Yes."

"You got it. Would you...um, want to move in with me when we get there?" As soon as the words slipped out, Cage almost groaned aloud. Could his timing be any worse?

"Yes." The emphatic nod of her head backed up her answer.

He hesitated. Since everything between them was going surprisingly well, maybe he should go for broke. "How about if we got married, too? Maybe it's too fast but I know how I feel about you."

"Yes." Karis pressed a kiss to his lips.

The grin that crossed his face spread through his whole body. "Really? You want to marry me? You're not just saying yes on autopilot?"

An adoring smile creased her face. "I know what I feel, too. You're the love I've been looking for since I stopped believing in fairy tales. I'm not saying yes on autopilot. I really would love to be your wife."

"Well, all right! Let's go home, get a ring on your finger, and start our lives." He helped her attach her torn strap, then took her hand in his and led her outside.

They emerged into the waiting crowd of security. The police took Miguel away, and his uncle frowned fiercely, shaking his head.

Once the red tape was behind them and they were waiting at the gate for their flight home, Cage kissed her softly. "Hey, fiancée. I love you."

She cupped his cheek, looking deep into his eyes. "You've made the dreams I stopped believing in come true. I love you, too."

Cage knew he'd never get tired of the view. "And just think, all the cupcake I want for the rest of my life. Hmm. I'm hungry right now…"

Karis laughed as they boarded the plane to start their perfect future.

ABOUT SHAYLA BLACK

Shayla Black is the *New York Times* and *USA Today* bestselling author of more than fifty novels. For nearly twenty years, she's written contemporary, erotic, paranormal, and historical romances via traditional, independent, foreign, and audio publishers. Her books have sold several million copies and been published in a dozen languages.

Raised an only child, Shayla occupied herself with lots of daydreaming, much to the chagrin of her teachers. In college, she found her love for reading and realized that she could have a career publishing the stories spinning in her imagination. Though she graduated with a degree in Marketing/Advertising and embarked on a stint in corporate America to pay the bills, her heart has always been with her characters. She's thrilled that she's been living her dream as a full-time author for the past nine years.

Shayla currently lives in N. Texas with her wonderfully supportive husband, her daughter, and two spoiled tabbies. In her "free" time, she enjoys reality TV, reading, and listening to an eclectic blend of music.

To be notified of new releases or sales,
join Shayla's private VIP Readers: www.shayla.link/nwsltr
Connect with Shayla online
Facebook: www.facebook.com/ShaylaBlackAuthor
Instagram: www.instagram.com/ShaylaBlack
Visit Shayla at ShaylaBlack.com!

Countdown

LEXI BLAKE

1

**SOMETIME IN THE FUTURE
DEEP IN THE HIMALAYAS**

BEN PARKER FIRED, TAKING DOWN THE LAST OF THE SECURITY. THE BLACK-clad guard hit the floor with a thud and Ben breathed a long sigh of relief. There had been twelve, a ridiculous number for a facility that was supposedly used to study the effects of climate change high in the Himalayas. But then Ben's higher-ups in the CFI knew what was really going on in this remote site deep in Nepal.

The "climate" scientists were actually virologists and engineers who had seemingly made evil their minors in college. Or greed perhaps, but given what they were brewing up here, he had to think it was pure evil.

A new delivery system for anthrax was being researched in this complex and Canada was going to make damn sure that was one research project that didn't get completed.

Ben was silent for a moment, waiting for any sound to reach his ear. The floors in this part of the complex were metal and any sudden movement rattled. Nothing. It appeared the intelligence had been correct and the facility had been evacuated except for security personnel and a few lead scientists. Now all he had to do was find the big bad guy and he could call it a day.

He touched the comm system attached to his left ear. It was sleek and small, nothing more than a dot that sat on the outer edge of his ear. He could walk around with it all day and no one would notice. "Tim, are you there? I'm past the inner perimeter. I need the code to get into the lab."

A garbled sound came over the line.

One of the best reasons to hide a lab in the middle of the Himalayas was the fact that technology sometimes went awry out here. He stared at the door in front of him. It was massive and made of four-inch-thick steel. He wasn't going to kick that sucker in no matter how many leg days he'd suffered through.

He knew he should have brought some damn C-4, but no, his handler was worried they would blow up the anthrax and kill the population of Nepal. There was no optimism left in his world.

He had one shot and damn but he hadn't wanted to take it. He'd wanted to get this thing done before the other team showed up. It would have made things infinitely easier, but it looked like there was no way around it. He hadn't come across anyone with the key to the inner sanctum. Behind that door was the part of the building not even security got into.

He glanced around, touching his comm again. "Tell me the damn Americans came through. I can't move forward without a code. I wasn't able to find anyone with the proper key card. You were right. All the scientists are gone. Huisman's in there somewhere and I think he's crazy enough to go down with the ship, eh?"

"Americans...code...coming. Sorry, there's a storm. Moving in... five...hang..." The line went dead.

Outside, the wind was whipping through the mountains. Tim and the team were roughly ten thousand feet below. He'd been forced to climb the damn mountain to get to the facility. He'd started in the dark, taken hours of moving quietly and steadily so they didn't see him coming. Though they were no longer worried about being seen, Ben didn't see his skinny-ass tech hauling butt up the mountain any time soon.

He stared at the door that separated him from the prize. From what he'd learned about the facility, this door led to the promised land—to the laboratory and the private office and residence of the man who had started this all. Dr. Huisman was in there somewhere, working on his plans.

The Chinese had gotten a foothold in North America, and Europe was rattling sabers. The world was changing rapidly and it was a renaissance time for the spy. Ever since the Mexican revolution had sent the entire continent into chaos, Ben had known he would wind up here. Maybe not this particular location, but in times when the whole world was on the brink, there was always some asshole willing to push them all over.

The world was a powder keg and if this new threat got in the wrong hands, Ben was worried it would blow sky-high.

And now he was literally one door away from reaching the prize, and the Americans hadn't come through with the code. They'd had one job. One.

He heard a slight squeak coming from the hallway to his left. He brought up his gun, ready to take out whoever came down that hall. Had he missed someone? Had their intelligence been off?

One breath in and he was focused.

And then he wasn't. A glimpse of pink hair made him stop. He lowered the gun because shooting this particular player wasn't what he wanted to do.

Nope. He sometimes wanted to throttle her, but mostly his intentions were far more sexual.

The woman he knew as Ms. Magenta stood at the end of the hall, dressed all in white for a change. She had on a huge white parka, but he knew what it hid—curves and hips and breasts he couldn't get out of his head.

The Magenta name was her play on her agency's time-honored tradition of calling its operatives Mr. Black or Mr. Green, or some other color that was meant to protect the operative's true identity. The woman in front of him was roughly five foot eight in flats and when she wore heels like she had on the mission in Macau, she could look him straight in the eyes.

Let other men covet petite, delicate females. He wanted this one. She was the Alpha female, cool and competent and often at odds with him. Maggie. Since he didn't know her real name, he called her Maggie.

He stared at her for a moment, trying to figure out which Maggie he was dealing with. Sometimes she showed up and he could feel how dangerous she was, how reckless and ruthless. Other times she nearly melted in his arms, coming so close to kissing him that he'd ached with the loss.

"Ben, I'm sorry I'm late." She strode up to him, pulling back the hood of her parka and setting free all that pink hair that was sort of her signature. He'd seen her with almost every color of the rainbow including her natural reddish blonde. There was something about the softness of her face that made him relax. She wasn't here to fight. "We had trouble with the helo, but it looks like you handled everything with your usual aplomb. That was a lot of bodies out there, buddy."

He loved that slight Texas twang that came out when she wasn't thinking too hard. He loved that it came out more and more when they were alone. But he frowned because they weren't supposed to be alone today. The US was still friendly with Canada, but the last thing he wanted was Maggie walking out of here with the prize.

The prize, in this case, was something he firmly intended to destroy.

"I didn't realize you were late because you're not supposed to be here at all," he returned.

She stopped a few feet away from him, her blue eyes narrowing. Ah, there was the dangerous girl. "You know we were responsible for getting the code. How did you think I would get it to you?"

"Text works." If she was here, she had a mission and it was likely to get that formula for the Agency.

She reached into her pocket and pulled out a card. "You need this along with the code. I took it off one of Huisman's men last night at a bar. He's still sleeping it off so I doubt he'll miss it. Now, if you don't mind, I'll open that door and we can be home in time for dinner."

Since they were on a completely different continent from home, he took it as pure sarcasm. She seemed to breathe sarcasm at times.

What was his play? He could fight her for the card, but she wouldn't give him the code. He could argue that she wasn't going with him, perhaps even slip in and lock her out.

And then she would take his balls off, and that wasn't how he wanted her to get introduced to his balls. He would have to get in, find the formula, and destroy it before they ever left here.

"Did you get the vaccine?" If they hadn't inoculated her against inhalation anthrax, there was zero way he was taking her with him.

She rolled those gorgeous eyes of hers. "Of course. Do you think I have a death wish?"

He'd seen her jump out of a plane at nearly 35,000 feet, so yes, he often thought she did. Of course, he'd jumped out after her because they were about to be murdered and she'd taken the only parachute.

Maybe he was the one with a death wish. His dick seemed incredibly stupid.

"All right, I'm going first," he said. "I don't know if Huisman is behind that door or not. According to our intelligence, he hasn't left the base in a week, but he sent home the rest of the non-security employees a few days ago. Be careful, eh? He might be a doctor, but he gave up on his Hippocratic oath a long time ago. He will be armed and he won't hesitate to kill you. Stay behind me."

She moved to the door, flashing the key card and punching in a five-digit code. "You know I love it when you say, eh. And hey, if you want to get murdered first, who am I to stop you? What's wrong with the comms? I can't get my team on the line."

So hers wasn't working either. It was good to know they were completely blind. "Apparently the storm is wreaking havoc on our electronics. Stay behind me."

He started to move through the room, catching sight of the SIG Sauer in her right hand. The whole three years he'd worked with her off and on, she'd always used that weapon, though there were far more technologically advanced guns out there. She always claimed if it had been good enough for her father, it was good enough for her.

The door closed behind her and he turned on the light. "According to the plans we stole, this is where Huisman works."

"This outer section is part of his office. The lab is in the back. It's a level-four biosafety lab so we'll have to change if we go in there," she explained.

Did she think he was a moron? "Yes, I got that intel. And we don't have to change at all. I'll deal with it and you'll stay out here and watch for any stragglers. And Huisman. I haven't found him yet. He's got to be here somewhere."

She stopped in the middle of the hallway, one hand on her hip. "I'm not going to sit out here like a good little girl and wait for you. I can bet what would happen. You would go in and the formula would mysteriously disappear."

He wasn't playing these games with her. He strode down the hallway. Huisman's compound was multi-tiered, but this was definitely the level with the most security.

So why were the doors all open?

"If you think I'm going to allow something that deadly to fall into your country's hands, you don't know me at all," she insisted as she followed him.

The door to the lab was closed, but there was a green light blinking above, indicating that it wasn't locked. The lab was on one end of the hall and, if he was correct, Huisman's office was on the other. Perhaps he should check the office first. He didn't want to get caught with his pants down.

"I don't know you at all, sweetheart. I don't even know your real name. The only thing I know is that you'll do anything for your country, including turning over a weapon of mass destruction when you would be better off destroying the formula." He strode down the hallway well aware that they were making far too much noise. He couldn't seem to help it around her. "And don't even talk to me about our countries. Let's see which one is known for being involved in every war it can send its troops into, and which one is known for maple syrup and delicious donuts."

"We have excellent donuts, too," she shot back. "And maple syrup.

Have you never been to Vermont? Name me one thing Canada has that America doesn't. Face facts. You're nothing but America North, buddy."

She irritated him to no freaking end. So why did he dream about her at night? Why did every woman he slept with morph into her at some point? He was young, fit, and in a job that seemed to attract women even though he couldn't talk about it. Somehow they seemed to know he was dangerous and it drew them to him. He should be having the time of his life, but no, all he could think about was a woman with pink hair who challenged him at every turn. "You know what we have that you don't, baby? It's called common sense. Sweet, sane common sense. Which is precisely why you're not stealing this formula."

He stopped at the doorway. Not because he was worried about Huisman getting the jump on them.

They weren't alone. Not that it mattered.

"Is he dead?" Maggie moved in behind him.

Yep. Dr. Emmanuel Huisman was totally dead on the floor of his office. Unless he'd managed to fake the bullet hole to his left temple. Ben kicked the revolver away from the bad doctor's hand anyway. Never hurt to be cautious in his line of work. More than one person had come back from the "dead" and tried to kill him.

"He must have decided to kill himself rather than face the Agency." Maggie stared down at him.

"Maybe he knew he was facing CFI." Canadian Foreign Intelligence. His group.

She laughed. "You've been around for five years, buddy. You're not known for being particularly ferocious when it comes to dealing with prisoners. You do tend to give them donuts and hope they like you enough to talk."

There was another thing his country had on hers. Niceness. The Canadian version of the CIA hadn't existed until five years before, when the Chinese and Russians had started moving in on South America and Mexico.

Maybe they weren't great at all things torture, but damn it, he wasn't going to allow his country to go down.

He stopped and stared at the desk in front of him. Huisman's office was totally different from the utilitarian rooms outside it. This office was luxurious and built for comfort. There were several laptops and a big, sturdy desktop that likely held the secrets of this facility. A monitor sat on the desk, a sticky note hastily attached to the side. It was barely clinging there.

Play Me

"I don't think we should go down that rabbit hole," Maggie said, her boot tapping against the floor. "Let's get into the lab and get out of here. If he wanted to monologue like a good villain, he should have stayed alive."

Somehow Ben couldn't see it going so smoothly. Huisman was the kind of man who tended to get what he wanted. If he wanted them to listen, he would have found a way.

Still, he agreed that he wasn't simply going to stand there and comply. He glanced around and saw there was another door. There was a room beyond the office.

He stepped in and found something the reports hadn't mentioned. Huisman had a beautifully decadent bedroom. He should have known the fucker wasn't sleeping on some military-grade cot. The whole space was white and cream-colored, dominated by a massive four-poster bed. He had to wonder what it had cost to get that gorgeous monstrosity up a mountain.

Was that a fucking Picasso above the bed?

"What is that?" Maggie stepped in behind him.

She wasn't talking about the bed. Right there in the middle of the room was a large piece of equipment with tons of wires and compartments attached. On top of it sat a digital clock.

The door behind them slid closed with a nasty hiss and Ben watched in horror as the clock blinked to life.

1:00:00

0:59:59

0:59:58

"Shit. It's a bomb," Maggie said.

Yes, the other quality the Americans possessed was the unquestionable ability to state the obvious.

He turned and tried to open the door. It held firm. "Try the key card."

She waved it over the security box. Nothing. Well, not nothing. They got nothing from the door. It didn't budge, merely blinked red to let them know it wasn't opening. But a monitor did slip down from the ceiling. It was perfectly placed to be seen from the bed. Ben moved back, taking in the monitor that was now full of Huisman's self-satisfied smile.

"Welcome, Benjamin," the man on the monitor said. He spoke in softly accented English, French being his native tongue. "I figured you wouldn't follow my very reasonable orders, so I had to set a bit of a trap to get you to hear me out. If you are not Benjamin Parker of Canadian Intelligence, I apologize. But I think it will be you. You and the American girl. I seem to find you together so very often. Welcome. You finally found me. I applaud you and you've managed to catch me at a delicate time. Even now you're at work in the outside perimeter, taking out my soldiers. I went cheap on the mercenaries. I suppose thrift really was my downfall. The good news is the bomb you are currently sharing space with is not cheap. It's quite expensive, filled with all the best uranium China could get to me. It's certainly enough to blow the top off this mountain. And it will be enough to send my enriched and hearty anthrax all over the country of Nepal."

"Why the fuck does he care about Nepal?" Maggie asked.

Huisman wasn't finished. "Why do I care about Nepal, you might ask? I don't, but the Chinese want it destroyed and they paid me an enormous amount of money to do it. The explosion will destabilize this part of the world. In addition to blowing off the top of this mountain, I've rigged something special up there. When my new anthrax hits the upper atmosphere, it will breed and form clouds. It will rain down on the people of this region. Imagine that. Not acid rain. Anthrax rain that only the Chinese and their select friends will be immune to. It will seep into the soil. Perhaps my new bacteria will continue to breed. It will be a brave new world, my friends. Unfortunately, you and I will not live to see it. I think I'll go out on a high note, but I wanted to leave you a bit of time to contemplate the end of your existence. This is my final gift to you, Benjamin. I give you the gift of time. What will you do with the final hour of your life? I think you will be like a rat on a sinking ship, scratching and panicking to save your own pathetic life. You see, there are worse things than dying. Au revoir, mon ami."

Ben felt her hand slip into his. He squeezed it tight.

They were so fucked.

⁓

41:34

The clock kept ticking.

"I think we should cut the blue wire." Maggie had been carefully inspecting the bomb that would likely end their lives. "The only problem is I'm fairly certain this sucker has a couple of land mines attached. I don't mean that literally, of course, but I think bad crap could happen if I clip the wrong wire. The red wire goes to something that looks like it's empty, so it's probably a gas."

"I wouldn't put it past him to release some sarin on us if we did something wrong." He could see what she was talking about. The bomb was a complete mess of wires. It would take hours to figure out where each of them went. Hours they didn't have.

Maggie sat up, pushing her hot-pink hair out of her face. She'd gotten out of the massive parka she'd been wearing and underneath had been a white jumpsuit that would have looked utilitarian on someone else. It just made her look like a freaking walking wet dream. "I could use a little optimism."

"I don't have any when it comes to that bomb. I think we should try to work on the comms. Neither one of us is a bomb expert." He'd tried everything he could to get that damn door open. It wasn't budging and he'd nearly taken off his own head by trying to shoot the locking mechanism. Luckily, he was excellent with some forms of technology. He touched the ultralight tablet he carried with him at all times and felt a thrill go through him as the TV screen switched from Huisman's face to a computer screen. "I'm in his computer system."

She stood, her eyes going wide. "How did you manage that? Can you get the door open?"

Probably not, since he'd shot the mechanism. Yeah, not his best moment. He started typing on the tablet. "The TV is a smart screen. It should be able to connect to any system with a signal. Huisman sprang for the best. The satellite connection is still working. It looks like he's shut down electrical to all the doors. No one can get in or out."

"Send out a message before his handlers figure out they should shut down the satellite." She was close to him again. He could smell the citrus scent of her shampoo. He lied to himself, trying to force his brain away from dangerous territory. She wasn't his type. He liked normal women. Women who didn't jump out of planes and have pink hair. Women who weren't incredibly skilled assassins. Women who didn't make his heart pound the way this one did.

He quickly typed a message to his handler. Tim was in a camp at the base of the mountain and they would all need to evacuate as quickly as possible. He sent it off but couldn't get through to Tim's mobile. He passed Maggie the tablet.

"Thanks," she said, turning away slightly. "At least I can warn my team."

"Where are they?" He knew next to nothing about her team. He'd only dealt with her.

"They're probably with Tim by now," she said. "They were taking the helo down the mountain after they dropped me off. My partner was worried about losing the bird. It's brand-new and it's capable of getting up to almost thirty thousand feet, but it's struggling with the storm. Langley will potentially murder us if we crash that chopper. It's their baby and we might or might not have had permission to take it out for this op."

Somehow it didn't surprise him. She was likely a massive pain in the ass to her boss. "You stole a helo?"

She finished typing and looked back up at him. "I think they will discover that we were simply mistaken about which helo we were supposed to take. It was really early and that requisition form can be hard to read before I've had a cup of coffee."

"Let me see if I can affect this bomb from here." He took the tablet from her and started poking around the system. "I have no idea how you get away with that shit. If I did it, I would be fired."

"It helps to have friends. We work with some of the best Special Ops teams in the world, and I happen to have grown up with some of those guys. I'm sure if times weren't what they are those relationships would cost me plenty, but I'm incredibly valuable for them now. My helo pilot used to steal cookies from my mom's cookie jar. Though I'm not the only one who seems to have connections. Why did Huisman call you friend?" If she was upset about the fact that they were locked in a room with a bomb big enough to take out a mountain, she didn't show it. She made a slow circle around the room, trailing her hand over the comforter on the bed. "Or more specifically mon ami."

"Because he's an asshole." He didn't want to go into this. It wasn't any of her business. He should leave it at that, but he found himself going on. "We were friends when we were kids."

Why had he said that?

"I knew he was from Quebec," she said, sitting at the end of the bed. "I didn't realize you knew him."

Frustration welled inside him as he pored over the system. Any way he went, he got blocked. Huisman had been a brilliant doctor, but he'd known computer systems, too. He might have gone cheap on the mercenaries hired to protect him, but he'd been smart enough to hire the best when it came to setting up his cyber security systems. Of course, it wasn't like Ben himself was some brilliant hacker. He knew just enough to think he could do things he obviously couldn't. That was why he had Tim. But he was worried Tim wouldn't be able to get into a closed system.

It was up to him. The whole fucking fate of this region was up to him.

"Hey, it's okay." She was suddenly behind him, her hands on his shoulders. "None of this is your fault. Unless Huisman was your secret lover and you cheated on him and that's why he hates the world."

He rounded on her. This was not the time to joke. "He was not my secret lover."

She shrugged, the motion making her breasts move. Gorgeous fucking breasts. Those breasts made his mouth water. They made his brain soft, because he was looking down the barrel of a massive, uranium-enriched gun and all he could think about was how he could see a hint of nipple through that white shirt. And it wasn't cold in here. It might be freezing outside, but Huisman had managed to keep it nice and toasty in his evil lair.

"I always wondered."

He turned, forgetting about the tablet for a moment. "You wondered if I was gay? I'm not gay. What exactly gave you the impression that I'm gay? If you say it's because I'm Canadian, I swear I'll be done with you."

Her lips curled up in the sexiest smile. "That sounds like something my dad would say. He's pretty rah-rah USA. Spent some time in the military. But no, your Canadianness doesn't make me question your sexuality, merely your choice of bacon."

She was so frustrating and he suddenly got the idea that he should show her just how not gay he was. "My choice of bacon is fine. It leads to far less heart disease than yours. Let me explain a few things to you, sweetheart. There's nothing wrong with homosexuality. It's a perfectly natural state. My natural state is different. I like women. I like breasts and hips and pussies. I really like soft, welcoming pussies, especially when they're attached to smart, sexy, dangerous women."

She held her ground and, yes, those nipples were definitely out and that had not a thing to do with the temperature. "Well, we've worked together a couple of times now and you've never once hit on me. It makes a girl think."

So arrogant. "So if a man doesn't hit on you, he's obviously gay? Maybe you're not my type."

"Oh, I'm you're type. Don't get me wrong, Ben. I can be arrogant, but I'm self-aware, too. I know perfectly well that I'm not every man's type. I'm a brat of the highest order and I was probably raised to have ridiculously high standards, but we're alike, you and I. If you prefer women, I'm your natural mate."

What was she trying to do? They had less than forty minutes before the world blew up and she was hitting on him? She wanted to do this now? "Natural mate? In your world do natural mates take the last parachute and leave the other to die? Do they shoot their mate in the shoulder? How about the throwdown in the alley in Beijing when you kicked me in the balls and stole the only invite to that auction the cartel was having?"

She rolled those gorgeous blue eyes. "Don't be such a drama queen. I took the parachute because I knew damn well you would follow me. If I hadn't, you would have stood there and talked that asshole to death. Excuse me for getting bored. And I shot you through the shoulder because that was the only way to kill the bad guy. His heart was behind your shoulder. I knew what I was doing and I wasn't about to let him drag you away and use you as a human shield. As for the auction…I know you won't believe me but I felt bad about that. I should have found another way but it worked out. That invite led to us all getting valuable intelligence. I'm sorry about…well, I'm just sorry."

He tried to keep his eyes on the monitor, but he could feel her moving behind him. "You halfway sound like you care, Maggie."

"I did and I do," she said quietly. "You're not going to be able to untangle that mess, Ben. We don't have near enough time."

She cared? About him? "I need some optimism."

That was the moment the lights went out. They were plunged into complete darkness. Ben reached out, putting the tablet down.

He stepped back, turning and reaching out for her. "Maggie?"

"I'm here." She moved close to him, bumping up against his chest. Her arms went around him. "I don't want to lose you. I can't see a thing."

He couldn't see a damn thing either, but he could already feel something. A chill went through the room. If the power had gone out, then the climate control would go as well. It was possible the venting had opened and they were about to get a big dose of what it meant to be twenty-three thousand feet above sea level.

The truth was even if he could get them out, it wouldn't matter now. They could try to climb down, but their time was running out and this was the kind of climb that took hours and hours without the aid of a helicopter.

And they couldn't hack into a system when the wireless was down.

He held her for a moment, taking in the gravity of the situation. His eyes adjusted and he realized something was still working. "Is the timer still ticking down?"

"Yes." She laid her head on his shoulder, the same one she'd shot. "It's on some kind of battery, but if I try to clip it, it looks like it triggers the system."

Naturally.

"And the sensor that connects it to the bomb on top of the mountain is very likely battery operated, too." It's what he would do. Huisman would have left nothing to chance. He'd set everything up perfectly. He'd even left them in the dark.

Like rats on a sinking ship.

How did he want to spend the last half hour of his life?

"I think I can see enough to get around now." Maggie took a step back. He heard her boots move across the floor. "Damn it. Well, the power going out didn't kill the security system. That door is not budging."

Because the man on the other side of it would have been very careful. Had Huisman hurried and hustled to make this happen? Had he realized he was going down and scrambled to catch the hunter in a trap of his own? Or had this always been his plan?

Ben rather thought it was the latter.

He heard a long sigh and then a single stream of light cut through the darkness. Maggie moved through the room, toward the big four-poster bed. She opened the nightstand and started going through it.

"Oh, look. The good doctor believed in safe sex," she murmured. "And a shocking amount of lube. Who needs that much lube? Ah, there we go."

She set down the small flashlight and there was the scratching sound of a match striking. She lit the candles that had decorated the room.

"Do you think he used this place as his pleasure palace?" Maggie asked as she filled the room with soft light.

Ben realized that he hadn't moved. Not an inch. Since that moment when Huisman's words had whispered through his brain—how will you spend your last hour?—he'd been locked in place, his focus shifting from survival to something else.

Her.

She turned, her pink hair still somehow so vibrant in the candlelight. It had softened all of her other features. "You okay?"

It was a ridiculous question. They were trapped inside a mountain that was going to blow up and decimate a whole lot of the population of their planet. He was not okay. "No."

Maggie stepped in front of him. "You need to have a little faith. We're stuck. There's nothing we can do, but our people know what's going on. They won't let this happen. I assure you that my team is taking that state-of-the-art helo up the mountain right now and they will move that bomb or they will find a way to ensure that it doesn't go off. They're the best. They won't let me down."

"But there's no way for them to stop the bomb that's five feet away from us."

She glanced over at it and sighed. "No. I don't think they can and they know what their priorities are. I've already assessed this and the most likely outcome is that my team takes out the big bomb and we die in here anyway."

"Yes, I think you're right." He wasn't going down like a desperate rat. He'd known this would be his fate. He would die on a mission, trying to save his country—the world, really. He reached out and did what came naturally. He touched her, touched that spun-sugar hair of hers. It was ridiculously soft against his skin. "I wish you weren't here with me."

"That's funny because I was thinking that there was no place I would rather be." She stepped in closer, tilting her head slightly up. "You took your time, Ben. You're not good at reading signals because I've been sending them out forever."

He let his hands sink into her hair, the sense of anticipation flooding his system. Yes, this was the way he would spend the last moments of his life. With her. Warm and happy with her. "Your signals suck, baby. All you ever had to do was this."

He lowered his head and brushed his lips over hers. So long. He'd waited forever to feel those velvet-soft lips under his. He moved slowly despite the fact that there was a bomb ticking down the time. It didn't matter anymore. That clock could move on and he would stay here, doing this, kissing her and exploring her like he'd wanted to from the first moment. Oddly enough, now that he was here, time seemed to slow and the destination wasn't half as important as the journey. If the world blew up, at least their bodies would mingle. No one would be able to tell the difference between them. In that moment, he was all right. It was a better fate than any other he'd been offered.

She moved with him, her mouth flowering open at the mere hint of his tongue. She welcomed him inside, her hands going to his hips. He felt her sigh as he deepened the kiss. Their bodies brushed each other and then she moved against him, bringing her breasts to his chest as she wrapped her arms around him.

Had they been anywhere else, he wouldn't have trusted the moment. He would have been on his guard, thinking she was trying to distract him. She was, but he wanted this distraction.

No. It wasn't the distraction he wanted and he hoped she wasn't using sex simply to get her mind off the fact that they were going to die.

"Maggie, I'm crazy about you. I've wanted to touch you since the moment I saw you. Well, most of the time," he whispered against her mouth. He dragged his tongue across her lower lip, loving the way she shuddered in his arms. "Sometimes it's like you're a different person."

She shook her head. "Don't think about that. That was all work. This is different, Ben. I want you so badly sometimes I can't stand it. My friends know it, too. They know you're the reason I haven't had a damn boyfriend in a year."

He kissed her again, drugged by her softness, the feeling of being able to lose himself in her. He took her mouth over and over again, thanking Huisman for being so slavishly devoted to his own comfort that he would have a bedroom built for sex even on this remote mountain.

He let his hands roam over her back and down to that perfect ass he thought about all the time. Maggie was fit and strong, but she had curves in all the right places. Her backside fit into the palms of his hands like it'd been made for him. He pulled her close, letting her feel what she did to him. "Do you have any idea how hard it is to work with you? I get this any time you're around."

She frowned at him. "Even when I'm busting your balls?"

"Okay, so there are times when you seem more pissed off than others." Sometimes she seemed deeply dismissive of him, as though she didn't remember or care about the times when they'd talked and worked together in harmony. Those tended to be the times he had to watch because he ended up shot or kicked in the balls. "I often wonder who hurt you."

Her hands moved up his chest. "One day I'll explain everything, but for now, please kiss me again, Ben."

One day would have to be had in Heaven or Hell, or wherever operatives went after they got their asses blown to bits, but he wasn't about to argue with her now. He gave in and kissed her again, their tongues sliding against each other.

He moved from her mouth to her cheek and down toward her neck. He wanted to kiss her everywhere, but that damn jumpsuit she wore covered her well and he couldn't find the zipper. "Baby, I want to see you. I want to touch you. I know we don't have much time, but I want to spend every single second we have left getting inside you. It's all I want now."

He wanted her more than breathing. If the door opened at this point, he would ignore it. He wouldn't waste his time trying to flee. He would spend it wrapping himself up in her.

She stepped back, the sweetest smile on her face. He loved seeing her like this. This was the Maggie who haunted his dreams. Not that she wasn't competent in the field, but this side of the woman seemed devoted to working with him instead of showing him what a dumbass he was.

"You know we have all the best toys, Ben." She turned slowly and he could see there wasn't a zipper anywhere and yet it was plastered to her body. It fit perfectly. "Nanites. They conform to whoever's wearing them. They're also resistant to bullets and weapons. Oh, push hard enough and you can still get a knife through there, but it gives me some protection."

Yes, the Americans did have all the best tech. "How do I get it off you?"

He didn't give a damn about how it worked except to get her naked. Normally he would ask a hundred questions because he'd never seen nanite tech like this before, but he couldn't care less. He was all about finally seeing how gorgeous she truly was.

"It's easy," she said. "It's voice-activated. Undress."

The white jumpsuit flowed down her body like a metallic cascade, unveiling her skin. Her hair spilled around her shoulders, falling almost to her nipples. The sight of her breasts made his dick harden even further. How hard could he get before he died from it? It didn't matter because he was watching as the nanites retreated and showed him her hips and the gorgeous spot between her legs. Her pussy was smooth and bare and he could see the glistening arousal there. Even the damn boots she was wearing disappeared into a cube that formed at her feet. She reached down and placed it on the nightstand. "Cute, huh?"

That wasn't the word he would use. "I take it that voice control is only for you. Because I could find a definite use for that. Damn, but you're gorgeous. Come here. It's cold and I don't want you to feel the chill for even a second."

"I didn't notice, Ben. I'm perfectly warm." She moved toward him, slowly, as though well aware of his eyes on her. "And I would never give you that code. I know what you would do with it."

He would have her naked whenever the mood sparked him, and it would spark him a lot. He would keep her on her toes, and the second they had any privacy at all, he would find a corner and give the command that would have her naked. "I don't have clothes that undress themselves. I think I need you to help me."

She moved right in, her hands going to the bottom of his sweater. "I should have known you would be needy. Lucky for you, I don't mind a little work."

She eased her hands under the sweater and thermals he was wearing underneath. Ben bit back a moan the minute he felt her hands on his flesh. She slid them up, running along his abs and up to his chest, and he was happy he'd kept up a hard-core gym routine because this woman deserved a lover who could keep up with her. He stared down at her while she stared up.

He wished he hadn't wasted so much time. They'd been on a dozen ops together over the past three years and now he wished he'd kissed her the first time they'd met.

She dragged the layers over his head and tossed them to the side. Then her hands were on him, palms flat on his chest as she leaned over and kissed the curve of his neck. Yeah, he wasn't feeling the chill anymore. A delicious heat stroked through his body as he allowed her to explore. She cuddled up against him, her nipples rubbing. He cradled the back of her neck as she kissed her way down his torso. She stopped briefly at the scar on his left shoulder, the bullet wound now raised and white.

"So sorry about that, babe." She kissed the scar and then ran her tongue around it before continuing down.

When she dropped to her knees, it took everything he had not to come then and there. There was something almost formal about the way she did it, as though she was offering him something he didn't entirely understand. He wasn't about to turn it down though. He watched in breathless anticipation as she unbuckled his belt and eased down the heavy fabric of his slacks and thermals. They'd kept him warm, but now the heat in her eyes would do the trick.

She glanced down as his cock came free. He bit back the need to beg her to touch him. He didn't care how much time was left on that fucking clock. He wasn't going to make this some rushed thing. It was their first time.

Their only time.

"I knew you would be beautiful, Ben. I win that bet."

He was about to ask her what she meant by that, but she leaned forward and gripped his cock in her hand. When she tongued his cockhead, he gasped and fought the urge to come. Nope. Wasn't happening.

She sucked the head behind those sinful lips of hers and he thought he was going to die. Heat sparked through his system and he felt his balls drawing up. That was all it took. She was so gorgeous, so hot and perfect that it was a fight to stay calm.

Her tongue whirled around his cock and he let his hands find her hair, sinking in and drawing her closer.

"Take more." He wasn't going to come in her mouth. No. He wanted to get inside her body, wanted so badly to feel that sweet pussy sucking him inside. But he would know her mouth, too. Fully.

"You have no idea what that deep voice does to me, Ben. One day we're going to have a long talk about my personal kinks, but for now just know that I can take orders. I want to please you."

Fuck, that did something for him. It made his heart speed up and his dick throb. He had a sudden vision of tying her up and torturing her body in the sweetest way. He would make her come again and again, and only when she begged him would he find his own release and relent. Then she would be his. His own spy girl with pink hair and cherry lips. She would fight against everyone except him because she would know he would protect and care for her.

Oh, the life they could have had.

"You please me in every single way, baby. Now take me. Suck me hard and fast and don't stop until I tell you to."

She licked her lips and settled back down, sucking him in long passes. So good. It felt so good, but he couldn't let it last. Her mouth moved over him, infusing him with energy like he'd never felt before. It hummed through his body and made him feel more alive than he'd ever felt before. He pushed into her mouth, taking control and feeling the moment when she surrendered. She let him use her mouth, sucking him hard and submitting in a way that nearly sent him over the edge.

This was what she wanted. She was trying to show him what she wanted from him. He tugged on her hair, just enough so she would feel it.

She came off him, her face tilting up and showing him red, gloriously swollen lips. Her blue eyes stared up at him as she waited.

She was waiting for him to take control. The idea made his cock jump and it damn straight made him want to show her exactly how good he could make this.

"Get on the bed and spread your legs for me. I want to see that pretty pussy before I eat it like a starving man." Something about her brought out the dirty talk. Sex before this had been good but polite. He'd been taught to be respectful and gentlemanly, but now he realized he could be both. He could respect the hell out of her and give her every dirty, filthy fantasy he'd ever had.

He kicked out of his boots, watching her while she spread herself on the bed. Her hair made a halo around her, but there the angelic references ended. She was a siren, calling a man to temptation, and he didn't care if it all led to tragedy.

"Touch yourself. I want you to rub your little clit and get it hot and ready for me. I want that pussy wet. I want to lick that pussy and get cream all over my tongue. Do you understand me?"

"You're killing me, Ben." She drew her hand down her body until she found her pussy and brushed manicured fingers over the pearl of her clitoris.

Ben stepped out of his pants and stroked his cock as he looked down at her. She was the sexiest thing he'd ever seen. So feminine and perfect. Sure, she had scars, but so did he. Those scars marked them, and if he'd had time, he would map her body. He would kiss every inch of her, moving from scar to scar and having the story of each one so he could know her soul as well as he would learn her flesh.

He climbed on the bed with her. "Give me a taste."

Maggie offered up her fingers and he brought them to his lips, sucking them inside. He was perfectly satisfied with the way she flushed. He sucked on her fingers, drawing the taste of her inside and letting it coat his tongue.

"You taste perfect, but I'm going to need more." He leaned over and took her mouth, giving the taste of her own arousal back to her before kissing his way down her body.

Her hands fisted in the covers as he sucked on one nipple and then the other, laving them with his affection. Her breasts were so beautifully sensitive, responding to him by puckering up.

He could stay there forever, but their time was limited so he kissed his way over the soft swell of her belly and down to where he'd wanted to be since the moment he'd laid eyes on her.

He breathed her in, the smell of her sex lighting a fire inside him.

"Please, Ben." The words came out of her mouth on a low moan as she spread her legs even farther.

What happened next would definitely please Ben. He lowered his mouth and covered her pussy. He settled in, loving the way she tasted, and he could feel her shaking under him. She was already so close. He could taste it, sense it in her little whimpers and cries. Her hands came up, fingers tangling in his hair, trying to keep him in a place he had absolutely no intention of leaving. Not until he was sure she'd been satisfied.

This was everything he'd wanted from her and more. He settled in, grinding his tongue over her clit as he eased his finger into her. She was so tight. Those muscles of hers clenched around him as he started to fuck her in time to the rhythm of his tongue. He curled his finger up inside her, looking for that sweet spot.

Her whole body stiffened and she came around him, her arousal flooding his senses.

And now it was his time. He got to his knees, stroking his cock. He glanced over at the condoms, but damn it, it was the end of the fucking world. Still, force of habit had him reaching out and opening the packet before he could really consider the fact that it didn't matter.

Then nothing mattered except the woman underneath him. Her skin had flushed to a gorgeous pink and he couldn't deny himself a second longer.

He pressed in, working his way in inch by inch. He couldn't breathe, couldn't think past the next thrust. She was silky and perfect around him. So tight he could barely move, but also slick and ready to take him. He pulled back out, her muscles sucking at him and sending a thrill through him like never before.

This was good. This was right. Finally the right woman at the right time.

It was perfection.

He fucked her hard, rubbing his pelvis over her clit and watching every expression on her face. Her eyes would widen with each thrust and she would clutch him when he retreated. He could feel the way her nails bit into the skin of his back, and it hurt so much that he wouldn't wake up in the morning and stretch and feel that pain and know she'd been right here with him.

He wanted tomorrow with her. All the fucking tomorrows.

He wanted to take this one moment and make it stretch forever, make it last until he couldn't breathe, couldn't take another single second.

But he was only human and long before he wanted it to end, he felt her tighten around him, her pussy milking his cock as she flushed again and called out his name.

He couldn't fight it. His balls drew up and his spine tingled. He gritted his teeth as he came harder than he'd ever come before. He unleashed himself and pounded inside her, the need to mark her as his own a primitive and undeniable instinct.

Pleasure coursed through him and he held himself tight against her, giving up everything he had.

He dropped down on top of her, giving her his weight as the blood pounded through his system in a pleasurable way. Her hands came up and she stroked his hair, sighing as she cuddled close to him. He buried his face against her neck and let peace flood him.

How could it all be ending when he'd just found her? He'd spent his whole adult life fighting for his country, but something had been missing, something hadn't been whole inside him, and now he knew what had always been missing.

Her.

A long moment passed and he realized she was shaking a bit. Cold. The cold suddenly bit into him.

"Baby, let's get under the covers. I want to hold you." He wanted to spend every second in her arms.

She smiled and kissed him briefly. "I can get with that. But go and get rid of that condom first. I do not want that slipping off and going everywhere. Sticky is not the new black."

Even here she teased him. He kissed her again and reluctantly pushed off her. "I'll be right back. Get under the covers. I want you warm."

Her lips curled up. "Yes, sir."

Something about the way she said sir made his cock spark all over again. He moved toward the door that would likely lead to either a bathroom or closet. He didn't care which. It wasn't like there would be some cleaning crew that would get embarrassed if he tossed a condom where Huisman stored his suits and shoes.

He glanced down and couldn't miss the red lights shining in the dim.

3:10

God. Three minutes. He opened the door and found himself in what seemed to be a gorgeous bathroom. The room was in shadows, the only light coming from the candles Maggie had lit. He pulled the condom off and dropped it in the trash and then tried the sink. The water still worked.

He wanted to touch her again, with clean hands. There wasn't time to make love again, but he could hold her. He could cuddle her close and kiss her over and over until the end.

Make love. He'd never used those words with the act before. He'd had sex, fucked, gotten laid, but he'd never made love.

He loved Maggie. She was the one woman in the world who held a piece of his soul, and he was about to lose her.

He forced the dark thought back because he wasn't going to panic. There wasn't anything that panic would solve, and he would spend his final moments in peace.

He would spend them with her.

He strode back out, barely registering the clock as he moved to her.

2:37

Two minutes and thirty-seven seconds left to hold her, to love her.

She was under the covers and she drew them back, welcoming him in. He immediately pulled her into his arms.

"I hate that I wasted all this time," he whispered, kissing her forehead. "I should have made a move, should have told you that first time that I thought you were the most gorgeous thing I'd ever seen, but you seemed so cold."

"About that," she began. She rubbed her cheek against his chest like a kitten looking for affection. "I'm glad you didn't because it would have been awkward."

"The second time I saw you I wanted to kiss you. Do you remember?"

She smiled against his chest. "I remember. We were in Croatia trying to track down that bomb maker and we had to pretend to be lovers. You danced with me."

Such a sweet memory. He'd thought she was gorgeous the first time, but the second time they'd worked together something had been utterly different. Something had slipped into place that had been missing before. "Your hair was flaming red and you were wearing that ridiculous green dress that had every man in the room panting after you."

"Including you?"

"Oh, so including me. That was when I knew I wanted you. You were distant before and then we clicked." They'd danced all night and brought that man down. Together.

Her head came up. "I should explain that. Why I seemed like two different people at times. Ben, I want to be honest with you."

Their time was running out. So fast. God, he needed more time with her. She looked over and her face fell.

1:10

She shook her head and wrapped her arms around him. "It doesn't matter. Just know that I always wanted you, Ben. I knew it from the moment I saw you. I knew you were the one for me and even though it was complicated, I was always going to end up right here. With you. This is how we end, Ben Parker. We end together."

He held on to her and found her lips with his. He kissed her again and again, this time with no expectations of anything but to die in her arms. His cock thickened, but he could ignore it in favor of telling her how gorgeous she was, how lucky he'd been to meet her, to know her.

To love her.

She wrapped her arms around him and held on.

For way longer than a minute.

What the hell was going on? He glanced over and the clock read 0:00.

It held for one second and then another.

And that was when he heard the clang of someone knocking on the door.

"I'm coming in. Dear god, please cover up and don't be doing something that will make me vomit," a familiar voice said.

"Oh, shit." Maggie turned and practically leapt out of bed.

The door came open and he was facing...well, he was facing a second Maggie, except her hair was a brilliant purple.

"Okay, sis, there's good news and bad news," Second Maggie said.

Maggie was reaching for her clothes cube. "I take it the good news is that we didn't blow up and that's awesome. How did you manage to shut down the bombs?"

"I didn't," Second Maggie said. "Tris did. He and that Canadian dude worked some serious mojo while Coop and I took the helo up and tried to take the bomb somewhere safe. Luckily we didn't need to because the geeks came through. By the way, the comm problem was totally one-way. We could hear everything, and also, there are cameras that fed out even after the power went off, so way to make a sex tape, sis. Dad's totally getting hold of that one, you know." She finally looked his way. "He's going to kill you, dude. And you should know that it was totally me who shot you and kicked you in the balls."

Yes, he could see that now. Damn it. She was twins. His head was kind of reeling because they weren't dead and now there were two of her and apparently she had some crazed father who wouldn't appreciate his sexual performance.

"Maggie?"

She was dressed again, the nanites covering her gorgeous body in an instant. She gave him a brilliant smile. "It's Kenzie. Kenzie Taggart."

His brain caught on that last name and his stomach kind of took a deep dive. That last name was iconic in the industry. It couldn't be a coincidence. "Taggart? Tell me he's not your father."

She sighed and rolled her eyes and looked like that perfect brat she'd called herself. "He's not that bad."

Ian Taggart was known as the single scariest dude in the whole of the intelligence community, and apparently he'd just made passionate, end-of-time love to the man's daughter.

The other Kenzie grinned but managed to make it slightly sinister. "Oh, he's so going to want to meet you, dude. Now let's go because we still have a crazy scientist to hunt down. I have no idea how he managed it, but he took a helo off the mountain twenty minutes ago while we were trying to make sure he didn't blow up the world."

Ben stood, not caring that he was naked. "Huisman is dead. His body is out there in the office."

"Nope," the twin said. "He faked it all and got out with the formula. We're starting from scratch. I believe you're wanted in a debrief and then our agencies are going to form a team. That should be fun now that little sister scratched her itch."

Maggie…Kenzie frowned her sister's way. "He wasn't an itch. You know that, Kala."

Kala sent her what seemed to be a sad smile. "I know. But we have to move. We have to get that helo back or Coop will be in trouble." Kala winked at him. "And nice package, Parker. I'm glad I didn't wreck it."

Kenzie turned his way and rushed to him. "I have to go, but I'll see you soon, Ben."

She kissed him briefly and then walked out the door.

Ben stood there utterly shocked.

"Hey, clothes, man." Tim walked in the room. "You might have made a sex tape but I don't need to see it up close and in person."

"Sorry." He was still looking at the door she'd walked through. "My clothes don't work on their own. Start talking. I want to hear everything."

Tim started the debrief as Ben dressed, but his mind was on something else. Someone else.

The game wasn't over. Huisman was still out there, but that was secondary in Ben's brain.

Kenzie Taggart could run. She could try to hide behind her legendary family, but he knew one thing.

That woman would be his.

ABOUT LEXI BLAKE

Lexi Blake lives in North Texas with her husband, three kids, and the laziest rescue dog in the world. She began writing at a young age, concentrating on plays and journalism. It wasn't until she started writing romance that she found success. She likes to find humor in the strangest places. Lexi believes in happy endings no matter how odd the couple, threesome, or foursome may seem. She also writes contemporary Western ménage as Sophie Oak.

To be notified of new releases or sales,
join Lexi's Mailing List: www.lexiblake.net/newsletter
Connect with Lexi online
Facebook: www.facebook.com/pages/Lexi-Blake/342089475809965
Instagram: www.instagram.com/Lexi4714
Visit Lexi at www.LexiBlake.net!

POWER *Struggle*

MARI CARR

1

"Had an interesting conversation at work today." Reed Donovan kicked back in his chair, taking a sip of the Scotch Carter had just poured for him. Carter enjoyed these occasional evenings with Reed, noticing how much more relaxed his stretched-tighter-than-a-drum cousin was these days. Carter knew exactly who to thank for the change —Frankie Carlyle, Reed's marketing partner and soon-to-be-wife.

"You and Frankie sexting through private messenger again?"

Reed grinned. "We did, but this conversation had more to do with you. It was with the one who got away."

Carter fell silent for a moment, digesting that information, pretending Reed hadn't just dropped a bomb. He didn't have to ask who Reed had seen. His cousin had taken to calling Bree Andrews the one who got away just a few weeks after she packed up all her belongings and moved to Paris.

He and Bree had been friends since their sophomore year in college and that relationship continued for six years, until Bree's escape from the States a decade ago. Bree had been there when he'd bought his bar with a loan from his uncle, and the first drink he'd served had been to her. He had been standing next to her the day she got the phone call that one of her clothing designs had been sold to a large fashion house.

They had been each other's confidants—and sometimes conscience—whenever they were in romantic relationships. There were no secrets between them, so he knew all about her love affairs, and she his. Both of them, demanding, passionate lovers, leaned heavily toward the alpha side in matters of sex.

However, they were wholly independent outside the bedroom and prone to push away anyone who needed a deeper emotion or closeness. As such, neither of them had found much success in long-term relationships. He could see now that they had provided the emotional support for each other back then while slaking their sexual needs with others.

Hindsight was twenty-twenty.

And then there was the day she learned her mother and sister had been murdered. Bree had clung to him for hours as she sobbed out her sorrow and he added a few of his own tears to the mix. Her pain that night had torn him to shreds, made him feel helpless.

He had been sitting next to Bree in the courtroom the day they'd read the verdict in Ronnie Bertrand's trial. Her stepfather had been sentenced to life in prison without hope of parole in the brutal murder of her family. Bree's testimony against him, revealing the years of abuse the three women had suffered at his hands, had gone a long way toward sealing the man's fate.

"Shocked you, didn't I?" Reed asked, pulling Carter from his memories.

Carter didn't bother to deny it. "Bree's in the States? To stay?"

"Yeah," Reed replied. "Moved back to Manhattan a couple months ago."

She hadn't called him. That fact tweaked even though it didn't really surprise him. In one impulsive night, he'd destroyed the most important relationship in his life. For years, he tried to get over her, to mend his broken heart with other women. And when that failed, he gave up and embraced his bachelor lifestyle.

Turned out, the one who got away was the only one for him.

"She wanted to hire me and Frankie to help promote her designs. She's setting up shop in the old NY of C."

"Tired of Paris?"

Reed shrugged. "We didn't talk about a lot of personal stuff. Although she did ask if you were still local, if you still owned the bar. Don't worry. I managed to work in the fact you're still single too."

Carter smiled at that, despite his best efforts to appear uninterested.

Reed snorted. "I gotta tell you, man, her poker face is better than yours."

Carter grimaced. "Pretending I'm not happy about her return would be a pointless endeavor where you're concerned. You know me too well. You know I'm thrilled."

"You're happy I'm back?"

Carter and Reed both looked toward Bree with surprise. Neither of them had noticed her walk into the bar.

Carter rose slowly from the table, drinking in every detail of her as he did so. Her raven-colored hair was longer than it had been when she left, but apart from that, there was very little about Bree that had changed. Age had only accentuated her beauty. Her long, lithe body was still curvy in all the right places, and her ice-blue eyes were as sharp as ever as they took a similar inventory of him.

He wondered how he was faring. He was no stranger to the gym, taking care to keep in good physical shape, but there was no denying there was salt added to the pepper in his hair these days.

Then Carter realized there was something else different about Bree. The way she was looking at him. She wasn't treating him to some distant, old-friends-reuniting smile. Bree was staring at Carter with a hunger he shared.

"Reed," Carter started, but his cousin cut him off with a knowing chuckle.

"You're excused."

Carter gestured toward the back of the bar, down the corridor that would lead her to his office. He grinned as the sounds of Sam Cooke's "Bring It On Home to Me" played.

Bree was familiar with the layout, having helped him decorate the place prior to the grand opening. She turned and led the way, her firm ass swaying in her tight black skirt as she walked gracefully in her heels.

Poise, class, confidence.

Bree had it all. She always had. It was one of the main reasons the two of them had always remained just friends.

They were too similar, too...controlling. Neither of them ever doubted the epic power struggle that would ensue should they give in.

And they hadn't been proven wrong about that. The night after her stepfather's sentencing, they'd returned to Carter's place and succumbed. Six years of pent-up attraction and desire came rushing out.

Carter closed the office door after she entered. Reaching behind him, he locked it, then leaned on it. So much for playing it subtle. He'd missed Bree, the ache in his chest never once subsiding until this moment. He couldn't let her leave again. Not until...

Until what?

"You've been back two months." The words came out sounding like an accusation. Carter needed to rein in his emotions, but it bothered him to know they'd been so close for eight weeks and she hadn't contacted him.

"I wasn't sure you'd want to see me after..." She paused.

"After you snuck out of my bed and disappeared without a word a decade ago."

"That night," she started, her gaze holding firmly to his, "was a mistake."

Carter fought like the devil not to wince. He knew what she said was true. He'd always known it. Regardless, it had been the best night of his life. Holding her, caging her beneath him, taking her, claiming her, fucking her. Everything he'd ever wanted had been in his arms that night.

And she'd run.

"And yet you're here now."

She nodded. "I am."

"Why?"

"Because mistake or not, I've relived that night a million times in the last decade, played it over and over so many times, I thought I'd go mad with...wanting you."

Carter pushed away from the door, the weight and significance of her words driving him toward her.

He reached up, taking her beautiful face in his hands. "I've missed you, Bree."

She smiled, the sheen of tears in her eyes. "I was wrong to run."

He shook his head. "No, you weren't." He had to give her that much, because hurt or not, he had to give her the same honesty she'd given him.

Bree had been on emotion overload after hearing her stepfather's sentence, and he'd watched her fight to deal with all of it—the anger, the sorrow, the happiness, the vindication. She'd been a live spark that night, and he'd been stupid enough to grab her with his bare hands, foolishly thinking he could contain the current.

They'd walked into his apartment and ripped into each other like rabid animals. He'd never fucked any woman so hard, with so much passion—and maybe even a bit of fury because he knew even as he took her, he'd never hold her. They had pounded out every bad feeling, going twelve rounds in the ring until they had both been knocked out.

For a full week after, Carter had felt the pain left from the deep scratches she'd put on his back and some serious soreness in his muscles. He didn't doubt for a moment that she'd carried around more than a few bruises as well.

It had been a brutal, beautiful struggle, but in the end, neither of them had won.

Bree grasped one of his wrists and turned her face, kissing his palm. "I'm not going to run away again. I can't."

It was all he needed to hear. He leaned close and kissed her, trying hard to keep the touch gentle, soft, even as every part of him was clamoring to consume her. Her reassurance that she wouldn't leave wasn't enough for the conqueror, the one who'd lost his treasure once before. He wouldn't lose her again.

Bree's lips parted and her tongue plundered, claimed. Despite his efforts to go slow, she had other ideas. She drove that point home when she bit his lower lip and he tasted the slight tang of blood.

He pulled away, his eyes narrowing. "Careful, Bree. This isn't a battle you'll win. Right or wrong, I'm still pissed off at you for leaving, for stealing ten years from us."

She tilted her head, no trace of remorse in her expression. "I didn't see you running after me."

He sighed and gave her the point. "I won't make that mistake again."

Bree tugged the hem of his shirt from his dress slacks and unbuttoned his shirt, then stroked his bare chest. He'd stripped off his tie and tossed it onto the desk just before Reed appeared. At the time, he had thought the night was winding down.

As she touched him, he kissed her, his hands sliding beneath her skirt, skimming along her thighs.

She perched on the edge of his desk as she parted her legs, inviting him closer. One night had been enough to prove their sexual appetites were in perfect unison. However, the rest...well...that remained to be seen.

He ran his fingers along her slit, the thin strip of lace of her thong already soaked.

He pushed it aside as he shoved two fingers deep inside her. She groaned, her head rolling back as her eyes closed. Unable to resist, he reached up and grabbed a handful of her hair, pulling it. Her lids flew open, her gaze finding his as he increased the pressure.

"It all changes tonight. You belong to me now."

Her eyes narrowed at his archaic phrasing, but he didn't let her fight him on it. Instead, he gave her what he knew she needed.

He added a third finger to her pussy, pumping hard as he said, "And I belong to you."

2

Bree clenched harder to Carter's shoulders as his fingers moved deeper, faster. She was already too damn close, ready to fly apart at the seams.

A small part of her still insisted on self-preservation, and it had convinced her she'd built the last time up too big, fooled herself into thinking her night in Carter's bed had been better than she remembered.

So much for that survival instinct.

She was a goner.

Bree pressed her head against his bare chest, her body tensing, right on the verge of...

Carter pulled his fingers out seconds before she got there.

Lifting her head, she saw him studying her, intently, intensely.

She shook her head. "Finish," she demanded.

He grinned, looking every bit like the dominant man she knew him to be. The problem was, she was no submissive. And he knew it.

The issue of their sexual preferences had come up one night at college. They'd both gotten a little too tipsy while watching a movie at her apartment. Rather than seek out their usual hookups, they remained in, talking long into the night.

Carter had told her about his latest sexual conquest, a girl named Veronica, who loved it when he tied her up, spanked her, and withheld orgasms until she begged.

Bree had been enthralled by the concept, turned on by the idea of absolute control. When she said the same to Carter, he had laughed and said that pretty much ensured the two of them would never be lovers. Neither of them was disposed to bend to anyone's will.

They had accepted that as wisdom and held true to that decision for six long years.

Knowing she and Carter were too similar to ever survive in the bedroom didn't prevent her attraction to him. If anything, the old adage of wanting what she couldn't have had kicked into high gear.

"Carter," she started.

He cut her off with a quick, hard kiss. "You're not coming until I'm inside you. Ten years, Bree."

A chink in the armor. She'd done that. Hurt him by walking away.

He'd opened a vein and she owed him the same. "I was afraid."

"I know. It was—"

"Intense," she added, needing the chance to explain. "I wasn't in a good place that night. I missed Mom and Traci. I hated Ronnie with such extreme loathing I could taste it. I fell into your arms, into your bed, and even as good as it was, I knew it wouldn't last. I've spent every bit of the last ten years in therapy, trying to fix all the shit my stepfather fucked up inside me. If I stayed, you would have wanted to be with me, maybe even marry me. And I knew, even though I loved you, I'd eventually push you away. I may have been able to give you my heart back then, but my trust was locked in a clenched fist that wouldn't open, no matter what."

"I understand."

One look in his rich chocolate-brown eyes proved that he did, and for the first time since she'd walked into the bar tonight, she had a sense that everything was going to be okay. The ten years they'd been apart melted away, and she was back with her best friend.

Which meant, she had no trouble slipping right back into another familiar role as well. She patted him on the cheek as she said, "So be a good boy and finish what you started."

Carter laughed. "I may be older, Bree, and I'm sure you're going to discover I've mellowed in certain aspects of my life, but in some ways, I'm even harder."

She let her gaze drift to regions south of his waist. "I'll never complain about harder."

His expression sobered. "You might."

Before she could question him, he had both her hands in his as something silky slipped around her wrists. She glanced over her shoulder and started to struggle when she realized his intention to bind her arms behind her back with a necktie.

"Hold still," he commanded.

She continued to fight him. "That tone doesn't work with me, Carter. Untie me."

"No."

Carter had the definite advantage. While she went to the gym to stay in shape, he clearly hit the weights to build muscle. His strength was undeniable and the knot he tied efficient and unbreakable.

"This is a very cute power play, but as you know—"

That was all she managed to say before he twisted her with a firm hand and placed her facedown over his desk. Cool air hit the backs of her thighs as he lifted her skirt. The chill was brief, replaced with heat when Carter slapped her ass five times in hard succession.

She was helpless to the onslaught as Carter held her down, his free hand pressing steadfastly against her back.

"Goddammit," she cried out, though his spanking didn't hurt as much as confuse her. She wasn't the type to let any man render her helpless. Jesus, if he'd tried this a decade earlier, she would have freaked out.

Tonight, she was an inferno, raging out of control. The blaze flaring even brighter when he used his foot to drag her legs apart. He pressed three fingers inside her, fucking her roughly with them.

She was back on the brink of coming within half a dozen forceful strokes. And now, like before, Carter knew the exact moment to withdraw to prevent her finding closure.

"You son of a—"

He spanked her again, the pain building up, provoking a need so overwhelming she started to scream. Carter's hand covered her mouth, muting the sound, the aggression only turning her on more.

She wasn't this woman. Wasn't the type to respond to controlling men.

Her reaction to Carter's heavy-handedness drove home just how effective her therapy had been. And how right she had been to come back to him.

He was the only man on the planet she trusted enough to allow such utter control over her.

"Be quiet, Bree. As much as I love the sound of your voice, there are still too many people out in that bar. I don't want to be interrupted until you've come at least three times. But don't worry. I plan to take you back to my place afterwards and make you scream all night."

Carter released her mouth and she pressed her lips closed tightly, not sure she could manage to hold back.

He tested her strength instantly, stroking her clit until she saw stars. She moaned, fighting hard to grab the orgasm he was intent on keeping from her.

Carter recognized her efforts, and the arrogant asshole actually chuckled.

"Tsk. Tsk," he warned as she shot daggers at him over her shoulder.

"Take care of business or I'll do it myself."

It was an empty threat and they both knew it. She was his captive, unable to do anything to help her cause along without him. In the past, she would have eviscerated any man for putting her in that position. With Carter, it felt like she'd finally come home after a lifetime away.

He gripped her upper arm and tugged her back to her seated position on the edge of the desk. Rather than ramp up the play, he slowed things down, unbuttoning her blouse with the patience of a saint. There was no hiding the hard-on he was packing in his slacks, but he appeared to be much better at denying himself the pleasure that was so close at hand.

Once her blouse was open, he reached into her bra and tugged her breasts up and over the lace, the ultimate push-up.

Bending his head, he sucked and bit at her nipples as she squirmed beneath him. She lost all track of time as Carter took his, tormenting her until she thought she'd go out of her mind.

"Please," she whispered at last, certain she'd expire on the spot if he didn't fuck her.

Carter lifted his head at the sound, and she saw something soften in his face. He untied her hands as he kissed her, then he unfastened his pants.

She reached forward to take him in her hands, but he gripped her wrists, tugging them away as he pressed her to her back on his large desk.

"Put your hands beside your head and leave them there."

Bree hesitated.

"I need to see, to know…"

She had told him she would give him her trust, but actions were more powerful than words. Bree placed her hands palms up by her head, the ultimate sign of surrender. Of submission.

"I'm yours," she whispered.

He lifted her legs, resting the backs of her knees over his arms as he guided his cock to her opening.

His eyes met hers. "No condom."

She nodded just once. Yet another way he wanted to claim her, mark her. "No condom," she repeated.

Carter slid inside, and everything else faded away.

Bree wrapped her legs around his waist as he pressed deeper. Once he was seated to the hilt, he paused, looking at her as if she were an illusion.

"I never stopped loving you," he admitted.

She smiled even as she felt a tear slide along her cheek. "Make me yours, Carter."

Her invitation set him free. Any restraint Carter had employed melted away as he pounded inside her. Just when she thought he couldn't go any deeper, he shifted her ankles to his shoulders and found a way to penetrate farther.

Bree wasn't aware how loud she was until she felt the same silk that had bound her hands, against her lips. Carter pushed the tie inside to mute her cries. She let him, preferring the gag to fighting to remain quiet on her own. The gag set her free, allowed her to give up her hard-fought control.

Her back arched as she came, but Carter kept thrusting, his thumb caressing her clit, drawing out her orgasm. As he fucked her, he flooded the room with loving promises and sexy threats.

"Mine," he grunted. "Always. Going to tie you to my bed forever if I have to. Spank that sexy fucking ass until you…realize…"

It would take time for him to understand she meant what she said. She wasn't going anywhere. But she understood his fears.

She dragged the tie out of her mouth, then cupped his cheek, even as she felt another orgasm begin to overtake her.

"Yours. I'm yours. I promise. Al—"

Her word was cut off by a groan of relief and, sweet Jesus, even a little pain. Only Carter had ever found the way to make her come this hard.

This time he came with her, erupting inside, filling her. They clung to each other tightly until the waves of their release subsided.

Carter rested his weight on his elbows, his softening cock still tucked inside her.

As he lifted his head to look at her, she finished the last word.

"Always."

3

Carter leaned over Bree's back as he stroked in and out of her, slowly, almost lazily. They'd been in his office the better part of two hours, and he'd already taken her three times. No matter how many times he came, no matter how sated he believed himself to be, she'd touch him or kiss him or whisper some sweet nothing in his ear, and he'd be rock hard once more and buried deep.

Bree grunted as he thrust in harder, and he worried that perhaps he was hurting her.

"Sore?"

She shook her head in quick denial. "Don't stop. I'm fine."

Carter kissed the back of her neck, even as he knew she was lying. "Bree. We have time. All of it."

"Keep going."

He had never responded to a woman's demands until her.

Until her, he would have said hell would freeze over before that happened. He had discovered his dominant streak in high school, and his need for absolute control had only grown since then.

"Bree," he whispered in warning, though he didn't stop moving, stop thrusting. He couldn't.

Her orgasm—he'd lost count of how many she'd had—struck hard and fast, neither of them expecting it. Her inner muscles clenched against his cock, and he was helpless to resist his own climax.

He remained inside her for several minutes afterward. She lay so quiet and still he thought she'd fallen asleep.

"I'm never going to get enough of you," she said, her voice husky, sexy as fuck.

Carter pushed himself upright, though it took some effort. Bree remained facedown, draped over his desk, naked, sweaty, gorgeous, as he dropped into his chair, feeling some painful effects of their efforts in his own stiff muscles.

Somewhere between their second and third time, they'd stripped each other of all their clothing, various articles scattered around his office.

"Let's get dressed and I'll take you home."

"That sounds—" Her cell phone rang before she could finish her response. She forced herself to stand, then rummaged through the purse she'd set on his desk after they'd arrived in his office. She pulled it out, her fingers clumsy, and she almost dropped it.

He started to tell her to ignore it, but something in her expression as she looked at the screen alarmed him.

"Bree?" he started, but she shook her head as she clicked to answer. "Hello?"

Carter listened with growing concern as Bree's demeanor changed. Whatever exhaustion she'd been suffering appeared to have vanished. She began picking up her clothes in sudden panic.

"How? When? I thought—" she said to the person on the other end. "I don't know. I haven't spoken to him since the sentencing."

Carter frowned and rose as well, dressing as she listened, then responded, "Donovan's Bar. West Forty-fifth."

Finally, she said, "I understand. I will," and hung up.

"What's going on, Bree?" he asked.

"Ronnie."

"Your stepfather?"

She nodded, looking shell-shocked.

"What is it? What happened?"

"He escaped from prison."

Carter went on instant alert as Bree kept rambling, her terror growing with each passing second. "They don't know where he is. He was being transferred from one facility to another due to overcrowding. The bus transporting him crashed. He got out, got away from the guards."

"When was the accident? Where?" Carter didn't like how pale she'd gone.

"Upstate. This morning."

"And they're only just now calling to let you know?" He hadn't meant to raise his voice, especially when she jumped. "Jesus, Bree." He reached out and pulled her toward him, holding her tight in his embrace.

"They wanted to know if I thought he'd come here. If he'd come after me."

Carter knew the answer to that question, but he didn't share his opinion. Bree already appeared to be in the early stages of shock.

"I told them I don't know. I mean, he was enraged after the trial."

That was an understatement. Her stepfather had looked her straight in the eye after her testimony and told her he would kill her if it was the last thing he ever did. It was that threat—made in the presence of the jury and the judge—that had sealed his fate.

Ronnie Bertrand was a crazy son of a bitch who placed no value on human life, especially not his wife or stepdaughters. Bree, a private person, had never told him the atrocities she'd endured growing up. He'd never heard any of those horrible stories until she was on the stand. Carter's admiration and respect for her strength grew a million times that day as he listened to one of the strongest women he'd ever known open up about things she'd shut away for years, in hopes of finding justice for her family.

"There's a chance he just saw a shot at freedom and took it, right?" she asked, hopefully. "He wouldn't risk that to come after me."

Carter wasn't betting her safety on that. "Until he's captured again, we're going into hiding. Together. I don't want you more than two steps away from me at any time."

"That's going to make bathroom breaks challenging."

He laughed. Bree might get knocked down, but damn if she stayed down long. Her indomitable spirit was already combating the disbelief and fear of a few minutes earlier.

"We're going to get married sooner rather than later, so we might as well knock down all the walls. Total intimacy."

She rolled her eyes. "Pretty sure of yourself, aren't you? A few mind-blowing orgasms aren't going to pave your way to the altar. I expect to be completely wooed and wowed and won over."

"So noted." Carter helped her finish dressing. "Come on. We're getting out of here."

"We can't. I told the police officer we would wait here. They're sending a guard to—" Bree's phone rang again.

"It's the prosecutor who put Ronnie away. Hello?"

Bree frowned as she listened for a moment. "I know. Someone from the prison just called and told me."

Carter felt his unease grow when she said, "What do you mean no one called?" There was a pause. "The phone was stolen?"

"We're getting out of here," Carter said, grabbing the cell from her. "We'll call you back," he said to the person on the other end.

Then he disconnected the call as her eyes widened. "What the hell did you just do?"

"Who made the first call?"

Her hands trembled as she pushed a strand of hair away from her face. "Ronnie stole a prison cell phone from one of the guards. The caller ID came up as Sing Sing. I thought the voice sounded... But I haven't heard it in so long... I thought my mind was playing tricks on..."

"You told him where you were. We're leaving. Now." Instinct was nature's true north and his was telling him to beat a hasty retreat.

Carter reached into his desk drawer, pulling out the Kimber he kept there for protection from anyone who might try to rob the bar. He had his concealed carry permit, and he was fully prepared to pull the trigger if Ronnie got within a hundred feet of Bree.

"A gun?" she whispered.

"Yeah. Bought it the week after the bar opened. Always thought it would be used to prevent a robbery."

"Have another one for me?"

He grinned despite his alarm. "You trained?"

She nodded. "Of course."

"I wish I did. We'll go out the back. My car is parked there." He rummaged through a box on the floor in the corner and tugged out a woman's scarf. "Lost and found," he explained. "Put this over your head and keep your eyes down. I want your face concealed as much as possible."

"We can't go to your place, Carter. I just told him I was here. He's going to know I'm with you. God, I shouldn't have come back. I've put you in danger."

Carter gripped her upper arms, forcing her to look him directly in the eye. "You are exactly where you're supposed to be. Don't you even think of trying to slip away to protect me. Believe me, you do that and you won't have to worry about your stepfather finding you. You'll have to worry about me."

He punctuated that vow with a hard kiss. Then he led her to the alley that ran behind the bar. Mercifully, he'd parked his car feet from the back door. They were inside without issue or threat within seconds. They rode in silence as he fought his way through New York City traffic. Ordinarily, he didn't drive to work, opting to take the subway instead. But his plan when he left his house earlier was to hit 220 after work. It looked like that was still the plan.

God help him when Bree realized where he was taking her.

Once they hit lower Manhattan, traffic lightened and he became more aware of Bree. She looked the picture of cool, calm, and collected, except for the fact her hands were clenched together white-knuckle fashion in her lap.

"It's going to be okay, Bree."

She nodded but didn't respond, so he didn't bother to say more. He was working overtime to mimic her fake poise as well. He wouldn't take another deep breath until he had her secured inside the club.

No. Scratch that. He wouldn't relax until her stepfather was back behind bars.

As they pulled into the parking lot of the club, Bree's curiosity won out over her fear.

"Where are we?"

"You'll see in a second. Put the scarf back over your head."

She complied, and he led her from the car to the club with haste. While it had its own parking, there was no sign denoting the large building as a place of business. Walking up the dozen or so steps, it looked more like they were entering a large brownstone as opposed to one of the most exclusive clubs in the city.

Carter placed his thumb on a keypad and the first door opened. Members gained entrance to the foyer through fingerprint.

Roger McMillan, dressed head to toe in black, was standing alone in the elegant foyer, next to the elevator. "Good evening, Mr. Donovan. I wondered if we were going to see you tonight."

Carter walked over to the ex-military man and leaned closer. "We're on full lockdown."

Roger paused for a split second before responding. "Weapons?"

Carter nodded. "Call in anyone who isn't already working. I want two men stationed here and at the back exit until further notice. The guests who are already here can leave, but no one else comes in tonight —member or not. Shut down the keypad."

"Yes, sir." Roger was the head of security at the club. They'd set up a certain set of safety parameters to protect the membership, but they'd never had to go to full lockdown. Even now, he could see Roger looking at Bree curiously, wondering if tonight's excitement was because of her.

Roger pushed the button to the elevator for them. As they waited, Carter turned back to the security guard. "I'll text you and the others a picture of the man we're working to keep out, once I get upstairs. If you see him, batten down the hatches and call the police chief directly. Don't engage unless absolutely necessary. You should consider this man armed and extremely dangerous."

Roger nodded, his fierce expression proving Carter had been right to hire him.

Once they were inside the elevator, Bree looked at him. "You own this place?"

"Yes."

"What is it?"

Carter took a deep breath. The answer to that was going to be obvious in about twenty seconds, when the elevator hit the next floor. "You'll see."

4

Bree stood stock-still, trying to assimilate what she was seeing.

"You brought me to a sex club?"

Carter took her hand and led her farther into the room, which looked to be a massive warehouse with high ceilings, low lighting, and every manner of expensive fetish furniture. The walls were painted a rich red, resembling a boudoir built for some billionaire sheikh.

Since her first question had clearly been rhetorical—there was no denying he'd brought her to a sex club—she lobbed another at him. One she definitely wanted answered.

"You own a sex club?"

"Yes. I do."

As far as responses went, that one was far too simple and unsatisfying. "Why?"

He grinned at her. "Because it's profitable."

Bree rolled her eyes. "You don't really expect me to buy that, do you?"

"I've never hidden my desire for wealth. Or control. I like being my own boss, Bree. The first few years after you left, I put all my energy and attention into the bar, but once I had the right people in place, it ran like a well-oiled machine. There was no challenge to it. I went out for drinks one night with my friend David and we came up with the concept of 220."

"I'm surprised by the high level of security. Is that normal for a sex club?"

Carter shook his head. "No. 220 has been operating for six years. In that time, it's made a serious name for itself as being one of the premiere BDSM clubs in the city. We cater to the extremely wealthy, those interested in the lifestyle but who—due to their public image or positions—need to keep those desires private."

"Politicians?" she asked.

"As well as actors and CEOs. We even have a certain prince who stops by whenever he's in the country."

"What does Reed think of your sex club?"

"He doesn't know."

Bree was surprised by that answer. Carter and his cousin were closer than brothers. "Really?"

"The truth is, there are very few people who actually know I own this business, even though 220 is, by far, much more lucrative than Donovan's. Let's just say I enjoy keeping certain aspects of my life personal."

"You play here?"

He nodded without hesitation. Despite their long estrangement, Bree was pleased by the fact they could fall into their same open, honest relationship. She never questioned anything Carter told her because, to her knowledge, he'd never lied to her. Not once.

"I do. Or"—he paused for just a moment—"I did."

Bree looked around the room, trying to take in everything. She had an academic knowledge of BDSM, but nothing practical or hands-on. She'd read books, watched movies, done a bit of Internet research—simply out of curiosity—and spoken in depth to a Parisian girlfriend one night who was very deep into the scene.

"Your past tense is for me."

Carter wrapped his arm around her waist, tucking her close so that he could whisper in her ear. "Anything and everything I did prior to tonight is past tense. My only plan for the future is you."

"And if I want to play here?"

"We will."

"And if I don't?"

He placed a light kiss on her cheek, amused by her questions. "We won't."

"Let me guess," she said sardonically. "You're always the Dom."

"I've spent a great deal of time here, finding play partners, women who enjoy being on the receiving end of my crop." Carter was watching her face very closely. She knew him well enough to appreciate his words for what they were. A test. He gave her an inquisitive look when she didn't take the bait, schooling her features. "You don't seem shocked by anything you're seeing, Bree. Have you—"

"No. I haven't." She started to say more, but another man approached them.

"Carter. I wonder if I might have a word with you in private."

Carter didn't seem alarmed. Instead, he said, "We were on our way to find you, David."

David. The business partner.

He and Carter must've met in the last decade because Bree didn't know the man.

"David, this is Bree Andrews. Bree, this is David Connelly."

"Nice to meet you," Bree said, extending her hand. Rather than shake it, David lifted it, kissing her knuckles, then giving her a wink when Carter reached over to reclaim her hand from his charming friend.

"Like that, is it?" David said with a grin.

"Yes," Carter replied, not smiling. "It is."

David looked at her curiously. "Wait. Did you say Bree?"

Bree's eyes widened with surprise. He knew her name? Then he proved he knew even more.

"Bree, the fashion designer? The one Reed refers to as the one who got away?"

Bree laughed, and Carter's expression softened as he looked at her. "She came back."

The smile David gave her was a mix of curiosity and genuine friendliness. Bree instantly liked him.

"Come on, Bree. I'll let Carter give you the grand tour later. For now...we need to talk. In private."

David led the way as Bree walked next to Carter. "You mentioned me?"

Carter shrugged. "Had a bad night a couple of years ago. Got drunk with Reed and David and said a hell of a lot more than I normally would have. I blame the bourbon."

They climbed a flight of stairs by a back wall and then entered an office. Unlike the elegance of the main room, this space was all business. Two desks set up on opposite sides of the room indicated that he and David shared the office and a large window stood in place of one wall that overlooked the action below.

"One-way mirror," David said when he noticed where she was looking. Then he turned to Carter. "Mind telling me why we're on full lockdown?"

Carter hesitated, and she sensed he was trying to come up with a way to explain to his friend without revealing her personal matters.

Bree appreciated his kindness, but she wasn't about to put Carter, David, or anyone else in this club at risk, armed with only a vague idea of the danger.

So she answered the question. "My stepfather murdered my mother and sister and was sentenced to life in prison. He escaped today and there's a chance he may come here, looking for me. Revenge for my testimony."

David tilted his head. "I see." He bent over the keyboard of his laptop and typed something. Once he found what he was looking for, he turned the screen toward her. "Two men escaped. Which one is your stepdad?" David asked.

Bree swallowed heavily as she looked at the arrest photo of Ronnie. She'd cut all traces of him out of her life a decade ago. Coming face to face with the evil man again was difficult, and while she was sorry she had put Carter in the line of danger, she was grateful she was with him.

What would have been a terrifying night alone was much less so with Carter. He made her feel safe, protected. "The one on the right."

David nodded, then turned the laptop back toward him as he clicked several keys. "I'll send a copy of that photo to our guards downstairs."

"I'm very sorry to put you and everyone here at such risk," Bree said, overwhelmed with the same rush of guilt. This was her nightmare. She was wrong to include others.

David's incredulous glance mirrored Carter's earlier, and she understood why the men were such good friends. They were cut from the same cloth. "220 is exactly where you should be tonight. This place is locked up tighter than Fort Knox right now. We'll keep you safe until your stepfather is back behind bars."

"How can I ever thank you enough for—"

"Something tells me you're going to keep Carter on his toes for the rest of his life." David's smile was pure mischief. "That show will be payment enough."

"Very funny," Carter said. "Bree and I will be in my private room. If anything happens—"

"I'll call you."

Carter nodded his thanks, and the two of them descended the stairs back to the main floor.

"Your own room?"

"One of the perks of ownership." Carter's hand was resting on the small of her back, but he slid it lower to cup her ass as he said, "Of course, we could stay out here and play."

She looked around, then pointed. "I wouldn't mind strapping you to that St. Andrew's Cross and having my wicked way with you."

His gaze narrowed, his tone sardonic when he responded, "My room it is. While we're there, we're going to discuss your knowledge of BDSM and set up some play parameters."

She reached lower, cupping his cock, which was rock hard, despite her bondage taunt. "As long as those parameters include me topping, we should be just fine."

Carter gripped her wrist, but rather than pull her hand away from his dick, he pressed it against him more firmly. "Touch it like you mean it," he taunted.

She closed her fingers around him as much as she could with his slacks in the way, but Carter didn't shrink away from her rough touch. Instead, he added to the play, reaching out and pinching one of her nipples through the silk of her blouse and the lace of her bra. Even those two layers didn't detract from the pain of it.

Bree wouldn't have expected to find pleasure in such things, but there was no denying his spanking earlier and this rough play had her body thrumming with a need that should have been well sated by now.

She had lost count of how many orgasms she'd had tonight after the fifth. And despite—or maybe because of—the fear she felt over the danger she was in, she wanted him again.

No. It went beyond that. Her need felt primal. Animalistic.

Every time she was with Carter, she felt the desire to dig her claws in, to leave scars. That couldn't be healthy, but the sexy man didn't appear to mind her marks.

She tightened her grip on his cock, prompting him to pinch her nipple even harder.

She gasped, but the sound soon morphed to a moan.

Carter responded to it by using his free hand to grasp the back of her neck and pulling her face toward his. The kiss he gave her was all-consuming, brutal.

Bree released her grip on his cock, moving her hands around his waist, pulling him to her as she added another layer of heat to the embrace. She pressed his cock against her by cupping his ass, swaying her hips side to side.

Carter released her and took a small step away. Bree tried to follow him, but he held her back.

"We need to get to my room. Now."

She didn't have a chance to reply as he grasped her hand and pulled her down a dimly lit corridor. The door to his room—like the front entrance of the club—opened by thumbprint.

As Bree walked in, it became instantly apparent that Carter hadn't exaggerated his desire for complete control over his lovers. There were straps attached to the four corner posts of a large bed, a spanking bench sat in one corner and a chain dangled in the center of the room.

Along one wall hung a shelf of interesting instruments—crops, spreader bars, rope, and more. An open chest at the foot of the bed held more intimate toys—dildos, vibrators, butt plugs, and nipple clamps.

"It's a veritable Kinky-R-Us store in here," she joked.

Carter chuckled. "See anything you like?"

She glanced at the chains hanging from the ceiling, then she went over to the shelf, picking up a narrow paddle. She didn't miss the look of hunger in his eyes when she tapped the palm of her hand with it lightly. "You would look very sexy, naked and chained there as I—"

"Bree," Carter interrupted.

"I haven't changed that much either, Carter."

He tilted his head as he appeared to consider whether or not she was telling the truth. "I just don't think you realize yet that you have."

"Meaning?"

"Take off your blouse."

She put the paddle down and her fingers were at the top button of her blouse before she could consider her actions. Then she just rolled with it because complying got her where she wanted to be faster. With him. Buried deep between her thighs.

Carter pointed to the spanking bench. "Kneel there."

Her eyes narrowed and she hesitated. Carter didn't move either. He simply gave her a look that told her he would wait all night if he had to. Something that would ensure both of them suffered.

She knelt on the leather pad but didn't bend her upper body over the flat surface. There were straps attached to the legs.

Bree recalled the reason they were here. Her stepfather was free. He was looking for her.

Carter stepped next to her, stroking her hair. The touch comforted her. Calmed her.

"I'm not tying you down. Neither one of us is wearing any of these straps or chains until Ronnie is behind bars."

Somehow he'd sensed her reticence and understood the reason for it—even when she hadn't. He wouldn't put her at risk, render her helpless until it was safe to do so.

But if it weren't for Ronnie, Bree had the uneasy—and shocking—realization that she would have bent over the table willingly for Carter.

Carter stepped behind her, her back to him. He continued to play with her hair, caressing it and the sides of her head, toying with her ears. It was sexy and sensuous. She'd never been so turned on by mere touches.

"Lean forward," he murmured after several minutes of his slow, relaxing head massage.

She leaned over the table, and Carter wasted no time lifting the back of her skirt, baring her ass. Bree hadn't bothered to find her thong back in Carter's office. She'd been too intent on getting dressed and getting the hell out of there.

She shivered when he ran his hand over her ass cheeks. Again, his touch was soft, gentle. After so much roughness from him tonight, she was struggling to keep up with this new style.

Bree had kept her hands bent beneath her on the bench, ready to use them to push her up and away if necessary.

"Put your hands down and grip the front legs of the bench."

"But you said—"

"I'm not binding them there. You're going to be a good girl and keep them there on your own."

She blew out a hard breath. "You might want to lighten up on that good girl crap because—"

His hand came down on her ass hard and she jerked, then tried to rise.

Carter bent over her, keeping her pressed against the leather, as he whispered, "Put your hands down."

His tone told her resistance would be pointless. And stupid. Carter wasn't a stranger. He was her friend, her lover, and the only man in her life she'd ever trusted. He'd never hurt her. God, more than that, he'd always love her.

Her hands slid off the bench, and she gripped the legs as he'd instructed.

She was rewarded with a kiss on the back of her head.

"You slay me, Bree."

"I love you."

Her words were met with a softly muttered "shit" that she didn't understand until he wrapped his hand around her upper arm and pulled her up from the table in one smooth, firm move.

Carter kissed her as if his life depended on it, and Bree tasted every sweet emotion she'd ever longed for. Love, acceptance, adoration, respect.

He released her, cupping her face in his. "I want to play with you, Bree, want to explore every single thing in here with you—from the top and the bottom, if that's the only way—but tonight..." He swallowed heavily. "Tonight I want to make love to you."

She dashed away a tear with the back of her hand. They'd had sex six ways to Sunday tonight, each experience mind-blowing and hot. But none of them were as appealing as what he was offering her at that moment.

"I want—"

Carter's phone rang, and Bree jumped at the sudden, unexpected sound.

Carter's face turned to stone as he pulled the cell from his pocket. "What's happening?"

He listened to whomever was on the line, his gaze drifting toward the door of the room.

"How is he?"

Bree's heart thudded painfully. Was someone hurt? Because of her? Suffused with guilt, she put her blouse back on, trying to button it. The simple act was made impossible by her trembling hands. Carter brushed them away, holding his phone to his ear with his shoulder as he quickly and efficiently buttoned her blouse.

Once she was dressed again, he tucked her closely as he wrapped up his call.

"He's here?"

Carter nodded. "He must have seen us leaving the bar and followed. He struck fast. Before we could get all our security measures in place."

"What do you mean?"

"He got the jump on one of my security guards at the back when he came into work. Holding a gun to my man's head, he was able to muscle his way in."

"Did he..." Bree couldn't make herself ask the question. If this guard died because she'd come here, she would never forgive herself.

Carter shook his head. "No. He forced him and the guard who'd already been stationed at the back door into the basement. Made one of them tie up the other, then he knocked the second out with a hard blow to the head. He took their walkie-talkies and weapons and locked them in the basement."

"So he's here? In the building?"

Bree had been fighting to keep her panic at bay. Freaking out wouldn't do any good. And while her head accepted that fact, the rest of her was revolting. She felt light-headed, nauseous, terrified.

Carter led her to the bed, helped her to sit down, then pushed her head down toward her knees. "Take it easy, Bree. David has most of the guests out and the guards are searching the building. The police chief has been alerted. Cops are on the way. We just need to lie low in here until they can grab him."

"You'll stay in here with me?" Bree knew Carter. He was a man of action. Hiding behind a locked door was not in his genetic makeup.

"Jesus. I'm not about to leave you in here unprotected." As he spoke, he picked up the gun he'd placed on the nightstand and switched off the safety.

Bree looked toward the door to the room. "Is that the only way in here?"

Carter glanced around as if looking for something. "No. But it's the easiest way."

"How else?"

Carter pointed to a long, heavy curtain. "Window behind there." She expected him to pull it open, but instead, he turned the spanking bench over on its side. "Crouch behind there, Bree."

As she moved, she asked, "Is the window locked?"

"No," a deep voice said, stepping from behind the curtain. "It's not."

Bree froze in terror as events unfolded in slow motion.

Carter lifted his gun as he stepped in front of her, but Ronnie already had his pointed in Carter's direction. Before either man could pull the trigger, there was a loud crash.

From the corner of her eye, Bree saw two policemen storm into the room, guns drawn. She tried to push Carter out of the line of fire as gunshots erupted. The sound was deafening as she knocked Carter forward.

Something flew by her as the two of them fell to the floor, but just before impact, Carter twisted, cushioning her landing for one brief second before turning to cover her with his body.

Another body hit the floor near them.

Her stepfather lay in a pool of blood.

She didn't spare him a second glance as all her attention, her focus returned to Carter.

Bree patted Carter's arms, his chest, her gaze flying over him rapidly as she searched for blood. "Are you okay? Did he—"

"What the fuck was that, Bree?"

She didn't stop touching him, looking. She had to be certain, had to make sure...

Carter gripped her wrists in his as he pressed them to the floor. He was scowling and his tone drove home his outright fury. "You put yourself between me and your stepfather. You could have been shot."

"Are you hurt?" She could've sworn one of the bullets whizzed right by them.

"No. Jesus, Bree. I should beat your ass black and blue for what you just did."

"Later," she teased, adrenaline giving way to uncontrollable giddiness as she glanced over at the cops. "When we're alone."

5

Carter shook his head. As always, Bree recovered quickly. Unfortunately, he didn't share her talent. Too many emotions were crashing down on him, and he struggled to keep them contained.

David entered the room, rushing over to help them both up. "Thank God. The cops got here and one of them said he thought he saw a shadow moving on the ledge. That's when I realized how he planned to get to you. I didn't think we'd get here in time."

Carter accepted his friend's hug, then watched as David offered the same to Bree. David really had been shaken up.

If Carter weren't still so overwhelmed with fear and terror and anger, he would have appreciated his friend's concern and relief.

Instead...

The police called for the morgue, then asked the two of them a million and twelve questions. Hours passed before the two of them were allowed to leave.

He led Bree to the office. David had returned there earlier and had asked him to stop by before he left so they could debrief.

Bree didn't realize he wasn't responding to her nonstop, somewhat manic chatter. It was funny how different their reactions to the same event were. In so many ways they were kindred spirits. But when placed in a life-or-death situation, they went in opposite directions. Bree relived the entire evening over, trying to use her words to deal with what had happened, fighting out loud to make sense of it all.

In the meantime, Carter kept it all in. He didn't fool himself into thinking it would remain there. The truth was, he was merely waiting until he had Bree alone. Then he intended to make sure she understood—in no uncertain terms—that her actions were wrong.

They were just outside the door when Bree realized he hadn't spoken a single word.

"Carter? Are you okay?"

"Not now, Bree."

"You're still angry? God, Carter. What did you expect—"

"Not now," he said through gritted teeth as David opened the door.

His friend had clearly heard enough to understand the razor's edge Carter was walking.

"Come on in."

Carter led the way, stalking into the room. He gestured for Bree to sit on the couch, but she remained standing, her arms crossed, her expression haughty.

Carter's jaw clenched as he struggled to calm down.

David leaned against his desk, attempting to break through some of the tension that was thick in the room. "I'd tell you two to head on home and we'll sort out this mess tomorrow, but I'm afraid the truth is, neither one of you is out of danger."

Bree glanced at his friend, confused. "What do you mean?"

David tilted his head toward Carter. "The man's about to blow. I heard your comments to the police. You shoved Carter out of the way, thrust yourself in the line of fire."

Bree nodded. "That bullet was meant for me."

Carter's head exploded. Alone or not, he couldn't keep it together one second longer. "Are you fucking kidding me? What part of crouch behind that bench didn't you understand? I wanted you out of danger, Bree. Not pushing your way to the front of the line. If that bullet…"

Her eyes widened. "So I didn't imagine it. Ronnie did fire."

Carter's legs gave out as he recalled her stepfather pulling the trigger at the exact second Bree pushed him. Carter hadn't had a chance to line up his own shot before Bree's unexpected shove from behind. It had only missed her by inches.

Fucking inches.

Carter rested his elbows on his knees, feeling the same panic Bree had suffered prior to Ronnie's appearance in the room.

"I almost lost you again."

"I'm sorry, Carter. I'm so sorry." Bree knelt in front of him. The Dom inside registered the submissive pose, but he was still too angry. He would never touch her as long as this rage roared inside him.

"Promise me. Promise me you'll never risk your life for mine again."

She shook her head. "I can't. It would be a lie."

Carter clenched his hands together. "Damn it, Bree. I need you to promise me."

"No."

Carter stared at her for several long moments, searching for some answer. Nothing came.

"Compromise."

She and Carter both turned to look at David. Carter had forgotten the other man was still in the room.

"What?" Carter asked.

"You're at an impasse. You've got two ways to go. Admit defeat and walk away from each other."

"No!" Bree said.

Carter grinned and for the first time since Ronnie fired his weapon, Carter felt the tightness in his chest begin to ease.

David chuckled. "Yeah. I knew you were going to reject that option. So the only other way is to compromise. The two of you are going to have to find ways to deal with each other. You're both too stubborn, too honest, and too controlling for your own good. If you can't figure out a way around this that works for both of you, I'm afraid you're going to be locked in this power struggle for the rest of your lives."

"I don't see a compromise," Bree said softly. "I'll never stand by and simply watch if you're in danger. I wouldn't ask that of you, so how can you ask it of me?"

Carter didn't know how to reply. His head might get the point, but his soul, his heart rejected it outright. David had given him shit for some of his more caveman beliefs. Not that his friend had much of a leg to stand on when it came to overprotective male instincts.

"Fine," Carter said at last, though it was probably the hardest word he'd ever spoken. "I won't demand the promise. Won't..." He blew out a frustrated breath as he forced himself to concede the rest. "Won't expect you to stand on the sidelines if we're ever in danger."

"Damn," David muttered. "Bet that hurt."

Carter shot his friend a dirty look, his scowl growing in the face of his friend's far-too-amused smile.

Bree didn't mock him, but instead acknowledged the sacrifice he was making on her behalf. "I really am sorry, Carter. I appreciate you understanding. Are we okay now?"

He shook his head and she frowned.

"But I thought—"

Carter grinned wickedly. "In order for it to be a compromise, both parties have to give something up."

Bree licked her lips nervously. "What do you want?"

"Your submission."

She narrowed her eyes, her refusal on her lips. He raised his hand to cut her off.

"Not forever. I realize that request is impossible for the long-term. However, the deal is this. Any time you put yourself in a situation that I consider dangerous, you agree to spend one night as my submissive. If I can't make you obey me outside the bedroom, by God, I will inside."

She rolled her eyes. "If I agree, you're going to have to find another word to use. Obey makes me want to cut your dick off."

David laughed.

"David," Carter said.

"Yeah?"

"Get out."

"That's cold, Carter. Here I am, giving stellar relationship counseling, and you kick me out just as things are about to get interesting."

Carter didn't take the bait, didn't even look in his friend's direction. "Lock the door behind you."

Once David was gone, Carter held still. Bree still hadn't agreed to his terms. Until she did…

"When you say submission," she started.

"No limits, Bree. You'll have a safe word. If there's anything that is a hard limit, say it now. Otherwise, you're mine."

"No one else. That's my hard limit."

He grinned. That one was easy. "I couldn't share you even if you wanted it."

"Paris."

"What?"

"That's my safe word. Paris."

"Your escape."

"From now on, it's just a word. In truth, I can't think of anything you would do that would make me say it."

He reached out, touching her for the first time in hours. "I have just enough sadist in me to want to push your limits on that."

"Bring it."

"Tonight's not the night."

"What?" she asked.

"I'm claiming your submission tomorrow night." His emotions were still too close to the skin, and until he had those under complete control, her submission would have to wait.

He ran his knuckles along the side of her face, enjoying the way her eyes closed as he did so. "Besides, I promised you something else tonight."

Her eyelids lifted, her bright blue gaze capturing his. "I love you," she whispered.

"I know."

She laughed.

Carter cupped her cheeks. "I love you too."

He stripped her clothing away as they kissed, then she spent several minutes undressing him, touching each bit of skin she bared with her fingers, her lips, her tongue.

Part of him was sorry he'd started this here rather than taking her home to his bed. However, even as the regret emerged, it vanished. He would never have been able to wait that long.

Carter laid her down on her back on the couch, coming over her. Bree's legs parted. He ran his fingers along her slit. She was wet, hot, ready.

If he pushed inside her now, it would end too quickly and he refused to let that happen.

Bree murmured a soft complaint when he lowered his head, taking her breast into his mouth. "Please," she pleaded. "I need you."

"I know. Soon."

Her hands found his hair and he expected her to tug it, to try to use her grip to force his face back to hers. Instead, she simply ran her fingers through it.

"Good girl," he whispered as he stroked her other nipple with his tongue.

She giggled softly. "God help me, I think I'm starting to like that."

Rather than respond, Carter moved lower, sucking her clit between his lips, teasing it with a light nip that had her hips lifting from the couch cushions.

"Carter," she moaned.

"Come for me, Bree. Give me one of those pretty orgasms." As he spoke, he pushed two fingers inside, keeping his movements measured, slow. They'd spent the first part of the night in a mad dash, clawing at each other like ravenous beasts.

Now, he wanted to show her there was more to this, to them. While they would always share a hot-blooded passion, there would also be moments like this. There was a time to consume, to conquer and take. And there was a time to treasure, to adore, to love.

When he applied more pressure to her clit with his tongue, she came apart at the seams. Once her climax waned, he withdrew his fingers and caged her beneath him again.

"Finally," she whispered.

He chuckled. "Yeah. You were really suffering, weren't you?"

"Come inside." She wrapped her legs around his waist and he let go, pressing into her with one hard, deep thrust.

Holding steady for just a moment, he stole one last long kiss. They set an easy pace, mimicking a boat on a calm lake, soaking up every minute of closeness they could.

With one last deep thrust, they came together.

Carter tucked her back against his chest, spooning her on the couch as they reveled in the aftermath of their brief trip to heaven. Both of them were crashing fast. Glancing at the clock on the wall, he wasn't surprised. It was just after six a.m. They'd pulled an all-nighter. He grinned at the memory of them doing the same thing in college, cramming for exams.

Bree sighed, the sound one of complete contentment.

"Happy?" he asked.

"So happy. What a night."

"You can say that again. What do you say we grab a few hours' sleep here and then we can go to your place, pack up all your stuff and move you into mine?"

She laughed. "So the wooing and wowing part of our courtship is already over?"

"That'll never end. I intend to spend the rest of my life laying claim to your heart."

"Just my heart?" she asked seductively.

He gave her nipple a quick pinch. "All of you."

Never one to be outdone, Bree reached back, adding her own pinch. To his ass. "Ditto."

Life with her was destined to be one long power struggle.

And he couldn't wait to get started.

ABOUT MARI CARR

Writing a book was number one on Mari Carr's bucket list and on her thirty-fourth birthday, she set out to see that goal achieved. Too many years later, her computer is jammed full of stories — novels, novellas, short stories, and dead ends and she has nearly eighty published works.

Virginia native Mari Carr is a New York Times and USA TODAY bestseller of contemporary erotic romance novels. With over one million copies of her books sold, Mari was the winner of the Romance Writers of America's Passionate Plume award for her novella Erotic Research.

∽

To be notified of new releases or sales,
join Mari's Mailing List: www.eepurl.com/NmRGf
Connect with Mari online
Facebook: www.facebook.com/MariCarrWriter
Instagram: www.instagram.com/MariCarrAuthor
Visit Mari at MariCarr.com!

1

MISSION ONE

PARIS, FRANCE

Drake McLeod felt his pulse quicken as he and his two fellow CIA officers in the nondescript van raced past Hôtel de Ville. Only a few more minutes before they arrived at Club Romantique, the hottest gay bar in the city.

His thoughts, which should have been hyper-focused on the mission, were split thanks to one of the men on his team—his ex, Chance Nicholls.

Things between them had been going great until Chance had given him an ultimatum. Chance had made it clear that he was ready for the next step in their relationship after both of them had received their dream assignments on Julie's team.

"Let's live together, Drake. We've been seeing each other for over a year now. It's way past due."

He hadn't understood why it was so important to Chance that they move in together. He shouldn't have been surprised. They were opposite in so many ways. Chance was carefree and always the life of the party, while he was serious and straightforward. Even their looks were reverse. Chance was blond and blue-eyed. Drake had dark hair and brown eyes. And he couldn't keep track of how many times their points of view were in conflict. That's what made it exciting to be with Chance. And the makeup sex was worth it all.

Still, Drake had been confused. Hadn't they had a terrific thing going already? Even though Langley had no official policy about officers dating, it was frowned on. He and Chance had been able to navigate those murky waters, but Drake was concerned that if they cohabitated, there would be no keeping it quiet any longer. As it was already, too many of their fellow officers knew.

He'd tried to use logic with Chance. "We need to keep our own places and be discreet so that Julie won't separate us." Julie Hudson was the chief supervisor of their team Rainbow Knights, the CIA's covert unit of highly skilled LGBT officers.

Logic had no impact on Chance. He'd argued that Julie had worked hard to recruit them on the team. "She won't care. I bet she already knows."

They'd fought all night long and come to a gridlock, neither willing to budge an inch. That's when Chance had broken his heart.

"I want a future, a family, the whole package—the proverbial house with the picket fence. It's clear you don't want the same things. Drake, I'm done. I can't do this anymore."

That was one month ago and those words continued echoing in Drake's mind. Longing to hold Chance in his arms at night and being with him on the job only added to his pain. It was sheer hell, but he knew he was right. Moving in together would expose their relationship, and Julie would have no choice but to reassign one of them to another team.

"Are both of your heads in the game?" Mick Kohler, who was behind the wheel, was one of those who knew about him and Chance. Mick didn't believe in happily-ever-afters, and he'd promised to keep quiet. "This is RK's first mission and I don't want it fucked up because you two can't work out your shit."

"We're professionals, Mick." Chance's tone was clipped. "Besides, this mission is a cakewalk. Drug the target and drag him out. No problem."

"Hope you're right," Drake told his ex. "But always expect the unexpected."

Chance looked at him with those big blue eyes. "Expectations? They can get you in trouble."

His gut tightened.

Mick took a left at the next intersection. "I'll say it again—keep your damn heads on this mission and your cocks in your pants."

"What's that supposed to mean, fellas?" Julie's voice came through the hidden comms in their ears. "Is there a problem?"

Damn. How long had she been listening? She was running the entire operation from their safe house a few miles away.

"No problem, boss." Drake tried to keep his tone casual. "Just the punch line of one of Mick's bad jokes."

"Cut the crap and focus."

"Yes, ma'am," the three of them said.

"Wiz and I have eyes into the club through their CCTV system."

"Guys, our target just entered." Wiz was Blake Stimpson's nickname. Top of his class at MIT, he was in charge of Rainbow Knights IT.

"What's your ETA?" Julie asked.

"Pulling up now." Mick parked the van in the spot they'd picked out earlier that day. It was in an alley at the back of the club, making it easy to capture their target, Johan Kuusik, an international assassin.

Recent chatter on the dark web had tipped off CIA analysts about Kuusik's arrival in Paris. It was believed that he'd been hired to take out a high-level diplomat at the upcoming international forum dealing with human trafficking.

As he, Chance, and Mick got out of the van, Drake's total focus returned to the mission. The club's pulsing music echoed in the streets, which became even louder when they got inside. The massive space was filled to the max with gay men of all shapes and colors, most quite handsome and sexy. Trying to find Kuusik in the crowd wasn't going to be easy.

"I'll head to the bar," he said in a low tone, knowing Chance and Mick would be able to hear through their comms despite the noise in the club.

Chance nodded. "I'll recon the dance floor."

"I've got the bathrooms." Mick grinned. "We'll flush him out, no pun intended."

After walking to the long marble-topped bar at the back of the club, Drake took a seat at an empty barstool and scanned everyone he passed. There was no sign of Kuusik, whose face he'd memorized from the photos in the dossier.

"Hey, handsome," the man with the goatee at the counter said to him. "How about I buy you a drink?"

"Thanks, but I'm waiting on someone."

"Could that be me?" another man behind him asked, shoving the barrel of a gun into his side. "I'm glad you waited for me, CIA. Don't turn around or make a scene. There are lots of innocent people who will get hurt if you don't do exactly what I say."

"Hello, Kuusik," he said, sending a message to the team through his comms. "Cool gun."

Chance's voice came in, "On my way to you now."

"Me, too," Mick said.

"How did you know I was coming?"

The killer laughed. "Nice try, but I know you're not alone. And you'll be the one answering the questions, not me."

Julie's voice came in next. "Be careful, Drake. Kuusik's skills aren't to be underestimated."

"McLeod, where are your buddies Nicholls and Kohler now?"

"Fuck. The bastard was tipped off," Mick said. "Kuusik even knows our names."

The concern in Mick's tone matched what Drake was feeling. Assessing the pressure of Kuusik's gun barrel in his side, he was confident he could turn things around and relieve the assassin of his weapon. But before he could make a move, gunfire erupted in the club.

Kuusik hadn't come alone.

As the entire place went into pandemonium, Drake heard something in his comms that made his blood chill.

"I'm hit, guys," Chance said.

A protective rage exploded inside Drake. In a move he'd practiced a thousand times during his martial arts training, he leapt from the barstool, kicking the gun out of Kuusik's hand.

The killer's eyes were wide with shock when Mick came up behind him, grabbing him by the coat.

"Got him, boss," Mick said.

More gunfire and screams. The panicked crowd ran for the exits. Some fell to the floor and were trampled.

"You and Drake get Kuusik out of there," Julie ordered. "Chance, I can't see you. You're in one of the CCTV's blind spots. What's your status?"

When he didn't answer her, dread filled Drake. "Julie, Mick can handle the package. I've got to find Chance."

"Go."

Drake turned to begin the search for Chance.

"Behind you, Drake," Julie warned, too late.

The man who had just offered to buy him a drink tackled him to the ground. As he battled Kuusik's accomplice, out of the corner of his eye he saw Mick get ambushed by another man. Kuusik got free, and two more thugs ushered him to the exit.

"How many of you fuckers are there?" Mick punched his attacker in the face, sending him to the floor.

Drake kicked Mr. Goatee in the gut, sending him gasping across the ground.

"Abort the mission," Julie ordered. "Local authorities are on their way. Find Chance and get the hell out of there."

He and Mick ran through the now nearly empty club. In a dark corner of the room, they found an injured and exhausted Chance pounding on three of Kuusik's men. At his feet were two more thugs he'd already neutralized.

Drake was filled with relief. "He's alive, Julie."

He and Mick stepped up next to Chance, helping finish off the remaining thugs.

"We've got to go, Chance," Drake said. "Are you okay?"

"I'm good. Just a flesh wound." He pointed to his bloodied jacket and then his ear. "These bastards broke my comms."

"We can debrief everything later," Mick said, still holding on to Kuusik's coat. "Let's go before the police get here."

They ran out the same exit Kuusik had escaped through.

As they made it to the van, the approaching sirens got louder. Mick drove out of the alley.

Drake looked at the increasing bloodstain on Chance's jacket. "Let me see where you were hit."

Chance nodded, opening his jacket, which revealed the scope of his injury.

"Oh my God, Chance. This is much more than a flesh wound." Drake took off his shirt, wadded it up, and pressed it against the hole in Chance's side to stop the bleeding.

Chance groaned and lost consciousness.

"Chance. Chance." Drake checked his pulse, which was ragged. "He's out, Mick. Hurry. He's still losing blood."

"I've already contacted Doc," Julie said. "He'll be here at the safe house waiting for you."

"On our way." Mick blasted through a traffic light. "Don't worry, Drake. Chance is a tough SOB. I'll get us there in time."

"Hang on, sweetheart." Drake had been on many battlefields and missions, but none had ever felt like this. Chance was his whole world.

Mick drove into the subterranean parking garage. What the locals were unaware of was the secret passage that was behind reserved spot number sixty-two.

Drake turned off his comms and kissed Chance lightly on the cheek. "I was wrong, sweetheart. I'll move in with you. Just don't leave me. I can't lose you."

Once the van was parked, he and Mick carried Chance to the hidden corridor that led to the team's safe house.

Julie met them at the door. "Doc's inside setting everything up."

She led them to the makeshift operating room, where they found the team's medical officer.

Doc looked like a surfer to most, long blond hair and sun-kissed skin. But Drake knew better. Even though he was only twenty-eight, he was uber-smart, having graduated from med school when he was only nineteen.

Doc pointed at the operating table. "Put him here, guys."

Julie's phone buzzed. She looked at the screen and her face tightened. "It's Collins."

Deputy Director Peter Collins was her immediate supervisor. He had adamantly opposed the formation of Rainbow Knights but had been overruled by the top person at the CIA and first woman director, Amanda Maddow. Even with Maddow's initial blessing, the disaster of this first mission definitely put the fate of the team in jeopardy, which Drake was sure pleased Collins. Julie would have her work cut out for her.

"We've got this," Doc told her. "Take your call."

She left and he turned to Drake and Mick. "I'll start the blood transfusion while you two scrub up."

The request wasn't unexpected, since every member of the team was required to go through EMT training. Julie wanted the Rainbow Knights to be self-sufficient in every situation.

"Drake, I know this must be difficult for you," Doc said, making it clear he also knew about his relationship with Chance. "I want you on monitors. Mick, you'll be assisting me."

During the entire procedure, Drake silently recited the prayer his mother had taught him when he was a child. "Our Father, who art in heaven..."

"Vitals, Drake."

"Blood pressure, seventy-seven over forty-eight. Pulse is 121. Respiratory rate, thirty-three."

"Let's continue," Doc said. "Suction here, Mick."

The sound of the pump sucking up Chance's blood echoed in Drake's ears.

"There's the little bugger," Doc said. "Gotcha."

Drake heard the clink of the bullet hit the bottom of the metal bowl. "Is he gonna be okay, Doc?"

"Yes, I would say so. The shot was clean, missing all his vital organs.

He's going to be fine. Even though he's lost a lot of blood, Chance is very strong."

"You can say that again," Mick said.

"I'll stitch him up. Then we'll monitor him until he wakes up, but I don't expect any problems."

Reassured that Chance was going to pull through this, Drake felt the tightness in his entire body suddenly release, causing him to lose his balance and almost stumble.

"Mick, get Drake a chair please."

"I'm okay, Doc." Drake steadied himself. "It's just such good news. Thank you."

"Nevertheless, sit down. That's an order."

He grinned. "I think I outrank you."

"Not in here, you don't. Sit."

"Yes, sir." He took a seat and kept watching the monitors as Doc finished the procedure.

Chance continued sleeping for another hour while they all kept close watch on him. Seeing his vitals improving let Drake breathe more easily.

Julie walked in. "How's Chance doing?"

"He's doing great," Doc said. "He should be waking up shortly."

As Doc continued filling her in on Chance's status, Mick came up beside Drake. "Breathe, buddy. You're holding your breath. Doc said he's gonna be okay."

"I know. It's just seeing him this way is tough."

Mick checked Chance's IV and then turned to Julie. "How did it go with Collins?"

"Are you talking about the son of a bitch I was on the phone with? He's the biggest asshole I've ever worked with in my life. There's something about that man... I can't put my finger on it, but one of these days I will. And when I do, he's going to be out the door in a heartbeat."

Mick smiled. "Tell us how you really feel, boss."

"To win this battle, we have to get Kuusik, because Collins is out to destroy us."

"How did Kuusik know we were coming?" Mick asked.

"That's what I'm wondering," she said. "How many knew about our operation? Me. You guys. Collins. Director Maddow. And two analysts. I'll work every angle to figure out how the details got into Kuusik's hands. In the meantime, we need to find him. The mission is still on."

"We know Kuusik likes young men," Drake said.

"Also dance clubs." Mick stepped next to Julie. "There's several besides Romantique that fit the bill."

"We'll start there," she said.

Chance began stirring. "Drake?"

He jumped to the side of his bed. "I'm here."

His eyes opened. "Did we get Kuusik?"

"Not yet, but we will. How are you feeling?"

"Like someone dug a bullet out of me. Are you here, Doc?"

"Right here, buddy." Doc moved to the other side of the bed. "And yes, I got the bullet. You're gonna be just fine if you follow my orders."

"If you think I'm staying in this bed all day, you're wrong."

"As a matter of fact, I want you to get up in a couple of hours, but you aren't leaving. That's an order."

"You and what army is going to stop me?"

Julie stepped next to Doc and leaned over. "This army, Chance. I didn't recruit you for just one mission. So you need to follow Doc's instructions to the letter and get back on your feet as soon as possible. Is. That. Clear?"

"Yes, ma'am." Chance nodded. "Very clear."

"We need to find Kuusik. Mick, you and Wiz are with me." She turned to Drake. "You're staying here with Chance."

Drake's jaw tightened. Why was she pulling him off the mission to watch Chance? Did she suspect that they had been in a relationship?

"Julie, he doesn't have to stay here," Chance said. "I'm in good hands with Doc. Besides, I can take care of myself."

"Fine. Drake, you're with us."

Drake wondered if Chance was still angry with him about refusing to move in together. This wasn't the place, especially not in front of Julie, to tell Chance that he'd had a complete change of heart. More than anything, he wanted him back in his life.

Chance looked at him. "You have a job to finish. Go get that fucker before he assassinates someone."

Drake nodded and squeezed his hand.

"Wait a minute," Mick said. "I left Kuusik's jacket in the van. I know it's a long shot but maybe we'll find something in one of the pockets that can lead us to him."

"Let's go get it." Drake rushed out the door with Mick to parking spot sixty-two.

They got to the van and Mick grabbed the jacket.

"You're not going to believe this. Kuusik's phone is in here." Mick held up a sat phone. "I hope this is the break we've been needing."

They ran back to the safe house, letting the rest know what they'd found.

Julie took the phone from Mick. "It's locked."

"If anyone can crack it, Wiz can," Drake said.

"You're right about that. He's still in the control room. I'll be right back." She left with the phone.

Moments later, Julie returned with Wiz.

"That was fast," Mick said. "Even for you, Wiz."

"The arrogant idiot used assassin for his password."

"We have to go now, guys," Julie said. "He's going to attempt to assassinate the French president at a ribbon cutting of the Hotel L'Gemme, which is in twenty minutes."

Chance sat up. "It will take at least that much time to get there from here."

"Not with him behind the wheel." Drake pointed at Mick.

"Damn right," Mick said. "Let's go."

"Get that bastard," Chance said.

Everyone but Doc and Chance ran out.

As promised, Mick got them to the ribbon cutting just in time. They remained outside the barricades and couldn't get closer because the French security in charge of protecting the president had blocked off the area.

Still, they could see there was a large crowd at the ceremony. The president sat with other dignitaries in chairs behind the podium. A speaker from the hotel chain was giving the introduction for the president.

"Circulez! Circulez!" one of the guards outside the blockade told them. "Il n'y a rien."

"Oui, Officier," Julie said in a nonthreatening tone.

The last thing she needed to do was draw attention to the team.

Drake and Mick walked one direction and Julie and Wiz walked the other, each duo scanning the area for any sign of Kuusik.

Knowing the killer would likely make the attempt when the president stepped up to the microphone, Drake prayed for a long introduction and looked for any spot where Kuusik could take his shot. There weren't many choices since the authorities had likely cleared the area hours ago.

Luck was on Drake's side when he saw light reflect off of the scope on Kuusik's rifle. The assassin was leaning out a third-story window in an abandoned building more than a block away at an odd angle that would make getting off a shot very difficult.

As Drake raced there, he imagined it had gone unchecked by the sweep of the authorities. They probably marked it off their list as too far away. But he knew Kuusik's reputation. He'd picked off an Asian general just last year on what most believed was an impossible shot.

"Kuusik is in that vacant building off to the south," he panted out as he closed the distance. "Third floor, the fourth window from the left."

"Copy that," they all confirmed.

"On our way," Julie said.

Behind him, Drake heard the applause that announced the president was moving to the podium. In front of him, Kuusik was about to fire.

Drake had no time to get closer for a better shot. He pulled out his gun and fired off every round at the third-floor window.

Hearing the pandemonium his gunfire had created, Drake saw the barrel of the rifle disappear. If he hadn't hit the assassin, at least he'd blocked his attempt.

Mick caught up with him, and they ran into the vacant building.

"Status," Julie ordered.

"Entering the building to apprehend Kuusik," Mick answered.

"Abort. Get out of there. Local authorities are headed your way now."

Drake didn't stop. Couldn't stop. The images of Chance bleeding in his arms and passing out kept playing over and over in his mind. Kuusik was the one responsible. Drake ran into the building, ready to make the fucker pay for what he'd done to Chance.

Just two steps behind, Mick grabbed him, turning off his comms. "What the hell are you doing, McLeod? You heard the orders."

Drake reached up and muted his comms. "Fuck the orders. This is for Chance."

"Okay. I'm game."

As the sound of approaching police boots echoed off the pavement, Drake realized he was too late. "I'll get him later. Let's go."

He and Mick ran into a bathroom, closing the door behind them in the nick of time before the police charged into the building. They escaped through a window, and luck was once again on Drake's side. He and Mick landed in an empty alley.

Running the opposite direction of the army of police, they alerted Julie and Wiz which way they were headed. Moments later, they were safe, driving away from the scene in the van.

"That was a little too close," Julie said. "But good job, team. The French president is safe."

"Thanks to Drake's quick thinking." Mick slapped him on the shoulder.

His words cut Drake deep. He'd let his emotions jeopardize not just his freedom but Mick's. One second later, they'd both have been carted away by the French authorities, their careers with the CIA over. The Agency would never claim them. That was the deal everyone who worked covert operations agreed to when they signed up. They were on foreign soil and would end up in a French prison, likely for the rest of their lives.

When Wiz parked in spot sixty-two, Drake was anxious to check on Chance, so he was the first out of the van.

Chance was sitting in a chair. Doc was standing next to him. They were watching the television, which was replaying footage of the events at the ribbon cutting.

Chance turned to Drake as the rest of the team came into the room. "Looks like the police took care of Kuusik for us."

"What are you talking about?" Drake looked at Doc. "Is he still under the influence of the drugs?"

"Nope. We just saw it." Doc pointed the remote at the TV.

The image of a young officer filled the screen. Under the image was the English closed caption.

"You are a hero," the female reporter said.

"No, madam. Just doing my job. When I saw the killer aim for the president, I just reacted like any of my fellow officers would have. I fired."

"And you were so far away on the street. You are an incredible marksman."

The officer clumsily grabbed the microphone from her.

Drake shook his head. "That guy couldn't fire his way out of a wet paper sack."

"I fired several shots, hoping I would hit him." The officer grinned. "Thankfully, I was successful."

"Liar! That son of a bitch is taking credit for Drake's shot," Mick said.

Chance grinned. "So Drake is the one who got him, not this up-and-coming officer."

"That's at least one good thing. Leaves us out of it." Julie was in her full-blown CIA supervisor mode. She liked missions that were neat and tidy, and this one was far from that. "Is Kuusik dead or in custody?"

"Neither," Chance said.

Doc muted the sound. "The police did find blood at the scene, but no sign of Kuusik."

Drake paced around the room. "No doubt he is already being slipped out of the country. The bastard got away. We failed."

"This isn't a failure, Drake, just a setback," Julie said. "We'll find Kuusik. I need to update Langley about the situation, and then I'm going back to the hotel."

"I'll drive you." Mick grabbed the keys from Wiz. "I could use a shower."

"Me, too." Wiz smiled. "And I'm good with your driving. Are you coming, Drake?"

"No. I'm staying here with Chance."

"Good," Doc said. "I'm starving. Haven't eaten all day. You can keep an eye on this difficult patient. I'll be back soon."

After everyone left and the coast was clear, Drake sat down next to Chance. "I'm so glad you're okay, sweetheart." He leaned over to give him a kiss, but Chance turned his head away.

"What the hell do you think you're doing? Have you forgotten we're no longer a couple? I told you I wasn't taking your games anymore."

"But, sweetheart, I—"

"Don't 'I' me, Drake. We're done. Over. Kaput."

"Please, sweetheart. Just listen to—"

"I'm done listening. I'm done period."

"So you don't want to hear that I want to live with you for the rest of my life."

"I don't want to hear any... What?"

"I want to live with you for the rest of my life."

Chance's big blue eyes widened. "You do?"

"Oh, yes. I've been a dumb ass, Chance. I finally get what you've been trying to tell me. I get it now. God, what an idiot I've been. No more. You're all that matters to me. I swear." Drake sighed. "Such a damn jerk. You deserved so much better. A moron. An imbecile."

Chance grinned. "Will you please just shut up and lean over and kiss me?"

Drake pressed his mouth to Chance's lips. As the kiss deepened, he could feel red-hot passion for Chance building inside him. "I want you, sweetheart."

"Honey, I wish I could but I can't."

"Don't worry. I've got this." He gently kissed his neck. "You just relax, enjoy, and let me take the pain away."

"I'd like that."

Drake got down on his knees in front of Chance, lifting his hospital gown, revealing his thick, long cock. "God, I've missed this."

"So have I."

Drake licked Chance's dick, wrapping his hand around his heavy balls. "Is this okay, sweetheart? I'm not hurting you?"

"God, no." Chance laughed. "Honey, you're a better physician than Doc will ever be."

"I'm going to be slow and careful, but if anything I do hurts you, tell me."

"I will, you fool. Will you just stop talking and keep going?"

"What my patient wants, my patient gets." Drake swirled his tongue around Chance's tip, finding a little tasty drop that hinted at more hot passion to come.

Swallowing Chance felt like coming home. How he'd missed him, missed this.

"Damn, that feels so good. Don't stop, honey. Don't ever stop."

He wasn't planning on it. Squeezing his balls, he sucked hard, hollowing out his cheeks.

Chance moaned.

Instantly, he let go of him with his mouth and hands. "Are you okay?"

"I'm okay, but damn, you're going to have to start all over."

"My pleasure." He slowly kissed Chance's muscled thighs, working back to his hard dick and loaded balls.

He bathed every inch with his tongue, relishing the taste of the man he loved, the man he would spend the rest of his life with.

"Oh, yes. That's it. Ahhh."

His passionate tone thrilled Drake, driving him wild. But he knew he couldn't unleash all his lust. He might hurt Chance. Gently, he resumed sucking on his cock. Up and down. Again and again.

"I'm coming, honey. I'm com... Ohhh!"

Drake sealed his lips around Chance's shaft, not wanting a single drop to be wasted. When he felt cream hit the back of his throat, he drank like a man who'd been dying of thirst. That's exactly what he had been doing since the breakup. Dying of thirst. Dying because of the breakup. Now that he was back with Chance, he would never feel that way again.

When Chance tugged on his hair, he asked, "You okay?"

"You don't have to keep asking me that. I'm fine. I want one little taste of you. I know I can't do more than that, but could I please have you in my mouth for just a little bit?"

"I'm not sure that's a good idea in your current condition."

"Please, honey. Just let me taste you. I have to taste you. It's been so long."

Unable to resist, Drake stood up. "Just a little bit." He pointed at his own chest. "That's this doctor's orders, understand?"

"Yes. Yes. Okay. Unzip. Now, before I rip off those damn pants myself."

He grinned, feeling his cock stiffen. Chance's playfulness in bed was something he'd missed most of all. Pulling down the zipper, he released his cock and directed it to Chance's hungry mouth.

"Mmm," Chance's lusty tone was the best music in the world.

"Okay. Okay. That's all."

"No. Just a little more."

"More will come later. Much more." Drake stepped back, holding on to his erect cock. "First, let's focus on your recovery."

Hearing the door to the room open behind him, Drake quickly stuffed his junk back into his pants.

"How's my patient doing?" Doc asked.

Now fully zipped up, Drake turned around. "He's doing great."

"Yeah, Doc. I'm doing great. You left me in really good hands."

"I knew you would be okay. Let me check your vitals."

Drake winked at Chance, a silent sign that conveyed I think we pulled it off.

"Huh. Your blood pressure is elevated. I'm not sure why."

"Uh... I just took a little walk around the room with Drake's help."

"A little walk." He smiled. "I haven't heard it called that before. It's a little soon for...walking."

INGLESIDE, VIRGINIA

Chance sat in the passenger seat of Drake's car, waiting impatiently for him to get one more box of his things. Drake had been adamant that he wasn't to lift a finger. Chance loved him for all his concern, but he really did feel great and capable.

He smiled. It hadn't been that long ago when he'd thought their relationship was over for good. Now? They were talking about getting a bigger place, and Drake was trying to convince him to adopt a dog. How could he be any happier?

Chance's phone rang. "Hey, Doc."

"I called to let you know that all your tests came back perfect. So I'm going to release you to resume your life the way it was." Doc chuckled. "You know, the walk you and Drake did back in Paris. Knock yourselves out. Run a marathon."

"Thanks, Doc. I've been anxious to get more steps on my Fitbit."

"I bet you have. I'll also let Julie know you're ready to resume your duty."

Chance sighed. "Thanks, but we're still benched."

"Yeah, we are. Damn. I wonder how long Collins will drag out his witch hunt."

"Too long, I bet." He saw Drake approaching with a box. "Drake's back, Doc. I can't wait to tell him the good news. I'll see you tomorrow."

After placing the box in the trunk with his other boxes, Drake got behind the wheel.

"Honey, you're going to love the news I have for you as much as I did."

"We're not benched anymore?"

"No. It's better than that. It's time for a celebration."

Drake smiled. "That was Doc on the phone. He released you, didn't he?"

Chance nodded and then leaned over and kissed him. "And I know just what we need to celebrate. That bottle of wine Emily bought me for my last birthday."

"Your sister definitely knows how much you love Pinot Noir."

"She knows we both love it."

"How about we stop and get some takeout from Antonio's Pizzeria?"

"After. I've been dying to make love to you since Paris. Let's go home first."

"You've always known how to pull a plan together. And you're not the only one who's been dying to make love." Drake revved the engine. "Fasten your seat belt, sweetheart. We're late for a very important date."

As Drake raced down the road, Chance laughed. "You might want to slow down a little, because I'd like to get there in one piece."

"You're right. You just got me excited."

When Drake merged onto the George Washington Memorial Highway, they saw a sea of brake lights in front of them.

"Damn," Drake said. "There must be a wreck ahead."

"It's going to be at least twenty minutes before we get back to my...I mean our apartment."

"I like that. Our apartment. Have you thought any more about looking for a new place for us? I really want a yard for the dog."

"I'm good with a bigger place, but I'm not sure about adopting a dog. The team won't be benched forever."

"We will if Collins gets his way."

Drake was right about that. Not only did Collins want to disband the Rainbow Knights, he believed there should never be any LGBT officers in the entire agency. What a bigot. Collins was taking advantage of Kuusik's disappearance, using it to undermine Director Maddow. Chance didn't care for Agency politics, but he knew that the team's future was in jeopardy as long as Kuusik was free. There wasn't anything he, Drake, Julie, or the others could do. Even their weapons would not be returned until Collin's investigation about the Paris mission was complete. The bastard's smug tone had infuriated Chance during their debriefing. "There is no doubt that a mole inside the Agency tipped off Kuusik. I believe my investigation, once complete, will prove that the leak came from inside Julie's group of misfits."

Drake kept one hand on the steering wheel while taking Chance's hand with the other. "Sweetheart, Emily loves dogs. I'm sure she would be thrilled to puppy sit if we ever get to go on another assignment together again."

"Just let me ask her first."

"Confession. I already did, and she told me she would love to." The rest of the trip home, Drake continued making his case for having a dog.

What a change Chance had seen in him. Before, Drake had been commitment shy about everything. It had been quite the undertaking to get him to exchange keys. Now, Drake was ready to jump in and start building their future together. It was a dream that had come true for Chance. Drake was his dream.

Once Drake parked the car, he jumped out, ran ahead, and yelled back, "We'll get the boxes later. Come on."

Chance laughed. "Oh, yeah. The plan."

He ran after him.

They both got to the apartment at the same time, each with their keys out. Since the sun had already set and his porch light was off, it was difficult to see the lock.

Drake stepped back. "Go ahead."

"No. You. This is your place too."

"My place. Your place. Unlock the damn door before I take you right here on the steps."

"You wouldn't."

"Oh, no?" He grinned wickedly. "Just try me."

Feeling heat roll through his entire body, Chance used his key to unlock the door.

They rushed inside.

Drake pushed him against the wall, kissing his lips and stripping off his clothes.

"Oh, no you don't. Paris was your turn. This is mine." Chance turned the tables, ripping off Drake's shirt, sending the buttons skating across the floor.

Now shirt free, they kissed each other hungrily as they made their way to the bedroom. They were full-throttle, blasting into sex from zero to a thousand in the blink of an eye.

Not taking the time to turn the lights on, they frantically peeled off the rest of their clothes and landed in the middle of the bed, caressing each other's bodies.

Chance gazed at Drake's big brown eyes, illuminated by the full moon's rays coming in through the window.

"I love you so much, Chance."

Hearing those words made him feel such overwhelming desire, such unrelenting want, and such primal energy. He opened his nightstand and retrieved some condoms and the bottle of lube.

"You're mine, Drake McLeod. All mine."

"Yes. I'm yours."

"Forever." Chance grabbed Drake and pulled him in close, devouring his mouth.

Drake parted his lips, inviting him to go deeper.

Chance sent his hungry tongue into his mouth as he reached down and wrapped his hand around Drake's hard cock, another part of him he wanted to taste. But he couldn't stop kissing him yet. As their tongues tangled together, he felt his pulse heat up inside his veins. God, his man knew how to kiss.

As his lips throbbed from the continued friction with Drake, Chance realized if he let himself go, this mind-blowing and body-igniting kiss would push him over the edge to release. He wasn't going to let that happen. He had other plans for Drake. Wicked plans that would cause his man to demand more, which he would gladly deliver.

Inhaling his scent, Chance began slowly nuzzling his neck and tenderly nipping at his earlobe. Drake's masculine aroma hypnotized him. How he'd missed his addiction, his smell of leather and spice. The more he inhaled Drake's essence, the more greedy lust surged through him, but he reined in his own desire, determined to give Drake every pleasure and want he'd ever dreamed of with the two of them together.

"God, that feels so good, sweetheart."

"You feel so good." Chance tightened his hand around Drake's cock while sliding down to dine on his chest, remembering how sensitive his nipples were.

"Mm." Drake's lusty moans were music to his ears, causing his own cock to throb and his balls to get heavy.

He tightened his lips around one of Drake's nipples and was rewarded with a hot groan.

"Sweetheart, I'm not sure I can hold back much longer," Drake panted out. "It's been so long."

"Take a deep breath, baby, because I have so much more to give you."

"I'll try." He inhaled deeply. "Damn, Chance. You are my wild man."

Keeping a tight hold on Drake's cock, Chance swirled his tongue around his nipple and then began slowly kissing a trail down his frame, enjoying his rock-solid body and six-pack abs.

When he got between his legs, Chance kissed the head of his cock, bathing his own lips in Drake's salty drop of pre-cum. Cuddling Drake's balls with one hand and fisting his shaft with the other, Chance swallowed his man's cock.

"Fuck. Your mouth is like heaven. Damn." Drake tugged on his hair. "I can't. Please, sweetheart. I've got to taste you."

Loving the anxious excitement in his tone, Chance kept on sucking but spun around so that his cock was positioned next to Drake's mouth.

When Drake's lips slid down his dick, Chance felt something that went beyond anything he'd ever experienced before. He knew at this very moment they were one. He'd always felt connected to Drake, but this...this was on a level far stronger and permanent. Transcendent. Nothing would ever separate them again. Their love would last for the rest of their lives. Forever.

In complete synch, they thrust their dicks into each other's thirsty mouths.

Chance sensed his man was getting as close as he was. He hollowed out his cheeks, taking every one of Drake's eager lunges. The pleasure continued, ramping up and up, pushing him to the very edge.

Unable to hold back any longer, he grabbed Drake's ass and gulped down every bit of him. In unison, they came, shooting cream down each other's throat.

Breathing heavily, Chance flipped around, bringing his lips to

Drake's. He pressed gently at first, but then Drake parted his lips, demanding more, which was exactly what he wanted too. He could feel his cock hardening again as he sucked on Drake's tongue.

"On your stomach, honey," Chance ordered, grabbing a pillow to put under Drake so that his ass would jut up in the perfect position.

"Like I said before..." He grinned. "You're my wild man."

Drake flipped around, placing the pillow just right.

Chance squirted out a generous amount of lube from the bottle onto his hand. He circled Drake's tight hole with his slicked fingers.

Drake began grinding into the mattress, heightening his own ravenous lust.

Chance slipped his index finger into Drake and was rewarded with a hot moan from him.

"Yes, sweetheart," Drake breathed. "Yes. Yes."

He added another finger to the first one and began thrusting into his ass, again and again, stretching Drake out and getting him ready to take more. When his man began thrusting back into his fingers, Chance slipped a condom down his dick.

Applying some lubricant, he fisted himself a few strokes and then got on top of Drake, positioning his cock between Drake's ass cheeks. "I love you."

"I love you too. Now get inside me. You're driving me wild."

"That's the plan, baby." Slowly, he pierced Drake's body.

"That's it." Drake shifted his hips higher, trying to take more of him.

But Chance, despite his own insatiable desires, pulled back slightly. "No, you don't, baby. I want to drive you mad with passion."

"Please, Chance. Fuck me. I need more of you inside me."

After teasing him to a point where neither of them could stand it anymore, Chance began thrusting hard and deep into Drake.

"Ohh. That's the spot, Chance. Yes. Yes. Yes."

"Take me, baby. All of me." He drove even deeper, even harder, his thrusts coming faster and faster.

"I'm so...so...so close."

Continuing to plunge into him, Chance leaned over Drake and felt his body's tremors against his skin. "Now, baby. Let's come together."

His final thrust was met with Drake shoving his ass back into him, joining their bodies even tighter to one another.

Their simultaneous releases exploded like a volcano that ended with both of them groaning out a primal sound of satisfaction.

After a few breathless moments, they flipped on their sides, facing each other.

Drake smiled. "That was...was...amazing."

"Yes, it was."

"No. You don't understand what I mean. You and I have made love many times and it was always great, but I've never experienced anything like what we just did. Ever. It was beyond wonderful, exciting, fabulous." He shook his head. "I don't know how to explain it to you. Did you feel it?"

Chance grinned. "Yes, honey. I felt it."

"What's different now? I've always loved you."

"Yes, you have. But Drake, you know you were holding back. Now you're not. Now you're all in, completely committed to me. And I am completely committed to you. That's the difference and that's why it was so incredible."

"You're right. That's it. It's not just me. Or you. It's now us."

"God, I love you."

Drake kissed him. "I love you too."

Suddenly, the closet door flew open and Kuusik emerged, aiming a Glock at the duo. "I enjoyed the show but this is getting sickening."

He and Drake sat up.

"Don't move, gentlemen."

"Hello, Kuusik." Chance assessed the situation, which was far from optimal. He and Drake were naked, on the bed, and under the covers without any weapons. "We weren't expecting you. Do you mind if we get some clothes on?"

"Nice try, CIA. Both of you stay right where you are and don't make any sudden moves."

"You're obviously here for a reason." Drake used his toe to tap out a Morse code message on Chance's leg. Your gun?

"Of course I'm here for a reason."

Chance tapped back: Nightstand.

Kuusik took a step closer to the bed but remained out of reach.

Drake sent the message: I'll distract. "You're pissed about Paris, aren't you?"

"Pissed?" The killer laughed. "I don't get pissed."

As Kuusik continued talking, Chance began easing—slowly so as not to alert the killer of his movements—to his nightstand.

"I'm too practical for that, McLeod," Kuusik said. "Besides, your lucky shot was only a flesh wound."

"That is your reputation, but you must have lost a bundle after we stopped you from completing your contract to kill the French president." Drake swung his legs off the bed.

"I said don't move!" Kuusik took another step in Drake's direction, which gave Chance his lucky break.

He grabbed his Smith & Wesson and fired off a nonlethal shot that hit Kuusik in the shoulder.

As he'd expected at this close range, Kuusik was knocked off his feet.

Chance and Drake pounced on top of him, forcing the gun out of the bastard's hand.

"Get off me, motherfuckers." Kuusik tried to break free of their hold but to no avail.

"Not happening, pervert," Drake said. "You got cuffs, sweetheart?"

"I sure do." Keeping his gun aimed at Kuusik, Chance returned to the nightstand and pulled out the handcuffs.

Using a belt to wrap around Kussik's ankles and the handcuffs on his wrists behind his back, they secured the asshole to a chair.

"That was too easy," Chance said, hoping to get under Kuusik's skin. "Drake, you want to be good cop or bad cop?"

"Bad cop, of course." Drake tossed him his jeans and turned on the light. "This motherfucker's men shot you in Paris at the club. You could have died. I can't wait to pound him into hamburger meat."

Chance knew that Drake wasn't lying, but he was professional. While he would love to rip Kuusik apart, he wouldn't unless it was necessary.

Kuusik's eyes widened. "You're Americans. You have to follow the law."

Drake leaned in close to him. "Americans? Yes. But we're also CIA. Some laws don't apply, especially to asshole assassins like you."

"The orders are clear, honey. We can bring him in dead or alive. It's your decision, Kuusik."

The bastard squirmed in the chair, which was a clear indication that he and Drake were getting to him.

They were both trained in all kinds of interrogation methods. This was just one of them.

"Maybe we should both be bad cops tonight." Chance pulled on his jeans. "I would really enjoy getting in some hits on your ugly face, but I'll start out easy on you. How did you know this was my apartment?"

"I have my sources, CIA."

Drake punched him in the throat, causing Kuusik to sputter and gasp. "If you're evasive with your answers, this is going to be a very long night."

Kuusik coughed and glared at him. "Fuck you."

"Allow me, honey." Chance punched him in the face, which felt so satisfying.

Kuusik spit out blood. "Fuck you too."

They were getting nowhere. Chance knew they needed to change tactics but wasn't sure how.

"We only ask because we already know how you tracked down this apartment." Drake pulled his shirt off the floor and put it on, buttoning it up very slowly.

"Bullshit."

Drake looked away from Kuusik to him and laughed, which Chance knew was all part of the game.

Chance returned the laugh. "He doesn't know."

Where was Drake going with this technique? Chance wasn't sure but was following his lead, anxious to find out.

"Our team figured it out," Drake said. "It was so easy to connect the dots. Paris. The French president's assassination. Who would benefit the most? And then you coming to the US to track us down?"

Chance looked at Drake and realized he'd already put something together in his mind. This wasn't a ruse. He'd actually connected the dots. What were they?

Drake continued, leaning in close to Kuusik once again. "That would take someone with a great deal of authority who could pull strings to get you in the country undetected."

"You're bluffing. You don't know a damn thing."

"No, Kuusik. You don't know a damn thing. Collins is in custody."

Kuusik's nostrils flared, an obvious tell that Drake had hit the target.

Collins wasn't in custody, but Drake had figured out he had to be the mole.

Chance kept the expression on his face flat, though he was reeling with the new information. It all made sense now. "We know everything, Kuusik. Collins has already confessed."

Drake sent him a wink before turning back to their captive. "If you had succeeded in Paris, the relationship between the CIA and France's DGSE would have been strained. Since Director Maddow has put so much weight into working with other agencies around the world, she would have been on thin ice with the current US president, giving Collins an opening to make a move to take her position. He also would have had the added benefit to discredit our team. But you didn't succeed."

The whole picture filled in for Chance. "That's when Collins sent you here to take us out. He has benched our team. He's the one with the grudge, not you. You're too practical for that."

"So, Kuusik, you have a choice." Drake sat on the bed, tying his shoes. "Collins has given you up and there will be no more paydays for you. Easy or hard?" Drake looked at Chance and smiled. "Is that all right with you, sweetheart?"

"I really hope he chooses hard." He slammed his fist into his hand. "I could go all night."

"Okay. Okay." Kuusik turned white with fear. "Fuck Collins. I'll tell you everything. Just don't hurt me."

"That's the right choice, though I am a bit disappointed." Chance hit the record icon on his phone. "Start at the beginning."

CIA HEADQUARTERS, LANGLEY, VIRGINIA

Chance sat in the conference room with Director Maddow, Julie, and Drake. The door opened and he saw the man they'd been waiting for walk in.

Collins had a stocky five-foot-eight frame, receding hairline, and thick eyebrows.

He frowned. "What's going on, Amanda? You can't reinstate Rainbow Knights until I finish my investigation. That's protocol."

"Please. Have a seat, Peter." The director stood and motioned to the empty chair between him and Drake. "We have some new intel to share with you."

Chance was impressed at how cool Maddow could be in this situation, but he wasn't surprised. She'd come up through the ranks at the Agency, proving her skills again and again.

"Fine. But I have a meeting with Senators Samuels and Reed in forty-five minutes. Make it quick," he said with blatant disrespect before taking his seat.

"I think you'll find this very enlightening," Julie said in a flat tone that kept her real motive hidden. If the director was cool, Julie was ice when necessary.

Maddow returned to her chair. "You've made it very clear to me and to your buddies on Capitol Hill how much you want to eliminate the Rainbow Knights team."

"That's common knowledge. Homosexuals have no place in the Agency. They are a liability."

"I think you will find it interesting, Collins, that these two homosexuals brought in Kuusik."

"What? When?"

"A few hours ago."

Collins's nostrils flared. "These two aren't released for duty yet."

"True, but I think we can make an exception since the assassin broke into their home." She clicked the remote.

Kuusik's image appeared on the large flat-screen in the room.

Per the plan, Drake remained seated while Chance stood and moved behind Collins. Both he and Drake reached for their guns.

"As you can see, they are interrogating him now, but we already know that Kuusik was working for you."

Collins panicked, started to rise, and reached for his weapon inside his jacket.

"I wouldn't do that if I were you." Chance shoved his Glock's barrel into the traitor's back.

Drake easily retrieved Collins' gun, slammed him into the chair, and cuffed his wrists. "There's more you need to hear, asshole. Much more."

"Officer McLeod is correct." Julie smiled. "The State Department and the Swiss government have frozen the bank account you paid him from. We know the balance is ten million dollars."

"Ten million dollars, Peter?" Maddow shook her head. "I'm sure when Julie's team digs deep they'll uncover all kinds of illegal activities you've been involved in."

"Fuck you, bitch."

"Actually, you're the one who is fucked." The director buzzed in the other officers, who immediately took Collins away.

The bastard's rants and curses never stopped.

When the door closed, they returned to their seats.

"That was quite satisfying." Maddow looked at Julie. "Now, about the other item we need to discuss with McLeod and Nicholls."

"Other item?" Chance asked.

Julie slid two folders in front of them.

"I don't have to open this, Julie. I know what it's about already." Drake stood. "I've decided that I'll leave the field and take a desk job."

"What are you talking about?" Chase and Julie said in unison.

"Let him speak," Maddow told them. "Go on, McLeod."

"It's obvious that you both know about Chance and me, especially after reading the report where we apprehended Kuusik. Chance and I are together, and we are going to stay that way. So, I've made up my mind. Chance is great in the field. He's the best the Agency has and deserves to remain with Rainbow Knights."

"Hold on, Drake." Chance stood and put his arm around him. "If anyone is going to take a desk job, it's me. Not you."

"Not either of you," Julie said. "Do you think you were fooling anyone about your relationship?"

"I think they did, Julie." Maddow smiled. "But may I remind you both that this is the place that uncovers secrets? We all knew."

"You both knew." Drake turned to Chance. "You were right."

Chance smiled. "Yes, I was."

"Sit back down, gentlemen," Maddow said. "Let's get to the actual item that we need to discuss."

They took their seats one more time.

"Julie, go ahead."

"Thank you. Guys, Director Maddow is promoting me to take Collins's position as deputy director of covert ops."

"Congratulations," he and Drake said together.

She smiled. "That leaves my previous position open. Now if you both will please take a look at what's in front of you, I think you'll see where I'm going with this."

Chance and Drake opened the folders and found something that thrilled them both.

"Two co-supervisors for the team?" Drake voiced his own question.

"Has that ever been done before at the Agency?"

"No," Maddow said. "But neither was an exclusively LGBT covert ops team until just a few months ago. Everyone thought I was nuts to give Julie the green light for the Rainbow Knights. But look what you guys have already done. The French president is alive. A notorious international assassin is in custody. And a mole inside the Agency has been brought to light. And that was just your first mission."

Julie's pride showed through her broad smile. "So, officers, what do you say? Will you lead the Rainbow Knights?"

Chance looked at Drake and their eyes locked for a moment. This was so much more than they'd ever hoped for.

"I say yes. What do you say, Drake?"

"Oh, yeah. We've already proved we're an unstoppable team. I have no doubt we'll be even more formidable as co-supervisors. Definitely yes."

"Congratulations, men," Maddow said. "You will still be reporting to Julie."

"Excellent," Drake said. "When do we start?"

"Right now." Julie stood. "I emailed you the files of the new recruits. You need to review them."

"The team is expanding?" Chance asked.

Julie nodded. "With two supervisors and more men, Rainbow Knights will be able to handle more missions."

The director's assistant, a twenty-five-year-old man, entered the room. "I'm sorry to interrupt, but I have the French minister of defense on your secure line."

"Thanks, Tim. Julie, this will be a good time to get your feet wet in your new job. Stay." Maddow looked at Chance and Drake. "You did great work and I expect no less from you in your new positions. We all have work to do. Julie and I will circle back with you later today."

As they walked out of the director's office, Chance grabbed Drake and planted a big kiss on him. "This is better than we both thought."

"That's for sure, sweetheart. On the way home tonight let's stop at Antonio's for dinner to celebrate."

"Well, that's one way to celebrate."

Drake laughed. "I like your plan better."

DRAKE TOOK ONE MORE GLANCE AT HIS TUXEDO IN THE MIRROR.

Mick looked out the window at Director Maddow's decked-out backyard, which was filled with CIA officers. "Quite the crowd you guys drew today."

"The more people who come the more nervous I'm getting."

Mick laughed. "Suck it up, McLeod. This is child's play compared to what you've seen in the field."

"Really? I don't get nervous in the field. There's no comparison.

Besides, you're the one who doesn't believe in relationships, and I'm guessing that's because you might actually be terrified of them."

"This isn't about me, Drake." Mick's tone sharpened for a moment. "This is your big day. And yes, I'm not a big believer in relationships—at least not for me. For you and Chance? You two are meant for each other."

The band hit the opening chord.

"That's your cue, buddy, to get into position."

He nodded and they walked to the den's double doors, which led to the backyard, and found Chance and Wiz.

"Sweetheart, you look incredible." Drake took Chance's hand.

"You just saw me last night, honey. I haven't changed." Chance had demanded they follow wedding protocol and not see each other until it was time to get married. "But I missed you so much. And you're the one who looks incredible."

"Yeah. Yeah." Mick smiled. "You both look gorgeous. Pay attention. You're up."

The band started the wedding march and Wiz and Mick opened the double doors for them.

Drake and Chance walked hand in hand down the red carpet to the wedding arch covered with multicolored spring flowers. They stepped up to Julie, who was officiating the service.

"We are gathered here to witness a special occasion, the marriage of Drake McLeod and Chance Nicholls. They are two of the finest and bravest men I've ever known. Gentlemen, please take each other's hand."

As they clasped each other's hand, Drake stared at the man he would spend the rest of his life with. He couldn't remember ever being happier.

"Drake and Chance have written their own vows." Julie turned to Chance. "Go ahead."

Drake could feel the slight tremor in Chance's hands, letting him know that he was nervous too. "You'll do great," he whispered to him.

"I can't imagine a life without you in it. You're the dream, Drake. My dream. Together we'll build a life, a future. With you in my life, I have everything. No matter what comes our way, I promise to stand beside you. I love you, honey, and choose you to be my husband, and I offer myself in return."

Drake was overcome with emotion at Chance's words. "Hard act to follow, but I'll try."

Everyone laughed, including Chance.

"I almost blew it, sweetheart, and lost you for good. The luckiest day in my life was the day I met you. I remember thinking how gorgeous and sexy you were. I was right, but I didn't realize then how amazing you are. I do now with all my heart and mind. I don't deserve you, but I am happy as hell that I get to marry you. I swear, now that I have you I will never let you go. I love you, Chance. Now and forever."

After the exchange of rings, Julie said, "By the power vested in me by the Commonwealth of Virginia, it gives me great honor to pronounce you, Drake McLeod, and you, Chance Nicholls, legally married."

Drake and Chance kissed and everyone, including Director Maddow and their entire Rainbow Knights team, cheered.

Suddenly, several cell phones started buzzing simultaneously, which Drake knew could only mean one thing.

He looked at the secured text about the new risk in Asia and turned to his husband. "I love you but—"

"But our country needs us. The honeymoon has to wait," Chance said. "I'll call my sister to get her set up to watch the dog. You assemble the team."

ABOUT KRIS COOK

Kris Cook was born in Monnett, Missouri, USA. His father was in the military, so Kris grew up in many locations, including: Missouri, Maine, California, Washington, Germany, Illinois, Indiana and finally settling in Texas.

Kris is a fiction author and novelist, writing in the romance, new adult and gay fiction genres.

His approach to writing is to dig deep emotionally with hard hitting and relevant current issues, striving to deliver books that have you ripping through the pages, catching your breath, and HEAs that will reach your heart.

∼

To be notified of new releases or sales,
join Kris' Mailing List: www.bit.ly/KrisCookNewsletter
Connect with Kris online
Facebook: www.facebook.com/KrisCookFanPage
Instagram: www.instagram.com/Kris_Cook_Author
Visit Kris at KrisCook.net!

WITH A *Vengeance*

ANISSA GARCIA

1

HER

Six months ago, my best friend and roommate was found in the river, her body lifeless. My heart hasn't felt the same since. Deep scars remain, ones that can't be seen but can definitely be felt. Rage mixed with sadness courses through me. Our boss, her lover, was a Jekyll and Hyde. She was his lover and she never knew the trajectory of his madness. But there was more to the story than she let on.

They claim it was a suicide. I know different. He's a powerful, rich man. Senator Branton Archard is as corrupt as most politicians. With Norah out of the way, he promoted me as his secretary, and I hate it. However, without hesitation, I took the job. My mission now is to prove the asshole guilty. It's taken longer than expected, and I'm nowhere close to finding the answers I'm searching for—what did Norah Cramer hold over Senator Archard? Is that what killed her? And if so, how will I ever find that proof? He belittles me, talks down to me, every day, and I take it. Because I know I'll eventually find him out.

Dark clouds loom as I stroll in Central Park. I stop and stare at the sky. The orange, yellow, red, and purple of the trees will sleep through the winter. I wish I could hibernate like them. I've been living in a haze —like everything is passing me by. My days and nights all seem to mesh together, filled with worry and work. I bundle my coat closer to me, the cold stinging my skin. The temperature has dropped significantly, and I should go back to my apartment, but I can't get myself to move.

Tears well up and slip down, staining my cheeks with trails of black mascara. I lean against Bow Bridge, staring at the water below. A sigh from a gentleman beside me grabs my attention. He's a few feet away and takes a long drag of his cigarette. Dark, thick hair waves on his head. Stubble covers his chiseled jaw. His profile's like a marble statue you'd see in Italy. It makes him look deliciously dangerous. The wool overcoat adds to his extreme good looks, as if he's a mystery to solve.

The smoke swirls from his lips as he puffs out, gazing into the distance. His Prussian-blue eyes set on mine and I shift. I'm caught ogling this beautiful stranger. I avoid his gaze and chip away at the already dwindling dark nail polish from my thumb. A few tears stream down again and I attempt to wipe them away in haste.

"Long day?"

The handsome stranger's standing beside me. His eyes focus clearly on mine. His hand is jutted out, the cigarette waiting. I reach for it; my shaking fingers clasp the burning death stick. My skin skims his, and I feel a stir in my heart, one that I can't explain.

"You could say that." I put the cigarette to my mouth and take a long drag. The nicotine fills my throat and rolls down my lungs. As I puff out, I can feel the tension dissipate. I hold back a cough, not used to the taste of smoke. I flick the ash down and hand it back.

He takes his own drag again and nods. "Me too." He breathes as he chuckles softly. "A city with over eight million people, and yet I've never felt more fucking alone."

I look to him as his velvet voice lulls me. He passes the cigarette back and I refuse. "I love and hate this city." I sigh, taking in the sunset. "The light, the trees, the buildings. Everything is so peaceful at this time of day...and then the night comes and..."

"Desolation," he finishes. I look up and his eyes are fixed on me.

"Smoking's disgusting, by the way," I say with disdain in my voice. He studies me as if he's confused, like I'm a marvel to him, then his mouth turns up slightly on one side. He puts out the cigarette on the rail and tosses the butt into a nearby trash bin.

"Want to get a drink?"

Shock tremors through me. Who is this man? "Why?"

"Why not?"

"You're a stranger."

He sounds amused as he begins, "That's the perfect reason to go and get a drink with me. We can talk it out."

"Talk what out?" I ask with suspicion.

"The reason why the both of us are fucking miserable."

He is hot. I'm lonely. I consider as my gaze sweeps over him. He's wearing a lush wool coat over a tailored suit, practically looking like a walking magazine ad. To not take him up on his offer would be insanity. "Okay."

He pushes his elbow out and I cautiously lean over to hook my hand around it. "I think it'll be best we remain strangers if this is going to be like a confession," he states as he leads me to a pub around the corner.

"Good idea." I don't need to be caught up in anything other than a fling. I'm too focused on my goal. I tell myself this as we walk.

The inside of the pub he takes me to is dimly lit, and we make our way toward the back. I can smell his scent as he takes off my coat. Cologne mixed with tobacco. It's heady and makes me weak in the knees. He removes his coat and orders lagers for the both of us. Dedication to his body is evident. Broad shoulders and a trim waist. What would he be like in bed? My stomach twists at the thought as he orders and offers to share some fish and chips with me.

We get settled, and he rests his forearms on the table, hooking his long fingers together. "Tell me, now. What's plaguing you?" That gaze is like lasers searing into me.

"Where to begin?" I shudder and take a sip of the frothy beer the waitress sets down.

"I'll bet I can guess why you were crying." No expression is given from me except a lift of my brow. "Your dog ran away."

I chuckle slightly. "No, no dog."

"Gerbil?"

I laugh louder, feeling my troubles lighten. "No. Nothing to do with pets."

He keeps his eyes on me. It's disconcerting. The fish and chips are set between us. He starts to munch on the food. I watch him, smooth and graceful in his movements. He picks up a fry and holds it to my lips. "I'm not really hungry."

"They're good." His eyebrow cocks up and I give a slight grin. "Come on, sweetheart, open those lips for me."

I try not to laugh but can't help it. My mouth parts and he slowly places the fry against my tongue. His finger glides across my lower lip and lingers before he then licks his own finger clean of salt. "Good?" he asks. I nod. "Good. Now, you lost your job?"

"No."

"Boyfriend?" I stay still. "Ah, a breakup."

"No, it's not that..."

His brows furrow, and a crease appears between them. "Divorce?"

"No. My best friend died."

His body stills and he breathes in as he takes a large sip of his lager. "I think we're going to need something stronger than just beer." He raises his hand and calls out for two shots of bourbon. "I'm so sorry. When did this happen?"

"Six months ago." His gaze lingers on me. He's so quiet, thinking things, judging me. "Do you pity me?"

"No. I know how it feels to lose someone." He watches me intently, his deep blue eyes so focused it's virtually easy to spill my secrets.

"I don't have anyone I can talk to. Confide in."

"Confide away. That's what we're doing here." He smiles and it pains me. He's so beautiful it's difficult to look at him. I wonder why the hell he's here with me when he could be out with some stunning runway model banging her into oblivion. I don't dwell on it, and take the opportunity to talk, which is much needed.

"She was my roommate and co-worker. We'd only known each other a few years, but we were close. And the thing is...I knew something was wrong. She tried to tell me she was in danger. I ignored it."

"What do you mean?" Concern swoops over his brow. He leans in close, the food forgotten.

"She drowned. They called it a suicide, but she told me she was pregnant. There's no way she would've thrown herself off a bridge. She didn't leave a note; there were no signs of depression. In fact, she was excited about the baby."

His thumb plays over his plump bottom lip in contemplation. "What about the father?"

I shake my head. "He's a scumbag."

His eyes darken as his form hardens. "You think he harmed her?"

I don't speak, giving him the nonverbal cues to an answer. He waits to respond as the waitress brings our shots. He grabs his and signals me to take mine. We both shoot the liquor down and I wince from the burn. "Want me to take him out?" he asks, a tiny hint of a grin playing over his angular, firm expression.

I think about it a moment and hum. "Not yet. I've gotta find the proof first. He's a crooked son of a bitch. I know there's some kind of evidence."

"And how do you expect to find it?"

I smirk and don't hold back, not sure if it's the alcohol that's making me bold or him. "He's my boss now. And I'll stick around the bastard until I find what I need."

"You're spying on him?" he asks, his tone astonished. His stern brow is furrowed, his expression intense. "That's dangerous, love."

I shrug, the booze heating my veins. "I have to do something. My friend said there was something she had of his. Something bad. I think she wanted to get back at him for leaving her once she told him she was pregnant. I just don't know what it is or how to find it. But I know deep in my bones he's the one who did this to her."

I've said too much. He's probably noticed my worry, and tries to lighten up the dark with a joke. "And when you do, then I'll take him out." He winks his twinkling blue eye. For a second I think he's serious, but he changes the subject quickly. "And you? No boyfriend troubles like that, I hope?"

I snag another fry as he signals the waitress for another round. "No.

The last guy I dated was unfaithful. Now I just have my slimy boss trying to hit on me all the time."

"Your friend's lover?" I nod. His jaw ticks as he takes a deep breath. "What a dick. You can't seem to catch a break, can you?" He jests, but his smile falters and he gives me that deep stare. There's something behind his veneer that I want to understand.

"My life could be a soap opera." I keep eating the fries, reminding myself I should take it easy and go to the gym. Archard likes me in tight clothes. He's already said things about the fact that I'm not as thin as Norah. He's a pig.

"I'm sorry that's happening to you. That's some tough times you've had."

"I try not to dwell on what I can't fix, and try to fix the things I can." Fuck Archard, I'm eating all the fries. "Why's your day shit, by the way? What happened to you?"

He runs his hand through his thick hair and shakes his head. "I don't know if I want to talk about it."

"Now that's not fair. You made me talk about me."

"I never agreed that I would though."

I huff out and roll my eyes. "You're sneaky."

That half grin of his appears again as he takes out his wallet. "Let's get out of here."

I watch as he drops a hundred on the table and shrugs his overcoat back on. He helps me with mine and then grabs my hand. I grasp it, and it's warm, large, and comforting. I know where the night will lead, and I'm ready. Ready to feel something exciting, something new, something amazing. I'm ready to take a leap into the unknown. To hell with the consequences.

2

HER

I'M STILL SLIGHTLY BUZZED FROM THE SHOTS OF BOURBON. BEFORE I KNOW it, we're in his apartment in Greenwich Village. This man is extremely wealthy. All I can do is sigh in relief that we didn't go to my tiny apartment in the Lower East Side. I stand in front of the large window, staring at the lights below. He approaches me, hands me a glass of alcohol. I anxiously clutch it, let the drink touch my lips and flow down my throat. It burns, but I need it to steady my nerves. I need this. I need him. I need to forget the year from hell.

He's taken off his coat, undone his tie, and is wearing a white button-down shirt. The cuffs are rolled up now and I can see his large forearms. I acutely study him. God, he works out. A lot. He's dauntingly large, masculine. My entire body screams in lust as I take another sip.

"So, what do you do that allows you to have a place like this?" I try to make small talk, but I know where all of this is leading.

"Financial things, analysis stuff," he dismisses. He still won't tell me about himself. What the hell am I doing? He could be a criminal.

"What kind of financial analysis stuff?"

"Stuff that would bore you." We both laugh for a moment as he sticks a hand in his pocket looking like a GQ model.

"Yeah, but even in a regular finance job you wouldn't be able to afford a place like this." He doesn't say anything and I shift. He could be a con artist, a drug dealer, with the mafia. As if he senses my unease, he finally answers.

"My parents died when I was two and left me everything. My uncle raised me. He worked on Wall Street and was extremely wealthy. He died from a heart attack a few years ago." He tells the story with no bitterness.

"I'm so sorry," I say softly.

"No need to be. I was loved. And I love what I do. But I get lonely." He approaches me slowly. "Tell me something, beautiful. When was the last time you slept with a real man?"

I gulp. My voice trembles. "Real man?"

His heated gaze runs over my face and to my lips. "Someone who knows how to please a woman."

"Uh..." I'm breathless.

He stays silent and I nervously gulp down the rest of my drink. He takes the glass from me and sets it on the table nearby. His body is hovering and his hands move forward. He brushes my hair back from my face gently, then runs his fingertips over my jaw down to my neck. Goose bumps rise over my skin.

"I want you to feel special tonight," he whispers as his mouth faintly grazes over mine. We aren't kissing, but my nerve endings sizzle. I imagine how those lips will run over my entire body and a small shudder releases from my mouth. "You seem delicate...I'll be careful."

"I'm not," I protest. "Don't be."

I move forward with urgency and our lips meet. His mouth devours mine. We both groan as our pace quickens. My arms clasp around his neck and I run my hands through his thick hair. I can feel his tongue peek through and touch against mine and my legs buckle. His hands grasp my waist and we fervently walk as he guides me toward what I imagine to be his bedroom.

We're losing clothing as we go. He's untucked his shirt after peeling mine off. I help him with his belt buckle as my back hits the wall behind me. He then pulls me away and rushes me toward a room. We both fall on the bed and I'm straddling him. His growl is deep as I push against his erection. He turns me over and suddenly stands from the bed. His eyes are sharp on me and his voice is commanding.

"Turn around."

I do as he orders, and he helps position me. My feet are rooted to the ground, I'm bent at the waist on the bed, and I'm ass up in the air. I'm intimidated but not scared. I want this, and he knows what I need. His fingers run from my shoulder to my hip. Both his hands graze the curve of my waist and he tugs me forward. I feel him kneel down and he kisses up my thigh. My breathing begins to pick up as I hear him murmur, "You're wet for me, aren't you?"

I moan and quiver as he pulls off my lace panties. His fingers caress between my legs—tentatively at first—but then dig inside of my folds. I lean into him and whimper. His mouth moves closer, and I cry out as he makes contact with my clit and traces up. His tongue dives into my pussy, his hands on my ass spreading me open for his assault. Oh God, he's dipping into me with his tongue, consuming me unlike anything I've experienced.

His fingers return, sliding in and out, searching for my textured spot. I grind against his face, his tongue, and I can no longer hold back. I clutch the sheets and the vibrations begin. I come violently against his mouth. My body spasms against the bed, toward him as he slows his glorious licks.

He rises and turns me over, kissing me. I can taste myself on him and I sigh. "That felt so good." I tremble.

He moves his hand down to my clit and rubs it. It's still swollen and beyond sensitive. "That was just the beginning. I'm hard as fuck for you. Now, where were we?"

I know I'm in trouble. I've just had the best orgasm of my life. There's no going back. And it feels fucking great.

3

HIM

I can't wait to have her, take her, fill her. That sweet, glistening pussy waits for me to complete it. I remove her black lace bra, and her breasts are perfect. Cream-pale with rosy nipples. I want to bite at them. I want to see my cock slide between those tits. I want to come all over her. There's no end to the things I want to do to this beautiful woman. She's quickly filling this pit inside me and it's a destructive need.

I lower my slacks enough to free my cock, and I watch her squirm as she moves her hand between her legs to stroke herself. I groan as I observe her. "What do you need?"

"I need to come," she whispers.

"You could make yourself come," I tease.

She speaks coyly. "I want you to make me."

I let out a breath, her voice so sweet. "Lick," I say, indicating my cock. I stand as she sits on the edge of the bed and runs her tongue from my base to my tip in one long motion. My fingers dig into her hair, and I hiss as she repeats her movement. It feels perfect as she traces lines along the underside of it. "Suck now," I command. She gives me a quick smile and takes me into her mouth.

I grunt as her head bobs between my thighs. My hips and legs vibrate with the curbed need to shove into her mouth. I indulge and push up until I hit the back of her throat. The noises emitting from her drive me up the wall. I pull her lips off me and guide her onto her back. I climb over her, press myself over her—my cock nestled against her folds.

She meets my eyes and licks her lips. Her mouth's greedy, but mine's greedier and we fight each other, devouring and tasting. "I want inside you," I say hoarsely. "You ready for me?"

"Oh God," she breathes. "Please, yes."

"Stay still," I warn. "Behave."

She bites her lip and nods. After covering myself with a condom, I press the head of my cock against her clit and brush down her entrance. She shivers as I move up, grazing her opening. Her expression's tormented and I want to kiss it away. A few more passes and I can't wait any longer. I lean forward, my body pressing, and finally slip inside an inch. I stop, my muscles quivering. Both of us stare at one another. She's so fucking tight, her pussy squeezes my tip, and her wet, slippery skin makes me want to sink in deeper.

She rocks forward, unable to help herself, and I grab her neck, my body shaking with the effort not to lose my load and come on the spot. "Stay still or I'm going to come before I want to, sweetheart. You're driving me crazy," I state sternly. Her breath is harsh and my tone turns her on as she whimpers.

"Hurry," she says and clenches her muscles around my tip again.

Fuck, she's going to kill me. I plunge into her with force. Moans become one as we rock against each other, our lips mingling. My mouth moves to her neck, kissing and biting.

"Right there, oh God, yes. I'm—" she cries, unable to finish her sentence. She doesn't need to because she's falling into spasms, her groans filling the air. Again and again, her pussy clamps down onto me, gripping and pulsing. Her fingers travel to her clit and she starts getting herself off for another go. She moves her hips slightly, enough to push me over the edge. My cock's so tight, my hips jerk, my stomach muscles jump, and then I let loose. I can barely breathe as my climax rips through me. The first woman to make me feel something in years.

Something more than just an orgasm. I fall limp on her body and force myself to stay still as I try to catch my breath. I want to memorize this moment—me inside her, the way she looks and how soft her skin is against mine. I move to her side and she lays her head on my chest, giving a contented sigh.

"Shit. I think you're a sorceress. You've got me under some spell," I slur, smelling her sweet hair. This woman with a beautiful heart, with a spirit as delicate as a flower, has taken me over. She's a burst of light in my dark heart. I can't ever let her know...She must never know I've been on her track for half the year. My secrets will stay locked up, safe and sound.

4

HIM

TWO MONTHS LATER

"Why, hello there, little one." I amble toward her and stir behind my zipper knowing she's so near. I bite the inside of my cheek to remind myself to calm the fuck down as she sits at her desk.

Her dark eyes meet mine and shock courses over her body. Her eyes dart to make sure nobody is around but us. "What are you doing here? How did you find me?" she whispers harshly.

One side of my mouth turns up. It's been two months since she thinks I last saw her. I've been keeping my eye on her, and I need to be closer now that I've had my way with her.

"I'm the new guy." I wink and point to the office opposite her desk. "I'm guessing this office is mine."

"You're Jake Cannon?" She blinks from those long, thick lashes. I want to make streaks of mascara run down her cheeks as she cries for more orgasms. "You're the new data analyst for Senator Archard?"

I want to admit I'm more than that, but I nod my head. "Is Branton in?"

She clears her throat, shifting in her seat, no doubt thinking of the way I filled her up and pleased her that night. "Mr. Archard is in a board meeting, then he has a lunch meeting."

"Are you going to show me to my office...Olivia?" Saying her name makes me want to nip the skin of her inner thigh and trail kisses to her beautiful, dripping pink pussy. My tongue wants to stroke her, taste her the way we devoured each other the first time—the one night I finally was able to bury myself inside a female and find a sense of rest, a small sense of peace.

"This way, Mr. Cannon." She leads me to the office. Her body is so tense, and she's on high alert. "It's basic, but if you need any supplies, let me know. Please be aware that my priority is to the senator."

I shut the door behind me and lock it. Her eyes meet mine, desire pooling in them. "So, tell me, Olivia. Have you thought of me since that night?"

She stands there, her hip jutted out, her chin up in defiance. "That's in the past."

Her attempt to escape me is unsuccessful as I wrap my arms around her waist and pull her hard against my throbbing body. I feel her shudder as my hand reaches up and cups her cheek. "Hey," I whisper, my lips close to hers. I know she can feel my straining cock. "Don't treat me like you don't know me."

"But I don't know you." Her voice trembles.

I lower my head, my lips touching the delicate shell of her ear. "I think we're well beyond being acquaintances, Olivia."

She pushes me away. "Just because you fucked me doesn't mean you know me. What the hell are you doing here, huh? You can't work for Archard. I...told you things." Fright breaks through her eyes. "Personal things. About me, about him. Are you his spy?"

I want to tell her my secret, but I hide it with my carefree façade. "If I told you I was, would you let me fuck you again?" I joke and lean toward her, my lips aiming for hers.

She stops me. "Are you here to mess up my cover? What the hell do you want?"

"Besides you?"

"Please, don't..." She rests her palms flat on my chest, holding me back. I can tell she wants me. I'm certain of it when she stares at my lips, her heart beating wildly against my chest.

"Don't what? Don't pretend that we didn't fuck each other?" I don't recognize my husky voice as I pull her closer. "Pretend like I don't want to sink inside you right now? Can't you feel how hard I am? How fast you turn me on?"

"It's been a long time." She sighs as my hand travels to the hem of her skirt. I hike it up and find the seam of her panties. She doesn't stop me.

"Too long, sweetheart..." I let my lips lower to her neck as I slide my fingers inside her lace panties. I smell her sweet honey scent, her soft skin pebbling as my lips brush against hers. "Too long since your sweet body was under mine."

She whimpers and it almost ends me as her hips piston against my hand. . "You're not playing fair," she tells me as her arms curl around my neck. "I...don't understand this. How are you here?"

I ignore her question. "You're soaked for me. I knew it." My fingers spread her wetness, and I circle her clit with pressure and speed. "I'm taking you here, love. I've fucking needed you, and you left without a word."

"I..." She can't finish her sentence when I reach down quickly and lift her skirt up around her waist. "What are you..." I shove her panties aside and she gasps as I push her into the wall.

"Tell me you want this, Liv." I stroke her softly as her panting quickens. "Say it, now, or I'll stop."

"Jake, we can't..." I remove my hand and she groans.

"Admit you want me." I pause and wait for her response. There's no fear in her gaze. She nods and I unzip my trousers. My cock springs out. I fumble quickly with the silver packet I dig out of my wallet and sheathe myself. Once covered, I run it against her drenched pussy and push inside her instantly and entirely. She moans loudly, and I place my palm over her lips. "Shh...those sweet moans are mine, love. Only mine." My free hand grasps her thigh to hitch it on my hip. My cock submerges to the root. I lick her neck and suck at her pulse point as she once again wraps her arms around my neck. "Feel me, Olivia. Can you feel me buried inside you?"

She whimpers in response as I buck my hips to hers. "Don't fucking leave like that again. You left. The morning came and you were gone." Again, I ram my cock inside her and pause as her inner walls squeeze. I remove my hand from her mouth and kiss her. She pants against my lips. I move quickly, pumping in and out of her. I'm glad our offices are separate from other workers, but if Archard can hear us, well, I don't give a fuck. I need her. She's mine. And if Archard tries to take her away from me, I'll have no issue killing him with my bare hands.

My body thrusts, filling her tight pussy with my aching cock. I look down and can see it glistening with her come as I pull out and push back in. My need to burst is close and I grunt, beads of sweat forming on my temples. Her sweet whimpers are filling my ears. She's close. Her breathing accelerates and she bites down on her lip as she bursts, her sweet body squeezing me as she tries to swallow her sobs of pleasure. I lose patience and my load. I slow my momentum as we both try to catch our breaths and I pull out. I can see I've left her a love spot on her neck and I smirk as if I've marked her, claimed her.

I watch as she adjusts her panties and skirt as I chuck my condom and tuck myself back into my trousers. She swaths her hair from her face and her cheeks are flushed with passion. She moves forward, clasps my collar in a move that shocks me. "Don't fucking do that again," she growls close to my lips.

I can't wipe the grin off my face. "Do what?"

"You wanna fuck? We find someplace else. Not here. Not again, do you understand me?"

I straighten my tie and clear my throat, "I thought I was your boss now."

"Not when it comes to fucking." She pauses, her dark eyes burning into my soul. "Besides, the senator is my boss. You tip him off about my plan, I'll have no hesitation poisoning your morning coffee. Got that?" She kisses me; her teeth grab onto my bottom lip and squeeze until close to breaking the skin. She releases me, then heads out the door. I stand and stare at her in awe. I'm in love. And I'm completely fucked.

5

HIM

It's been over two weeks—and every single time Olivia passes by my office I want to pull her in, lock the door, and take her sweet body. Today she's wearing a tight red skirt and white silk blouse with black stockings. I've spent ten minutes straight staring at the straining buttons at her chest. I've had to adjust myself several times and ask Branton to repeat what the fuck he was saying during our current meeting. Who the fuck cares? At the moment, I don't. Why? Because the little minx hasn't given me the time of day since she found out I'm partially her boss.

She's rebuffed me at every opportunity. I can't take it much more. I want her more than I've wanted anyone. She's my fantasy come to life, and I'll be damned if I let her just walk away from what we'd shared.

The meeting lets up and I stay still, my eyes watching her like a hawk awaiting its prey. Grabbing her notepad, she turns, her eyes barely giving me a glance. I refuse to stand for it any longer. I follow as she walks briskly toward the elevators. When I stand beside her, I can tell she's tense as she continues to stare straight ahead.

"Olivia..." "Don't."

"Don't what?" "Don't do this."

"You don't know what I'm going to say."

"You don't have to say it for me to know." She moves away and heads toward the door for the stairwell. I trail behind her. "Jake, don't follow me."

I want to tell her what I'm doing here, but it's not the time. It's never the time. The stairwell is eerily empty and dark. I yank her arm and pull her against me roughly. I can hear her intake of breath and it shatters my resolve. "Stop denying me."

"You're my co-worker."

"I'm your lover."

"Lover?" Her lips turn into a grin as she stares up at me with those beautiful mahogany eyes.

"Yes, Olivia. At this point, you're more than just a fuck. I'm consumed by you. I need you. My body craves you, sweetheart, and I want to bury myself inside you until you shatter."

I hear a small moan escape her lips and I push her against the wall. The notepad she grips tumbles to the ground. My lips instantly take her mouth and her whimper shoots straight to my cock, making it harder. I push my pelvis against her so she knows how I'm eager and fervent for her body.

"You want to fuck me?" She reaches her hands between us and quickly unzips me. I spring free and her fingers clasp over me. The dripping of my pre-come is spread by her dainty fingers, and my lips clasp on the lobe of her ear. I bite at it and it sends a chill over her body. My hands cup her tits and I want to rip that blouse off her body. I move my hands down and hike up that tight little skirt that's been driving me fucking wild. She's only wearing those thigh-highs with clasps. Fuck.

"I'll never get enough of you..."

"Why? Tell me why," she whimpers as my mouth moves over her neck. I can smell her honey scent in my nostrils and it's making me drunk with lust.

"Why?" I ask.

"Why don't you get enough of me?" she asks breathlessly. I take out the condom that's been burning a hole in my wallet waiting to be utilized...for her. My cock rubs against her wet folds and I push inside her warmth. It envelops my cock with perfection.

"Because you feel fucking incredible." I thrust against her and she grunts. "Feel like...you make me..." I plunge into her again. "God, you make me able to..."

"Able to what?" She clasps her hand around my neck and bites my earlobe as my body speeds up, pushing in and out of her.

I look into her deep dark eyes and can't take it. My chest aches and I'm dizzy from our scent, our bodies melding. "To...deal with myself." I bury my head in her neck as I lose myself. I need to wait...but I can't. I can't take it. My groans are stifled by her skin. I burst and know that, from this moment, I'm lost. I'm so lost in this woman. I look into her eyes and see compassion in them. I quickly move away from her and tuck myself back in, running my hands through my hair to try to make myself presentable. I lost control. I never lose control. I watch as she lowers her skirt, shifts her body, and clears her throat.

"I'm sorry..." I say with remorse. "I never come before a woman."

"It's okay..." I stay silent as she fixes her hair. "I do, however, want an explanation on what you mean by what you said."

"I don't— I can't..." I shake my head and look away from her. "I can't talk about it."

"I don't know what's going on, Jake, but I can't trust you if you don't trust me." She crosses her arms and her perfect tits are perked up and I feel myself getting hard all over again. What the fuck's wrong with me?

"I can't talk about it."

"Can't or won't?"

I shake my head and bend to grab her dropped item from the floor before we make our way back into the office. I need to clean myself and get my head cleared. This is too dangerous. She's breaking me down. The lump in my throat is thick and I don't want to deal.

"This is why I haven't gotten close to you, Jake. You're hiding something. When you're ready to talk, I'll be here. But not for long."

I open the door and she walks past me quickly. And I feel oddly more alone than I've ever felt in my life.

6

HER

ONE WEEK LATER

I QUIETLY MAKE MY WAY INTO SENATOR ARCHARD'S OFFICE, HOPING FOR A miracle. He's gone for the day, and the pesky Jake Cannon finally got the hint that I won't leave work anytime soon. He's left the office early. It's odd working with the elusive, handsome man I slept with, but compartmentalizing my work and my love life is necessary. I can't get distracted from my goal.

There has to be something on Archard. Norah had mentioned something about a file. Perhaps that was long gone, along with her, but there had to be a trail. I'd been trying to figure out the password to his computer for months. Luckily, flirting with the guy from the IT department paid off, and he gave me something I could use. I hover over Archard's keyboard and glance at the instructions laid out. I follow the protocol and within minutes I've unlocked the screen.

Triumph rises within me as I reach into the handbag sitting beside me on the desk. My heartbeat speeds up as I dig for the flash drive. I snap it into the desktop and begin to copy and paste files upon files of my boss's records.

"That's not a good idea, love."

I'm startled and jolt back as my heart pounds against my rib cage. "Jake." My voice falters as he approaches. I tell myself to stay calm, act blasé, and give away nothing as I stand tall with my shoulders back. "What are you doing back in the office? I thought you left for the day."

He approaches and stands beside me, never once glancing at the computer screen. "What the hell do you think you're doing, Liv?" His voice is a harsh whisper. "This is extremely risky. And you won't find anything on there about Norah."

I tamp down my irritation. "I've got to try, Jake. There might be something, anything to implicate him. A clue..."

He shakes his head, his eyes pitying me. "No, sweetheart."

Awareness blazes through me and I step away with caution. "I never told you her name..." His body tenses as he tries to close the space between us. "Stay back! Stay away from me." I glance at my purse. I have mace in it but I can't reach it. My only option is to bolt for the door, but I'm in heels, and he'll catch me before I can get far.

"Liv." He's blocked my way and I won't get past him if I try.

"Don't call me that!" We're circling the desk like a game of cat and mouse. I want to beeline toward the door. My eyes dart between the exit and him.

"Don't try," his deep voice rumbles. "I'll only catch you."

I sprint fleetingly, but it's no use. He's wrapped around me immediately, my arms pinned to my sides, my back against his chest. I try flailing, wriggling, thinking of a way to get free. "Stop it," he growls, holding me down. I jerk my head back and make contact with his chin. He groans but only tightens his grip. "Olivia, that's enough! Stay still."

My breathing hitches in my chest as I breathlessly speak. "Are you gonna kill me?"

A rough laugh escapes his mouth. "What?"

"Are you one of his lackeys?" I struggle in his arms, hoping he's not allies with my boss. "You killed Norah, didn't you? Have you been following me?"

"I didn't kill Norah, woman. Calm yourself. I'm not going to hurt you." He loosens his grip and rests his mouth on my temple, giving me a sweet kiss.

I push forward, rush to the end table, and pick up a large glass vase with flowers. I hold it up high, ready to hurl it at him if need be. "Explain yourself, Cannon! How do you know her name? What do you know about Branton Archard?"

He steadies his breath and rests his hands on his hips. "I'm investigating Archard." I lower the vase, in shock, but keep it in my hands.

"What?"

"I've been looking into him for a while." I scrutinize him, doubt his confession. He sighs, looks at the door, as if nervous someone's about to walk in. "We need to talk, and it's not safe here."

I'm planted on the spot. "I have questions."

"I know you do." He stares at me, the silence unsettling. "Let's go, Liv."

"How can I trust you?" I lift the vase again with intent to throw. "How do I know you're telling the truth? You could kill me the moment I turn my back."

His face twists as he rubs over his jaw with his hand. "I've been shadowing you for over half a year and I haven't hurt you yet." I gasp, my blood curdling as he leans forward and yanks the vase out of my hands and sets it back in place. "Get your shit, Olivia. I'm taking you home."

We don't say a word to each other as his driver takes us to my tiny apartment. I sit on my ratty couch as he shifts around the kitchen. "I guess I shouldn't be surprised that you know where I live?"

He slightly grins as he sets the kettle on the gas stove and walks toward me. He sits on the arm of my sofa and gazes down on me. "Ask me what you want."

I give him an inscrutable glare. "Are you even a real data policy analyst?"

"I'm with the FBI."

Hurt flares through my body. My heart sinks. "Is your name even Jake Cannon?"

The confidence in him leaves. His eyes are downcast as he shakes his head. "No."

"What is it?"

He hesitates telling me, as if at war with himself. "It's Hunter Reed."

I try not to let his lie affect me and choke back tears. "Why were you following me?"

The kettle whistles and he gets up to make the tea. He returns with two cups and hands me one. "At first I thought you were with Branton—that you were his mistress. I was solely looking for any lead I could possibly find. My partner and I've been investigating him for over a year."

I don't notice the tears trailing down my cheeks until he reaches forward to wipe one away with the pad of his thumb. I jerk my face away. "Where were you when Norah needed you? He killed her and you didn't see that?"

He chokes on his words as he continues, "I knew he was bad, Liv, but I had no idea he was capable of having women murdered. We weren't paying attention to his lovers. We kept to the business aspect."

I try to breathe through the pain in my heart, and take a sip of the English breakfast tea, but it doesn't comfort me. "I knew you were hiding something, but why start working with Archard now?"

He shrugs and puts his cup on the table. I follow suit. His jaw tightens, and he's locked his fingers together. "Because I fell for you."

My heart tightens. Anger lances through me. "When exactly did that happen? When you were stalking me? When you approached me in Central Park? Or when you fucked me?"

"I wasn't stalking you, Liv. I kept my distance and didn't look into you until recently."

"Well, isn't that reassuring." I rise from the couch and pace the tiny space behind it. "How am I supposed to believe anything you say?"

"I thought you were with him." He approaches me and I back away, unsure of trusting him or myself around him. "I thought you were his. I trailed you because you were a person of interest. But you were there at the park and crying and I just...I had to know more."

"So you used me to gain information."

"I wanted to comfort you." He's compressing his irritation, trying to get his point across. "You didn't see what I saw. You were crying, hurting, but when you opened up to me...that was everything. Olivia, I'm doing this for you. I'm protecting you. That's my new purpose in all of this. And now, more than ever, I want to get this bastard. I want to nail him, and I want you safe. That's why I got the job. It took me months to set everything up to work for him. I'm risking it all for you."

I chew my lip and stop him before he can get close. "I can't trust you for anything other than working this case. I'll help and give you whatever I can. But don't even think I'd give you another shot."

His sad eyes focus on mine. "I'll earn your trust somehow, Liv."

I ignore his confident statement. "What do you need from me to get this asshole?"

"Well, as I said, you're not going to find information in that work computer. Is there any other reason he'd have Norah killed?" He runs his hand over his scruff, and exhaustion is evident under the circles that darken his wary eyes. "Can you recall anything at all, Liv? You were her roommate. She must've said something, given you something. Anything."

My eyes close briefly. "She mentioned a file, but I've racked my brain trying to locate something, Jake— Hunter...sorry. I don't know what to call you."

"Stick with Jake in public."

We're both quiet. I'm in my head processing everything that's happened around me. He's staring at me. My heart speeds and I'm entranced at the light he brings in the dimness of the room as he closes the distance between us. His fingertips skim over my jawline before cradling my face, and his mouth descends. Our meeting of lips is tender, but I try to pull away and he holds me, his mouth challenging me for more. I sigh as my hands make their way to his hair, tugging him closer, the world around us fading. I quickly come to and pull away. "I can't..."

"I know." His voice is rough. "I will make this right though."

"I'm not sure you can."

7

HIM

Without a lead, there's no way we can implicate the senator in Norah's death. However, there's a shitload of other things we're piling up on him, and I've got to find a way to nail the bastard for the big kill.

I sit on the bed beside my brunette beauty and study the way she sleeps, her eyelids fluttering as she dreams. I refuse to leave her side, much to her chagrin. Now that my partner and I've looked into Branton's exes and seen how they disappear, I won't risk Olivia becoming a victim. At first she was nothing more than information, but my lust became something different. And the night she opened up to me brought me to my knees. Will she ever trust me?

Her breath picks up. Moans release from her throat, and before I can nudge her awake, she's startled. A gasp releases from her and her eyes open. "Sweetheart, you're fine," I whisper as she regains her breath. "You were having a dream." I reach over slowly, my hand caressing her soft skin. I lean forward and place a kiss on her shoulder. She trembles, tears flowing from the corners of her eyes.

"I dreamt of her."

My chest tightens as I try to hug her. She only sits in my arms a moment before leaving them. "What did you dream?"

Her voice is weak. "It was a party, and she was happy."

"Wherever she is now, perhaps she's happy there."

She says nothing. She's deep in thought, perhaps lost in the dream. Her body stiffens and she turns on the night lamp beside her. "I have an idea on how to get a confession from Archard."

"What?"

Her dark eyes look into mine, a gleam in them as if her mind is made up. "I'll be the bait."

I won't lie that I had considered asking for her help. Bringing her on as an informant could be useful, but being bait is an entirely different deal. "Absolutely not."

"Why?"

I shake my head. "Over my dead body. I won't let you put yourself in that danger."

She chuckles. "He's been signaling me for months. Just wire me, and I'll let him make his move, reject him, then ask about Norah." "And if he doesn't take it? We could ruin our whole case. We don't even have enough evidence on his corruption, fraud, extortion, let alone killing his mistresses."

Her excitement can't be contained. "But that's where I can say that Norah told me about it and then he'll confess."

Worry floods through my body. "No. I forbid it, Liv. I don't want you getting hurt."

Her eyes narrow. "You can't forbid me from anything. You're not even my boyfriend. Hell, you're not even my real boss."

"You'd be interfering in an ongoing investigation."

"So, what? You'll arrest me?" We both pause. "I have to get back at him for what he did. I have to. He killed my friend."

Her eyes well up, gutting me. Every time a tear falls, my heart breaks for her. "I don't want you to join her. I care about you too much."

I'm not sure she believes me after my colossal deception. "I don't want him doing this to other women, Hunter. It comes to an end. Please, help me."

8

HER

I'VE STAYED AT HUNTER'S THE PAST FEW DAYS, FOR SAFETY REASONS. Tensions are high at work. Archard can tell I'm not my usual self, though I do my best to act nonchalant. The demands on me are high, and he's had me stay well into the evenings to finish work, which has left Hunter more than paranoid.

Today is no exception. I'm working around the clock. Hunter pulls me aside as I head to the copy room. He carefully pans the area around us and runs his hand into the neckline of my blouse. My body stiffens and I clasp his wrist to stop him. His eyes meet mine. "I'm not trying to make a move on you."

He lifts his other hand and holds up a small pin shaped like a daisy. I look down as he lifts the material and tacks it on my right side. "It has a camera and microphone. I have one too." He points to his silver tie bar with a circular shape at the end of it. "I have an earpiece and can hear what's going on and communicate with my partner, Boyd. He's running surveillance." "Well, then. I'd better watch what I say." He doesn't smile at my attempted joke.

"Don't bait him, Liv. Not until we find something more on him. Please." He's worried about me, and my heart melts. As much as I want to deny him, he's done this for a reason. I can't fault him for that. I cup his cheek and give him a tender kiss, surprising him.

"Fine. Now let me get back to my job." I kiss him again, then once more.

A small groan exits his lips. "God, I miss you. Try to get out early. I'll meet you at the deli across the street for some dinner?"

"I'll see you at seven." I give him a hesitant smile. Little by little, I'm opening to the idea of giving him another shot. I've connected to him on a level I never knew existed. But avenging Norah takes precedence and I'll do what's necessary.

I get back to work until, hours later, Archard's slimy voice breaks through the phone's intercom. "Olivia, I need you."

I press the button and reply. "Yes, sir. Be right there."

I finish up the notes on a file and shut the folder. I glance at the view outside and see the sky has turned dark. The office is empty, and all I hear is the buzz from the lights above. I knock and await my instruction to enter. Branton Archard sits behind his large desk, instructing me to shut the door. His hands steeple as his green snake-like eyes follow my moves.

"Take a seat, please."

I nervously await his instruction with a pad and pen resting in my lap. His salt-and-pepper hair is slicked back. Not a great look for his receding hairline. Many have called him handsome, charming—it's what drew Norah to him—but virtuous? He's far from that. I wait for him as he glares, a typical thing he does to intimidate others. However, that look was never directed at me until now.

"You've been acting off the past few days, Olivia. How are things?"

Surprise hits me at his concern. "I'm fine," I say without emotion.

"Yeah?" He stands from his chair and ambles around the desk, resting himself in front of it. He crosses his arms and is an arm's length away from me. "How's your love life?"

Another attempt at coming on to me. I'm almost used to it by now, but I try to keep myself in control of baiting him the way I want. "I usually keep those things private and out of the workplace."

"Really?" He nods. "This would suggest otherwise."

He turns the screen of his computer around and a black-and-white video of Hunter and me is playing. We're in his office and at each other like rabbits. "Or how about this one?" He presses a button on his keyboard and the scene switches to the stairwell. There's no sound on the videos, and they aren't clear quality. I give a breath of gratitude that I'm covered by Hunter's body, but my cheeks redden in embarrassment. "Interesting, isn't it?"

"We—uh, I don't know…"

His head tilts, giving me a look of pity. "I understand office affairs better than anyone, my little Olive. In fact, I find you and Cannon intriguing to watch. I've had those videos for a while now, but I let you have your fun. However, this video from a few days ago? Well, it's my favorite." He presses the keyboard again and it shows me skirting around his office, checking his computer, and Hunter attempting to stop me.

My heart is racing, and though my plan was to broach the subject of Norah eventually, this is an unexpected turn. Hunter had said the office wasn't secure. I wish now I had believed him. Archard turns the screen back and smirks. His eyes land on me again and they're dangerous. "What were you looking for, Olivia?"

I straighten my shoulders, steeling myself, ready for the fight. "I was looking for evidence."

He huffs, his smirk still painted on his face. "Evidence of?"

Months of holding in my pain starts to spill. "I know about your affair with Norah."

"And I know about your affair with Cannon."

My face heats. "She was pregnant. I know she didn't commit suicide. You had her killed."

"That's a serious accusation."

His voice remains calm, his eyes cold. It sends chills down my spine and my heartbeat spikes. I need his confession. "I worked with her. I lived with her. We were best friends. She told me everything. I know everything about you, and I have proof."

I'm giving him the bait. It wasn't the plan, but I hope it's all caught on video. Archard rises, moves to his desk, and opens a drawer. He holds a black handgun and points it my way. "Olivia, I didn't want to have to do this." I rise instantly, blood rushing to my head. "Don't run. Sit down."

I slowly descend back onto my chair. My breathing speeds as he strolls over. "You wouldn't kill me." I stay calm, try to gather the will to fight, to do anything that will keep this man at bay. "A dead body in your office? You wouldn't risk it."

"But you're distraught. Your best friend committed suicide. You've turned to me for affection and I've denied you. You can't take it anymore. The heartache, the pain." He points the gun to my head and signals to the legal pad and pen on the floor. "Write it down."

I don't move. If I buy time, Hunter will come, so I just glare, refusing to give in. "What?"

"Your suicide note."

"Fuck you. Never." I gasp as the cold barrel of the gun hits my temple. What if my camera isn't working? What if Hunter and his partner are too late? I'll do what I can to get what they need. "Do you know how much shit I have on you? I guarantee if I'm not alive, it will make it to the FBI."

"You mean Cannon? You think I don't know he's an undercover agent? I've got a plant, darling. His partner, Warren Boyd, came to me a few days ago. He works for me now. You don't think I have people on my side? Money always talks."

Dread prickles over me as he presses the barrel deeper into my temple. I whimper, my heart aching over the deception. If his partner's working for Archard, there is no way I have a chance out of this. Archard gives a fake laugh, then runs a fingertip over my jaw. "Funny. Norah refused to write a suicide note as well. You're not crying the way she did though. You're more of a fighter. Luckily I disposed of that file she gathered on me…just like I disposed of her. I kept you close to make sure she hadn't told you anything. You had me fooled for a good while too. Great work, Olivia."

My breathing catches in my throat. He's confessed. But it doesn't matter because Hunter's partner is working surveillance. "The fraud, the extortion, I have it all. You don't think she was stupid enough to keep it to herself?"

Archard's clammy hand reaches out and grasps my jaw. He squeezes tightly as I wrap my hand around his wrist. The barrel presses in farther. "You're lying. Write the fucking letter, Olivia."

"No!"

"Fine." He overpowers me, making my hand grasp the grip of the gun. His fingers wrap over mine. His other hand digs into my hair and he yanks my head back. His weight is on me. I'm too small for him, too weak. He forces the muzzle to my head as I attempt to push it away. "Stop fighting. There's no way you're getting out of this. Accept it."

I feel my finger close to the trigger. I'm hoping with all hope that somehow, someway, someone will catch this asshole. Even if I'm gone. I close my eyes as I continue to fight, the pain in my head growing as he pulls my hair.

The door bursts open, and the weight of Archard, the pressure of his hand over mine releases. He raises the gun and shoots, the sound blasting near my ears. I see a body collapse and cry out as I realize it's Hunter. "No!"

Archard points the gun to me and two more shots ring out. Archard stumbles back and falls against the desk. A man in a black shirt and jeans rushes to Archard and kicks the weapon away from his reach. Words are exchanged into a two-way radio as I fumble to the ground and crawl to where Hunter props himself up against a wall. He's bleeding profusely below his shoulder. His blue button-down shirt is soaking with crimson. He hisses as I place pressure on the wound. "You're here." I'm breathless as he nods slightly. "I was scared I'd never see you again."

Hunter grunts as I press harder. "You stood me up."

"I didn't intend to, Reed." I turn to look at the man who has cuffed Archard, despite his bullet wounds. "Is that your partner? Boyd?" Hunter nods. "I thought he was working with the senator."

"Pretending." The pain creeps through his voice. "We decided to give the bastard incentive. See if he'd take Boyd as bait instead of you."

I look back at Hunter and shrug. "Smart." He closes his eyes and shifts. His breathing is getting heavier, and when he opens his eyes, they begin to gloss over. I cup his jaw with my free hand. "Don't you give out on me, Hunter."

He gives a tired huff. "He might've hit an artery."

My eyes sting and my ability to stay strong wanes. "You'll be fine. It's okay. Everything's going to be all right."

"He's losing a lot of blood." Boyd had called for backup and an ambulance. "Keep the pressure on him. Keep him talking."

"Hey, you can't leave me, all right? It's not allowed."

He gives a half smile. "Does that mean if I'm okay you'll marry me?"

"Well, let's start dating first, and we'll go from there." His eyes close and panic wells within me. "Hunter? Oh God, no. Don't. Please!" Tears sting my cheeks. "Hunter, don't leave me! I'll marry you. I'll be with you."

His eyes open and he grins. "You don't have to beg, Liv. I'll say yes."

I huff out and want to smack him, but only lean forward and give him a kiss. "Don't do that, jerk!"

"You love me," he whispers. The paramedics arrive and instantly push me aside. They get Hunter on a stretcher and work on him. I know then and there that I do.

EPILOGUE
HER

After Hunter's extensive surgery, I'm let in to the room to see him. I sit beside him, holding his warm, strong hand in mine. Is it possible in such a short amount of time to fall in love with someone? My heart tells me yes, but my brain tells me I'm insane to think it's possible.

I watch as Hunter's eyes flutter, the stillness of his body, the quiet hum of machines reminding me how I almost lost him. The care he's taken with me, to protect me has gone over and beyond necessity. I feel strangely as if Norah's watching over me.

His brow furrows and a strangled grunt buried deep in his throat makes its way out. I lean forward and brush the hair off his forehead. He's hot to the touch and his heart rate is rising.

"Relax. You're fine," I whisper and press my lips to his temple.

"I ache everywhere," he croaks out.

"You lost a lot of blood, but the surgery went well. You should have full use of your hand, but they'll want to do some therapy regardless."

His hand squeezes mine and he focuses on me. "I'm glad you're okay, love. I thought I'd be too late."

"No, we're both going to be fine. And Boyd found the file in a hidden baseboard in Archard's desk."

Hunter breathes in deeply and exhales slowly, his eyes closed. "Good. He'll be going away for a while hopefully."

"Thank you for helping me with this, Hunter." Tears prickle my eyes. "We got him."

He gives a lazy smile. He's heavily sedated and needs more rest. I try to pull away but his hand grips mine tightly. "Hey," he mumbles. I wait for him to speak. "I meant what I said, you know."

His eyelids are hooded. He's falling asleep. "What's that?"

"I'd marry you in a heartbeat, Olivia."

I place my other hand over his. "We'll talk about it later. You're too medicated right now," I say gently.

"Olivia." His eyes have opened and he's alert. "I solve things for a living. My brain is always on, figuring out cases, mysterious happenings." He pauses. "But our first moment at the park, the moment I spoke to you, I knew you were it for me. There was nothing to figure out. No searching. No questioning. No mystery other than what steps I could take to make you mine."

Tears spill down my cheeks as he continues. "I knew you were the girl. Tell me this isn't one-sided."

I give a half sob and half laugh. "It's not. I love you, Jake Cannon-slash-Hunter Reed."

His face lights up. "I knew it."

I reach forward and press my lips to his. He groans and I pull away. "I'm sorry! I'm hurting you."

"Yeah, but I'll deal. And I love you back."

My mission to prove Senator Archard guilty was successful. It wouldn't have happened without Hunter. The anger in my heart over Norah's death has started to subside, and it's replaced with the ability to appreciate what I have now. I have him. Somehow, it feels right. Like we were meant to meet, as if Norah brought him my way, and all is well.

ABOUT ANISSA GARCIA

Anissa Garcia earned her bachelor's degree in Speech Communications and English. She held an array of jobs including Public Relations Manager for Barnes and Noble. Wanting a change of pace, she attended The American Academy of Dramatic Arts, and trained full-time in theatre for two years. After working in Hollywood as an actress and casting assistant, she relocated to Austin, Texas, and began writing freelance for Cosmopolitan and other publications. When not writing stories, watching movies, or drinking a latte, she loves to daydream about romantic fictional men.

The Promise Series is available now.

To be notified of new releases or sales,
join Anissa's Mailing List: www.bit.ly/AnissaNews
Connect with Anissa online
Facebook: www.facebook.com/AnissaGarciaAuthor
Instagram: www.instagram.com/AnissaGAuthor
Visit Anissa at AnissaGarcia.com!

HARD Asset

KYM GROSSO

1

THE POUNDING BEAT OF THE MUSIC FILTERED INTO THE STREET AS EVAN stepped out of his black Maserati. He brushed past the line of partygoers, flashing the highly coveted silver feather that had been given to VIP guests. Evan Tredioux had secured an invitation to the elite gala through a military buddy who'd recently become a senator. A casual mention of the party over cocktails at a five-thousand-a-head fundraiser opened possibilities. A few texts later, and he'd been assured an invite.

Dom Marretta, CEO of Tri-Trylle, hosted the lavish, once-a-year event that served to bring together the country's top influencers. From LA to New York, nearly a hundred of the most relevant men and women gathered to celebrate, to see and be seen. Film stars, beacons of industries, scientists, athletes, musicians, and the ultra-interesting all indulged in champagne and top culinary delights.

For weeks, Evan had suspected sensitive data had been systematically stolen from Emerson Industries, where they'd engaged government contracts, developing top-secret state-of-the-art technologies. Discrepancies in dates assigned to the files raised red flags but he had no proof. Without concrete evidence, he'd been reluctant to alarm his friend and boss, Garrett Emerson, but had made up his mind to go to him tomorrow and tell him everything. Suspecting he'd been followed for the past few days, Evan had planted a thumb drive of sensitive data with a known white hat hacker, Selby Reynolds, who worked for his friend Lars Elliott. Both individuals were highly competent hackers, and most importantly, they could be trusted should he go missing.

It was well known that Dom Marretta had his hands into selling secrets. From gossip to the latest software developments, he stole, traded, and lied and covered it all up like a pro. Three years ago, Marretta had been implicated in an attempt to steal data from Emerson Industries, but the key witness went missing as did several pieces of evidence, so it never even made it to trial. Evan suspected if he did a little snooping at his personal office, in his home, he'd find at least a clue as to who was messing around in their data.

Adding fuel to the fire, Evan had been tipped off by a friend in the government that an asset would be in attendance tonight, but he couldn't say who. It was suspected foreign nationals were planning a meeting and Marretta had his sticky fingers in the pot. Evan didn't know if the suspected targets were in attendance or guilty of planning any crimes against the state. They could have been planning to trade cookie recipes, for all he knew, but he suspected they'd share information regarding stolen data and technologies. If his suspicion was correct, Emerson Industries' own prototypes could be utilized against ally armed forces. Much of their data still reflected theories but it was light-years ahead of their adversaries. Given the volatile state of affairs, leaked secrets, even small ones, could lead to aid for terrorist attacks.

Arriving fashionably late ensured Evan that the intoxicated host and the partygoers were relaxed into the night, less likely to notice his activities. Successfully passing through the security check, he strolled into the foyer and brushed past a group of men who spoke French, discussing their most recent visit to LA. As he stepped into an enormous living room, a dark and sensual mood filtered throughout; muted conversations had been swallowed into the driving bass that reverberated throughout the contemporary space. Dimly lit bubbled glass light fixtures dangled from the ceiling, illuminating a sea of undulating bodies moving to the music.

Evan gave a cool smile, making his way through the crowd. He spotted a perky blonde at the bar, and her presence set off a cautionary alarm. Although he recalled that she'd occasionally skydived with their group, there was nothing particularly remarkable about her that would garner an invitation and he suspected she had ties to Marretta.

As he stepped outside onto the back porch, he scanned the secluded property. Lanterns of various sizes lit up the perfectly manicured lawn. He glanced to a half dozen topless women who floated in the pool upon glittering golden blow-up swans, their incessant laughter echoing into the night.

Evan reached for a glass of champagne offered by a waiter and kept moving, carefully negotiating the room like a shark seeking its prey. More of a whisky-straight-up sort, he wasn't much for the bubbly, but for tonight, he'd blend. While pretending to watch the seductive mermaids, his peripheral vision drifted to the third-story window. Shadows danced in the light behind a curtain, alerting him that the party wasn't limited to the first floor. Interesting.

As he made his way toward the living room, he caught sight of the dominating billionaire. At six foot two inches, Dom Marretta was slightly shorter than Evan. Wearing a fitted royal-blue suit, the ruthless host appeared as if he were a supermodel. But Evan knew otherwise. Although Marretta had never spent a day in jail, he'd been suspected in thirteen deaths, not to mention the countless missing persons once in his employ. Anyone stupid enough to sue him found their lawsuit quickly dismissed courtesy of his legal eagles and bought judges.

"Evan." Marretta gave a boisterous wave.

"Dom Marretta. Finally we meet. Thanks so much for the invite, buddy." Evan's lips curled as he approached. Long ago he'd learned to control his emotions. The surge of anger that pulsed through his veins was tempered by the deliberate decision to remain calm. As he extended his hand, Evan's eyes locked on Marretta's, and he forced an easy laugh, appealing to his host's misogynistic tendencies. "Nice work on the pool scene. Those are some sweet birds ya got going on."

"Nothing but breasts. Haha, I knew you'd be a ladies' man."

"That I am. Excellent party."

"It appears we have mutual friends," Dom mentioned casually, ignoring the compliment.

"You know how it is. Leaving the force never breaks bonds. Our brothers are everywhere."

"So I hear. So I hear. Well, whichever friends you have must have the utmost respect for you for mine to trust them. You are aware of the rules?"

"Absolutely." Evan had been briefed. No gifts. No weapons. No smoking. No guests of guests. No fucking the help. And no matter what you see, illegal or not, you look away and keep your fucking mouth shut. Talk about what happened at the party or who you saw, there was a good chance you'd end up missing. Evan nodded and smiled. "No worries. Just here to enjoy the swans."

"Those are some fucking hot swans, yeah? Who's a pretty bird?" he laughed. His attention drifted to a set of redheaded triplets congregating in the foyer. "If you'll excuse me, some fresh ones just flew in and I think they'll be looking to join my flock. Cardinals. Three is my lucky number tonight."

"Enjoy." Evan smile faded as Dom turned his back to him. Women were a known weakness to the billionaire, his indiscretions regularly splashed across the tabloids.

Evan glanced to a balcony above the foyer, where guests mingled. He noted the guards blocking access to the hallways, and reasoned he'd have to devise a ploy to pass them to join the private party on the third floor. Thriving on challenges, Evan ascended the winding staircase, its intricately designed wrought iron rail twisting to the top. As he reached the landing, he smiled, scanning the scene for a patsy.

It took only seconds before selecting the perfect diversion. A thin blonde sipped a martini at the bar, engaged in a conversation with a twenty-something man whose muscles bulged through his two-sizes-too-small white T-shirt. The transparent material stretched tightly, his erect nipples and chest hair protruding against the straining fabric. The beauty gave a pained smile as he slid his palm over her shoulder. His voice boomed throughout the room, and although he drew the occasional side eye from the crowd, no one intervened.

Evan inwardly laughed, giving a nod to a group of gorgeous women in the corner. No time for ladies tonight, he advanced toward his mark. He casually slipped his hand inside his pocket, sliding a finger into the hidden compartment. The size of a pencil eraser, the wisp of poisoned paper adhered to his finger. Initial testing of the organic prototype had proven successful to incapacitate an adult within fifteen seconds. Odorless, dissolvable on contact, the stamp activated upon contact with blood, saliva, or sensitive mucous membranes, such as the mouth or genitals, and of course, tonight's option, upon ingestion. The short-lived results of one dose lasted exactly ten minutes. Victims never recalled the incident or the means of deliverance, and no long-term effects had been observed. Heart rate and other vital signs remained intact yet no known antidote existed to revive the intended unconscious state. The wafer-thin weapon had been utilized in human trials, but the neophyte technology was only available to government agencies.

Evan eyed the man's cocktail as he set it on the bar, and increased his pace, advancing toward his target. His gait swayed as he pretended to be drunk.

"Pete. Pete...it's me, Patrick," Evan's words slurred as he stumbled toward the mark. Patrick had always been a favorite alias and slipped off his tongue as truth. As he lifted the stranger's drink, his finger dipped into the beverage, releasing the poison. Evan lifted it to his lips and continued. "It's been what? Three years since we ran the San Fran marathon. No, no...wait...was it two years ago?"

"What the hell, man? That's my drink there, asshole."

"Oh, yeah, sorry. My bad." Evan glanced to the glass and set it down gently, careful not to spill the liquid. He curled a finger at the bartender. "Hey, can I get a rum and Coke? I went to the john and someone jacked my drink. Can you believe that shit can happen at a shindig like this?"

"You sure you want another?" the muscle-bound stranger asked with a condescending tone.

"Two years, right? Geez, it was foggy that day. I could hardly see." Evan paused to accept his drink from the barkeep and took a sip. "I'm getting ready to run Boston this year but I usually stick to the West Coast."

"You've got the wrong guy. Look, I'm busy here." His eyes darted to the blonde, who nervously played with her hair. Evan wondered why the girl bothered staying and wondered if she was entertaining the casting couch.

"Yeah, yeah. No worries. Have fun." Even held up his glass and nodded, turning away. He gave a closed smile as he took a step toward the balcony railing. In his peripheral vision, he watched as the man gulped his drink. Evan eyed the guarded hallway and silently counted the seconds. Ten. Nine. Eight. Seven. Six. Five. Four. Three. Two. One.

The high-pitched scream echoed, drawing the attention of those guests on the second-floor landing. As guards and partygoers swarmed around the fallen body, Evan slipped away unnoticed. Quickly making his way down the hall and up a side stairway, he bounded upward to investigate.

EVAN REMAINED IN THE SHADOWS, TRAVERSING THE HALLWAY WITH stealthy precision as he attempted to avoid the detection of the overhead dome security cameras. All eyes would be on the victim, attempting to wake him. Vital signs would register normal. Evan expected guards would relocate him to a private location while they tried to wake the guest. They'd hesitate to call the police or paramedics, reluctant to disrupt the event. In exactly nine minutes, he'd wake and they'd send the drunken guest home in a cab.

Evan drew closer to the third floor, and the faint whispers of an argument grew louder. As he approached the door, he recognized the female and stopped cold, listening.

"I thought you said you'd be able to help us get the data," the unfamiliar male growled.

"I told you that I worked there. I'll get you want you want, but it comes at a price," the female responded.

"Five million cash. It's what we're willing to pay. This is not news. Take it or leave it."

"And I told you, I don't just want money. I want names," she replied.

"Names?" he laughed. "Are you fucking kidding? These people are everyone and no one. Names will get you killed as soon as you blink."

"Names are part of the price," she demanded.

"You've got a death wish, lady. My contacts...there's no fucking way they want this shared with the likes of you. And now that Mr. Marretta and I have approached them, arranged for this exchange, we're all at risk. You're going to get us all killed."

"I don't give a shit what you think. Names are and have always been part of the deal."

"What kind of shit are you into? Blackmail?"

"I'm a collector of sorts. But for the sake of your boss, let's call it protection should any of these folks decide to come after me. If everyone plays nice, we have no issues. The clients get what they want. I disappear quietly. Everyone's happy. The terms of this deal are nonnegotiable." She sighed, shook her head in disgust, and took off toward the door. "Look, if you can't make this happen, I'm out of here. I want to speak with Mr. Marretta. I tire of dealing with the B team."

Evan held his breath as the sound of her heels clicking grew louder. He glanced to his watch. Seven minutes.

"Where the fuck do you think you're going?" the male demanded.

"Get your fucking hand off of me right now, or neither you or Mr. Marretta will ever see me again," she promised, her voice terse.

"I'm going to tell you what's going to happen right now. There's a party going on downstairs." The imposing thug gripped her arm and tugged her toward him.

"What are you saying?"

"I'm going to teach you a lesson in how Dom negotiates. How I negotiate."

"I'm warning you right now," she told him, her voice firm but calm, "get your fucking hands off me or you'll regret it."

"You know what I want to know? Why did Dom let you into our circle? Why does he trust you anyway? You're a dumb bitch who just wasted our time. We already arranged this deal and now you're fucking around. I've got news for you. My time is expensive." He jerked at her limb, shaking her like a rag doll. "And this pussy right here is payment for my wasted time. I'm going to split you open, little girl. Give you something to remember me by and then you're going to get the data for me. You'll be thanking me when I'm done."

"Do it," she challenged with a laugh.

Evan's heartbeat sped up at her words. What the ever-loving fuck was she doing?

"Here's a bit of advice. Scream all you want. No one's going to hear you. I promise only to bruise you where they can't see. This time."

"Yeah, that's not gonna happen, asshole. How 'bout you scream for me?"

The sound of flesh meeting flesh sounded and Evan tore into the room. Blood gushed from the large thug's nose as the female broke free of his hold and smacked him across the face with a glass statue. Her attacker rushed forward, shoving her into the wall, and without missing a beat, she kneed him in the balls, driving him to the ground.

"Your mama didn't teach you any manners, did she?" she seethed, fire in her eyes.

"You're both dead," the male grunted, catching sight of Evan.

"We all gotta go sometime. But not today." Evan shrugged with a smile and landed a fist on his jaw. A loud thud sounded as her assailant fell unconscious to the floor.

"Evan," the female whispered, her eyes wide on Evan's.

"Raine."

"I've got this," she insisted. "You've got to go."

"Like hell you do. You're going to get us both killed. What the fuck do you think you're doing?"

Raine rolled her eyes and tugged down her white spandex dress. She reached for a matching pump that had fallen off her foot, slipped it on, and glanced around the room. "My purse."

"Forget your goddamned purse." Evan checked his watch. Two minutes.

"I've got it," Raine responded, lifting it up off the floor.

"We've got to go now."

"Fine," she agreed, reluctance in her tone. "Come on. We can get out the back."

"Jesus, Raine. Just how the hell do you know this place so well?" Evan asked. He slid the backs of his knuckles across the emerald sofa, depositing a smear of blood onto its fabric and poked his head around the doorjamb to check for guards. "It's clear but not for long. My car's parked a block away. Let's go."

"To the left," she instructed.

"Yeah, I've got it." It was only a matter of seconds before someone saw the video of him in the room upstairs. Evan led them into the shadows toward a staircase farther down the hallway. "Goes to the kitchen, yes?"

"The caterers are in there but we should be able to slip out the alleyway. They'll be looking for us though. We are so fucked," she gritted out as they bounded down the flight of stairs.

As they reached the kitchen, Evan blocked her from going farther.

"What the hell are you doing?" she whispered.

"Hold up." He peeked into the room. Several cooks and waiters buzzed around the area, all focused on their work. Evan's eyes met Raine's. "Out the back door and to my car. Follow me. If they come for me, run as far as you can get on foot. I will come for you."

"I don't need saving."

"Sweetheart..." He gave a small smile, recalling how she'd handled the guy upstairs. "After what I saw tonight, I'm tempted to agree but you and I are as good as dead if we don't make ourselves scarce. Now."

Evan took her hand in his, shoving away the electricity that tingled in his palm. Tonight they'd have it out, and one way or another, he'd find out what kind of shit she was into. For months he'd wanted to fuck his lovely coworker, but after overhearing her conversation, it was likely he'd kill her by his own hand or she'd be spending a long time in a government lockdown facility. A shame, really, but business was business.

As they tore into the kitchen, he dragged her, weaving through the sea of uniformed staff. A pan dropped, releasing a loud clang, and he looked over his shoulder, noting the five armed guards barreling toward them.

"Move," Evan told her. "Sorry, buddy." He snatched a silver tray out of a waiter's hands, and puff pastries flew into the air as he sent it hurling at the barrage of goons who screamed at them to stop.

"This way." Raine pointed to the back exit.

Evan tugged a carving knife from a cook, shoving through the crowded kitchen. The swinging doors banged against the wall as he shouldered them open. A few cooks who stood smoking in the side alleyway made no move to stop them as they ran away.

"Keep going. They won't fire shots here at the house," Evan told her.

"Yeah, they'll find us later and kill us." Raine tore her hand from his as they broke into a sprint down the street.

"Here." Evan shoved his hand into his pocket and depressed the remote, unlocking the car.

"I'm not getting paid enough," Raine remarked at the sight of his expensive vehicle.

"Seems to me you're doing just fine with the money you're demanding." Evan didn't bother opening the door for the woman who had attempted to illegally sell data that didn't belong to her. "Get the fuck in."

"What crawled in your bed and died?" she asked, rolling her eyes. She opened her door, jumped in, and slammed it shut.

"Are you fucking for real, Raine?" Evan blew out a breath and shook his head, tossing the knife to the ground. He opened his door, slipped inside, and started the engine. "No, you know what? Don't say another fucking word. But you go ahead and think about what you're going to say."

"About what?" Raine's face tensed as she glanced in the side mirror. Headlights flashed in the distance. "We've got company."

"The truth. That's what the hell what." Evan shifted into gear and slammed his foot on the accelerator.

The wheels squealed, and the scent of burnt rubber permeated the car's interior. Evan wrenched the steering wheel to the right, taking the vehicle around a hairpin curve and down a side street. His eyes flashed into the rearview mirror, noting the lights flashing behind him.

"Whatever shit you're into, you're in it deep. I want to know what shit. Whose shit. And how far you're swimmin' in it…" Evan paused as he raced into an underpass. Switching lanes, he passed several cars until they emerged from the tunnel. He slammed on the brakes, sending the car spinning, and by the time they stopped, they faced the other direction. Spotting a dark alleyway, he sped into it and shut off the lights.

"Just because I didn't kill you back there for offering to sell government secrets," he continued, "that doesn't mean I won't. You have secrets, sweetheart, but so do I. My guess is that you aren't carryin' but be prepared because I'm searchin' your ass for weapons when we get to our destination."

"And where exactly is that?" Raine kicked off her shoes and twisted to look out the back window. "That's them there. They passed. Jesus Christ, you're right about one thing, we're in some shit."

"Correction, sweetheart. You're in some shit. I'm not the one sellin' what doesn't belong to me."

"I would never do anything to hurt Emerson Industries or this country, and you fucking know it." Raine glanced to her blood-splattered dress and sighed. "Damn. I'm never gonna get that out. I just bought this. And I looked good in it too."

"You're cold, girl. I'll give you that." He shrugged and fired the engine on. "Tell you what. If I find you're telling the truth, that what you were doing was something other than what I thought it was, then I'll buy ya a new one. But I can promise you this. Lie to me? You're goin' to lose a lot more than an overpriced dress."

"It's not what you think," she protested.

"Just stop. You just sit there and work on your story. Later. I want the truth. All of it."

"But..."

"Not another word." Evan shifted hard, his thoughts racing as he tore down the I-5.

Raine Presley. What the hell was she doing tonight? Not for a minute would he have pegged her as a corporate spy. A fearless skydiver, Raine had joined Club Altura a year after starting her employment at Emerson Industries. As the chief security officer, she reported to Garrett on paper, but it was Evan who oversaw her work.

For months Evan had fought his attraction to her. Office dating wasn't an option. Not dipping his pen in the company ink had been a hard-and-fast rule that had served him well. A moment of pussy could be sweet as sugar but bitter as fuck the minute it turned. Although technically he wasn't her boss, the managerial lines blurred, and it could easily be argued he'd pressured her into it.

As the months progressed, their unsated sexual chemistry morphed into a heated, quick-witted banter that only served to fuel his desire for her. Despite the ongoing fantasy and temptation, logic warned him to stay away.

Evan had found it particularly difficult to resist her at Club Altura events. From skydiving to rock climbing, the members skirted the edge of death and openly explored their sexuality within the confines of Garrett Emerson's beachfront retreat. He found it interesting how the attractive executive would flirt yet never indulge in the more adventurous sexual activities. While Evan had publicly played with women, engaging in the occasional fling, he'd often catch her watching, a craving flickering in her hungry eyes.

He glanced to Raine who checked her phone. He noted the emerging bruises on her skin, a small trickle of dried blood on her shoulder. His mind churned as he recalled how she'd fought her attacker. He'd been in the military and had witnessed violence firsthand. She'd defended herself with an effortless precision and accuracy, which told him she'd been trained. The question was by whom and for what purpose.

Evan focused on the road and sped toward San Diego. They'd have only hours to secure extra protection, decide next steps. Dom Marretta would want answers as to why he'd gone snooping at his party. Evan would claim he'd simply wandered in search of a restroom. As for Raine, he still couldn't be sure of the consequences of her actions. Once they arrived at his house, he'd either get the truth or, if not, he'd turn her over to the authorities himself.

2

Raine stepped into the darkened foyer and released the breath she'd been holding for what seemed like forever. Evan Tredioux. What the hell was he doing at the party tonight? She'd been close to gathering the names of over a half dozen suspects, ones who sought to harm the country. Marretta's henchman had unexpectedly double-crossed her, refusing to give her the names she was promised in exchange for the data. As soon as he'd laid his fingers on her, she'd been set on taking him out, well before Evan made an appearance. She could have hidden her skills from him, but she'd chosen to defend herself first and then come up with a defensible lie.

Raine's father had been in the CIA, so she was no stranger to the life. Concerned that harm would come to his family, her daddy had trained her to kill when she'd been ten years old. Living in fear most of her childhood, Raine had deliberately chosen a different life, a safe one. She'd studied hard throughout school, landing herself a full scholarship to Harvard. Her mother had prayed she'd major in finance or law, land herself a rich husband. But Raine had decided long ago she wouldn't rely on anyone but herself. She'd majored in technology and secured a coveted internship at L-Tech. Within a year, she'd transferred over to Emerson Industries, quickly climbing the corporate ladder to lead their security team.

When Dom Marretta had approached her in a coffee shop, she'd immediately decided to take it to her contacts in the government. Ever since, she'd been a spy for a covert government organization. As she was deep undercover, neither Garrett nor Evan knew of her deception. It was true; she'd stolen bits of harmless information from Emerson Industries and delivered them to Marretta to show good faith. She'd systematically proved her worth to him, slowly earning his trust. But tonight, he'd blown her off, instead choosing to delegate negotiation for payment to an underling.

As she reflected on the evening, she considered if there was a bright side it was that Dom would review the security footage and observe her taking out one of his best men. Although he'd be pissed that she'd insisted on the names, he'd always known it had been part of the deal, and she'd earn respect for her actions. Evan, however, was a complication. She'd have only hours to figure out how to explain his presence.

With spies everywhere, Marretta would find them eventually. Before that happened, she'd have to get the hell out of wherever Evan had taken her and go back to the event on her own. She'd save face by doing so, but if he suspected she'd told Evan about their criminal activities, he'd swiftly order both their deaths. Raine would play it off as keeping with her cover. She'd tell him that she'd been as surprised as anyone to see Evan and had decided to go with him to distract him from the deal, draw attention away from the gala.

As Raine ran through a litany of plausible lies in her mind, a door slammed behind her, causing her to startle. Evan. He'd press her for answers. She'd have to tell him just enough to satisfy him without divulging everything, exposing her mission.

"Whatever you're thinking, it better be good," he commented.

"I'm not thinking anything," she lied.

Her anxiety rose as Evan pecked a code into a pad on the wall, activating the home's security system. There was no way she'd escape without him knowing. She'd been trained in fighting, not disabling alarms.

"I don't know what's going on, Raine, but I want answers starting now," he told her and switched on the lights.

"But I..." She lost her words as Evan stripped off his shirt, revealing his tanned, corded muscles. With his back turned, he waved a hand at her to follow him.

She struggled to concentrate, a rush of desire threading through her body. For as long as she could remember, she'd fantasized about making love with Evan. Chills danced over her skin as she recalled the last time they'd worked on a joint presentation, the delicious scent of his cologne enticing her senses as he'd peered over her shoulder.

Despite the opportunity to act on sexual impulses at Club Altura parties, Raine had been hesitant to engage in the activities. Her attraction to Evan had been unrivaled by any other man. He was the only one she'd ever wanted. She suspected if she slept with him, it was likely she'd want him forever. Pursuing him would only lead to heartbreak. If by some miracle Garrett didn't fire her when the mission was all over, it wasn't likely Evan would ever look at her the same way again.

Raine had seen him with women at the lavish events and often retreated. She loathed the jealousy that curled in her chest, but she'd been careful not to show it, afraid to damage their relationship. Logic told Raine to forget him, but the fantasy to be in his arms and bed lingered.

"Raine," she heard him call to her, breaking her contemplation. He spun around, pinning her with his penetrating blue eyes. Her heart pounded in her chest as he stalked toward her.

"I'm sorry. I...I..." She averted her gaze, afraid she'd confess how she felt. Raine glanced to her arm and sighed at the sight of the dried blood. In her adrenaline-fueled escape, she hadn't noticed the scratch.

"Are you sure you're okay?" he asked, his voice softening as he approached.

"I...uh, yeah, I'm fine." A myriad of emotions twisted through her as he drew closer. Relief she'd survived. Fear he'd grow angry. Arousal.

"Raine..."

As he closed the distance, she stepped backward, her shoulders brushing the wall. She licked her lips as he pressed into her.

"I've known you for what? Five years now maybe?" he asked.

"Four." Raine's green eyes drifted up to meet his. He towered above her, the heat of his body emanating onto her skin. "What are you doing?"

"There hasn't been one project where I haven't been able to rely on you to hit a home run. Everything we've done has been successful. There isn't one jump we've done where I wouldn't have trusted you to pull my cord. And then tonight..."

"It's not what you think... I can explain."

"Tell me I didn't hear what I heard tonight."

She closed her eyes, releasing a breath as he flattened his palms on the wall, caging her with his arms.

"Selling data? Demanding names? Why does someone do these things? Stealing. What the hell were you doing?"

"I..." Her lids lifted, her gaze slowly meeting his. She'd craved him since the first time they'd worked together, and now he thought her a liar, a thief. This was never her intention when she'd agreed to help the agency. "It's complicated."

"I bet it is. But you'd better fucking tell me right now or I'm calling the police. Don't even fuck with me, because I'll know if you're lying."

"I told you. It's not what you think. You know me," she insisted. It wasn't as if she didn't get why he thought she'd betrayed him, Emerson Industries, and the country. Raine's chest tightened as her words danced on the tip of her tongue. "I'd never sell our secrets to someone like Dom Marretta. I can't tell you what I'm doing but you have to trust me."

"Who?" he asked with a raised eyebrow.

"What?" she stammered. Her heart pounded as Evan leaned in close, his eyes locked on hers.

"Who do you work for?"

"You know who I work for. Emerson Industries. The same place you do."

"What you did tonight...taking out that asshole. That wasn't the kind of guy just anyone can take on. You've been trained. So again, sweetheart, who?"

"I... Evan...please, I can't tell you but I swear to God I didn't..." Raine closed her eyes and sighed, his warm breath teasing her ear. Desire twisted through her body and she lost concentration. Tell him anything he wants to know. For so long, she'd denied herself pleasure. "I...I work for our government. I can't tell you who. I need the names of those guys they were selling the data to. That's all I can say, but you have to believe me. What you saw tonight, it's not what you think."

"Ah, a truth. Finally. Do you see how easy it can be? But still, my little thief, I want to know who. Who in the government do you work for? And what in the hell are these terrorists going to do with the data? Why would the government allow you to give it to them?"

"I can't tell you that. Jesus, Evan. You were in the military. You know I can't say." Her heart pounded in her chest. So close, her hands reached toward him, her palms pressed against his chest as his lips grazed her ear. "I swear to you though. The data was scrubbed. Please."

"Why don't you ever play at Club Altura?"

"What?" Raine stammered, shocked at the change of subject.

"The entire time you've belonged. I've never once seen you with anyone. Not even once."

Raine froze as he moved to tilt his head toward hers, his eyes on hers.

"Why is that?"

"I...I... It's just I've never wanted to..."

"I've seen the heat in your eyes. You want to, all right," he pressed.

"Why are you asking about this? I need to make a phone call and then get back to the party," she insisted, attempting to deny her body's response to him.

"Because, I know what you want, Raine," he said, his voice low. "I've always known."

"Please let me go. Dom wants the info I have. I need the names. I have to do something right now. Don't you understand how close I am to getting those names?" Anger flared in her eyes, yet as he inched closer, arousal flooded her body. "Evan..."

"The club. Not everyone plays openly. But you? Never. Not once."

"I don't want to talk about this." She pushed on his chest but he didn't budge.

"I do. Why? I want the truth."

"Why don't you ever choose me?" she countered, surprised at her response. As the words left her lips, she was helpless to stop them. "So many late nights. We've been working together forever. You never ask me... Not once did you... I just thought that maybe..."

"Maybe what?"

"That you...me..." She couldn't bring herself to articulate her fantasies.

"Say it, sweetheart. That what?" He gave a devious smile.

"Please," she sighed, closing her eyes. Raine's body prickled in awareness as he brought his lips to her ear once again.

"I've wanted you," he whispered. "So many nights."

"No," she responded, shock in her voice. "You never..."

"Because we work together. But at the club, you never play."

"Maybe that's because the one person I want to play with...I can't..." she breathed.

"Tell me what you want. Tell me, the truth."

Raine shuddered as his lips brushed her neck, and she found herself unable to keep her thoughts at bay. "I've always wanted...you... but you never..."

"I don't mess with people who report to me. But don't ever think I didn't want you," he told her.

"But...you..." Gooseflesh broke over her skin as he peppered kisses along her neck.

"You're fired." As Evan's lips crushed onto hers, Raine melted into his arms. His tongue swept into her mouth and she kissed him back with an urgent fervor. She shivered as his palms glided over her shoulders, trailing over her sensitive neck, sending tendrils of desire through her body. With a deliberate sensual control, palms cupped her cheeks, deepening their kiss, his lips making love to hers.

As Evan tore his lips from hers, he rested his forehead on Raine's. "I don't get involved with people who work for me."

"I...I can't promise when this is over I'll still be here." As her senses returned, logic warred with her arousal. After tonight, it'd be unlikely she'd still be in San Diego let alone working for Emerson Industries.

"One night, Raine. Right now, I'm going with my gut here, trusting that you wouldn't steal. Whatever the hell you've got yourself into, I can't even think of letting you back in the doors of Emerson. Not until I know everything. Not until someone in the CIA, FBI, or NSA comes to me. Hell, after what just went down back there—"

"I've already got what I need," she confessed. The agency had given her dummy files to pawn off to Marretta in exchange for names. They were a mishmash of scrubbed data, with tidbits of fake information she'd created.

"One night," he repeated.

"One night," she nodded, taking a deep breath as her heart fluttered. *I'm going to regret this.*

She'd lied, all right. If she made love to him, once would never be enough. She'd always known that. After years of working and skydiving together, their relationship meant more to her than she'd admit. She never thought it possible to fall in love with someone she'd never kissed, yet when his lips had met hers, her heart crushed, confirming her suspicion. Her feelings ran deep, and there was no way she'd be able to stop the rush of emotion that had been kept at bay. Still she willingly dove down the rabbit hole, praying she would survive.

Evan lifted her off the ground and cradled her to his chest. Raine wrapped her hands around his neck, molding her body to his, engulfed in his warmth. She closed her eyes, her mind churning as he carried her. Maybe the agency would vouch for her. Maybe he'd trust her again. Maybe she could stay in San Diego. Maybe he'd choose her and her only. Maybe...

The patter of water droplets broke the contemplation of her thoughts, and she blinked open her eyes. Her hands clutched his shoulders as he set her on her feet. She reached to remove her dress, and his firm voice stopped her cold.

"Raine."

"Yes," she whispered, her hands trembling.

"Don't move." He hooked his fingers around the thin spaghetti straps of her dress, dragging them over her shoulders. He never took his eyes off of hers as he tugged the fabric off her body, allowing it to pool to the floor. "Do you have any idea how long I've waited for you?"

"No..." Raine's heart skipped a beat as Evan spoke. Every single day, working side by side, the anguish of pretending she didn't want him had nearly killed her. But it had been nothing compared to watching him with other women, denying herself his affection, silently swallowing her jealousy.

"Our late nights." He gave a sexy smile and set his palms on her hips.

"I wanted to..."

"Jesus, you're gorgeous...always have been, but it's your mind that has always drawn me to you."

She gave a flirtatious smile, recalling their incessant banter. "Well, what can I say, sir? I can't let the boss think he knows everything."

Raine knew he was dominant. She'd watched him at Club Altura, taking control of his flavor of the month. While she'd never been submissive in the least in the office, regularly challenging him in the boardroom, the rush of jumping out of a plane at thirty-five thousand was nothing, she imagined, to the sting of his hand on her bottom.

"You've got quite a mouth on you, sweetheart."

Raine sucked in a breath as he reached for her hips and yanked her toward him, rocking his erection into her pelvis.

"This is just the beginning. That little mouth..." He dragged his thumb over her lower lip. "Let's see what you can do with it."

"What are you doing?" She gasped as he lifted her by the waist and set her into the warm spray.

Her heart pounded against her ribs as she watched him strip off his pants, his enormous cock springing forth. Evan kicked off his pants and stalked toward her. She breathed in anticipation as he closed the distance.

Raine sighed as his lips smashed onto hers, her body coming alive at his devastating kiss. His tongue swept into her mouth, tasting, probing. As he broke contact, she protested. "No..." Breathless, her body quivered in his arms.

"That little mouth of yours...I know exactly what I want to do with it," he told her, commanding her attention. He brushed his finger under her chin. "On your knees."

"What?" The shower mist clung to her lashes as she blinked up to meet his gaze.

"On your knees."

Shock rolled through her at his demand, but her pussy tightened in response, flooding in arousal. Raine had never considered doing anything like this for anyone, submitting. In the office, she'd just as soon tell him to go fuck himself. But in the shower, nude and vulnerable, her traitorous body reveled in his command.

"Did you hear me, little one? You've been enough trouble for tonight. Now, on. Your. Knees."

Raine shivered, his voice washing over her strong and clear. She did as she was told, her palms curling around the backs of his thighs as she knelt on the floor. With a heated gaze, she licked the moisture from her lips, waiting for his instruction.

"I've wanted you for the longest time. Now you're going to show me what you can do with that wicked little mouth of yours."

She reached for his cock, but he reprimanded her.

"Ah, ah, ah. No touching. Just open your lips, the ones that enjoy back talking me." He stroked himself as if baiting her to disobey.

Raine trembled, her mouth widening. As he dragged the thick head of his cock along her lower lip, her tongue darted over his wet slit, tasting his salty essence. Her pussy contracted, an ache throbbing between her legs.

"You've wanted this for so long and so have I. Tonight..." He inched his shaft inside her warmth. Raine moaned, sucking him as he slid his cock inside her mouth. "I'm going to make love to you all night. You'll never doubt that I've always wanted you."

Raine's heart caught, hearing his words. So much more between them than just lust. He'd known it, too, and whatever happened after they made love, she was certain they'd forever be connected.

"Fuck," he sighed, sliding himself in and out of her mouth.

She tightened her lips around his shaft, sucking hard while

resisting the temptation to take him in her hands. Increasing her speed, she swallowed his hard length until he groaned.

"Aw, no...not coming in your mouth," he insisted.

She ignored him, lapping at his cock. A firm grasp into her wet hair, the sting to her scalp warned her to obey. As he tilted her head backwards, she released him with an audible pop, licking her lips. Inwardly she laughed, aware that it was she who still remained in control, but didn't dare speak a word.

She squealed as he reached under her arms and pulled her to her feet. His mouth slammed on hers, his devilish tongue sweeping against hers. Sucking and tasting, he demanded her presence, and Raine reveled in his control.

"Ah," Rained moaned into his touch. As he palmed her pussy, the tip of his finger feathered over her clit.

"How long have you wanted it? To make love? All those nights at Club Altura? The office?"

"Oh, yes," she breathed into his kiss. She dug her fingernails into his shoulders as he shoved a thick digit into her core, stretching her open.

"How long have you waited to be fucked?" he growled into her ear, taking the lobe between his teeth.

"So long. So fucking long," she responded.

"You're all mine tonight." Evan moved his lips to her chin and nipped at her lower lip. "This mouth." As he palmed her ass and teased his finger over her back hole, she shivered in his grip. "This too. You ever been fucked here, Raine? Because tonight this is mine too."

"I...I...I've never..."

"Do you want me to fuck your ass?"

"I...I..." Raine's head fell backwards onto the tiles as he bit at her neck. She'd never talked dirty to another man, but her body responded, his crass language further driving the passion between them. He increased the pace, fucking her pussy with his hand.

"Hmm...let me see how tight you are."

Raine sucked in a breath as the tip of his finger probed her back hole. The dark fantasies she'd always harbored rushed to the forefront of her mind and her pussy contracted around his fingers, pulsating to the sensation.

"That's it, sweetheart. Jesus, I need to be in you."

As he stroked her clit, his fingers filling her, she succumbed to his pleasure. The overwhelming desire to confess her emotions stirred, but she reined it back, simply allowing her senses to fill her mind. Pleasure. Desire. Lust. Evan Tredioux was a cliff she'd willingly base jump off, and as she fell, she'd embrace the complete lack of control.

"You see, I've always had this talent for reading you," he continued, fucking her with his fingers, his lips on her neck. "All those late nights. The body responds in ways you don't notice. Your breath, the way you stretched your neck when I'd come close to you. The hunger in your eyes, watching me at the club."

"Oh, God." Jesus, he knows. She was so close to coming, and her embarrassment faded as he flicked the pad of his thumb over her clit.

"That's right, sweetheart. I saw you. Do you know it took fucking everything I had not to play with you? To pretend I didn't want you? But this..."

"Please don't stop," she cried.

"This tells me everything."

"I...I..." Raine panted as her body shook, the climax rocking through her. Exposed, she'd own the truth of wanting him, desiring him. He'd peel away the layers and reveal the honest truth of her thoughts.

"But tonight you lied so I'm going to give you a little pain with that pleasure."

"No, no, no," she pleaded as he removed his fingers from her pussy and ass. Empty, she trembled as the tendrils of her orgasm rolled through her. As he turned her around, bent her forward, placing her hands on the wall, she continued to beg. "Don't stop. What are you doing?"

"I promise, Raine. If you know nothing else, know that I will take care of you. Stay right here. Let me get a condom."

"I'm on the pill. Clean," she said, breathless.

"You sure about this?" he asked.

"Yes. Please...just...I can't wait."

"Trust?"

"I'm sure. Please...just don't stop," she pleaded.

"All right then. Let me see that beautiful ass of yours." He smiled, pleased as she bent over and spread her legs wide, her hands flattened against the wall. She wiggled her bottom at him, and he continued his instruction. "You like this, do you? I want to hear it then. Ask me to fuck you...nicely."

"Um...what?" she stammered.

"You heard me. Ask me." His fingers glided down her back, stroking her skin.

"No...I can't..."

"Now, Raine," Evan demanded.

"Ow...ah," she cried as he slapped her wet ass, the delicious pain sending a spear of erotic pleasure to her pussy. *Oh, my God. He knows everything. He knows what I've watched him do, what I want.*

"Stop thinking. Just let go," Evan told her, and another firm slap to her bottom sounded. "You've wanted this. I've wanted this. And now... we are finally together."

"Fuck me...ah yes" she breathed as the broad crown of his dick pressed into her core, stretching her. She widened her stance, accepting him, allowing him to slide deep inside her pussy. As she bent over, water dripped down her hair into her face. Her lips drenched, her tongue darted over the moisture.

"Raine..." he began but lost his words as he withdrew and slowly pressed back inside her.

"Yes...please, Evan," she pleaded.

Raine braced her hands onto the tiles and grunted as he slammed inside her. Her body tightened with desire with each hard thrust. She wiggled toward him, attempting to get him to go faster, but he continued his restraint. Evan twisted his palm into her wet locks and tugged, reminding her of his control. Her lips parted with a smile as his fingers gripped her shoulder and he slid inside her once again.

"You're so fucking tight. Fuck..." he grunted.

"That's it, yeah." Her core fisted his cock as he pounded into her. She gave a ragged breath with each delicious stroke.

As he released her hair, her head lolled forward. His fingers teased down her spine. "This, though."

Raine's heart pounded in anticipation as his thumb trailed down the crevice of her ass. She startled in response to his touch. As he teased her puckered hole with his slippery finger, another layer played to her arousal.

"Do it. Please...ah, yes." The dark pleasure blossomed, and she found herself begging.

"Easy, now...ah yeah." Evan slowed his pace.

"Ev...Evan," she panted as the tip of his thumb penetrated her ass, a twinge of pain radiating through the tight ring of muscle. Slowly, he pressed inside until he'd filled her completely.

"That's a girl. See how good that is." He gently worked the ring of muscle until she relaxed into his touch.

"Yes, oh God...don't stop."

Slowly he rocked inside her, gradually increasing the pace.

"I...I... please..." Raine lost focus as his fingers slid through her slick folds, teasing her swollen nub. With his thumb inside her ass, and his other hand playing at her clit, she sucked in a breath. So full and overwhelmed with sensation, she tilted her hips, moaning as her climax teetered on the edge. As he withdrew his cock and thrust inside her, a rush of fresh arousal surfaced, hurling her toward her orgasm.

"Aw fuck, Raine. You feel so good," he praised, pressing his thumb into her back hole in tandem as he fucked her.

"Please...please...do it...like that. Ah, yeah...it feels so good." His fingers danced over her clitoris, increasing the pressure. As he rocked into her pussy, Raine's body shook, the wave of ecstasy claiming her. She screamed his name as her orgasm rocked through her, holding firmly to the wall as Evan gave a final thrust, his grunt echoing in the shower.

Raine went limp, releasing a sigh. As he removed himself and gently lifted her into his arms, her chest tightened in emotion, a hot tear running down her cheek. Never in her life had she let a man speak the way he had to her, fuck her the way he'd done, and her heart crushed, aware she'd beg him to do it again. She wanted Evan in her life, and not just for a night. Her mind raced at the thought of losing him, barely noticing as he laid her on the bed.

Raine curled away from Evan as he pressed his lips to the back of her wet hair. A warm towel draped over her body, and she attempted to shove her feelings away. You'll never have Evan, a voice in her head told her. Fuck him. Enjoy it. Then get back to work. He was a player. And she was a spy. Some things, no matter how much you wanted them, weren't meant to be.

3

The second he'd kissed her, he knew he shouldn't make love to her. Every late night. Every inside joke. The sexual tension that had built over four years wouldn't be sated in one night.

Fucking feelings. Jesus Christ. The moment her soft lips touched his, it confirmed his worst fear. He'd seen the way she'd watched him at the club, knew the moment he pushed her, she'd willingly submit. She'd come undone under his touch. He'd deliberately fucked her from behind, avoiding the surge of emotion he suspected he'd feel if he looked into her eyes.

He'd pulled his dick out and lifted Raine into his arms without saying a word. Although she attempted to shield her face, the tears trailing her cheeks told him that their relationship had transformed forever. She'd play it off as nothing but he knew their one-time friendship had been permanently replaced by a ravenous craving that wouldn't be satisfied by a one-night stand.

Evan set her gently in the bed and returned to the bathroom to turn off the water. He glanced in the mirror and shook his head. Guilt teemed through him, as he was aware he'd crossed a line. Jesus fucking Christ, you're an idiot. What if she was lying? Although his gut told him she was telling the truth, doubt crept inside his mind.

He shook off the thought and returned with a towel. As Evan approached, he smiled, finding her curled onto her side. His little badass spy had fought a three-hundred-pound thug but now hid from him. It wasn't as if the intimacy hadn't grabbed him by the balls, but if he'd learned anything in his lifetime, you had to man up and face your fears.

"Hey." Her reddened eyes flashed up to him and she gave a small smile. Gently grazing the towel over her skin, Evan spoke as he dried her. "You all right?"

"Yeah, I'm fine," she replied, her voice shaken.

"Raine."

"Yeah?"

"You're beautiful. Tonight, it was amazing."

"It was unbelievable. I've never felt like that before," she confessed.

"Come here." Evan tossed the towel aside and lay onto his back. Sliding his arm underneath her, he cradled her to his chest. He stared up at the full moon through the ceiling skylights and sighed. "Tell me what you're thinking."

"I'm thinking...I don't know..." She hesitated.

"It's okay to be honest. We worked together all this time. Jumped too. Trust. It's something we always had. I have to believe whatever you're doing, you wouldn't do it without giving it serious consideration. I've never seen you do anything without carefully weighing the consequences."

"It's just...I've only dated one other person from Emerson."

Evan knew she'd dated his friend, Chase Abbott, well before she'd ever taken over as Emerson's chief security officer. But he had insisted they were nothing more than friends and had gone as far as to encourage Evan to ask her on a date.

"Chase and I. It was never serious. We're just friends. We definitely didn't play openly at Club Altura. I'm not like that. Or at least...I don't know. Maybe I am. Maybe you were the only one I wanted to play with."

"But you wanted this tonight. Us."

"For the longest time," she confessed, raising her eyes to meet his.

Raine sighed and laid her cheek back onto his chest. "What we just did... God, it was amazing. But you know I'd never be the one to initiate. And you..."

"You knew I didn't date people at the office."

"Yeah. People talk. And frankly, as much as I wanted this, to be together, I didn't want to risk my job. I love working at Emerson. When this thing with Dom came along...I didn't ask for it to happen. But I couldn't ignore the opportunity to take him down either, to go after a few bad guys. My Dad was in the CIA. I may not have wanted a life of danger, but I'm not a coward. I love my country. So after I got involved with the Feds, I had to finish what I started."

"Yeah." Evan couldn't commit to understanding a situation without having all the facts. Until she divulged everything, he couldn't comment further. Saying he trusted her was as far as he could go.

"You don't believe me." Her voice faltered in disappointment.

"I want evidence. I want to know the name of the organization. I want to talk to them."

"All I can promise is that I'll ask them. You were in the military. These things...involvement with the Feds...I can't just go breaking protocol no matter how much I want to tell you." Raine pushed up on his chest and looked him directly in his eyes. "When this is over, I'll tell you one way or another. I promise you. I swear to God I'm not lying."

"Didn't you ever want to play at Club Altura?" Evan changed the subject, determined to peel away her layers.

"Truth?"

"Yeah. Truth."

"I don't know. It's not like I'm a prude. It's just that, I don't know. I just started going to the events a few years ago. I was working with you. And I just had this idea...that you and I, we'd had this connection. So it just felt like if I did that, if I had sex with someone else, like maybe that would say something to you."

"I had sex with other people. You watched." Evan detected the flash of pain in her eyes but she quickly recovered, forcing an impassive expression.

"You chose to do that."

"They weren't members of the club."

"Why did you do it? If you wanted me, was it is a message?"

"Not deliberate. But you?"

Raine sighed, trailing her finger over his chest. "I've wanted you forever. But we couldn't... You never attempted to kiss me or anything. And then I saw you with the women. And I don't know. I questioned if that's something I want. Not everyone does those things. If I was going to do it...it would only be with you. No one else."

"What I did, you know it wasn't serious. I'm not seeing anyone. You know how it is there," Evan attempted to explain. He'd never given a thought to what he was doing at Club Altura as long as it wasn't with an employee.

"Things just got to a point where I knew..." She blew out a breath and hesitated.

"Knew what?"

"I'd want more. One night. I get that's what we said, but Evan...I don't want to be a one-night stand. I don't want this to be the end of us," she confessed.

"It doesn't have to be." Evan weighed his next words, careful not to make empty promises. "If Marretta doesn't kill us both, and the Feds you're working for spill the truth, then we can see what happens. Whoever it is you work for, these assholes should have come to Garrett and me instead of you. I'm not going to bother asking you any more about the situation, because I get they'll come down on you, but tomorrow, Garrett and I will find out who it is, and the shit will hit the fan. It's not like we haven't cooperated in the past. This is some bullshit. They put all of us in danger."

"Marretta's going to try to kill you." Her voice fell to a whisper. "You don't know him. I've seen things." She shivered in his arms, calming as he ran his hand down her shoulder. "He's a monster."

"I'm not letting you go back to him. I don't give a shit what agency you're working for. It's too dangerous." Evan released an even breath, attempting to conceal his anger.

"I don't have a choice." She sighed. "Besides, I'm close to getting this done, getting names. Dom will respect me for what I did. He'll question why I went with you, but I'll lie. He'll buy it. I'll get the damn names. They'll get some shitty dummy file. By the time they run the data, double- and triple-check, I'll be out of there. You should know, though, if I don't leave here soon, the Feds will come for me. You'll be charged with holding me. They'll make up something. There are dark recesses of our government. Invisible agencies. They report to few and do what they want. They don't even register with most senators or representatives. No one knows about them."

Evan considered her words. It was true that there were ultra-secret operations, spy agencies that never surfaced, let alone went public. They'd sooner make her disappear from the face of the earth than allow her to refuse to complete the mission.

"I'll go with you," he said.

"I can't put you in danger," she replied.

"I may not be able to control what's going on tonight, but Garrett and I, between the two of us, we can rein this situation in, find out the organizations that are driving this effort and get you out."

"Do you have any weapons here?" She glanced around his bedroom and smiled. "Wherever here is?"

"More than you'd know what to do with, sweetheart."

"All right then. We'll play it your way but you have to stay far behind. If they see you, we're both dead."

"You'll deny that you knew I was following you."

"I can do that but he'd probably kill us. They'd definitely kill you, Evan. I can't let that happen." Panic laced her voice.

"I know what I'm doin'. Not my first time at the rodeo. I'll be invisible."

"We've got to get out soon. I have a few contacts of my own who expect me to report. And if the Feds show up, it's not going to be a good situation. We're going to be fucked. I need to get back on the job. I'll get the names and get out." Raine shoved up onto her elbows, attempting to leave.

"Not so fast, sweetheart." Evan rolled Raine onto her back, and she squealed in laughter as he pinned her arms to the bed. He settled between her legs, his cock lengthening as she arched her back, her breasts brushing his chest.

"Hmm...I like you this way."

"Vulnerable?" she asked.

"With me. That's how."

A broad smile crossed her face. "Me too."

"We've always made a good team, you know that?"

"The best. No one could mess with us in the boardroom."

"We'd make a better team now."

"Are you saying you'd like to change the terms of this agreement?" She raised an eyebrow, giving him a sexy smile.

"I'm thinking..." he laughed. "Yeah, I'd like to renegotiate."

"I'm open to hearing your proposal, Mr. Tredioux."

"After this mess is cleaned up, I want a proper date." Evan's lips moved to her neck, tasting her delicate skin.

"Yes," she laughed.

"But you can't work for me. I was serious about the being fired part."

"Hmm...that much I expected. Ah..." She wriggled underneath him, rocking her pelvis against his thickening cock.

"If you're telling the truth, I'll go to bat for you with Garrett. If not, no dinner date."

"I'm not lying. Besides, who said dinner was our date?" she countered.

Evan laughed. Although she was gorgeous, her wit was something he'd always found particularly attractive. "Rock climbing. Then dinner. No arguing. Dinner is always required for a date."

"What girl can resist rock climbing? Ahh..." she moaned as he peppered kisses down her breast, a nipple slipping between his lips. "Evan..."

"You're beautiful," he murmured, his mouth full.

"Please..."

"I want to taste every inch of you," he told her as he released her swollen tip.

With his cock painfully hard as steel, he resisted shoving himself inside her. Slowly, he nipped and sucked at her abdomen, shifting himself downward, between her legs.

"That's a girl. Let me see that beautiful pussy of yours." He trailed his lips over her mound and spread her labia open with his thumbs.

"Evan," she cried as he stroked his tongue through her slick folds.

He lapped at her clit, tasting her sweet essence on his lips. Lifting her bottom with one hand, he speared his tongue into her core. While flicking her swollen bead with his thumb, he fucked her pussy. She bucked wildly, but he held firm, his fingers gripping her ass. Raine screamed his name, and her head thrashed as her entire body quivered, her hands gripping the sheets as he relentlessly milked her orgasm.

As her cries faltered, he rose above her, settling his cock between her legs. He licked his lips, his hunger flaring in his eyes. With a deliberate motion, he stroked the tip of his hard length through her slick folds, teasing her clit.

Emotion rose in his chest as he gazed into her eyes. He prayed like hell she was telling the truth, that every shred of intuition that told him she was innocent was on point. He shoved the thoughts to the back of his mind as she mewled, and glided his palms over her full breasts. Slowly, inch by inch, Evan eased his cock into her tight core. Raine opened to him, her knees falling to the sides, moaning as he filled her completely.

As he rested on his forearms, his fingers tunneled into her silken locks. He kissed her with passion, releasing the emotion he couldn't articulate. A master of restraint, Evan finally let go, making love to Raine. Her magical kiss weaved a spell, and in that moment, he knew he'd fight to keep her in San Diego.

As he increased his pace, thrusting inside her, she tilted her hips to meet his. She wrapped her legs around his waist, drawing him deeper. With his forehead to hers, their heated gazes silently communicated the feelings neither would dare speak. His breath quickened as he drew closer to orgasm, his pelvis grazing her clit.

"Evan...oh, God. I...I..." Raine panted.

"Fuck...yes..." Evan grunted, unable to control the climax that rocked through him. His seed exploded deep inside Raine as her core quivered around his cock. Waves of ecstasy rippled through him, and his lips smashed onto hers, muffling her screams of pleasure. He gave a final thrust before gently slipping out of her and rolling to his back, keeping her close to his chest.

"Raine, I need you to know—"

"I don't want this to end," she interrupted, her breath ragged.

"Nothing will happen to you," he promised, inwardly cursing the situation.

Evan held her tightly, swearing he'd keep her alive. He'd decided to call on his good friend Dean Frye, who was an assistant district attorney. They'd have to work fast. The longer she took to get back to Dom Marretta and give him the data, the more likely it was he'd doubt her story.

Exhausted, Evan closed his eyes and pressed his lips to her hair. As she fell asleep in his arms, he considered the array of weapons stocked in his home. Garrett joked he was paranoid, but Evan preferred to think of his enthusiasm as actively prepared.

He smiled as her lips touched his chest, reminding him of the secrets that lay in his heart. His lioness would fight to the death. He'd seen her in action and had no doubt she'd push the limits get the names. But no matter her confidence that Dom would believe her, that she'd be safe, Evan couldn't take that risk and let her go it alone.

Raine imagined a life without espionage or danger. When she'd agreed to the mission, the element of death had seemed worth the risk. But within Evan's embrace, she questioned everything, her career, her decisions, her life.

As he'd made love to her, she could feel every thread of his emotion. The connection they'd built over time, as friends...now lovers, was stronger than ever. Nothing would ever be the same.

Her heart constricted as she snuggled against his chest, attempting to memorize the exact way it felt. His masculine scent. The strength of his arms. The pace of his breathing as his chest rose and fell, the rough pad of his fingers trailing over her arm.

Evan had always represented power and intelligence, a charismatic rainmaker. The man who'd haunted her dreams had finally become reality. After tasting his passion, she refused to give him up without a fight. She'd go to Dom tonight, give him the data, and complete her mission. But if he so much as laid a finger on Evan, she'd shoot him dead without blinking an eye. Evan was hers and no one, not a mob boss, not the government, would take him away.

As sleep claimed her, dreams of rock climbing danced in her head. A summit. Dinner for two. A kiss. Evan Tredioux.

EPILOGUE

As Raine pulled away in the cab, Evan switched on the ignition of his car. He'd called in a favor with Dean and arranged to have an undercover cop drive her to Marretta's mansion. Although the police were on alert, they'd been cautioned not to interfere with the covert action.

Raine had already texted Marretta, alerting him that she'd arrive within a few hours. She'd fed him a lie about Evan accidentally finding her upstairs, that he'd insisted she leave the party and she'd only gone along with him so he wouldn't cause a scene. She'd claimed Evan had taken her to a diner in San Clemente, where he'd interrogated her for hours over coffee but eventually bought her story. Marretta had insisted the deal was still on and agreed to give her the names and money. Although he'd appeared satisfied with Raine's explanation of the night's events, Evan's intuition told him something was wrong. With the way they'd torn out of his house, there was no way Marretta would let her off the hook so easily. But Raine insisted that she knew Marretta better than he did. With the Feds minutes away, Evan had no choice but to let her go about her mission.

In the obscurity of the night on the I-5, Evan had lost a visual on her cab nearly ten minutes ago. The police vehicle, disguised as a taxi, had been outfitted with a tracking device. Evan had deliberately kept far behind, remaining invisible in case Marretta had eyes on the cab. He glanced at the blip on his cell phone as it inched toward LA, his stomach dropping when, in an instant, the car disappeared from his screen.

As he tapped at the glass, praying it was a malfunction, a loud horn sounded behind him. The tractor trailer had come up from behind in darkness, and he knew he was in trouble. The flare of its headlights glared into his rear window, blinding him as he sped to avoid the impact. The crunch of metal scraping metal sounded, and as the car spun off the highway, he wrestled with the wheel. Darkness claimed its victim, and the only thought in his head was Raine.

"What did she say? Fucking tell me now." The deafening command rang in his ears.

"I'm going to kill you," Evan promised, his naked body slumped forward, blood pooling in his mouth. He'd been in and out of consciousness for hours. Tied to a bar on the ceiling, he forced his mind into survival mode, resorting to his military training.

"What's your relationship?" the captor barked. Landing a solid blow to Evan's ribs, he laughed as crimson body fluid splattered onto the floor.

"Fuck you," Evan grunted, breathless from the impact.

"What did Raine tell you?" His attacker spun, punching him hard across his jaw.

Evan's vision blurred, the jolt of pain spearing through him. He blinked, taking in his surroundings, spying his weapon of choice.

"I'm going to kill you," Evan spat again, formulating his plan. Dean and his buddies were waiting for a text from him. When it didn't come, they'd rain hell down upon Dom Marretta and his henchmen. The tracker would provide evidence as to where Raine was delivered.

"Wrong, buddy," the stranger laughed. "You're not going anywhere. You're already dead. You just don't know it."

"I'm going to kill you," Evan repeated, choking on his own blood.

"Evan Tredioux is about to die an untimely death. Skydiving accident. You're not going anywhere. We're going to keep you as long as we need you."

Confusion swept through Evan as the needle pierced his neck. If there was one thing he knew better than anyone, it was skydiving. The swirl of the drugged haze filtered through his bloodstream and Evan swore retribution. They might be able to hold him captive but he'd eventually get out.

His captors? Dom Marretta? The people who bought the data? They were all dead men living on borrowed time. They'd fucked with the wrong man and soon they'd all wish they'd never heard his name.

ABOUT KYM GROSSO

Kym Grosso is the New York Times and USA Today bestselling author of the erotic paranormal series, The Immortals of New Orleans, and the contemporary erotic suspense series, Club Altura. In addition to romance novels, Kym has written and published several articles about autism, and is passionate about autism advocacy. She is also a contributing essay author in Chicken Soup for the Soul: Raising Kids on the Spectrum.

In 2012, Kym published her first novel and today, is a full time romance author. In 2012, Kym published her first novel and today, is a full time romance author. She lives in southern California where she enjoys writing sexy stories near the beach.

To be notified of new releases or sales,
join Kym's Mailing List: www.kymgrosso.com/members-only
Connect with Kym online
Facebook: www.facebook.com/KymGrossoBooks
Instagram: www.instagram.com/KymGrosso
Visit Kym at KymGrosso.com!

Revenge on the Rocks

JENNA JACOB

1

Victor LaCroix cursed as he slammed the gearshift of his truck into drive and sped out of Haven, Texas.

"That cantankerous cunt is making me drive fifteen fucking miles—one way—just to buy a goddamn bottle of whiskey," he snarled. "Fuckin' bitch."

Of course, he wouldn't have to make these trips if he simply apologized to Gina Scott, owner of the Hangover—the only bar in town. But Victor didn't apologize to anyone, particularly women, and especially not that woman.

"She can suck a big, fat dick! I'd rather die than grovel to that slut," he spat. "The bitch is crazy. No sane woman would threaten a customer with a baseball bat and throw a tactical knife at his head."

And that's exactly what she'd done to him, too. Six months ago, he'd walked into her bar, short-tempered and in a surly mood. Victor couldn't remember what had pissed him off now, but it didn't matter. The sassy bitch had no business running a bar. That was a man's job. So maybe he shouldn't have told her to find a man to keep her in her place, but sometimes the truth hurt. It was no excuse for the radical feminist to go schizoid.

His contemptible grudge for the woman had fed on itself ever since.

Victor could still see the rage stamped on Gina's face, still hear her cold and brittle words:

The only things I need from a man, I can buy from the store and put batteries in. You may think I'm a weak little woman who needs to be coddled and taken care of, but I don't. Apologize and enjoy your drink, or lift your wrinkled ass off my barstool and get the fuck out.

He'd refused to accept either offer, and that's when things turned ugly.

Victor had spent the rest of that night at home in his trailer, sipping cough medicine instead of whiskey and plotting his revenge.

Of course, he'd passed out before he could exact said retribution, but the plan had been swirling in his brain ever since.

Pride and animosity kept him from visiting her bar again. A bruised and battered ego forced him to make the thirty-mile jaunt for booze, wasting valuable time and gas in the process.

"Women," he barked with a sneer. "They're nothin' but whores."

An unwelcome image of his mother flashed in his head.

"Especially that nasty crone. Damn demanding, alcoholic, ball-busting bitch. The only decent thing she ever did was give birth to me," he growled.

Following on Mommy Dearest's heels was the vision of his late wife —now resting in a shallow grave behind his trailer.

"That sick cunt should have kept her legs closed instead of offering her pussy to the town mechanic, Cletus. That whoremonger's damn lucky he's still alive."

Victor's anger and blood pressure soared.

"It's past time for that trash-mouthed, skanky bartender, Gina to disappear, just like my snatch-assed wife."

The vile words had no more left his lips when an explosion split the air.

His truck spontaneously swerved across the pavement.

Victor gripped the steering wheel and pumped the brakes as he watched chunks of rubber shoot into the air in his rearview mirror.

"A goddamn blowout. Cocksucker!" he bellowed.

He steered the truck to the packed-dirt shoulder. After inspecting the damage, he tossed the jack and spare to the ground.

"You're gonna pay for this, bitch."

Gina Scott wiped the condensation left by a bottle of beer from the bar's surface. The tinkling sound of the bell above the door had her lifting her head in time to see the chime fall to the floor. Her attempted repair of the alert had failed again.

"Dammit!" Nash—second youngest of the six Grayson brothers—cursed as he bent and plucked the bell from the floor. "I thought you fixed this damn thing, Gina."

"I thought I did, too." She shrugged. "Guess I should have used thicker wire."

Gina held out her hand as Nash strode toward her. He placed the bell in her palm and she tucked it beneath the bar. As the man sat down in front of her, she twisted the cap off a beer and passed it to him. She didn't bother asking what he wanted. Gina knew her customers well, especially the Grayson brothers.

In fact, she knew one of the nipple-tightening, sexy brothers in a toe-curling, sexual way.

Nate Grayson was her current lover, and twelve years her junior.

Gina tried not to fixate on how she was robbing the cradle. Instead, she chose to focus on the inexplicable chemistry they shared both in and out of bed.

She'd never meant to steal his virginity either. Nate had vowed to remain pure until marriage, but after a bitter altercation with Victor LaCroix, months ago, one thing led to another. Quarrelling with the asshat had left her weak and vulnerable. Two emotions Gina loathed. Nate had offered her comfort and she'd accepted. They'd spent that night in her bed feeding on one another like animals. Sex with the young stud was earthquakes, rockets, and freakin' volcanoes...the best she'd ever had. She couldn't stop making horizontal magic with him even if she'd wanted to. He'd ruined her for all other men and Gina was addicted to Nate in ways she didn't want to admit.

It would be a sad day when their affair was over. She knew it wouldn't last forever, a reality that made her stomach twist. Nate was too young. He had his whole life ahead of him. Someday he'd want to settle down and raise a family…want all the things Gina couldn't give him. Turning an expectant glance at the door, she hoped today wasn't that day.

"He's finishing up at the ranch. He'll be here in a few." Nash smirked.

Her eyes widened. Her heart sputtered and her throat went dry.

Busted!

She and Nate had gone to great lengths to try and keep their relationship private. Haven was a small town filled with a bevy of gossip-mongers who thrived on spreading rumors. Until now, the only Grayson brother privy to her and Nate's affair—as far as Gina knew—was his older brother Sawyer. But Nash's comment had her suspecting all the brothers knew that she and Nate were regularly fucking each other's brains out.

At a loss for words, Gina didn't know whether to play dumb, ignore Nash's remark, or thank him for the information. Opting to neither confirm nor deny a thing, she sent him a tight smile.

"You do know he's in love with you, right?"

Love?

Nash's declaration assailed her like a slap in the face.

With a wave of her hand, she dismissed his comment. "He'll grow out of it."

"I knew it," he snarled. "You're going to break his heart, aren't you?"

Gina bristled.

"That's a hateful thing to say. In case you failed to notice, Nate's a grown man who knows the difference between love and…"

She let the words die on her tongue. She hadn't discussed their affair with anyone. No way was she going to start now, especially with his brother of all people.

"Casual sex?" Nash supplied. His cocky grin irked her. "He'd held on to his virginity for a reason. He gave it to you because you're special to him, even if it's meaningless to you."

His insult scalded and sent her hackles rising.

"Ever since Sawyer and Brea's wedding last week," Nash continued, "all Nate's talked about is marriage."

Surely he isn't assuming that I'd be his bride...is he?

Tendrils of fear slid through her.

Gina had walked down the aisle once. It had turned out to be a living hell. She swore she'd never make another monumental mistake like that again.

"Nate will find a nice girl to settle down with someday."

Saying the words out loud left Gina feeling as if she'd just impaled a knife through her chest.

"And you're not a nice girl?" Nash pressed.

Gina scoffed. "You don't take a woman like me home to meet the parents."

"Why not?"

"Because I have a mouth like a sailor. I own a bar, and I'm twelve years older than Nate. I'm sure Norman and Nola Grayson have higher expectations for their son than the likes of me. Besides, Nate will want a family someday. My baby factory was surgically closed years ago."

A pang of regret pierced her heart. Gina's hysterectomy hadn't been by choice, but a necessity, to save her life. Ghosts of her past slipped out of the dark shadows in her mind. She quickly shoved them away. Now wasn't the time or place to revisit the gruesome life she'd left behind. Though she hadn't found the peace of mind she so desperately needed yet, she had found safety in Haven. It was a start.

Nash leveled an angry scowl at her. "Don't pass judgment on my folks. They're not the pretentious snobs you paint them to be. If my parents thought you and Nate were in love, they'd welcome you with open arms. Those are your own insecurities talking."

Yes, they were. Self-doubt had her by the nipples. The blades of vulnerability enveloping her scraped every inch of her flesh. But what chafed more was that the young man across from her, the one barely old enough to drink beer, possessed sage and profound insight beyond his years.

"Maybe. But you and I don't have a stellar track record when it comes to love."

Nash didn't say a word. In fact, he refused to even look at her. He simply tipped back his beer and drained the bottle.

Gina inwardly scolded herself for reminding him of the woman he'd loved and lost. Nash and Megan had been high school sweethearts and had been engaged until she pressed him to set a wedding date. Cold feet, insecurities, or pure, mule-headed stubbornness had caused Nash to balk. Rumor had it that after several heated arguments, Megan tossed back his engagement ring and slammed the door in his face. The two hadn't spoken to each other since. Even now, when they happened to cross paths at the bar, the air would turn arctic.

Of course, anyone with eyes could see they were miserable apart. But until Nash pulled his head out of his ass, misery was destined to be his only company.

"You could have Megan back in a heartbeat, you know that, right?" Nash turned his head, pinning Gina with a stony glare. "What's wrong, pot? Don't like it when the kettle calls you black?" She bit back a knowing smirk and twisted the cap off another beer. When Nash didn't acknowledge her jab, Gina shook her head. "Guess I'm not the only one who needs to own up to their insecurities."

"Fuckin' leave it alone," he grumbled.

"Exactly," she bit out. "Fuckin' leave me and Nate alone."

She set the beer in front of him, then turned and walked away.

Inside the frigid standing cooler, Gina sucked in a deep breath. She needed to chill out, or she'd rip Nash to shreds with her vicious tongue. Her head told her he was only looking out for his big brother, but rationale did nothing to quell the flames of annoyance licking her heart like a tiki torch.

Gina shoved a keg of beer onto its side before rolling it out of the cooler. Kicking the door closed behind her, she wrangled the heavy canister around the corner. When she looked up, she saw Noble, Nate's twin brother, behind her bar helping himself to a draw. She knew it wasn't her lover because the familiar tingle wasn't sliding down her spine.

"What the fuck do you think you're doing?" she barked, dressing him down.

Noble's eyes widened. "Getting a beer."

Turning on the charm, he flashed her a devilish grin. She suspected he'd used that same wicked smile to seduce the panties off every single woman in town. The tall cowboy with his striking handsome features and decadent chiseled body looked exactly like her lover in every way. The only telling difference between the twins was that Noble flaunted his suave, seductive prowess. Nate oozed his sexual confidence in the privacy of her bedroom.

Clutching his beer, Noble moved in close to her. He slung an arm around her waist and dropped a kiss to the top of her head. "Lighten up, sunshine. I knew you were busy."

~

NATE HAD SPENT THE DAY SADDLING, UNSADDLING, AND GROOMING horses on the family ranch outside of town. He'd rotated the animals to ensure that each child who attended Camp Melody—a respite for terminally ill and special needs kids—enjoyed a fresh but not too spirited mount.

The early October weather was unseasonably warm, and Nate had sweated a storm. He was anxious to grab a shower when dinner was done and head into Haven. But his brothers Nash and Noble seized the two bathrooms first, forcing Nate to wait an extra thirty minutes before he could scrub the smell of horse from his body.

Even his lingering annoyance with his brothers couldn't take the spring out of Nate's step when he hopped from his truck. Pocketing his keys, he strode toward the Hangover as excitement strummed through his veins. He was seconds away from laying eyes on the woman he'd been dreaming about all day. The woman he loved, Gina.

When Nate entered the bar and found his woman wrapped in the arms of his twin brother, rage born of jealousy consumed him. And when Noble kissed the top of Gina's head, pure possession pumped through his veins.

"Get your fucking hands off her," he bellowed as he ate up the floor in long, angry strides.

"Uh-oh." Noble grinned with a playful wink. "Looks like we've been caught, darlin'."

Nate knew his twin was only busting his balls, but it didn't placate the fury inside him. The Grayson boys had grown up bantering, teasing, and tormenting the hell out of each other, but this time Noble had crossed the line.

"Caught? Caught doing what?" A look of alarm crawled across Gina's gorgeous face. As she peeled out of Noble's grasp, she landed an open-handed slap to his chest. "Take your paws off me, asshole! I'm not one of your bed bunnies. And get the fuck out from behind my bar."

Nate was proud of his feisty woman for taking his dickhead twin to task. Noble flashed a triumphant grin, then joined a laughing Nash on the other side of the bar while Nate fought the urge to pound Noble's face in.

As if sensing his wrath, Gina sent him a gentle smile. "Nate, can you help me drag another keg from the cooler?"

"Sure." He narrowed his eyes at his twin. "Touch her again, asswipe, and I'll beat you fucking bloody. Got it?"

All traces of humor left Noble's face. He raised his hands in surrender. "I was just messing around, lover boy. No need to get your tampon sideways."

Nate grabbed Noble by the shirt and leaned in close to his face. Tension pulled his muscles up tight and hard. Fury rippled outward in powerful waves. "Fuck around with someone else. Gina's off-limits."

"Sorry, man. I didn't mean anything by it."

Nate released his brother's shirt.

Nash let out a low whistle and slapped Noble on the back. "You just got shit on."

"Shut the fuck up, or I'll shit on you," Noble countered with a smack on the back of Nash's head.

Ignoring the idiots, Nate locked eyes with Gina.

The rage inside him instantly melted, replaced by hunger and need. He flashed her a carnal smile and followed her to the back room. His eyes were glued to the sway of her ass and Nate moved in behind her, cupping her tempting cheeks. Gina stopped abruptly, then pivoted and pressed herself to his chest. Her tight nipples scraped the flesh beneath his shirt and he repositioned his hands on her ass. Aligning his hips to hers, Nate rocked into her, letting Gina feel his ready erection.

"I missed you, too," she whispered.

Lifting onto her tiptoes, she pressed her lips to his.

Though Nate had kissed her a million times, each time felt like the first. Sliding a hand to her hair, he fisted her mane and tilted her head back before delving his tongue deep inside her silky mouth. He ached to strip her down, slam her up against the wall, and drive balls deep inside Gina's tight, velvety pussy. Swallowing her tiny whimpers, Nate knew she wanted it just as badly.

"Two a.m. can't get here fast enough," he murmured as he nipped her neck.

"Maybe it'll be a slow night and I can close early." Her breathless words came out low and sultry.

"I'll be your bouncer tonight and kick everyone out at midnight."

Her throaty laugh nearly did him in. She looked up at him with pale blue pleading eyes. "But I want you now."

"I want you now, too." Nate pulled the fabric of her T-shirt down and dragged his tongue over the soft swell of her breast. "Want you to melt all over my tongue as I lick your sweet pussy and nibble on your clit."

Gina exhaled a blissful sigh. "You make it hard for me to work."

"You make me hard, just breathing."

Gina grinned and arched her heated pussy against him.

The air stilled in his lungs.

His cock swelled impossibly harder.

After giving his virginity to Gina, Nate understood his brothers' fascination with sex. But he was more than infatuated with her pussy; he was obsessed with everything about her...heart, mind, body, and soul.

Nate knew all the reasons they had to keep their relationship secret, but he was tired of hiding in her room, waiting for her to close up the bar before he could show her affection. That's why he'd decided to take things to the next level. The engagement ring he'd purchased for Gina two months ago was burning a hole in his pocket. Unfortunately, he hadn't yet told her he loved her. A blunder he planned to remedy, tonight.

"Nate."

Her mournful whimper made him smile.

She was as desperate to soar to the heavens as he was.

"What's wrong, baby?" he taunted, grinding his cock against her cunt.

"I'm as wet as you are hard."

"I know," he growled. "I can smell your tart juice and it makes my mouth water."

Gina stared up at him with that sexy pleading gaze that always turned him inside out. Her cheeks were flushed. Her breathing was shallow and ragged. He couldn't wait to tease and torment her body... couldn't wait to hear her scream his name as she exploded all over his dick.

It was going to be a long fucking night.

"If you two are going to stay in the cooler doing the nasty, I'm going to fetch myself another beer," Noble yelled from the other room.

"Fucking asshat," Nate mumbled under his breath.

Gina giggled before kissing him quickly. "I need to go back out there. The sooner I get everyone liquored up, the sooner I can lick you up...and down, and up and..."

Nate issued a guttural groan. "You're killing me, woman."

He begrudgingly pulled away from her. Her nipples were hard like gumdrops as they poked from beneath the fabric of her shirt. It took all the willpower he possessed not to drag the material off her body and latch his lips onto them. Gina dipped a glance to his cock and instinctively her pink tongue swiped at her bottom lip.

"Which keg do you need me to haul out for you?"

Dragging her gaze from his body, she pointed to the silver cylinder in the corner. Nate hefted the heavy barrel onto his shoulder and headed out of the room. While Gina poured Noble another beer, Nate placed both kegs inside the small cooler beneath the bar and tapped them. He loitered on his haunches, staring at her ass, dreaming about the night to come before rising and joining his brothers.

Nate's hopes of long, sweaty hours dragging orgasm after orgasm from Gina's hot body were dashed as the place filled with customers.

Megan unexpectedly sidled up beside Noble. Nate hadn't seen her arrive. Ignoring Nash altogether, she flashed Gina a smile. "Rum and Coke, please?"

"Are you married yet?" Nash asked, staring at Megan's reflection in the huge mirror behind the bar.

She sent him an irritated scowl. "You know I'm not."

Her tone was curt and clipped.

"Why not?" Nash smirked. "When you tossed your ring back at me, you said you were going to find someone else to marry. What happened?"

Nate watched the exchange with a sideways glance. He wanted to smack his brother upside the head for being such a prick. When Megan's chin started to quiver, he wanted to do a whole lot more than smack the dumb shit. Now he wanted to beat the fuck out of Nash.

Tension filled the air.

"Make it a double, please," Megan called out.

Gina nodded and filled the glass three-quarters full with rum.

"You plan on walking home tonight, right? We both know you rarely drink and that one alone will surely knock you on your ass." Nash finally turned to face his ex.

"How I get home or who I go home with is none of your business."

His brother bristled and clenched his jaw. Nate knew exactly how deep the teeth of jealousy sank into the skin. Anguish flared in his stubborn brother's eyes. But instead of trying to make amends with the woman he loved, Nash simply stood. He tossed a wad of bills on the bar, then turned and leveled Megan with a sardonic sneer.

"Just make sure you have a ring on your finger and a wedding date set before you let some fucker crawl on top of you. We wouldn't want your pristine reputation tarnished by some dickless prick knocking you up and skipping town, now would we?"

Megan tipped back the glass and emptied the contents as she flipped Nash the middle finger. She slammed the empty tumbler on the bar, turned on her heel, and stormed off to join her friends at a table near the jukebox.

"Fuck," Nash spat. "I need one of you to be sure she gets home safe. All right?"

Nate exchanged a quick look with Gina, who gently nodded.

Dammit! Instead of taking care of his own woman, Nate was going to have to babysit his brother's ex-girlfriend.

"I'll take care of her," Noble announced with a wolfish grin.

"You touch her...you die." Nash glared.

"What is it with you two?" Noble chided. "I've never seen more possessive bastards in my life. I'm not going to poach, even though I should. Someone sure as fuck needs to make you wake up and smell the fucking roses...force you to open your damn eyes and stop being such a hard-headed prick. You keep fucking up, and you're going to lose her for good."

"I already did." Nash stomped away and blasted out the front door.

"And this is why I'm never falling in love." Noble shook his head in disgust.

"It's not so bad." Nate flashed Gina a smile.

A look of terror slid across her face. The glass of white wine in her hand slipped from her fingers and crashed to the floor.

"Fuck!" Grabbing a towel, she dropped out of sight behind the bar.

"Need any help?" he asked.

"No. I-I got it."

There was fear in her voice. Nate worried his fingers over the ring in his pocket. Maybe he was moving too fast, but he shoved the notion away. They were made for each other, and dammit, he loved Gina.

When she stood up once again, she looked frazzled and nervous. She dragged a hand through her hair, sent him a tight smile, and went back to work.

Nate could watch her all night, and often did. While some saw Gina as brash and crude, he saw past her façade and recognized the graceful, poised, and independent woman beneath. Everything about her turned him on. She was a self-assured and strong woman who needed an even stronger, self-assured man. Nate was that man.

At eleven thirty, Noble called it a night. Taking on the brotherly duty assignment on his own, he hauled Megan and a couple of her inebriated girlfriends home before heading back to the ranch. Nate stayed perched on the barstool taunting Gina with murmured sexual innuendos. He liked watching her blush, liked seeing the hunger flare in her pale blue eyes, liked the way she bit her bottom lip and squirmed at the dirty things he promised to do to her.

An hour later, after most of the customers had left, Nate slipped upstairs to Gina's apartment, unnoticed. Lying naked in her bed—cock stiff, throbbing, and weeping—he breathed a sigh of relief when he heard her close and lock the front door.

When she entered the room, a broad smile spread over her sinful lips. "I just love coming home from work to find a naked man, with a massive hard-on, in my bed."

Shucking off her clothes, she crawled onto the mattress beside him. His cock leapt and leaked. He'd been waiting all night for this. Nate fisted a hand in her strawberry-blonde curls and pulled her lips to his. The kiss wasn't slow and sensual, but fierce and possessive. He couldn't drink her in fast enough, deep enough, or thoroughly enough.

"Wrap those pretty plump lips around me, baby. I need to feel your wicked mouth."

He guided her head down his body as Gina dragged her tongue along his flesh. He basked in her kitten-like moans as she nipped at his hot skin. Pausing, she swirled her slick tongue around his nipples and flicked the tips. He sucked in a hiss.

"Paybacks are going to be hell on you tonight, baby."

"I'm counting on it, cowboy," she purred.

Nate's laugh morphed into a groan when she wrapped her luscious lips around his pulsating dick. Silky, wet heat surrounded him. The swirl of her tongue and the sublime suction pulling at him made Nate's eyes roll to the back of his head.

"I love the things you do with your mouth," he murmured.

I love you. Nate wanted to say the words, but he was too lost in the sensation of Gina working her magical tongue up and down his aching shaft. She was burning him alive with her wicked skills...sucking, laving, and gently scraping her teeth over each thick, throbbing vein.

All too soon, his balls were churning...his seed was boiling. He commanded her to stop in a hoarse and raspy voice. But she didn't. He yanked on her hair, pulling her off him, only to be met with a sly grin stretching over her wet, swollen lips.

Gina arched her brows in a manufactured look of innocence. "What's wrong, sugar?"

"I'm going to explode in your mouth if I don't take a minute to settle down."

"You say that like it's a bad thing."

"Nothing you do to me is bad."

"Wanna bet?" She shot him an evil grin before sliding a finger inside her mouth.

When she pulled it back out, her digit was covered in glistening saliva, just like his cock. Pulling against his hold, Gina swallowed his shaft once more and cradled his balls in her palms. She massaged his sac, applying the perfect amount of pressure and friction, inside and out. Nate couldn't hold back. He grunted and rocked his hips. Pumping in and out of her mouth, he gripped her hair tightly as Gina swallowed him to the back of her throat. Releasing his sac, she traced the wet finger around the gathered rim of his ass.

The sensation startled him but felt fucking good. "What are you—"

His question morphed into a yell when she thrust her finger deep inside him.

She rubbed some magical spot that sent a burst of fire to engulf him.

Flames exploded up his spine.

Lights flashed behind his eyes.

Every muscle in his body grew taut.

With a feral roar, he jettisoned down her throat like a goddamn geyser. Thick ropes of come exploded from his cock, showering her hot mouth.

Gina issued a guttural moan as she sucked and swallowed every creamy drop.

Consumed in a blinding ecstasy he'd never felt before, Nate rode the mind-bending orgasm as she milked him dry.

She slowly eased her finger from his ass and lifted from his cock before flashing Nate a wide grin. "Bad things feel pretty damn good, don't they?"

Unable to form words, he simply nodded and stared at her in awe. While he wasn't sexually savvy like his brothers, Nate was more than willing to let Gina teach him all the naughty things she knew.

"Are you okay?" She softly chuckled.

"I think so," he choked out. "That was… Why didn't you warn me you were going to stick your finger up my ass?"

"Would you have let me?"

He shot her a scowl. "No. Probably not."

"That's why I didn't warn you." She laughed. "You're not mad, are you?"

"Mad? No. How could I be mad after that?"

"Good. If you want to, you can play with my ass."

"Oh, yeah?" Intrigued by her offer, he arched his brows.

"Uh-huh." She nibbled her bottom lip and gazed at his cock. "You're really big, but if we take it slow and use lots of lube, I think I can fit you up my ass."

That prospect had his sated cock growing hard again. "You want me to fuck you in the ass?"

She nodded shyly.

Oh, hell yes!

"Do you have lube?"

"Yes," she whispered softly.

Gina climbed off the bed and walked to her dresser. Bending, she opened the bottom drawer. Nate glanced at the condoms he'd placed on the nightstand, then rolled to his side and lifted onto an elbow. From his vantage point, he spied a virtual treasure trove of sex toys.

"You've been holding out on me, woman. Bring some of those babies over here. I wanna melt your spine the way you just did mine."

She turned, wearing a deer-in-the-headlights expression. A deep red blush painted her cheeks. "Wha...which ones?"

"Your favorites, of course."

Her blush grew a deeper crimson.

Nate chuckled. "Sweetheart, you just had your finger up my ass and invited me to work my dick into yours. We passed shy a long time ago, don't you think?"

"Are you sure you want to do this?"

"Yes. Are you?"

She pinched her lips together and nodded.

He'd never seen this timid side of her before, but Nate liked it. She woke a sleeping primal beast inside him and the damn thing roared to life. Climbing out of bed, he bent and lifted Gina into his arms. He kissed her hard as he carried her back to the mattress. His salty seed still stained her tongue, but he didn't mind. A whole new feeling of sexual empowerment had him by the balls. He was ready to take charge.

Easing her feet to the floor, he smiled. "Climb back onto the bed and get on your hands and knees. I'm taking you to the stars."

Excitement zipped across her eyes.

Yes, she wanted him to take control.

Nate wouldn't disappoint her.

Striding back to her secret toy chest, he selected a thick rubber dildo, a pretty pink vibe, and a tube of lube. When he turned around, he nearly swallowed his tongue. His brave and amazing Gina was positioned exactly how he'd instructed. Her swollen and glistening folds had his cock stretching and growing painfully harder. Nate stared at her tiny puckered opening and wondered how in the hell he was going to squeeze his dick through such a small and fragile hole without tearing her apart. The idea of causing her pain made his gut clench.

As if sensing his reluctance, Gina glanced over her shoulder and sent him a tender smile. "I know you haven't done this before, but—"

"I don't want to hurt you."

"You won't. I trust you, Nate."

He trusted her, too, trusted that if she couldn't accommodate his cock, she would tell him to stop. Nate set the items on the edge of the bed before quickly tearing open a condom. He smoothed the latex over his aching cock with one hand and caressed her supple, warm butt cheeks with the other.

Without a word, he dragged his fingers up her center, then dipped inside her hot tunnel.

Gina gasped and softly purred at his touch.

The scent of her heated spice filled his senses.

His mouth watered.

Nate's cock jerked, eager and ready.

The hungry beast within broke free of its chain. He gripped Gina's ass. Spreading her cheeks apart, he lunged his mouth over her inviting folds. Using the flat of his tongue, he lapped and licked as her familiar spicy flavor coated and ignited his taste buds. He wanted to eat at her all night, but the invitation to explore her dark, forbidden passage urged him to move forward.

While he explored her smooth, slick cunt with his fingers, Nate dragged his tongue up and over her puckered hole. The muscles of her pussy clutched around his digits. Gina bucked and groaned as he teased her tiny passage.

"You like being my dirty girl, don't you?"

"Yes." Her breathless cry went straight to his cock.

Nate couldn't wait to feel her tightness strangle him. Easing back, he removed his fingers and watched as her tunnel clutched at the emptiness.

"Easy, my nasty little princess. I'm going to fill you up...fill you full and stretch you tight...make you shatter for me," he assured in a soft growl.

"Nate," she wailed.

He watched a shiver ripple through her and smiled as he picked up the vibe and turned it on. Dancing the tip lightly over her clit, Nate teased and tormented her swollen nub before burying the wand inside her needy pussy. Gina whimpered and rocked her hips, sensually riding the pseudo cock like she rode him night after night. His dick jerked as if jealous of the plastic phallus, but Nate tempered his impatience. Soon, he'd be wedged inside the heavenly, tight splendor of her ass.

After pulling the vibe out, he placed the bulbous head of the dildo to her pussy lips. He coated the rubber tip with her glistening juices before he began working the heavy slab in and out of her clutching tunnel.

"Take the vibe and press it to your clit for me," he instructed as he passed her the wand.

Like a good girl, she settled the buzzing toy atop her sensitive nub. The walls of her pussy gripped the dildo and held it in place. Nate coated his fingers in lube, then slathered the cool gel over her crinkled opening. Sliding the dildo in and out of her pussy, he pressed the tip of his finger through her tightly gathered flesh.

"Yes. Yes. Oh, god. More! Please, Nate. I need more."

Adding more lube, he drove his finger deep inside her ass. Her smooth liquid heat engulfed him and when her velvety muscles started to suckle his digit, Nate wanted to howl. But it was Gina's desperate keening cries that nearly did him in as he drove his finger in and out of her blissfully tight ass.

"Oh, god. I'm— I can't..." She screamed and shattered.

Bucking and wailing, she gripped at his knuckle. Nate wanted to rip the dildo from her cunt, plunge deep inside her pussy just to feel her walls spasm around him. He feared he wouldn't recover as quickly if he came again so soon.

"That's it. Come for me. Come long and hard. I'm going to wring you dry of orgasms tonight."

"Yes. More. Stretch me. I need your cock," she gasped. "More...more fingers."

Sex with Gina had always been incredible, but this...this was amazing. She'd never been so wild and uninhibited before. He loved it... loved her for showing him how unrestrained she could be.

"I'll work you wide so you can take every inch of me. I'm going to fuck you so hard you won't sit for a month...make you scream until you won't be able to talk."

"Please..." she moaned.

It was both torture and bliss as he worked two, then three fingers into her taut dark hole, thinning her fragile tissue. Nate's dick stood at attention, throbbing and aching in demand.

It was now or never.

A ripple slid down his spine as he fisted lube over his cock. Coating the condom thoroughly, he moved in behind Gina and removed his fingers. He aligned his fat crest to the opening of her ass and gently pushed against her snug rim.

Gina cried out and Nate instantly pulled away.

"No," she wailed. "Don't you dare stop! Fuck me, Nate. Fuck my ass, dammit."

His sweet, snuggly kitten had turned into a full-blown hellcat.

It turned him on even more.

Sweat dripped down his face as he inched his thick crown through her narrow ring. He was instantly surrounded in her hot, tight heaven. Gina moaned and Nate growled.

Adding more lube, he painstakingly fed inch after inch of his strangled dick inside her. It seemed to take forever before he was finally fully seated within her scorching tightness. It took all the will he possessed to keep from fucking her silky nirvana with a frenzy, but Nate persevered even when her molten walls fluttered and gripped, adjusting to his invasion.

With the vibe still pressed to her clit, Gina's shoulders slumped to the mattress. Reaching between her legs, she began fucking her cunt with the dildo. Nate bit back a roar as the fake dick rubbed against him against the thin membrane inside her.

Gripping her hips, he closed his eyes and sucked in a trembling breath as he fought to hold back the pressure of his mounting orgasm.

"Faster, dammit!" Gina rasped. "You're burning me alive."

Without thinking, Nate drew back his hand and slapped her ass. "I'm in charge now, sweetheart."

Gina yelped first, then began to purr and moan. When she wiggled her hips as if silently begging for more, Nate couldn't help but grin. "You need me to spank you like a bad girl, don't you?"

"Oh, god," she mewled.

Nate landed another swat before he eased back and shoved inside a tiny bit harder.

"Answer me."

"Yes," she answered in a long-suffering moan.

Oh, hell. *This just keeps getting better by the second.*

He could barely contain himself. Picking up the pace, he began fucking her in earnest as he alternated between drawing his palms over her orbs and slapping her supple flesh. Nate couldn't keep from moaning each time she tightened around his dick.

Driving in and out of her ass, Gina's heightened cries told him she was close again.

"Such a sweet dirty girl." He grunted. "That's it...take my cock...take it up your ass, my gorgeous, nasty princess."

"Nate," she cried out again.

"You want to come for me again, don't you, sweetheart?"

"Yes. Oh, god. Yes!"

"Me, too. Come for me, Gina. Shatter all over me, baby."

She screamed his name as she bore down and fragmented, taking him with her. Her muscles clamped around him with such force that Nate saw stars. Gripping her hips in a vise-like hold, he slammed in and out of her as he exploded with another spine-melting orgasm.

She might very well be the death of him, but he couldn't think of a better or more blissful way to go than balls deep in her ass.

GINA LAY IN A BONELESS HEAP ON THE BED. QUIVERING AFTERSHOCKS rippled through her sated body. Nate had eased both his cock and the dildo from inside her. He'd taken the vibe and turned it off before returning to her with a warm, wet cloth. His murmured praises echoed in her ears as he cleaned her up. All Gina could do was softly purr. She couldn't even form words yet to thank him.

Slowly, her brain cells began firing once again and a wave of embarrassment slid through her.

I did not just do that with him, did I? Yeah, I fucking did. Son of a bitch!

With an inward groan, she closed her eyes, wondering if she'd scarred him for life.

Gina had planned to introduce the innocent boy to a little ass play, slowly, not give him the whole damn lesson at once. She'd wanted to work him up to a bit of slap and tickle before moving onto bondage with some silk scarves. Never had she intended to baptize him by fire so soon, but to her delight, Nate had adapted well and even taken full control. And it was her fantasy come true. While she wasn't into the whole Master/slave thing, she liked a bit of spice here and there. He'd more than welcomed her hidden kinky side.

Nate joined her on the bed. Wrapping his arm around her waist, he rolled to his side and cradled her against him.

He pressed a soft kiss to the top of her head. "Are you all right?"

"Mmhm," she answered sleepily.

"Yeah, me, too. That was amazing."

She grinned, relieved that she hadn't totally freaked him the hell out.

"I'm going to enjoy making love to you like that every night of my life."

"What do you mean...every night of your life?" She lifted her head and raised her lashes.

"I mean forever, Gina. You and me...forever." He stroked his hand up and down her arm. "I love you. I want to marry you and make you my wife."

No. No. No. This can't be happening!

The happy, sated glow suffusing her instantly vanished.

Ice chugged through her veins as a foreboding wave of panic swelled within.

You're going to break his heart, aren't you? Nash's premonition merged with Nate's misguided vow of love and marriage and echoed in

Gina's brain. No matter how gently she tried to let him down, Nate was going to be crushed. She was sure to devastate him.

"Nate," she began softly, unable to mask the sorrow in her voice. "I'm much too old for you, sugar."

"No, you're not. Age is just a number."

"It's not only the difference in our ages…it's…"

She felt as if she were running naked through a minefield while trying to dodge bullets.

"What else is there?" His tone was harsh and defensive.

Gina struggled to choose the right words. "I know you think you're in love with me, but—"

"I am in love with you, goddammit!" He sat up quickly and pinned her with an angry glare. "Are you saying that you're not in love with me?"

"I-I-I like you…like you very much. We've had a lot of good times together, but—"

"Good times?" He launched from the bed and jerked his jeans off the floor. "Is that all this has been for you…good times? Christ, was this all some kind of premeditated plan? Did you what…one day decide to take my virginity, have some good times, then kick me to the curb? 'Cause I gotta tell you, this isn't much of a good time for me right now. Was I nothing but a challenge, or just a convenient boy toy for you to play with?"

His accusations were stripping the flesh from her bones.

"No. You're my friend…a good friend."

A humorless scoff rolled off his tongue. "How many other good friends in town have you fucked, Gina?"

The pain in his eyes and the disgust lining his face sliced her heart in two.

Letting him go shouldn't hurt this badly…why was her soul breaking inside? If she was honest with herself, she already knew the answer. She simply didn't want to acknowledge the fact that she'd fucked up and had fallen in love with him.

How?

How could she not? Nate was kind, funny, honest, and treated her like a queen.

When?

She couldn't hide behind lies anymore. Gina knew she'd started falling for Nate from the very beginning. She'd foolishly believed that her vow to never love again would supersede emotion. She'd been wrong.

Gina had no one to blame but herself for the two hearts that were breaking tonight.

While she desperately wanted to wrap her arms around Nate's rugged neck and pledge her love to him for all time, she couldn't. Couldn't steal any more of the compassion and tenderness he'd so generously given her. Couldn't saddle him with a commitment he'd one day loathe and regret.

Though it felt like a white-hot knife through the heart, she knew it was better to hurt him now than chain him to a lifetime of misery. Somehow, Gina had to find the strength to end her affair with Nate, tonight.

"A few, but they didn't mean anything…not like you, but I-I can't do permanent relationships. It's not you, Nate, it's—"

"Spare me." He pinned her with a feral sneer as he buttoned his jeans. "Don't feed me that 'it's not you, it's me' bullshit. Tell me the truth. What the hell were we doing together? Fucking? Is that all you thought this was? I didn't. I thought we were learning about each other so we could build a life together. Obviously, I'm just a living, breathing form of another battery-operated boyfriend you have shoved in your goddamn drawer."

"You were always more to me than that." Biting back tears, she crawled out of bed, tugged on her robe, and cautiously moved toward him.

Nate shook his head, held up his hands, and took a step back. "Answer me. What the hell have we been doing together?"

His caustic tone sent a shiver through her. Gina dragged a hand through her riotous curls and let the lies that would ensure him a happy life roll off her tongue. "We were having fun."

Nate clenched his jaw. His nostrils flared. And his whole body turned rigid as he pinned her with an icy glare. "Having fun. I see. Well, it has been fun. And now that I've made a fool of myself, it's time for me to go. Thanks for everything. I'm sure you'll find another friend to have fun with in no time. Take care of yourself."

As he turned and headed toward the door, Gina wanted to stop him. She wanted to wrap her arms around him and beg him not to go. Tell him that she loved him, too, but she couldn't. All she could do was stand there and try to keep from coming apart at the seams as he stormed out the door, slamming it behind him.

Tears filled her eyes.

Her body trembled.

And Gina felt her heart shatter once again.

She flopped down on the edge of the bed, covered her face with her hands, and cried. Consumed by the pain of losing Nate, and the guilt of hurting him so deeply, she sobbed like a child. She held on tightly to keep from falling back into the bowels of hell she'd once clawed and scraped herself out of. The price of reclaiming her soul and discovering her own identity—after the mental abuse delivered by her ex-husband, Barrett—had cost her dearly.

She'd struggled to survive his emotional torture and often wished that Barrett would lose control…take his abuse to a physical level. Then she could show the world what kind of pain he was inflicting on her psyche. He'd finally fulfilled that wish, but it had cost her the precious life growing inside her womb when he'd kicked her down the stairs. The emergency hysterectomy saved her, and when she was released from the hospital, she packed her bags and left to find a new beginning.

But losing Nate paled in comparison to that nightmare. She hadn't loved Barrett, not the way she did Nate.

The walk down memory lane singed her soul.

Drying her eyes, she stood and made her way downstairs to the bar.

After pouring a double of Jack on the rocks, Gina sat down at one of the tables and tipped back her glass. She welcomed the burn, hoping it would extinguish or at least ease her blistering heart.

Victor peered out from the alley between Toot's Café and Dresher's Hardware, keeping his eyes locked on the Hangover. Even though the lights had been turned off over an hour ago, he was biding his time. He knew Nate Grayson—the pussy-whipped, ass-licking twit—was still inside. No doubt he was slapping his dick inside Gina's sloppy cunt that very moment. The thought made Victor's stomach sour. He'd taken a blast of shrapnel to his crotch in Vietnam. Though they surgically reattached his dick, he could piss, but his cock never got hard again. Victor held a great deal of contempt for men who could still get it up.

Suddenly, the door of the bar flew open. The Grayson kid stormed to his truck and took off out of town. Victor narrowed his eyes, hoping to catch a glimpse of the bar owner, but the lazy slut hadn't even mustered the courtesy of walking her meat-maggot to the door.

"This will be like shooting fish in a barrel," Victor snickered.

Darting a glance up and down the street to ensure he was alone, Victor patted the hankie in his pants pocket—the one doused in chloroform, and slowly eased from his hidey-hole. Keeping close to the buildings on Main Street, he quickly worked his way toward the bar.

"No more driving thirty fucking miles. No more flat tires. No more cunt to contend with," he spat under his breath.

Gripping the doorknob, he gave it a gentle twist. Much to his surprise and joy, it was unlocked.

I just hit the fucking lottery.

Biting back a cheer, he quietly pushed the portal open and eased inside. Careful to keep the latch from snapping out against the strike plate, he held the knob and quietly released the mechanism. It slid into place without a sound.

The neon beer sign behind the bar cast an eerie shade of red over the room. Scanning the area near the bar, Victor was delighted to see Gina sitting in a chair, alone. An empty glass lay on the table in front of her. Her eyes were rimmed red. If Victor could have gotten hard, the sight of her distress would have given him more than a chubby.

Aw, looks like the lovebirds might have had a quarrel. Bitch is going to suffer a hell of a lot more before I'm done with her.

Inching closer, Victor inadvertently stepped on a squeaky floorboard. Gina snapped her head his way. A look of shock and a hint of fear glided over her face.

He flashed her a horrible smile.

"We're closed, LaCroix. Go home."

Victor slowly advanced, intently studying her body language. He could see the tension drawing up her shoulders...watched her slide a gaze to the bar. He knew she wanted Martha...the Louisville Slugger she kept tucked away there. The same weapon she'd threated him with months ago. Moving in a wide arc, he blocked her path. She'd have to go through him to retrieve the ominous bat.

"I said we're closed."

Her voice didn't hold the same level of irritation. No, Victor could hear her fear...smell it in the air. It made his heart race, his gut flutter, and his mind fill with all the agonizing pain she'd endure for him.

"I didn't come here for a drink, you stupid slut. I came here for you."

As he lunged toward her, Gina launched from her seat, shoving the wooden table onto its side to block him. Like an Olympic sprinter, she raced up the stairs to the second floor.

"You can run, you evil cunt, but you can't hide. Not from Victor LaCroix." He let out a maniacal laugh as he climbed the steps two at a time. "I'm going to catch you, you miserable bitch. And then we're going to have a party...a pain party. You'll be the guest of honor."

He reached the entrance of the room she'd disappeared into and was met with a door slammed in his face. Victor stepped back, raised his leg, and kicked with all his might. The hollow wood splintered.

Gina screamed as she raced toward the nightstand by the bed. Unsure if she was going to pull a gun on him, Victor ate up the distance between them.

"Get away from me, you crazy son of a bitch," Gina yelled.

But it was too late. Victor wrapped his arm around her waist and yanked her back flush against his chest. He reached inside his pants pocket and withdrew the chemical-laced handkerchief and pressed it over her face.

She fought like hell and he enjoyed it immensely.

The sound of her muffled screams made his blood sing.

She kicked and writhed, pulling the sheets off the mattress. He heard the lamp tumble to the floor and shatter.

Victor laughed in her ear as he turned his head to keep from inhaling the toxic fumes.

"Fight all you want. It ain't gonna change nuthin'. You're mine now… all mine, and may God have mercy on your soul, bitch."

NATE SAT IN HIS TRUCK PARKED ON THE DRIVEWAY OF THE FAMILY RANCH. Fueled by fury, tears stung his eyes. But he refused to bitch out and cry. Instead, he gripped the steering wheel and tried to calm his ragged breaths while mentally wrapping a tourniquet around his bleeding heart.

His plans of happy ever after with Gina had been destroyed. He'd been an idiot to believe she'd loved him, too. But dammit, the time they'd spent together meant something to her. He saw it in her eyes. What he didn't know was why she insisted on dismissing her feelings for him so vehemently. Confusion swirled in his brain.

"You're not going to solve anything tonight. Best to go back and talk to her tomorrow," he mumbled to himself.

Climbing from the truck, Nate trudged toward the house. His feet felt like cinder blocks, his eyes like sand. The acrid smell of smoke on the wind had him scanning the fields. Turning his attention back toward the house, he spied Nash sitting on the deck, cigarette in hand. Nate scowled and hurried toward his younger brother.

"What the hell are you doing? If Mom catches you smoking, she'll tan your hide."

"Ease up off me. I ate enough shit tonight from your girlfriend."

"What are you talking about?"

"Gina...your fuck buddy. She was busting my balls about Megan earlier."

"First of all, she's not my girlfriend or my fuck buddy. Second of all, you should listen to her and pull your head outta your ass and patch things up with Megan. You two are so pathetically miserable without each other it's ridiculous. Both of you are in a contest to see who can hold on to their stupid pride the longest."

"Get off my dick. Better yet, take yours back to town and stick it in Gina."

Nate grabbed his brother by the front of his shirt, hauled him off the porch, and slammed a fist into his jaw. Nash flew backward and landed on his ass in the yard.

"Don't ever talk like that about her again. She's not a whore."

"Hit me again and I'll throw you a beating you'll never forget, you little bitch."

Nash stood, flicked his cigarette butt in the air, and brushed off his jeans before storming into the house. Nate seethed as he watched his brother's retreat.

Both of them had demons to battle now.

He trudged into the house and crawled into bed. It seemed he'd been asleep but a minute when his alarm sounded. Rolling over, Nate turned off the annoying buzzer and groaned as he rolled out of bed. Scrubbing a hand over his face, he stumbled to the bathroom. When he glanced up in the mirror, the haunted reflection staring back made him cringe.

"This is going to be a long-assed day," he grumbled and climbed into the shower.

As predicted, the day dragged on and on.

When dinner was done, he carried his plate to the sink where his mom, Nola, was loading the dishwasher.

"You've been quiet all day, sweetheart. Something troubling you?"

"No, Ma. Everything's fine," Nate lied.

She set the pan she'd been rinsing down and picked up a wooden spoon, then smacked him on the ass with it.

"What the hell was that—"

"Lying isn't allowed in this house," she scolded. "What's wrong?"

"It's personal, Ma."

"That's all you had to say." She lifted onto her toes and kissed his cheek. "If you need to talk, I'm always here for you, son."

"I know. Thanks. Dinner was great."

She sent him a smile but concern still lingered in her eyes. As he turned toward the hallway to claim one of the showers, Noble and his youngest brother, Norris, shoved him out of the way and raced into the bathrooms.

"Goddammit!" he spat.

Thirty minutes later, Noble exited the bathroom wearing a towel around his waist and a taunting grin curled on his lips. "I'll be happy to keep Gina company for you until you haul your slow ass to the bar."

"You put one hand on her and you won't live to see tomorrow."

Noble threw back his head and laughed. "You couldn't give me a black eye, pussy, and we both know it."

When Nate drew back his fist, Noble ducked and raced to his room.

"Now who's the pussy?"

As the hot water pounded at his aching muscles, Nate rehearsed the things he intended to say to Gina.

He'd done everything wrong last night. She'd hurt his feelings and instead of manning up and talking things through, he'd done what all the Grayson brothers did…he'd lost his temper and lashed out. He needed to knock the chip off his shoulder and find out why Gina was afraid to love. In the wee hours of the morning, he'd finally realized there wouldn't have been such hurt in her eyes if she didn't love him. The anguish he'd seen told him the time they'd shared was more than simple fun.

She'd lied to him and Nate aimed to find out why.

"And if I don't get my ass moving, I'll never get the answers I need," he griped to himself.

With a towel wrapped around his waist, Nate gathered up his dirty clothes and hurried to his bedroom. He could feel the cell phone in his jeans vibrating and hastily pulled the device out as the call ended.

Hoping it had been Gina, he checked the display only to discover he'd missed six calls from Noble.

What the fuck? Nate wondered as he quickly dialed his brother back.

"You spend more time in the shower than a woman," Noble spat.

"You call more than a nagging wife. What the hell do you want?"

"You need to get your ass over to the Hangover. Gina's gone."

"What do you mean gone?" Nate's heart sputtered and then began thundering like a drum in his chest and ears.

"I mean someone's taken her…kidnapped her. There was some kind of struggle because the place is a wreck. Jasper's here now, but dammit, man…someone's got her…taken her against her will."

The room spun. The drumming in Nate's ears grew into a deafening buzz as his stomach threatened to purge the supper he'd just eaten. Swallowing back the bitter bile rising in the back of his throat, Nate trembled.

"I'm on my way," he barked.

Panicked and filled with fear, he threw on his clothes, tugged on his boots, and then ran to his truck. In a cloud of dust and gravel, Nate barreled down the driveway before skidding onto the paved road. Slamming his foot down on the accelerator, he sped like a bat out of hell toward Haven.

A block from the bar, the street and sidewalks were crowded with people. News of Gina's abduction had traveled fast. Gripped with terror, Nate bolted out of the truck and ran toward the building. Before he could reach the bar, his older brother Sawyer, and his new wife, Brea, intercepted him. Sawyer gripped Nate's arm and dragged him into the alcove of the flower shop four doors down from the Hangover.

"Get your fucking hands off me," Nate spat. "I need to get down there."

"No. You need to chill out if you don't want the whole damn town knowing about you and Gina. It's not only your reputation you need to protect," Sawyer tersely explained. "Noble called me when he couldn't reach you. Brea and I arrived on the scene the same time as Jasper. He's still inside doing his cop thing, but he asked us if we knew if anyone had a grudge against Gina. I drew a blank then, but I have a sneaking suspicion who took her. I'll need to talk to—"

"Who the fuck would want to..." The nasty confrontation she'd had months ago careened through his brain.

"Victor LaCroix," the two men said together.

"But that was ages ago. It doesn't make sense. Why would he wait until now to... Fuck! I need to get over there."

Before he could take a step, Sawyer's strong hand splayed over Nate's chest, pinning him against the wall.

"You're not going anywhere near that demented prick's trailer. Let me talk to Jasper and tell him to drive out to Victor's place and look for Gina."

Sawyer was out of his fucking mind. Gina could be dead by the time the cop decided to pay LaCroix a visit. If her life was to be spared, it had to be now! Sawyer knew Nate wanted to haul ass to the bastard's mobile home, and would no doubt hog-tie him to keep him in Haven. Nate had to choke down the urgency rising inside him and pretend he was on board with his brother's suggestion.

"You're right. LaCroix might kill her if anyone but Jasper shows up." Nate hoped his act was at least partially believable. "Go tell Jasper about the scene we witnessed at the bar. Tell him now. Light a fire under his ass."

"Okay," Sawyer replied. "You two wait here. I'll be back."

As his brother walked away, Nate glanced back at his truck. It was only a couple of yards from him. If he could distract Brea, he could sprint away and be out of town before she could alert Sawyer.

Dragging a gaze all around, Nate looked for someone or something to draw Brea's attention. That's when he spied Emmett Hill, the town's slightly delusional Bigfoot hunter and World War II veteran, hobbling toward the crowd. The old man's coveted 1945 Browning A5 shotgun was slung over his shoulder.

"I'll be right back," Nate announced to Brea. "I want to ask Emmett if he saw anything unusual."

"You mean besides Bigfoot?" Brea asked wryly.

"Yeah." Nate forced a chuckle, then turned and ran toward the elderly man.

"What's all the ruckus down yonder?" Emmett asked.

"Not sure," Nate lied. "Mind if I borrow your shotgun?"

"What fer?"

"I-I..."

"You saw him! You saw that big, hairy bastard, didn't you? Where is he? Where is the pesky Bigfoot?" Emmett slid the gun off his shoulder and peered down the alley through its scope.

"No. I didn't see Bigfoot, but I need to save Gina. Someone kidnapped her from the bar and—"

"Goddamn bikers. I heard 'em…heard a whole mess of them loud-assed motors rumbling through town yesterday. Damn Devil's Angels or whatever they call themselves. I bet they took her and—"

"It wasn't bikers," Nate exhaled, trying to hold on to his quickly evaporating patience. "I think Victor LaCroix has her. I need your gun. Mine are back at the ranch."

"Never leave home without your weapon, boy. Didn't your daddy ever—"

"Emmett!" Nate cut him off. "Are you going to give me your gun or not?"

"Victor LaCroix, you say?" Nate nodded. "Never have liked that sum'bitch. He's got lifeless eyes, like a shark. Never trust a—"

"Emmett!" Nate growled. "I need your gun."

"To hell with it. I'm going with you. If anyone's gonna put a bullet in that bastard LaCroix, it's gonna be me."

Nate suspected that the old coot couldn't hit the broad side of a barn anymore, but there'd be time on the drive for him to figure out a way to claim Emmett's gun.

"Great. Get in my truck. Let's go," Nate instructed.

Darting a nervous glance Brea's way, he was relieved to find her staring at the still-growing crowd. He'd get an earful from both Sawyer and Jasper, but Nate didn't care. Gina was all that mattered. Nate would move mountains and give his own life to save her.

Victor LaCroix was a dead man.

Gina had woken several times, briefly. Each time, Victor had pressed the cold, chemical-filled cloth to her face. When she floated to the surface again, sunlight streamed in from a gap in the curtain.

Her head was pounding.

Terror thrummed through her veins.

A vile-tasting rag had been shoved into her mouth, and duct tape covered her lips.

She lay tied to a dirty, sweat-stained mattress.

Her fingers were numb, but circulation was the least of Gina's worries.

Victor LaCroix paced back and forth at the foot of the bed. His features were twisted in rage.

Gina was on the verge of a full-blown panic attack as her fear mounted. She didn't know when the crazy fuck was going to snap and physically unleash his hatred on her. God only knew what kind of terror he had in store for her, but she was certain it was going to be brutal.

When he stopped and gazed down at her with an evil smile, her heart nearly leapt from her chest.

"The weather forecast isn't calling for rain until next week," he announced.

What the fuck? He knocked me out, hauled me to his filthy trailer, and tied me up to talk about the goddamn weather?

"Not much of a chance, only thirty percent for Monday and forty percent on Tuesday. Guess I'm gonna have to keep you around and play with you over the weekend."

Gina struggled to align meaning to his cryptic statement.

Victor laughed, obviously pleased that she didn't understand.

"You ain't the brightest cunt in the bed, are you?" he snarled. "I didn't think you were to begin with. Let me explain it to you, nice and slow. See, we're going to have to wait for the rain to come so it'll make the ground nice and soft. That way, I can dig you a big ol' comfy grave right next to my cunt-faced wife, Mable." Hatred gleamed in his cold, brown eyes. "After I slice you up, I'll toss you in beside her, and you two worthless bitches can spend eternity next to each other. Doesn't that sound like fun?"

Panic surged like lightning through her. Dread tingled up her limbs and down her spine. Gina closed her eyes and inhaled a shallow breath through her nose as a loud knock came from the other room.

Victor jerked his head toward the sound. Rage crawled across his face once more.

"You make one sound, whore, and whoever's out there is gonna be added to your grave. You got it?"

Gina nodded. She sent up a silent prayer that someone had come to save her.

Victor leveled her with a warning glare. "I'm not fucking around, bitch. Not a goddamn peep."

She nodded again, sending the pounding in her head to a sickening level.

The knocking from the other room increased.

Gina released a mighty exhale through her nose as Victor turned and walked away.

"I'm coming. I'm coming. For fuck's sake, keep your boxers on. Can't a man live in peace?"

Gina heard the squeak of a door. She held her breath and listened intently.

"What the fuck do you want, you crazy ol' fool?"

"I see old age hasn't taught you any manners yet." The old man's voice was hauntingly familiar. Gina closed her eyes and tried to place it with a face.

Emmett Hill.

She didn't know what the crazy but sweet old man was doing at Victor's trailer, but Gina hoped it wasn't to get himself killed.

"Manners are for pansies. You didn't answer me, Emmett. What the fuck are you doing here?" Victor barked.

"What I always do…hunting Bigfoot, you stupid buffoon."

"Well, he sure as fuck ain't here sipping tea with me, so go away."

"Now wait a cotton-pickin' second," Emmett squalled. "Did you see anything strange out here last night?"

"What do you mean?" Victor's tone was laced with fear.

"I mean this."

Gina didn't know what Emmett was talking about, but then again, she seldom did.

"What the fuck is that?"

"It's hair off a Bigfoot, you igit," Emmett scolded. "I found it over yonder on that tree branch."

"You stupid sum'bitch. That's nothing but dog hair."

"Oh, really? Well, then what's that?"

All of a sudden there was a huge explosion. The trailer shook and Gina's muffled scream resonated in her ears.

"Don't move, cocksucker, or I'll blow your brains out!"

Gina knew that voice by heart.

Nate!

Oh, thank God.

She screamed beneath the gag and thrashed on the bed. The ropes cut into her flesh, but Gina didn't care. All she wanted was to make enough noise to draw him to her.

"You're a dead man, Grayson. Nobody breaks into my house and holds a gun to my head," Victor bellowed.

"Go... Check out this filthy piss hole," Nate said.

"I'm on it," Emmett replied.

"Where's Gina? I know you took her. You've got five seconds to tell me where she is before I shove this shotgun down your throat and blow your fucking head off."

Pull the trigger! Pull the fucking trigger! her mind screamed.

Emmett poked his head into the room. His smoky blue eyes widened before they filled with sorrow. "I found her. She's alive."

"Get back out here," Nate yelled.

"Let me free her first."

"No. Come help me tie this fucker up. Then I'm going to need you to keep this gun at his head," Nate yelled.

"Sorry, sweetie, but I think your boyfriend wants to rescue you." Emmett shot her a wink and hurried away.

In the distance a siren wailed.

Tears spilled from her eyes.

Relief flooded her veins.

The terror slowly began melting from her body.

Long seconds passed before Nate rushed into the room. He stared at her and paled. Then his features turned stormy and his eyes filled with tears as a howl of rage and anguish tore from his throat.

He rushed to her side and yanked a knife from his pocket.

"Hang on, baby. I'm going to cut you free," he whispered.

Nate made quick work of the ropes before he gently cradled her against his chest. Gina couldn't feel her limbs and she struggled to peel the tape from her mouth.

"Let me," Nate whispered. "I'm sorry, love, this is going to hurt."

He quickly yanked the duct tape off. Gina spit the rag from her mouth. She let out a cry and pressed her numb fingers to her lips. She wasn't surprised to find them bleeding, but she didn't care. Nate clutched her, burying his face against her neck as she sobbed.

"I was so fucking scared." His voice cracked and Gina knew he was crying, too. "You're safe now, baby. I've got you. I love you...love you so much."

"Oh, god, Nate. I love you, too," she wept.

He pulled back and sent her a watery smile. "I knew it! I fucking knew it!"

"But—"

"Shhh. Not now. We'll figure the rest out later. Right now, I just want to hold you."

He wiped her tears with the pad of his thumb, then bent and placed a feather-soft kiss to her painful lips.

"Did Victor...did he..."

"No. He didn't rape me. You saved me before he could"—a tremor racked her body and another flood of tears spilled free—"cut me up and bury me next to his wife."

Nate cupped her cheeks and gazed into her eyes. "No one is ever going to hurt you again. I promise."

Gina closed her eyes and nuzzled against him, drinking in his vow, his warmth, and his love.

"Come on, baby...let's get you home."

He wrapped her in the sheet, lifted her off the bed, and carried her out of the room. They passed Emmett and Jasper—who was slapping handcuffs onto Victor's wrists—and stepped out into the cool evening air.

Nate had saved her from death...saved her from a life void of love. Gina had found her peace of mind...found her future, right here in his safe, strong arms.

And she was never letting go.

ABOUT JENNA JACOB

USA Today Bestselling author Jenna Jacob paints a canvas of passion, romance, and humor as her alpha men and the feisty women who love them unravel their souls, heal their scars, and find a happy-ever-after kind of love. Heart-tugging, captivating, and steamy, Jenna's books will surely leave you breathless and craving more.

A mom of four grown children, Jenna and her alpha-hunk husband live in Kansas. She loves reading, getting away from the city on the back of a Harley, music, camping, and cooking.

Meet her wild and wicked fictional family in Jenna's sultry series: The Doms of Genesis. Become spellbound by searing triple love connections in her continuing saga: The Doms of Her Life (co-written with the amazing Shayla Black and Isabella LaPearl). Journey with couples struggling to resolve their pasts and heal their scars to discover unbridled love and devotion in her contemporary series: Passionate Hearts. Or laugh along as Jenna lets her zany sense of humor and lack of filter run free in the romantic comedy series: Hotties of Haven.

To be notified of new releases or sales,
join Jenna's Mailing List: www.bit.ly/JennaJacobNewsletter
Connect with Jenna online
Facebook: www.facebook.com/AuthorJennaJacob
Instagram: www.instagram.com/Jenna_Jacob_Author
Visit Jenna at JennaJacob.com!

SEDUCING *Danger*

KENNEDY LAYNE

1

Landon Smyth wanted the woman currently in his sights, and he was a man who always succeeded in obtaining his desires.

She was a vision to behold...absolutely mesmerizing as she tapped her French-manicured fingernails in rhythm to the beat of the Dutch Caribbean island music. He took his time trailing his gaze up her long, tanned legs in appreciation to where her left hand rested against the provocative cut of her flowing white skirt.

No wedding ring.

There was no sign of a tan line on the ring finger of her left hand. Considering the number of Europeans here on the island, he made sure to check her right hand as well.

His mystery woman was completely lost in her enjoyment of a local steel drum band entertaining the tourists who were visiting the tropical island of Aruba. He'd seen her countless times mixed among the crowds both at the resort and in the various markets over the past week. Unfortunately, he'd been conducting business and hadn't afforded himself the time to introduce himself until now.

Landon was going to ensure that was no longer a detail he left unattended.

He couldn't have possibly asked for a better locale to enjoy some time to himself than this hidden treasure of an all-inclusive resort on the Caribbean's friendliest tropical island. It was the major reason he would be signing on the dotted line to acquire a controlling interest in this commercial property and additional rights for the two adjoining properties if everything went through as he expected in tomorrow's meeting.

The opportunity to buy into such a paradise, where the sun was always shining, the white sand was constantly warm, and the light breeze off the ocean felt like a lover's caress, was golden. It was rare such a gem could be found where the sliding glass door of a patio led directly to the beach, where the white caps came up to dance on the shoreline mere feet from the guests' rooms. He certainly didn't intend to spend his last night here in paradise by himself if at all possible.

Landon confirmed once more that his mystery woman wore no wedding band to indicate that she was taken, nor had he seen her in the company of another man these past five days. Hell, she'd been alone every single time he'd caught a glimpse of her.

Was that her intention? To enjoy her solitude?

He would have to chance interrupting her solitude to see if she was receptive to his company.

There was only one way to find out.

"Jerry," Landon called out over the other patrons at the bar and the low bass tones escaping the large speakers positioned near the stage. The majority of the tourists crowded around the bartender were in true vacation mode as they danced with umbrellas in their cocktail drinks and lost themselves in the familiar music. They were making the most of their rather expensive all-inclusive package. It was worth every penny and more, just like his business decision to invest in this small piece of nirvana and several of the other properties dotting this picturesque shore. "You've been working the night shift all week. Do you, by chance, know what drink that beautiful guest over there has been enjoying?"

Jerry flashed a toothy smile when his line of sight followed the direction Landon had gestured with his glass of rum, Coke, and lime twist. The stunning woman was now swaying gracefully in time with the music while her long black hair did the same, though the light trade winds coming in off the ocean caused a few silken strands to caress her sun-kissed cheek.

She'd been watching the band entertain the tourists for the past thirty minutes, and he found himself once again wondering about the color of her eyes. Brown? Green? Or were they blue, like the turquoise tint of the early evening tide rolling in behind her?

"She does not drink alcohol, sir." Jerry was currently twirling a bottle of rum in his nimble fingers so that it landed label out to help the patrons choose from the various types of alcohol provided by the resort. His movements were fluid as he adorned a stemmed cherry alongside an orange slice. He slid the cocktail across the bar to another patron before reaching for another glass. "She prefers still Voss water chilled with a wedge of lemon."

Landon was becoming more and more intrigued with the sexy brunette with each passing minute. He took a healthy drink of his rum and Coke as he studied the mystery lady who'd captured his attention. This distraction was downright infuriating, and there was only one way to solve that conundrum.

Within seconds, the mystery woman's chosen beverage was placed before him, accompanied by a friendly wink of encouragement. Landon took a moment to stare at the nonalcoholic drink in perplexity. He'd recognized the wristband she was wearing as the designated one for those customers who paid to have alcohol in their package. Why wasn't she enjoying that particular amenity she'd paid quite a lot for?

"Hello," a feminine voice purred right before a lovely blonde filled his vision. There was no denying her beauty, but there was only one woman on his mind this evening. "I was hoping you'd buy me a drink."

"Actually, I was just on my way to join someone else," Landon replied somewhat apologetically, not wanting to hurt her feelings. "Enjoy your—"

"I'm sure she can wait. She's been there for quite a while already." The blonde feigned a demure smile as she reached for the glass of filtered water. Landon wasn't surprised at her boldness, but he also wasn't a man to play games. He clenched his jaw when she went so far as to take a sip of the water he'd specifically ordered for another woman, leaving a red lipstick stain on the rim. Her somewhat surprised gaze dropped down to the contents in disappointment and amusement. That was, until she decided to use the nonalcoholic drink to her advantage. "I'm quite certain my company will be much more entertaining."

"Would you care to dance?"

Landon didn't have to look to know his mystery woman was behind the lucrative offer, though her suggestive proposition had him doing just that. The white summer dress she wore was accentuated with a teal flower tucked behind her right ear, though it wasn't needed. Her exquisiteness alone outshined the vibrant color.

She was even more stunning than he'd originally thought.

No other woman on this island could hold a candle to her beauty.

And her voice? The intoxicating sound was like a sip of fine whiskey...smoky and smooth. The distinctive resonance only made him want to hear more words escape her sensual lips. She'd covered them with a dash of pink he found enchanting, but he sought the answer to the question that had been on his mind all week.

Blue. Her eyes were a startling blue so unlike the water over the reef. The vivid color of the mighty ocean didn't hold a candle to the gorgeous shade that he had no doubt captured the interest of many men before him.

"I'd like that very much," Landon responded quietly, speculating what motive she could possibly have to approach him now. He gave the blonde a cursory glance as he held out his hand toward his mystery woman. "Shall we?"

Landon stepped past her, guiding them to the designated dance area in front of the band that was now playing a softer rolling ballad that enticed other couples to enjoy the intimate ambiance. He turned and drew her into his arms, the intoxicating scent of lilacs and another floral fragrance greeting him as the length of her body melded into his as if they were made for one another. He wrapped his right arm behind her to pull her even closer as they swayed to the music.

"I guess a thank you is in order." Landon savored this moment as she tilted her head to catch his words over the soft melody. The humidity in the air rose another degree. "You saved me from what could have been a very bad encounter."

"All in a good day's work," his mystery woman replied softly as she placed her soft palm against his, following his lead as he slowly guided her around another couple. Her blue eyes sparkled as if she had a secret she wasn't willing to share. "Didn't your mother ever tell you not to talk to overly forward strangers?"

"As a matter of fact, she did," Landon countered amiably, enjoying this light banter after such a complicated week. "Which is why you're now required to tell me your name. It should be obvious I can't fly back to the mainland and tell my mother I ignored her advice. She'd be devastated."

Her light laughter at his rationale rang through the air, joining the soft melody and causing him to wish they weren't surrounded by people. He could admit to being a selfish man when it came to certain things. She was definitely on that list. He wanted her all to himself, and he would make no apology for that.

"Kelli," she finally answered with an infectious smile. "You can call me Kelli."

"And I'm Landon Smyth. It's nice to meet you, Kelli. See?" Landon pointed out as he slowly weaved them throughout the other dancing couples. "Now we are no longer strangers."

"It's nice to see a man who cares so much about his mother's feelings."

Landon drew her closer, if that was even possible, when a woman who obviously had too much to drink stumbled backward toward him. Kelli's breasts pressed against his chest, and he didn't miss her quick intake of air at the intimate position he'd drawn them into. A physical attraction this palpable couldn't go overlooked for long.

There was no need for more words when they both recognized where this evening would end—his bed or hers. It was inevitable.

Landon allowed himself to finally unwind and appreciate this blissful setting he'd all but ignored this past week. There was a light breeze steadily blowing in off the ocean as the moon and stars lit up the night sky with their radiance, heightening the sensual mood of the evening, which he intended to enjoy very much with the beautiful woman in his arms. They thoroughly appreciated the ringing melody of the first song and were well into the second when he could no longer just hold her in his embrace.

Landon released her hand so that he could softly stroke his thumb across her lower lip. Damn, but he needed to taste her. He dipped his head and captured her lips. He savored the faint taste of strawberries and wanted more, already recognizing that one night with her wasn't going to be nearly enough. He couldn't resist running his tongue across her lower lip before pulling away and resting his forehead against hers.

"Let's continue this in my private suite, Kelli."

2

KELLI GARRETT HAD NEVER ONCE DEVIATED FROM ANY ASSIGNMENT EVER given to her in the two years she'd been working as a private security contractor. She'd learned long ago during her stint in Navy intelligence that no task was ever taken lightly and to leave no detail ever done half-assed, nor to ever stray from one's objective. Yet she couldn't bring herself to walk away from the one man she'd just spent days surveilling as a favor to a lieutenant commander she'd served with during her later years in the service.

It should have been an easy debt to repay—simply observe and deflect any obvious threats.

After all, she was basically given an all-expense-paid trip to a Dutch Caribbean island for an entire week while ensuring Landon Smyth's physical safety. She'd enjoyed the sunshine while her charge had been in meetings, savored delicious meals at fancy restaurants she otherwise would have avoided, and taken long, relaxing midnight strolls on the beach to ensure he was all tucked in for the night.

Nothing too taxing for her extensive skill set.

In all honesty, this had been one of the easiest assignments she'd ever undertaken right up until she had to run interference.

She should have fucking known better than to think she could coast through the remaining two days of this milk run without the shit hitting the proverbial fan.

Landon's father had been rightly worried about a business rival—Curtis Pynaker—using unconventional, and in all likelihood questionable, means to stop what could be the real estate deal of the century for their firm. Mr. Smyth also believed that this adversary wasn't beneath blackmail to get what he wanted, though Landon disagreed.

The lesson here for everyone involved was that parents were always right.

"Let's continue this in private, Kelli."

The sensual vibrations of Landon's voice sent goose bumps chasing each other in zigzag patterns over her sensitive skin. It didn't surprise her that he had that effect on women, considering his sex appeal was off the charts. It was easy to see that he rivaled the Kennedys in good looks and charm. She had little choice in taking this to his room.

To be truthful, Landon had not been exactly what she'd been expecting upon catching the same flight as he had out of Los Angeles bound for Miami then Aruba. He'd gone out of his way to aid an elderly woman down the ramp when boarding and even spent time entertaining a toddler who had been restless before takeoff. He'd actually given up his luxury town car to two parents who were late to their daughter's wedding due to a flight delay at MIA. The vehicle had been specifically sent by the resort owners to the airport to welcome him to the island.

Landon Smyth was the entire package, but he was Kelli's charge—not her date.

There was no mixing business with pleasure, at least in her line of work.

Yet here she was…standing in his warm embrace actually entertaining the thought of joining him in his room for a roll in the hay.

"Kelli?"

She blamed the blonde provocateur who'd obviously been paid to seduce Landon with every intention to either stall him for tomorrow's meeting or somehow set him up to look bad in front of the resort's longtime family owners. She was the sole reason that Kelli found herself in the arms of the man she'd dreamt about for the last five nights.

The right thing to do here would be to walk away once she'd gotten them safely back to his room.

Kelli found the strength to look back at the bar, not surprised in the least to find the blonde watching them with an eagle eye. She was just waiting for the right moment to close, not wanting to miss out on the large amount of cash she'd probably earn should she succeed in her task of getting Landon tangled in her web.

An opportunity to prevent this woman from ruining a man's reputation had been presented to Kelli with sparkles and a pretty bow. She would take what was being offered before creating a valid excuse as to why she couldn't stay the night with Landon and bowing out gracefully.

"I'd like that very much," Kelli whispered with more honesty than she'd wanted to convey.

She closed her eyes as a shiver of arousal traveled down the back of her neck. Landon had leaned into her and pressed his lips against her ear so only she could hear him whisper his response.

"Shall we leave then?"

It was impossible for her body not to respond to the sexual electricity generating between them. He never once let go of her hand as he slipped through the couples on the dance floor to the small wooden boardwalk parallel to the beach. The relaxing sound of the waves crashing against the sand could be heard as the murmurs of the crowd and the beat of the music faded in the distance as they departed.

Kelli would have given anything for this walk to Landon's room to be legitimate. Unfortunately, only she was aware that it was simply a ruse to keep him safe until those real estate papers were signed and the pressure was off.

She casually glanced over her shoulder to see the blonde pull out her phone, no doubt notifying Curtis Pynaker of the delay in their cunning plan to interfere with Landon's business. The question remained...just how far would Mr. Pynaker take this corporate conspiracy?

Blackmail? Kidnapping? Murder?

Neither she nor Landon said a word as they walked hand in hand under the soft moonlight shining on the wooden planks defining the edge of the white sand beach. The light ocean breeze coming in off the water brushed against her shoulders, much like the way Landon's thumb was caressing the backside of her hand. It was a promise for more that she wouldn't be able to accept, much to her chagrin.

Kelli wasn't surprised when Landon lightly tugged on her fingers, veering them from the path to where an opening separated two buildings. The patio doors to each room that led directly to the sandy beach purposely did not contain a method in which a guest could enter by key. It was a security measure that went mostly unused by tourists who were too trusting—they often left their glass doors open for easy access from the beach during the day.

Each structure was assigned a block number, and he was staying in building eighteen hundred. He didn't know that she was in the room next to him, nor would he if she had her way. She would see to it that he was safely deposited inside before she came up with a reasonable excuse as to why she couldn't spend the night with him.

Kelli thought she had her carnal cravings under control and hadn't expected her heartrate to accelerate when Landon's dark eyes met hers as he inserted his keycard into the card slot. The not-so-innocent action initiated the faint sound of the electronic lock unfastening right before he turned the handle.

He slowly opened the door, almost as if he could sense her hesitation. It didn't surprise her, considering she was well aware of how gentlemanly he could be. Only she didn't want him to be a gentleman at the moment…and that was the problem.

Kelli swallowed hard as she stepped past him, the heady scent of his cologne enveloping her in his sphere. Landon had left on his bedside lamp, which currently cast the room in a golden hue that all but beckoned her into his bed. She resisted, stopping just shy of the spacious area where she was likely to change her mind and violate her principles. Staying in the small foyer was the wisest thing she could have done.

"Would you care for a drink?" Landon asked, catching her off guard when he came up behind her and ever so leisurely ran the backs of his fingers down the length of her arm.

Kelli should have been paying more attention. She inhaled slowly, trying to clear her mind for what needed to be done.

"I was thinking that maybe we could—"

Oh...

Kelli gasped, arousal awakening every nerve in her body when Landon's warm lips pressed against the side of her neck. He pressed his palm against her abdomen, pulling her back against him. There was no hesitation on his part as he finally whirled her around and captured her lips, commanding the moment in a manner she was unaccustomed to when it came to simpler men.

She was usually the one who took control during situations like these, just as she should be doing now. Yet the firm hold he had on her now that he'd slid his fingers underneath her long hair was enticing. He was a man who knew what he wanted and wasn't afraid to go after it with all the power that he possessed.

Landon turned them so that her back was against the large mirror attached to the wall. He finally released her lips and trailed his own across her jawline, not stopping until he lightly bit the lobe of her ear. The sharp little pain he caused had her arching her back. She needed more of what he was giving, and this small taste of what he could offer wasn't nearly enough for her.

Kelli's body and mind fought for the dominance she normally expressed. Had it just been her, with no outside influence, her intellectual awareness would have won out—it always had before. That's what made her so good at her job, yet Landon wasn't playing fair. Unfortunately, he didn't know that he had to.

"What is it about you that has me losing all sense of reason?" Landon murmured before once again pressing his lips to hers as she fought for balance and the answer to his question. It was the other way around as far as she was concerned. She couldn't gather her thoughts. His touch was too seductive. "All week...you're all that I thought of. I need more than just the taste of your lips, my elusive little siren."

Kelli had a moment of realization when Landon had brought up this past week. She was able to inhale enough oxygen to clear her mind momentarily and step away from him. The heavy patio drape wasn't closed, but instead only the sheer curtain covered the window. He had a habit of leaving his room like this at night, giving anyone the opportunity to look inside and monitor his comings and goings.

"We need to close this," Kelli managed to say without hesitation. She quickly walked around the bed and drew the heavy fabric over the sheer material of the drape, giving added security to a room she needed to vacate before she lost her sanity. "We wouldn't want someone catching an eyeful or even taking pictures."

"That's good to know," Landon said with an understanding smile. She was confused momentarily; that was until he clarified his meaning. "You're not into exhibitionism. Duly noted."

Another shiver of arousal shot through her, and not only due to his words, which had conjured up an image of the two of them making love on the beach where anyone could see them in a salacious act of self-destruction. No, he'd been waiting for her when she turned around and instantly wrapped an arm around her waist to pull her close. Her awareness was at its peak, and her nipples hardened beneath her dress as the front of her pressed against his chest.

"Are you?" Kelli asked, more to give herself time to extricate herself from this situation. His answer all but told her she was staying, because he had somehow become the man she couldn't walk away from.

"I'm the man you need me to be," Landon replied sincerely, slipping a finger under the strap of her dress so that it slid easily from her shoulder. He maintained eye contact as he softly brushed his lips against hers while waiting patiently for her response. "What do you want tonight, my little siren? Your pleasure is my command."

Kelli needed to walk away. She should have walked away. Instead, she slipped one side of his blue tie through the already loosened loop, letting it drop to the floor in answer to his question. She worked each button through the tiny openings until she could part the starched material, revealing his contoured chest and ripped abdomen she'd had the pleasure of looking at during his daily swims.

Now?

Kelli granted her muscles the approval they needed in order to touch him.

One night.

She could slip away in the morning.

One night of hot sex, guilty pleasure, and much-needed relief was what she would allow herself before continuing to do her job as she'd been assigned. She would then disappear, leaving him to his wealthy lifestyle of excellent food, expensive cars, luxury homes, and lavish trips.

Kelli gradually ran her fingers down each of his biceps as his undershirt fell to the floor, joining his shirt and tie. How was it that a man who worked in an office every single day of his life could have the physique of a god? It didn't matter, as long as she got to enjoy the product of all his hard work.

"I'm glad to see we're on the same page." Landon allowed her to remove his belt, but she only got as far as unfastening the button on his dress pants when he surprised her by taking her and carefully, yet quickly, laying her on the soft sheets of his turned-down bed. He leveraged himself with one elbow as he grazed his thumb over her bottom lip. "But we have all night."

"And I don't want to waste a second of it," Kelli whispered, pressing against his shoulder so that she could take command the next few moments. After that? He could have his way with her. She just needed to remove the holster she'd secured around her right thigh before he discovered she was armed and started to ask questions. "Let me enjoy myself, Mr. Smyth."

It was obvious that Landon didn't like the way she'd addressed him in her attempt to keep this from becoming too personal. He'd be correct in his assumption, but something told her from the first moment she laid eyes on him that he was different from all the other men she'd met in her life.

Kelli took her time enjoying his upper torso. She used her lips, tongue, and fingers to explore every ridge of his chest and abdomen. The lower she brought herself, the more aroused she became by her attention to his body. His fingers were tightly tangled in her hair just firm enough to keep the sensation at a constant hum throughout her body. Her nipples were rubbing against the soft material of her dress while her pussy had become rather damp at the provoking thoughts of his cock filling her over and over until release.

It wasn't long before the rest of his clothes were discarded and she was able to continue discovering what he liked and disliked. She took that opportunity to reach under her dress and remove her holster, carefully lowering it to the floor when she'd done the same with his pants. The coast was now clear for her to enjoy the rest of the evening without fear of being caught in such a compromising position.

Kelli never expected him to roll her over onto her back, so that he was once again looking down at her with that perceptive gaze she'd come to recognize. Her heart stopped briefly at the thought he'd caught sight of her weapon.

"Do you always have to be in control?" That question alone had her heart racing once more, wondering if he had something deliciously naughty in mind. She received an answer when he lightly started to trail the fingers of his right hand up her inner thigh, starting from her knee. "Don't answer that. There are certain things we must find out for ourselves."

Landon dipped his head and pressed his lips against that sensitive spot on her neck she hadn't even known was there. He had taken ahold of both her wrists in his left hand, locking them together above her head.

"Spread your legs," Landon murmured, though his request sounded more like an order. What was it about him that had her melting against her will? "Where have your panties gone? Did you go without? I like that idea, little siren."

Landon's hand brushed over her folds in the lightest caress possible. He dipped one finger into her cream before bringing her juices up and over her clit. His touch was feather soft, and he gently rubbed the slickness over her swollen tissue until she wanted to scream at him for wasting time. She didn't want to be crass, but he was purposely dragging this out when all she wanted was for him to enter her.

"Landon..."

"I think that's the first time you've said my given name." It was almost as if he rewarded her by ever so slowly sliding his finger inside her, causing her to arch her hips for more. She had every intention of aiding him, but he tightened his grip on her wrist before she could move. "Relax, Kelli. Let us both enjoy this part."

Landon kissed her as he continued to manipulate her clit with his fingers until she was very close to coming, only to then gradually remove the pressure to introduce two fingers and leisurely thrust them inside of her until that impending orgasm became elusive.

He did this over and over until she could no longer take it, finally breaking his hold on her at the same time she shifted so that she was straddling him. She placed her hands on his shoulders, trying her best to even out her breathing to ask a very, very important question.

"Please tell me you have condoms." Kelli did her best to quell the desperation in her tone. Landon's smile grew as he started to reach over the bed for his pants, but she quickly put a stop to his good intention. "I've got it. No worries."

Kelli leaned down, stretching her arm so that she was able to drag his clothes closer to the nightstand. She quickly retrieved his wallet while at the same time positioning her holstered weapon in between the bedside table and bed. He never noticed her achievement as she finally shifted so that she was upright.

Landon reached for the gathered material of her dress, but she couldn't wait anymore. She quickly acquired the condom and tore open the foiled package, shifting down so that she had complete access to his long, thick shaft.

"Always in such a hurry," Landon lightly chastised, grabbing her wrist after she'd rolled the latex over his cock. He pulled her to him, the bottom of her dress lifting so that the material was around her waist. "It's a good thing we have all night, or you might have found yourself tied down to my bed."

He kept putting these wicked images in her mind, instantly causing her body to want more. She didn't hesitate to position herself over his tip and sink down inch by inch until he filled her to the point of a slight burning sensation that literally almost triggered her release. He was so thick that she hadn't been quite sure she could take all of him, but she managed to in this position. It also helped that he had wrapped his hands around her waist and helped guide her down slowly. It was when he tightened his grip and wouldn't allow her to move that she met his dark gaze in almost desperation.

"This isn't over." Landon had his own plans that involved more than this brief moment in time, yet Kelli understood that it was in both of their best interests to leave after they were able to extinguish this flame that had been burning all week. She had to believe that this would quench their thirst, even if he chose not to think that himself. "Agreed?"

Kelli couldn't bring herself to speak or nod in agreement, so instead she leaned down so that she could kiss him. His soft lips immediately parted and accepted hers. Their tongues played until he finally released his hold on her hips and brought his hands up until his palms were cradling her breasts.

She leaned back, leveraging herself on her knees so that she could lift herself off his cock...only to descend once more. Her sheath contracted around his shaft, signaling that her body couldn't take much more without exploding into a million pieces. She set the pace while his thumbs stroked over her hardened nipples, triggering that ever-sweet, piercing arousal to shoot from her breasts to her overstimulated clit.

The faster she took him inside of her, the firmer he pressed on her nipples. He was now rolling those sensitive nubs in between his thumbs and index fingers, pressing harder and harder until her body finally shattered.

"Oh!" Kelli leaned her head back as ecstasy rained down over her skin while her sheath contracted around his cock, eliciting wave after wave of intense pleasure. The explosive orgasm stole her breath, and she dug her fingers into his shoulders to ground herself. "Landon, that was..."

"Not enough. Just the beginning," Landon practically growled as he took her wrists and drew her down until her breasts were pressed against his chest. The rich tone of his voice stirred another wave of arousal, signaling he was more than accurate in his assessment of—

Click.

Kelli instantly reached for her weapon, withdrawing her firearm from its holster before Landon even realized someone was trying to enter his room through the patio door.

Everything happened at once. Landon tried to move her out of harm's way, preventing her from palming her weapon in her right hand. His explicit curse words were muffled by the shattering glass and she was able to identify the barrel of a Glock pushing aside the drape, though she didn't give the intruder time to find his or her target.

Kelli squeezed the trigger.

The telltale wet thud of the bullet entering flesh was unmistakable. Unfortunately for her, the hired hitman was already fleeing the scene. Splintered glass coating the carpet blocked her path to give chase, though she was able to draw the heavy curtain back to see the damage.

She briefly considering going out the front door and attempting to track her target down from that angle, but there was no way in hell she could leave her charge unprotected in his room. Her gunfire already had tourists coming out of their rooms to see what had taken place.

"Damn it," Kelli murmured, doing her best to smooth down the material of her dress just as one of the vacationers asked if he should call security. She gave him a few short directions as she turned to address Landon, who was already standing while holding a sheet around his waist. His gaze went from her eyes to her weapon, then back again. Shit. How was she going to explain this and not sound unprofessional? "Landon, I should have told you—"

"Told me what, Kelli?" Landon demanded, all but ignoring the gathered crowd outside and the shattered patio door. He took a step forward before shaking his head in disbelief and then running a hand through his hair as he tried to connect the dots. There were too many for him to join, and it didn't surprise her when he finally demanded to know her identity. "Just who the fuck are you?"

3

"...Check the local hospitals. We'll have the staff be on the lookout for anyone with a gunshot wound or any sign of blood on the towels." The uniformed policeman closed his notebook, signaling to the other officers to wrap up their questioning of the guests. "I'll see to it that you and Mr. Smyth have an escort from the resort to the lawyer's office tomorrow morning."

Landon tried not to take his omission from the conversation personally, though that was really hard to do at the moment. His anger had ratcheted up to fury by the time Kelli Garrett had explained exactly who she was and what her true role had been this past week. No matter that his father had called in a special favor from a retired military friend to hire her for his protection, she had overstepped her professional bounds and become intimate with him.

"I appreciate that, Officer Farro," Landon responded for Kelli, stepping forward to shake the man's hand. "I'd like to leave for the meeting promptly at nine o'clock."

It was more than apparent that Kelli had already tagged him as a rich, incompetent fool who'd inherited his father's business. All she knew was what she'd read on a sheet of paper. It was not only an error but a small piece of the puzzle that comprised who he was. Hell, she didn't even truly know him as a man even though they'd just fucked in his bed. Well, she was about to find out exactly whom she was dealing with.

Landon had taken a few moments to himself before the police arrived to wash himself off, dispose of their used condom, and throw on some of the clothes he'd been wearing earlier. The resort already had his new room waiting for him, though Kelli wouldn't allow any of the staff to move his things just yet. She insisted they would see to it themselves. They had even been provided a golf cart to use. That was fine by him. It was time for them to have a little chat.

"Go collect your things," Landon directed her once the police had left the room. The only one who could overhear their conversation was the groundskeeper who was currently boarding up the patio door. "I'll be out in a minute."

"I'm sorry?" Kelli appeared rather taken aback by his request, though she shouldn't be the least bit surprised. At least three hours had passed since the shooting, so it had to be going on one in the morning. Did she think he was just going to let bygones be bygones? "You're now aware of who I really am and what I've been hired to do. An attempt has been made on your life. I'm not leaving you alone until you've done your business and you are sitting in your first-class seat on the way back to Los Angeles."

Landon had opened the closet door with the intention of grabbing his business suits, but her comment about first-class and the fact that she hadn't once personalized her job had him changing course. He grabbed her wrist and had her back against the wall before she could inhale to make another declaration.

"What exactly am I to you?" Landon asked, capturing both her wrists in one hand and pressing them against the laminated wood above her head. His lips were inches from hers, and he made sure those blue eyes of hers were trained on his. "Was I nothing but a job to you? Did you get off knowing that I had no idea my father hired you to protect me while we fucked? Or better yet…did you fuck me to keep me safe? I'll be sure to let my father know you went above and beyond in fulfilling your duties."

Landon had already anticipated that Kelli would try to pull away from him, so he leaned his body into hers right as he stated his intentions. It didn't get past him that she kept herself in good shape. Her muscles were toned and she was a lot stronger than she let on, most likely a conscious decision on her part. It no doubt gave her the edge over most enemies she might encounter.

"Tonight…" Kelli's voice trailed off and it was then he thought back to when she approached him at the bar. A sick feeling stirred in his gut and he abruptly stepped away from her as she confirmed his suspicions. "I recognized the blonde from some intel that was given to me regarding Curtis Pynaker's known associates. It was more than obvious she was hired to approach you, most likely delaying your signing or exposing you to some type of scandal so that Pynaker could make a competing offer."

"So you thought you would sacrifice yourself for the greater good?"

Landon was stunned that his business rival would take things this far, but he was even more disgusted that Kelli would go to the lengths she did in order to defuse a potentially dangerous situation. He'd thought she was special.

Did she go to this type of extreme with all her clients?

All Kelli had to do was come clean with him. He wouldn't have liked that his father had gone behind his back after they'd discussed this possibility before leaving Los Angeles, but he would have at least been on an even playing field. Right now, they weren't even playing in the same league.

"It's not like that," Kelli argued with a shake of her head. She'd lost the flower in her hair long ago. She took a step forward, but he'd already turned his back and crossed the room to grab his cell phone from the nightstand. "Yes, I needed to intervene, but all I had intended to do was dance with you. I didn't mean for things to—escalate."

"What? You didn't mean to accidentally fuck me?" Landon wasn't in a forgiving mood after being made a fool of when this had all been avoidable. Now that he was convinced his father was right—which really pained him to admit—he would hire his own protection detail. He was done with this conversation, so he swiped the home screen on his phone and initiated a call to his father. "Don't bother packing, Kelli. Stay on my company's dime and enjoy the rest of your vacation. Think of it as a mission bonus. It's the least I could do for you after you saved my life."

"Don't be such an ass," Kelli exclaimed, quickly taking his cell away before he realized her intention. He would have taken it back had she not put the phone to her ear. She never wavered her determined stare as she all but challenged him to try to stop her from having her say. "Mr. Smyth? Yes, this is Kelli Garrett. There's been an incident, and Landon now knows I've been hired as his protection during this trip. No, no. He's fine. Yes, his meeting is still scheduled for tomorrow morning."

Landon observed Kelli as she continued to speak with his father, going into more details about what had transpired this evening. She even turned away from him, wrapping one arm around her waist as she took three steps to the right and then three steps to the left. She was looking down at the sandals she'd put on before the police had arrived. Even he was aware of the defensive posture she'd taken, the only sign that this evening's events had any effect on her.

Kelli was conveniently leaving out the fact that things had gotten rather personal between them. Honestly, he could see how things had spiraled out of control now that she'd monopolized his phone and given him some time to think. He had pressed her pretty hard. He had time now to go through the past week, recalling each and every moment he laid eyes on her.

Their attraction wasn't one that had been forced. He truly desired her, in spite of the fact that she had withheld her true identity. As for her response to his touch? That spoke for itself and he wasn't quite ready to walk away from her.

"Dad, we'll talk about this when I get back home," Landon said to his father once Kelli had handed him back his phone. A quick glance ensured that the groundskeeper had finished boarding up the patio door. "There are some things I still need to take care of this evening."

"What do you still need to do?" Kelli asked him after he'd disconnected the call. Once again, she was trying to take charge of the situation. He was getting to know her better with each passing second, and that included her physical response to him closing the distance between them. "Landon?"

"I only want to know one thing." Landon didn't touch her. He stopped inches from her, coercing her to tilt her head back so he could see for himself that she hadn't played him for the sake of her job. "Was it enough for you?"

Kelli's lips parted in surprise at his candor, but she was already aware that he wasn't into playing games. He never had been, and he never would be. Her blue eyes darkened in response to his question, giving him his answer…but he needed to hear her response. He was a straight shooter and they had a little more than twelve hours before they parted ways.

"No, not quite," Kelli whispered, closing her eyes almost in regret. "It wasn't enough, but we both know it's unwise to continue to mix business with pleasure."

"I've personally never tried that cocktail," Landon admitted honestly, finally giving himself permission to touch her. He brushed his hand over her cheek and then slid his fingers behind her neck, waiting for her to look at him. She finally lifted her lashes in acceptance. "One night. Until we have our fill, and then we can both walk away satisfied."

It was easy to see the internal battle going on in her mind as she continued to hold back, but she'd already given him her answer earlier. Her admission that their time together wasn't enough was all he needed to initiate a seductive night of complete and utter release.

"We'll need to take off your dress," Landon directed as he stepped back and led the way as he unfastened the first button on his shirt. "You had your time of enjoyment, little siren. It's time for mine."

4

WHAT THE HELL WAS SHE THINKING?

Kelli should be telling Landon to pack his suitcase. They should be heading to the new room the resort had provided. She certainly shouldn't be reaching for the shoulder straps of her dress and slipping the strips of material down her arms, but his assertion that this was only for one night was something she couldn't possibly turn down.

One night of bliss.

She didn't want to wake up tomorrow with the regret of not having enjoyed the time given to them.

They were both aware that they ran in different social circles. She wouldn't fit into his life, and he wouldn't want to live in hers.

We have our fill, and then we can walk away satisfied.

"After we are done, you need to allow me to do my job," Kelli stipulated, wanting to clarify that she still had an assignment to complete. "That means listening to what I say from the moment we leave this resort to when I see to it that you're safely on that flight to Los Angeles."

"I can handle that," Landon conceded rather confidently, shedding his shirt and not hesitating to reach for his belt buckle. The rise of his right eyebrow told her that there was a but to that concession. "But as I said…you'll have to let me be in charge tonight."

Kelli would have loved to say that the humidity in the air had risen, but the heat she was experiencing had nothing to do with the temperature and everything to do with her reaction to his words.

Yes, she was his...for tonight.

"Come here." Landon had waited until she'd stepped out of her sandals and her dress had fallen to the floor. It wasn't the kind of material where she could wear undergarments. It had been a struggle to conceal her holster, but she'd been able to make it work. As it was, she wasn't about to let her weapon out of arm's reach. "You can put your weapon underneath the pillow...where your hands will remain until I say otherwise."

This attraction Kelli had for him was only growing stronger with each passing minute as she realized that there was more to him than what was written in his dossier. The men she dated tended to defer to her decisions, and Landon was anything but a submissive type.

Kelli forced her trembling knees—which weren't only unsteady due to the remaining adrenaline rushing through her bloodstream—to move until she was standing in front of him. She truly thought he would reach out and touch her, but he stood there in all his glory with his hands at his sides and a penetrating stare, which allowed him to see more than she would have preferred.

"We should get started."

Kelli's movements weren't as graceful as she would have liked them to be as she crawled onto the bed, slipping her holstered weapon underneath the pillow as he'd instructed. It was very liberating to lie down on her back and lift her arms to gently rest them on the goose down pillow.

Her breasts were now exposed to his scrutiny. From the hunger darkening the deep color of his eyes, she could see his approval. He wasn't even touching her, yet she was becoming even more aroused by observing his passionate, intense demeanor.

"Spread your legs."

Landon was giving these short, terse commands and she was involuntarily obeying. It was hard to explain, even to herself, but this was what her body and mind needed to balance her everyday life.

Kelli allowed her knees to fall open to his inspection. She couldn't stem her quick inhalation when the backs of his fingers softly ran up the side of her knee, over her hip, and around her breast. What made his light touch even more exhilarating was how he never once broke eye contact with her as he explored her body.

Her responsive reaction when his warm hand settled over her mound took them both by surprise. She brought one hand down with the intention to wrap her fingers around his wrist, only to find that he had done so with hers.

"Arms up on the pillow," Landon murmured as he settled over her, leisurely seeing to it that she was positioned like before. He slowly descended until all she could see were his penetrating dark eyes...right before his lips closed over her clit.

"Landon!"

Kelli arched her back and dug her fingers into the pillow, completely aware that she was quickly on the verge of an orgasm. He was doing something amazing with his tongue, but he wasn't consistent enough with the concentrated pleasure to send her over the edge. It was pure torture, yet there was something freeing to hand over her will and allow him to decide the route she would take to reach her destination.

Landon had taken two fingers and slowly inserted them inside her pussy. His fingers were crooked in such a manner that each stroke swiped across that sweet spot, taking her even higher than before...but not enough for her to break. Was it possible to even soothe the extreme state she was in? She hadn't realized she'd started to close her legs to try and make him do more until he caught her in the act.

"Open to me, little siren, or I'll keep you like this for hours."

A crashing wave of desire washed over her as she whimpered in his conquest, wanting more than anything for him to grant her that elusive orgasm. She had to literally force herself to separate her legs even farther than before in order to control her movements. The cool air rushed over her clit right before he added a third finger to her pussy. The varied temperatures sent her straight to that torturous height she couldn't seem to step off in her need to acquire that elusive orgasm.

The sweet anguish became even more so when Landon took his tongue and lightly traced her clit in circles, causing the swollen nub to throb in time with her heartbeat. It wasn't enough. She cried out when all pleasure ceased. It was as if time stood still.

"Turn over," Landon directed rather harshly, his rich tone telling her that he was just as affected as she was by their passion. "Elbows and knees."

Kelli managed to do what he asked, though her limbs were weak with desire. She'd just gotten into position when she heard the tear of a foil package. She wasn't sure where he'd gotten another condom, and she honestly didn't care.

Need consumed every part of her. She leaned down on her elbows instead of her hands, just as he'd asked. It was then she realized this position would give him leverage while allowing him to enter her with ease.

Kelli didn't even have time to brace herself for his thrust. He'd settled in behind her and slammed his cock into her until there was no more room.

She was full.

The burn of her adjustment was seconds behind, but by that time Landon had already pulled out. He thrust back into her, instantly rubbing that sensitive area with his cock and triggering a tidal wave of pleasure. By his third stroke, she was screaming his name.

So this was paradise...

LANDON STARED AT THE LAST PAPER IN FRONT OF HIM THAT WOULD CLOSE the deal of the century for his father's legacy. His signature would give their company the edge they needed to move into a brighter future here on the island, yet his John Hancock would bring to fruition this trip... and his brief affair with the beautiful woman currently standing across the room from him.

They'd fucked all night long.

By morning, it had turned into more than just another casual encounter.

He knew it, she knew it...yet their lives were on different paths.

"I was sorry to hear about your competitor," Matthew Campbell stated as he set his coffee cup down on the conference table. He adjusted his tie before addressing this morning's news. "We'd heard rumors of Mr. Pynaker's business dealings being rather underhanded, which was one of the many reasons we chose to go into business with you and your father as a sole partnership. We prefer to keep our distance from his kind. Last night's attempt at stopping this particular deal crossed the line, and I was glad to hear the individual who tried to break into your room was eventually apprehended."

Landon forced himself to sign his name by the large X, thus concluding his business in Aruba. He then quietly laid the borrowed pen on the stack of papers before pushing his chair back and extending his arm in acknowledgment.

"Let's just say it was very satisfying to learn that the man and his female partner from last night decided to cooperate with the local police about their involvement with Curtis Pynaker." Landon shook Matthew Campbell's hand before nodding his appreciation toward the real estate agent who'd brokered this amazing deal. "The man will ultimately get his due, and both of our businesses will continue to flourish. It's been a pleasure doing business with you, Matt."

"Same here, Landon."

"I'm needed back in the States directly," Landon informed him, buttoning his suit jacket, "but my assistant will be in touch regarding the initial funds for the renovations we spoke about during the week. Once you've settled on a general contractor, we can get things started."

Matt made some notations on his notepad before addressing a couple of things that could easily have been done over the phone in the coming days, but Landon appeased the man by staying a few minutes longer to tie up loose ends. It wasn't long before he was standing before Kelli, still amazed by the change in her demeanor.

This woman standing before him with her hair pulled back at the base of her neck and wearing a pantsuit where her jacket concealed her weapon was not the same woman who was in his bed last night. No, that femme fatale was simmering just below the surface and he wanted to be with her again.

"I had my assistant check on my flight. There are still seats available if you'd like to accompany me to Los Angeles," Landon offered, watching her closely as they walked down the long corridor to where the elevator banks were located. "I've heard that Curtis Pynaker is posting bail, so we can't be too careful. I might need protection all the way home."

A small smile began to form on Kelli's sensual lips, reminding him of how she looked after achieving her third orgasm last night. His cock stirred as they came to a stop in front of the elevator. She pressed the down arrow without looking his way, alerting him to the fact that she would stick to their agenda. He had to wonder if she was afraid she'd change her mind.

"Curtis Pynaker's movements are being monitored and you just closed your business deal." Kelli looked up at the red numbers ascending in order, purposely avoiding his stare. "I'll see to it that you make it on your flight and then I'll return to Washington, D.C. My next assignment is in Iraq."

Landon couldn't help but grit his teeth upon hearing what her next assignment entailed and the fact that it would take her out of the country. It wasn't that she couldn't take care of herself, but there were other factors involved that she might not be able to control...just as he hadn't been able to control the lengths to which a business rival would go to in order to prevent a merger that resulted from today's signing.

"My father was right about something," Landon confirmed, reaching out to ensure that the elevator doors stayed open long enough for both of them to step inside. He pressed the button that would take them to the lobby before continuing. "Our corporation is growing and becoming more competitive. We're going to need to hire a security staff and someone to oversee some of our future ventures."

"I'm sure you and your father will choose your employees wisely."

Landon wanted more than that, and she was well aware of that fact. He reached out and hit the switch that would bring the elevator to a stop. Sure enough, the cable lines caught and held them fast as the emergency stop switch rang a warning. He was quicker, backing her up against the laminated wall and trapping her in between his arms.

"Last night wasn't enough."

"It has to be for both of us," Kelli whispered somewhat woefully, finally lifting her lashes to reveal her blue eyes so clouded with indecision. "I signed a contract with a government contractor, and I have to see it through. I have a reputation to protect."

"There are ways to—"

"It doesn't matter if there are loopholes in the agreement." Kelli lifted her hand and pressed her cool palm to his cheek in her bid to gain his understanding. It wasn't working and his anger started to simmer. "I gave my word. I won't go back on that now. Besides, you seem to forget that I followed your every move this past week. I remember distinctly overhearing you discuss employer and employee relationships. You don't cross that line, Mr. Smyth. I'm not the only one with a reputation."

I gave my word. There were so many facets to Kelli's personality. He hadn't come close to seeing and learning them all. He would have enjoyed getting to know her better, but there were obligations she needed to fulfill. He understood that more than most.

"It was truly a pleasure, Ms. Garrett," Landon murmured before he gently pressed his lips to hers in farewell.

5

SEVEN MONTHS LATER...

"I'M NOT GOING TO HIRE SOMEONE TO OVERSEE SECURITY WHO HASN'T served in the military," Landon exclaimed, effectively shutting down this conversation. He and his father had gone through several resumes in their bid to construct a security team now that their corporation had officially doubled in size and currently had more lucrative deals on the table. "I'll have Susan bring in another round of applicants next Wednesday. We'll start from scratch. What we need here is leadership, someone who has the credentials that the rest of the team can identify with."

"This one has military service," Richard Smyth pointed out, holding up a thick manila folder. He opened it to the front page and started to read off the applicant's accomplishments.

"Dad, I think we need to call it a day." Landon pushed his black leather chair back on its wheels and stood in exhaustion, bringing to close another long week. Recently, he'd been working fourteen-hour days and most weekends, this one included. "My flight leaves for Aruba in three hours and I still need to go home and pack."

Aruba.

Landon couldn't think of the Dutch Caribbean island without seeing his blue-eyed brunette lying naked on his bed.

Yes, his.

He'd thought of little else since they parted ways at the airport.

"I think we should pick someone from our existing group to start heading up the security team." Richard tossed the dossier onto Landon's desk. He wasn't in the day-to-day business decisions, but he did like to be included in major changes within their family organization. "You shouldn't be going back to Aruba without security, so I've made an executive decision."

"Dad, you don't have the authority anymore to make an—"

Landon broke off his declaration when his father swung open the office door to reveal the woman who'd taken over his thoughts every waking moment for the last seven months. She was wearing the same exact dress she had been the night she'd asked him to dance, thwarting whatever plan Curtis Pynaker had in mind.

Kelli Garrett was breathtaking as she stepped into the office and paused long enough to embrace his father in a warm hug.

Was that a blue flower in her hair?

His curiosity went by the wayside at the familiar way Kelli was addressing his father, as if they were old friends. Exactly what had he missed?

"Meet the head of our new security team," Richard said rather proudly, a broad smile on his face as he grabbed the doorknob. "I'll leave you two to sort out the details of the trip, and I'll see you both next Wednesday."

And just like that, Kelli was standing by herself wearing that beautiful, white formfitting dress with nothing on underneath. Well, most likely besides her holstered weapon.

"Lock the door, Kelli." Landon had already started to remove his jacket, well aware that neither one of them was leaving this office without some sort of satisfaction. "It appears we have an interview to conduct."

"Technically, I've already been hired." Kelli turned the small lever on the door handle anyway, securing them inside. Her blue eyes practically sparkled as she leaned back against the wooden structure. "No interview needed, though there are details that will need to be sorted out before we continue with this...relationship."

"Such as?" Landon asked, tossing his jacket over the arm of his chair. He took his time pushing away the various items on his desk, giving them a wide clearing for what he had in mind. "Wages? Hours? Responsibilities?"

"I was thinking more in terms of guidelines for a professional work environment," Kelli responded, reaching under her dress and removing that ever-present holster. She set it gently on top of the bookcase without ever breaking their gaze. "I keep you safe by you simply following every instruction I give you during the course of your trip."

"Agreed, with one exception." Landon began to loosen his tie. "I allow you satisfaction in the bedroom by you simply following every instruction I give you during the course of our sexual endeavors. We can further agree to an equal partnership in our marriage."

Kelli had just slipped out of her heels when the last word registered, causing her to slightly stumble. It was quite adorable to finally see her somewhat taken aback by his declaration.

"There's this clause we have here at the office about employer and employee relationships, so I took it upon myself to discover a loophole that would allow us to continue to explore our relationship." Landon shrugged out of his shirt, discarding it over his jacket as he reached for his belt. "By the way, you didn't return my calls when you arrived back in the States."

"I was busy accepting a business offer I couldn't turn down," Kelli explained, still regarding him warily as he unzipped his pants. "Landon, we can't get married. We hardly know—"

"You said it yourself, little siren. I follow your directives during our business trips, and you follow mine in our love life and we're equal in our relationship. It's a fair exchange, though I can see where we would want a six-month probation to iron out the kinks."

"Was that a pun?" Kelli's light, addictive laugh rang out through the room as he slowly closed the distance between them. "Mr. Smyth, I've already negotiated my contract. But I'm open to making a few concessions."

"And the six-month probation period?"

They both were aware that he was talking about a short engagement. He needed an answer before they took this any further.

"Yes, I definitely agree to those terms," Kelli whispered happily as she wrapped her arms around his neck, lifting herself up on her tiptoes so that her lips were inches from his.

The tightness he'd experienced in his chest over the last seven months eased, finally allowing him to breathe in her sweet fragrance. Everything was right in their world. He wrapped his arm around her waist with every intention of taking her over to his desk to seal their contract.

"Then let's finally put this deal to bed, little siren. We have a plane to catch."

ABOUT KENNEDY LAYNE

Kennedy Layne is a USA Today bestselling author. She draws inspiration for her military romantic suspense novels in part from her not-so-secret second life as a wife of a retired Marine Master Sergeant. He doubles as her critique partner, beta reader, and military consultant. They live in the Midwest with their teenage son and menagerie of pets. The loyal dogs and mischievous cats appreciate her writing days as much as she does, usually curled up in front of the fireplace. She loves hearing from readers

To be notified of new releases or sales,
join Kennedy's Mailing List: www.kennedylayne.com/newslettertext
Connect with Kennedy online
Facebook: www.facebook.com/KennedyLayneAuthor
Instagram: www.instagram.com/Kennedy_Layne_Author
Visit Kennedy at KennedyLayne.com!

Enforce Her

A LEATHER, PIPES & PASSION SHORT STORY

ISABELLA LAPEARL

1

RAMBLER

I WOKE AT THE CRACK OF DAWN, SWILLED DOWN A POT OF COFFEE, AND SAT impatiently on the porch to wait for Doc.

He was late.

He'd offered to give me a ride to the motorcycle consignment auctioneers in Palm City to pick up a sweet 1946 Harley Davidson EL Knucklehead Bobber I'd paid for with the money I'd earned from my last black op mission in Afghanistan six months ago. I was champing at the bit to lay eyes on her, swing my leg over her sleek body, and take her for a long ride. I needed this. I needed peace and wind pouring over me so the wounds of war might finally scar over.

When Doc showed, he was driving up in the shitty flatbed Chevy he loved. It was definitely not a pavement princess. In the back, his pit bulls, Sadie and Gracie, barked a greeting as he pulled up in front of the house. I loved Doc's dogs, but Sadie had been specially trained to assist vets. She woke Doc from any PTSD-induced nightmares and gave comfort.

Now each of them stood wagging in place, leashes secured to the guardrail in front. They peered at me over the sides, wearing big grins, tongues hanging out as they staunchly guarded "Dad's" truck.

After a hearty slap on the back, Doc and I pulled out for the hour-long drive back to Palm City.

When we arrived, the Mandel twins were already there and drooling over my new ride. Eric and Evan—brothers and fellow vets from our biker group—were known as "Spic" and "Span." They'd earned their nicknames because in their Ranger squad they'd been known to clean house as a sniper and spotter, respectively.

If anyone could see us, they'd probably think we rarely laid eyes on each other, given all the fist bumps and man hugs. But we were simply brothers in an elite group of eight combat-hardened veterans who had been tested by the blood of war and had learned the hard way never to take friendship—or the future—for granted.

"You've got so many bikes now. You must be running out of room, Rambler. Where the fuck are you going to put this one?" Eric asked.

"You know that big-assed coffee table in my family room?"

"Yeah, but—"

"Dude..." Evan howled, shaking his head with a grin.

"You know he means it, right?" Doc asked.

They were too busy pissing themselves laughing to realize I was dead serious.

I crossed my arms over my chest and scowled. "Damn straight. The table's out and the bike is in."

We stood around yapping for several minutes about the twins' new lady, Mazie. They looked genuinely happy for once, and I was thrilled for them, if a bit envious. It wasn't that I hadn't looked for a woman who fit in my life. I just hadn't found anyone I clicked with for more than a night, except...

Well, she was gone. It didn't matter now.

Doc and I agreed to meet the twins later that night for pizza and beer at Lorenzo's. As we solidified our plans, my beauty was wheeled out into the Florida sunshine, all ready to ride home. What a sweet sound she made—a low, throaty growl guaranteed to draw attention.

"She sure has a great set of pipes," Evan complimented. "Wanna swap?"

"Fuck off, Span." It was my turn to laugh. "A grown-up lady like this has no use for a pup like you. She needs the feel and touch of a grown man."

That had them all snorting again, but I was done talking. I wanted to ride.

"I'll follow you back—"

"No need, Doc. I got this." But I knew I was wasting my breath. I could tell by the set of his mouth that he'd already made up his mind.

"Too bad." He turned away and headed back to his truck.

The twins followed me out of the parking lot on their CVOs while Doc and the pups brought up the rear. We split up once we hit 714. Spic and Span headed east toward Stuart, back to their woman. Doc and I veered west, back to Lake Okeechobee.

The ride was sheer bliss. Wind in my face, the vibration and rumble of fine machinery. Best of all, nothing else intruded. It was a gorgeous day to enjoy the stretch of road known as the Hundred Year Oaks. The trees along each side had grown up and over the pavement in a canopy. The twisted limbs of evergreens allowed the play of sunlight to dapple and spill through.

The day was perfect—until we turned down the private road and started toward my place. Around a slight bend, near the lake, we found a Land Cruiser on its side in the watery ditch.

I pulled up to the wreck on my bike. Doc stopped his truck a moment later. But I didn't wait for him, just headed straight down the bank and into the murky water. I could hear the dogs barking as he grabbed his go-bag and followed me.

The SUV, half-submerged in the swampy water, looked disturbingly familiar.

I was already wet up to my thighs and at the vehicle when Doc yelled from the bank. "Is there anyone inside?"

"Don't know yet."

Doc made his way into the water to join me, MedPac in hand.

The windshield was shattered, which meant I couldn't see shit through the web of glass. I climbed up onto the vehicle and managed to wrench the driver's-side door open.

Then I saw her—suspended by the seat belt and trapped inside.

Though her head was slack and turned down, her lovely long blonde hair covering her face, I knew exactly who this was.

Ella.

My gut was churning. My heart racing. Memories rushed back, blinding and brilliant.

The first time I'd laid eyes on her, nearly a month ago, she'd instantly given me a hard-on from hell.

The guys and I had been on a ride, heading home from Tampa. We rounded the curve and found her bent over in the back of her truck, ass sticking out, and a shock of red panties shining in the sun between her luscious thighs. Her legs had nearly blinded me, all tanned, shapely, and teetering on a pair of black stilettos. Providence had been smiling on me that day because the smokin'-hot babe had a flat tire. I'd been more than willing to be the man who helped her—with whatever she needed.

Though the back view of her had been damn fine, when she'd turned and stood, she'd pegged the needle on my make-you-come meter. Her long platinum hair had been clipped back in a black bow, and the curls spilled around her shoulders in a soft tumble. Her gorgeous oval face looked smooth and flushed. Her huge baby blues had all but weakened my knees. But it had been her soft pink mouth that had sent my filthy mind south and unleashed a host of dirty desires I ached to shower all over her sinful body.

I'd peered over my shoulder and noticed the rest of my buddies had pulled over as well. They'd looked just as dumbstruck by her beauty as I was.

When I'd climbed off my bike, she'd sent me a wary expression. I'd probably looked rough and disreputable, but I'd aimed to change her opinion of me—fast. I didn't want to hurt her, just give her the time of her life.

"Need help with that tire, miss?" I asked softly. "Looks like you're having trouble."

"We'll be happy to fix it," Dozer offered beside me.

Her expression changed, now somewhere between surprised and relieved. "Please. That would be great. I'm Ella."

After those quick introductions, we'd made short work of her flat. Meanwhile, Ella met the rest of the gang. That day, for the first time, I really wished I'd been alone.

Spic and Span hadn't yet hooked up with Mazie. The horny twins had been all over Ella like bees to fucking honey. Even Doc had been in the bloody way, acting like a goofy, wet-behind-the-ears school kid.

It had been fucking embarrassing. And funny as hell.

Sparks wasn't even in the same league as Ella, yet he'd flirted like he considered himself a studmuffin and a half. Not even close, since—thanks to a diet of pizza and energy drinks—he had a short, round body and needed two vest extenders to keep the leather on. That day, his head had seemingly gone even softer than his belly.

I'd stood staring at the man and bitten back a growl. Though he was no looker and he wore thick, Coke-bottle glasses, Sparks had skills. If he wanted, he could turn an ATM into a slot machine. The good news for me that day? He seriously lacked in the art of seducing a woman. Still, he'd given it his all, and the bastard had me wondering where the hell our tech geek had gone.

But the most embarrassing display had come from Junior, our resident Mr. Fix-it. He was a decent-looking dude, and a millionaire to boot, but he dressed like a homeless wino. I'd seen the shy smile on his face when he glanced Ella's way. He'd been doing some stupid Southern boy routine, spouting off lots of "ma'ams" as he offered to get his flatbed and tow her vehicle back to his shop.

I'd seen Ella first, and maybe it wasn't right or mature, but I wanted to slap him upside the head with a tire iron for not recognizing that.

Only Casey, our handy supply expert, had seemed less impressed. He'd been quiet and observant, happy to help but not at all interested in flirting. I'd wondered if maybe he was gay, not that I gave a shit. But how anyone could ignore the gorgeous beauty was a mystery to me. Then again, Casey had always been too quiet. Maybe the sly bastard had finally found his One and was already in love?

Whatever the case, he'd been the only friend I hadn't wanted to beat the living shit out of that day.

As we'd helped Ella get rolling again, there'd been something about her that got to me—deep down in an uncomfortable sort of way that I hadn't been able to explain. I didn't want to. That would have meant I'd have to confront it and give it a fucking name. It was more than attraction or mere like. I'd wanted to grab her, kiss her, stake my claim on her, and never let go.

I wasn't anywhere near ready for that commitment shit. Was I?

When Casey—of all people—invited her to join us for lunch, I'd nearly choked. But Ella had other ideas. A huge smile that could have melted the sun lit up her face when she'd locked her big blue eyes on me and had sauntered my way.

"I could join you for lunch...or you could take me for a ride."

You could have heard a pin drop. I'd struggled not to swallow my tongue and find a coherent reply. But elation and thrill had rocked me. I couldn't manage a verbal answer, so I'd simply nodded. All I could think about was her on the back of my bike in that tight skirt and fuck-me pumps while the rock-hard steel rod trapped in my jeans screamed for joy.

Fate had been smiling on me that day.

My bliss had been short-lived when she opened her pretty little mouth again. "Let me just put on my jeans and sneakers, then I'll lock the car. Won't be but a sec."

When she'd disappeared inside her vehicle, the guys had stood mute for a whole ten seconds before they burst out laughing, as if they'd been privy to my fantasies of Ella and her little skirt. I'd bitten the inside of my cheek to hold back the grin that threatened to spill over my face.

Doc had brought order to the chaos. "The lady has chosen, lads. I say we make tracks and leave them to it."

"Why the hell would she want to ride your old man fucking rigid when she could perch her hot...err, pretty backside on the padded seat behind me?" Dozer demanded.

"And miss the vibration my bike will give her?" I'd preened. "She wouldn't."

"You dirty bastard," Dozer groused before he'd flipped me off.

Casey had let out a laugh when he and Dozer had climbed onto their bikes.

Sparks had looked totally perplexed. "What the fuck just happened? Seriously, someone please explain how he ended up with the girl?"

"Come with Uncle Junior, and I'll explain the birds and bees to you." Junior slung an arm around the man's shoulder.

Sparks had shoved the man's arm away. "Oh, fuck off."

As raucous laughter ensued, Spic and Span had given me fist bumps when they passed.

"That was beautiful, man," Eric murmured.

"Legend," Evan echoed.

Moments later, my buddies disappeared in a roar of engines and a cloud of dust.

Ella stepped out of her Land Cruiser and looked around. When she discovered the others had left us alone, she pinned me with a look of hunger, potent and needy. In that instant, my cock had been ready to explode.

I'd taken her hand and brought her palm to my lips, pressing a soft kiss to it. When she shivered, I'd felt a surge of triumph, but I suppressed it, setting her up with goggles and gloves, instead. Feeling all kinds of eager, I'd waited as she climbed onto the bike behind me.

"Hold on tight. I don't have a backrest. I don't want you sliding off."

"Oh, okay. Like this?" She snuggled forward, plastered her hot body against my back, and pressed every warm, soft curve against me.

"Yeah," I managed to growl out. "Just like that."

I'd only driven a few miles when I'd felt the roll of her hips with each breathless rise and fall of her chest.

Fuck! She's coming, and I'm missing the show.

After pulling over on familiar, deserted ground, I'd flipped her in front of me and gotten an eyeful of her desperation. I hadn't been able to wait anymore, so I'd taken advantage of her panting pleas, stripping off half her clothes and letting my mouth wander all over her body. After another screaming climax or two, I'd lifted her off the bike and carried her to the abandoned boathouse by the lake.

"Ella? Baby?" I questioned as I set her down.

"Yes," she said breathlessly.

That had been the only word I needed to hear.

When I'd delved between her splayed thighs, she'd been soaking wet and ready. God, she'd been so pretty and soft everywhere. I'd meant to take my time with her, but everything about her revved me up.

We'd kissed as I yanked off my clothes and tore away what was left of hers. In seconds, I'd sheathed up and plunged deep inside her.

Oh, shit. I'd reveled in the grunts and squeals she made as I bucked and thrust inside her. She gave herself over to me so utterly, so completely and sweetly. Never before had I made love to a woman who'd felt as if she could become my nirvana. It had been mind-blowing. She had been everything. That night had been beyond.

So seeing her unconscious now, helpless and injured, was killing me. I told myself I couldn't get involved with her again. She'd nearly torn me up when she left me the first time.

But my heart wasn't listening.

"Get your fucking ass over here, Doc," I shouted. "It's Ella! She's pinned in. We need to get her out."

"Is she breathing?"

"Yes."

"Is she bleeding?"

"Yes, but I can't see from where."

I did a cursory look and saw a nasty gash in her hairline. Her pretty face was covered in blood, which dripped into the water that had filled the cab.

"Looks like a fucking head wound."

"Don't panic. They bleed like a motherfucker," Doc reassured as he darted up behind me and tried to push me aside. "Move over and let me look."

I wasn't budging. "There's not enough room. Hang on. I need to get her out."

"Wait. Let me give you something to support her neck first."

Doc passed down a neck brace from his kit. I carefully slipped it around her throat. Making sure I had a good grip on Ella, I yanked my knife from my pocket and slashed through the belt.

"Help me, Doc. I'm backing out."

"Careful now. I'm right here. Try not to move her more than necessary."

Together we managed to lift her from the vehicle, out of the canal, and up to the bank. Doc went straight to work putting pressure on the bleeding wound. I doubled back to retrieve the backpack I'd seen floating in the cab. She'd probably want that later.

I dropped her pack down beside Doc and silently watched him work. Mind racing, I peered down at her and wondered what the hell had happened. What had gone wrong?

Ella had stood me up two weeks ago. I hadn't seen or heard from her since. I'd tried to reach out. Nothing. Even now, I couldn't deal with how shitty and wretched that had made me feel.

As I crouched beside her, even seeing her tugged at my heart, but knowing she was injured…I couldn't deal. A whole mess of thoughts raced through my brain. Obviously our couple of weeks together had meant more to me than her, but our shared moments were burned into my mind's eye like a jumbled collection of still frames. The sounds of her laughter mingled with the cries of her passion and echoed in my ears.

Now here she was again. Why? And why did I still feel so raw and angry and confused?

Because she's your Kryptonite.

She'd tied me up in knots—something no woman had ever done. Then out of the blue, she'd vanished. Her absence had unraveled my world, torn me to shreds, leaving me gutted and hemorrhaging.

Seeing her again had split those wounds wide open once more.

"What do you think, Doc? Will she be okay? Do I need to call an ambulance?"

"Apart from the cut to her head that could probably use a couple of stitches, she doesn't appear too badly hurt. I'm not sure the ER can do a lot for her, except charge her an arm and a leg to tell her she's got a concussion. But I'll feel better when she comes to so I can ask her some questions."

"Yeah, I have some questions I want to ask her, too," I mumbled.

Ten minutes later, we managed to get Ella to my place and lay her out on my kitchen table. Doc did a double check for any other possible injuries and came up negative. As he tended to her head, I turned to bring the dogs onto the porch. After making sure they were okay, I retrieved Ella's backpack from Doc's truck.

That's when I saw the stacks of money. She'd been carrying a shitload of cash. I did some quick math. This was the kind of money average people wrote cashier's checks for.

My heart stopped. What the hell was she up to?

Head swimming, I brought the pack inside and dropped it on the floor at my feet. Doc looked down and paled.

"Is that what I think it is?" he asked incredulously.

"Oh, yeah. It's exactly what you think."

"What the fuck is going on here, Rambler? Open the pack up properly. How fucking much is in there?"

"It's none of our business, man. She didn't ask for our help."

"Really? What the hell was she doing on your road, then?"

Admittedly, since I lived in the middle of proverbial nowhere, it was a good question. "I'll be sure to ask her when she wakes up."

"Don't tell me you're not curious."

I totally was, but I stared at him, stoic and stubborn.

"Don't be a dumb fuck. If you won't look, I will. I want to know what else is inside."

Well, shit.

With a sigh, I reluctantly unzipped the half-open bag and spread it wide.

"Son of a bitch! That's a lot of Benjamin Franklins. W-what the hell is she, a bank robber?" Doc actually stuttered.

Ella might have broken my heart, but she didn't have a criminal bone in her body. "It could be a blackmail drop. Or a kidnapping ransom."

Doc whistled. "Something is definitely up."

The dogs began barking in alarm, a tone that told me it was a warning and someone needed to get a gun. I didn't question the canines' instincts; I simply complied.

That's when I heard the sound of a big car pulling up outside.

As one, we stepped onto the porch. A big black Caddy, complete with a gold grill and tinted windows, came to a stop. Two Russian-looking mobsters poured from the backseat, wearing identical off-the-rack suits. They made a performance of facing us with legs spread and hands crossed over their balls. They looked like a cheap cliché.

Talk about surreal. I swear I looked around for a fucking movie camera.

Doc and I exchanged a WTF stare before facing them. Sadie and Gracie continued their barkfest, yanking at their chains, throwing spit, and snarling at the intruders. Their warning was crystal clear: stay back.

Goon One stepped forward and sneered, pointing to the dogs. "They are guard dogs, yes?"

Just as I suspected, the voice was laced with an accent that screamed Eastern Europe and manufactured badass.

Neither Doc nor I answered.

When he realized he was shit out of luck on replies, the smile disappeared. He backed up, and Goon Two gave us his best shot.

"We know the girl is here. Give her to us and we go. You live. Everybody is happy."

"I've a better idea," I said. As Goon Two turned to face me wearing the same sneer as his partner, I flashed him an acidic smile. "How about you both climb back into your pimp-mobile and get the fuck off my property before I blow your brains out."

His sneer turned down into a frown. "Our business does not concern you. This woman has taken something from our employer and he will have it back."

The dumb fuck actually unbuttoned his coat and exposed the piece he carried, as if he imagined that would scare me.

I pulled out my .45 and aimed the barrel between his eyes. "Maybe we have a language barrier. Do you not understand fuck off?"

Goon One appeared to have more sense. He gripped his partner's arm and pulled him back, muttering something in Russian.

As they inched toward their car, they wisely never exposed their backs to us, but Goon Two added a parting shot. "We'll be back."

Doc and I looked at each other as they climbed in their car and roared out of the driveway.

"What the fuck, dude? Does he think he's the Terminator?" I asked with a chuckle.

Doc shrugged as he settled Gracie and Sadie down. "No idea. What the hell..."

Then he left me on the porch and returned to his patient. To Ella, mysteriously injured on my property after weeks of total silence. And now she had Euro-trash thugs after her.

Waiting until Doc closed the door, I reached into my back pocket and pulled out my cell phone. I found Sparks's number and hit send. He answered on the first ring.

"Yeah?"

"I'm home and I'm thinking it might just be what the doctor ordered if y'all came over for a bug hunt."

"You don't say. What's on the menu?"

"Remember that Flat Tire beer we helped by the road about a month back?"

"I do. Very tasty. I would have liked a drink of that."

"Fucker," I grumbled. "Just so happens, I have it right here. Oh, and I have White Russians, too. It might be a good idea to make sure everyone brings plenty of mixers."

Sparks's chuckle told me he knew exactly what I was saying. "Sounds like our kind of party. Can't wait."

"I didn't ask before, but I think it's time to check out that brand of Flat Tire, see where it comes from. I'm having a powerful thirst for more."

"I can do that. What time do you expect this party to start?"

"Oh, it already has, but I wouldn't be surprised if it gets a bit rough and crazy before the night is through."

"Thanks for invite, man. I'll pass the word and make sure everyone comes with enough to go 'round."

I hung up. The call for reinforcements had gone out. Now it was time to wait.

2

ELLA

I awoke in darkness feeling something cold pressed against my eyes. As I reached up to push it away, a warm hand covered mine and gently eased my fingers aside.

"Leave it be. You're safe."

I knew that voice... Rambler? "Where am I? What happened?"

"You were in an accident, lass. You cut your head. I've given you a cold compress for the swelling." The faint accent of the other male voice sounded a lot like Doc.

"We found you on the road to my place, Ella. Were you looking for me? Need my help with a problem?"

I tried to turn my head, but the dull pain there sharpened. I moaned. Ugh, I couldn't think.

"How did I get here? Rambler, Doc, is that you?" Since I couldn't see, I needed confirmation. My thoughts were fuzzy, my head swimming in a fog.

"Yes. It's us," Rambler confirmed. "I'm surprised you remember the sound of my voice."

I couldn't miss the hard edge of his tone, but I did remember him. I couldn't forget a single thing that had happened between Rambler and me. I'd tried...and failed.

"Easy on her, man. Ella, try to relax and lie still. We're going to help you," Doc murmured in soothing tones. "You've been in an accident."

Suddenly, I remembered—just like I recalled the terrible reason I'd been in my Land Cruiser driving way too fast. A flash of terror exploded in my gut. "Did you find a backpack?"

"You mean the one filled with all the money?" Rambler left the question hanging.

Dread gripped me. I winced, then regretted moving at all. The drawl in his tone told me he was just this side of pissed off.

But I had much bigger problems than Rambler and his wounded pride. Worse, my beat-up body was telling me I wasn't leaving anytime soon. Panic gripped my lungs, knotted my stomach. Staying wasn't an option. No matter how crappy I felt, I had to leave—now.

Again, I reached for the cloth over my eyes and struggled to sit up. A gentle but strong hand pushed me back.

"You're not going anywhere just yet." Rambler's low voice might have meant to soothe me, but there wasn't an ounce of calm in his tone. "Care to tell me what you're doing with all that cash? Are you in trouble?"

"I'm fine," I lied.

What else could I say? My problems weren't his. I didn't want to involve anyone in my danger, especially a man I cared about far more than I should. How could I explain to him that I'd forced distance between us two weeks ago because I refused to drag him into my mess and risk his life?

"Right. And I'm the Easter Bunny," Rambler scoffed. "We'll get to the money later. Now that you're awake, maybe we should take you to the hospital, have you checked over."

If he did, Niko would find me for sure.

"No. I told you I'm fine. Thanks for everything, but... Look, it's my money. I didn't steal it. I just need to get out of here. Will my SUV still run?"

"It's totaled. And you're not leaving." I could almost hear Rambler gnashing his teeth as he spoke in that Alpha voice that sent shivers up my spine. He meant business. "Something is going on with you, and we're going to get to the bottom of it. Start talking."

I pressed my lips together mulishly.

He growled. "Who are you running from this time, Ella?"

I heard his unspoken question loud and clear: Why did you run from me?

"We didn't save you from that wreck just to throw you to the wolves. And we never thought you stole any money." Doc tried to set me at ease. "Just tell us what's going on. Maybe we can help."

I wish. No one could help me. It was years too late for that. And now I was out of options. I reached up to shove the compress aside again. Strong fingers curling around my wrist stopped me.

I grunted in frustration. "Can you take this damn thing off, please? I don't like not being able to see."

Someone sighed, probably Doc since the sound was more concerned than irritated.

"All right. Lie back and keep your eyes closed until I tell you to open them, lass."

I nodded carefully. The dull ache in my head told me it would be wise to rest another five minutes before I attempted to flee.

With gentle hands, Doc lifted my head and began to peel away the bandage and compress. "If you feel sick, let me know."

The second he moved me, a wave of nausea slid through my belly. I swallowed it down. "How long was I out?"

While Doc removed the bandages, Rambler took my hand. The memory of his calloused palms on my body made me tingle.

"Maybe twenty minutes," Doc explained. "I had to put a couple of stitches in your head."

"Well, first we had to pull you from your vehicle," Rambler cut in. "Otherwise, you might have been gator bait."

I shivered at that possibility. "Thank you."

"Okay, you can open your eyes now," Doc instructed.

I lifted my lids a fraction. My vision was blurry, but I managed to blink and focus on the small but functional room. The relief was immediate—until I caught sight of the men.

Rambler and Doc both hovered over me. They looked concerned, and guilt tore through me. The edge of anger on Rambler's strong face only made me feel worse. I wished he'd look at me the way he had when we'd been together, when he'd laughed with me. When he'd utterly possessed my body and made love to me.

Those days were gone.

Still, I couldn't stop staring. Rambler was taller than his buddy, and a few years older. He kept his sandy-blond hair from his rugged face with his signature camo-print skullcap. His mustache and beard hugged the angles of his sharp jaw. His piercing stare was more than disconcerting.

The past came rushing back, how my flat tire had led to knowing exactly what this man's soft beard between my thighs felt like.

It had been a typically hot, sticky Florida day. My tire had blown out and I was stuck on the side of the road, digging around in the back of my car for a jack. I was sweaty, disheveled, and pissed off with the world because no one had stopped to help.

Eight riders had suddenly appeared and pulled over. Each had been wearing hungry grins. But then one man had stepped off a huge bike and whipped off his aviators, his smile wide—stark white teeth against tanned skin—and he'd nearly stolen my breath. Confidence had radiated off his rugged body as he strode toward me on dusty leather boots. He had deep-set hazel eyes that bored into me with such intensity I'd had to look away, but not before I noticed how his black T-shirt strained across his chest and framed his large, muscular tattooed biceps. His big hands had been encased in weathered leather gloves. There wasn't an ounce of fat on the man anywhere from his lean hips to his long legs, covered in blue jeans that had molded perfectly to every packed inch.

And just like that, Rambler had taken my breath away.

At first, I'd been intimidated by so much raw, masculine muscle and black leather, but after introductions were made, I'd calmed. The bikers had quickly changed my tire, but I couldn't keep my eyes off Rambler, or ignore the palpable draw that pulsated between us.

When the boys had invited me out with them, something bold and daring had blossomed inside me. I'd brazenly asked Rambler to take me for a ride. Maybe I'd been searching for an escape from the fear, from always looking over my shoulder. Or maybe I'd simply been lonely and needed the strength and sensual power this man exuded. At the time, it hadn't really mattered. He'd taken me up on my offer, and I'd climbed onto the back of his stunning bike.

Arms wrapped around his steely body, I'd held on for dear life, convinced that any minute I'd fly off the back and scrape my ass raw on the road. Surrounded by hardness—both his body and the firm seat—every bump, slide, and vibration had ignited my clit.

The delicious ache that had hummed over my sex sent heat and demand singing through my body. I'd grown utterly saturated in seconds flat.

At first, I'd rocked imperceptibly, but the faster he drove, the harder I'd ground against the metal seat. Consumed with throbbing vibrations, my need had torqued up unbearably. I'd closed my eyes and rested my head against his shoulder as I'd drowned in the lovely, quivering shockwaves. My hands had slid from his waist and cradled his thick leather belt until the climax rolled over me like a freight train. I cried out and dropped both hands, wrapping them around the solid, thick bar of hot flesh between his thighs.

Lost in my own bliss, I hadn't remembered him pulling over. I just had a vague recollection of the trees, the lake, and the nearby boathouse. Rambler had somehow swung me around his body until the handlebars were at my back. My feet had rested on the seat behind him, and my legs were spread wide and locked around his hips.

I'd never felt so wanton, passionate, and desperate to feel a man inside me than when he'd ground his hard cock against my still-throbbing cunt. He'd driven me mad as he'd held me so tight I could barely breathe. Then he'd laid claim to my mouth in a feral kiss. My lips—both sets—had been swollen and so sensitive, the conflagration of fire that had built inside had felt as if I was all but combusting. He had me begging.

"Please. Oh, Rambler, that feels so good. I need more."

"I'll give you more, baby." His voice had dropped to a deep rumble, a velvet-sounding baritone that reverberated through me. I'd melted. He'd leaned forward and roughly pulled apart my shirt, sending the buttons flying with an odd-shaped knife he'd held in his hand. Before I'd been able to suck in a gasp, he'd flicked his wrist, and my bra landed in pieces on the ground.

"You owe me a new bra."

Quick as a flash, he'd slipped a finger down the inside of my jeans, snagged my panties, and lifted the seams clear of the denim. I'd held my breath and watched as he'd carefully slid the blade through the soft silk on both sides and tugged my panties free.

He'd wadded the fabric in a fist and brought it to his nose before he'd drawn in a deep breath. "Now I owe you panties, too."

The heated gleam that blazed in his eyes had me swallowing back a gasp. An instant later, he'd slurped the hard bud of my nipple into the wet heat of his mouth and sucked hard. I began to howl, the need for more overwhelming me.

At the same time, he'd reached up with one hand and dug his fingers into my hair, grasped a thick section, and pulled. I'd screamed as he bit down on my nipple and lashed it with his tongue.

As he'd broken the suction, an animalistic smile had crawled across his lips. "Fuck, you're delicious."

He'd quickly pocketed the knife and gripped my pussy through the soaked crotch of my jeans. Seconds later, he'd latched onto my other nipple, attacking it with equal fervor. A loud groan had escaped my lips as I'd thrust my pussy at him, shocked to discover that I was primed and ready to come again. Rambler then shoved his hips against me hard and ground his cock with the perfect amount of friction against my soft, wet sex.

I'd exploded. Deep, pulsating shockwaves of pleasure had poured outward in a blissful, heated rush. I'd thrown back my head and howled his name.

The huge grin that had suddenly appeared on his face promised more.

I remembered thinking, Oh, my god. He'll ruin me for anyone else.

That premonition had invaded my brain before he'd stripped away the sodden jeans, pushed me back against the bars, and told me to hold on tight. With wide hands, he'd gripped the insides of my knees, parted my thighs, then paused and taken a moment to admire the wet warmth he'd made of me.

His intention had been clear.

Rambler would not be denied.

I'd held my breath and watched in fascination as he dipped his beautiful head and covered my pussy with his greedy mouth. Then that incredible, ferocious, wildly beautiful man had proceeded to feast. He hadn't done it with polite interest but a controlled intensity. He'd suckled and devoured my fleshy sex as if I were a succulent peach. He'd coaxed one climax after another from me.

Then before I'd even realized what was happening, he'd lifted me into his arms and headed toward a boathouse. When he'd placed me down on my hands and knees and moved in behind me, kicking my feet apart, I gasped. My heart soared when I heard the soft snick of his zipper and the tearing sound of a wrapper.

"Thrust your ass out and put your head down."

His command had made me even wetter. When he'd pushed deep and full inside me, I'd braced my palms firmly on the floor, fingers digging into the wood, and wailed.

Gazing at Rambler even now, the recollection of our shared raw passion still reflected in his eyes and set me on fire. I could still feel his calloused hands cupping my hips, hear his strained voice as he told me how sexy I looked while he stroked deep inside me that first night—and all the incredible nights that had followed.

Biting back a moan at the memories, my tunnel clutched and my juices spilled.

Rambler's nostrils flared. A knowing smirk kicked up one corner of his mouth.

Oh, yes. He knew exactly what I'd been thinking.

I quickly wiped the sensual images from my mind and turned

toward Doc. Though not as tall as Rambler, he was just as fit and good-looking with a shocking mop of auburn hair. Pale skin framed vivid green eyes and a friendly smile. His slight accent hinted at his Scottish descent.

I felt safer here with them both...but I'd left Rambler for a reason. I couldn't afford to linger now.

I tore my gaze away and pushed up to my elbows. Though stiff and sore, I didn't feel foggy anymore.

"I didn't say to get up," Doc groused.

"I have to. Besides, I'm feeling much better now."

"That might be, but you took a nasty bump to the head. Lie back and rest. I insist." He guided me back down.

With an impatient sigh, I relented.

In a possessive show of force, Rambler moved in alongside his friend, compelling me to look at them both. My mind warred between gratitude that they'd saved me again and resentment. My only window of escape had closed. A burst of panic and fear exploded within me. My plane had departed without me. Still, there might be time for me to arrange another, but I couldn't do it here.

Rising to my feet, I sent them a tight smile. "Thank you both, but I—"

Rambler and Doc both reached for me as I wobbled. Together, they eased me back down to the bed.

Rambler didn't let go. "Whoa. You're not going anywhere yet, girl."

"But I feel fine. Honest."

"Great. Then you can give me some answers," he snapped. "You owe me that much."

Guilt pelted me from all angles. I couldn't avoid the conversation anymore, but they wanted answers I couldn't give them.

"He wants what's best for you, as I do. You will stay in that bed and rest," Doc growled.

Taking orders from Rambler was one thing, but when Doc started putting in his two cents, my temper ignited.

"I don't need you to watch over me. I said I'm fine," I snapped indignantly.

"Is that right?" Rambler was suddenly in my face. His warm breath drifted across my mouth.

Goose bumps exploded across my flesh at his firm, commanding tone.

"We're not going to force you to stay. I'm sure you'll run off the minute you get the chance, just like before." Rambler's smile was arctic. "But you can either talk or I can call the cops and report the accident before we take you to the hospital and get you checked out."

"Good idea. I'll grab her backpack full of cash," Doc volunteered. "We'll let the cops figure out what the hell to do with it. Not our problem."

Their words cut like dual knives. Their ultimatum left me no choice. I had to say something. Guilt helped my decision along. Fate or divine intervention had made our paths cross again for a reason.

"Look, the money in that bag belongs to me. It's my life's savings. I'd like to stay…but I can't."

I'd already put them in enough danger.

Anger lined Rambler's face, but it was the pain in his eyes that crushed me.

I looked away. "Let me pay you for your trouble."

Both men bristled at my offer.

Rambler leaned in with a growl. "I don't want your money. I want answers, baby."

I bit my lip to hold in tears. "I'm sorry you have to keep coming to my rescue, but I have to leave, get as far away as I can before—" When I realized what I'd nearly admitted, I fell mute.

"The Russians find you? It's too late for that." Rambler shook his head. "We've already had a little visit from two of them. How do they know you?"

Niko's goons found me again?

The panicked sensation of stepping off into an abyss swamped me. Oh, god. Oh, god. Now what?

My last thought before I sank beneath the wave of welcoming blackness was that I'd tried so hard to spare Rambler this terrible danger. And just like my mission today, I'd failed.

IT WAS DARK WHEN I WOKE UP AGAIN, THIS TIME ALONE.

What else could I possibly expect? I'd walked away from the man I'd fallen in love with without explanation. Yes, I'd done it to save his life but he didn't know that. I couldn't even afford to spend time lamenting my situation. But I did anyway.

The last time Rambler and I were supposed to hook up at the Regency Cinema in Stuart, we'd laughed that we were finally planning a real date. All we'd done so far was spend our time in bed.

I'd arrived a half an hour early, waiting for Rambler in the parking lot while enjoying a frozen custard. When he'd texted that he was on his way, I'd checked out the two cars beside me. They'd both been empty. I'd grinned as I'd slipped off my panties from under my dress, just in case he'd planned to do naughty things to me inside the theater.

I hadn't seen a reason why I couldn't have my cake and eat it, too.

Since Rambler had come into my life, I'd been deliriously happy. The man was dazzling, amazing. I'd been so utterly miserable for so long, and each moment I'd spent with him had brought me back to the living.

When I'd heard the familiar sound of his bike, I'd looked up and watched him glide into the parking lot. He'd pulled into an empty space a couple of rows away. He hadn't seen me yet, so I'd decided to saunter over to where he'd parked, let him get a good view of my dress as I headed his way.

But as I'd started in his direction, I'd noticed two of Niko's men sitting on a park bench, watching me with those somehow menacingly blank expressions.

The bottom had dropped out of my world.

A voice in my head had told me that if I truly cared about Rambler, I had to save his life. Walk away and set him free.

My heart had screamed out a mournful no!

Ultimately, I didn't have a choice.

When I'd turned and peered at him as he sat astride his bike, phone in hand, I'd been so swamped with the searing pain of loss I couldn't breathe.

My phone had dinged and I'd glanced down at the message Rambler had sent.

Where are you? I'm here in the parking lot. Are you inside? I can't wait to taste your lips, baby girl.

Crushed, I shoved my phone back in my purse. There had been no point in answering his text. I had to leave, get out of town. Out of the state. I'd done this before, and I didn't understand why I felt so bereft this time. Our relationship—while amazing—had been brief and based on passion and sex.

Or at least that's what I told myself.

But I'd known with each tear that had spilled down my cheeks while I drove away that I was lying to myself. The love we had shared had been both fierce and fragile, and I had shattered it into a million pieces, along with my heart. Hoarse, ugly sounds had wrenched from my throat. I could feel the joy that had burned so bright inside me melt away, replaced by my old friends terror and uncertainty.

Even as I'd absently wiped my nose, I hadn't been able to take my eyes off him, reflected in my rearview mirror. I'd tried to will him to look up so I could see his beautiful face one last time. As if he'd heard me, he'd raised his head and scanned the parking lot. I committed each angle and plane to memory and added that singular moment to the collection of time I'd shared with him, each second now branded in my brain. That would be all I'd have left of him…of us.

When I'd pulled out of the theater parking lot, I'd felt as if I'd left a part of myself behind.

Niko's goons had simply lifted their heads and smiled at me.

In hindsight, I should have paid more attention to that. But then, I'd been upset. Until then, I'd foolishly thought I'd managed to escape my former life. The peace and happiness I'd found in Florida had been nothing but smoke and mirrors. I'd stupidly let my guard down, grown careless, and had let Rambler deep inside my body and my heart.

I sat up in bed and exhaled a heavy sigh.

We've already had a little visit from two of them…

Even remembering Rambler's words sent a surge of panic ripping through me. I clutched the sheets as my heart rate tripled. The signs had no doubt been there this whole time. The bastard probably knew exactly where I'd been all along. But how? How had Niko found me? He couldn't have traced my car. I'd bought it on eBay the week before I ran. I'd abandoned his precious Lamborghini in a parking lot at the local mall the day I skipped town. I thought I'd taken every precaution before heading south from Brighton Beach, New York. Obviously, I'd missed something.

Had he somehow planted a tracking device inside me?

Now you're just being paranoid, my subconscious chided.

Nothing made sense. I didn't know why his goons hadn't tried to snatch me that day at the theater. Maybe Niko had simply ordered them to find and observe me so he could come and kill me himself. That sounded like something he'd do—with pleasure.

I honestly thought he would when I left Stuart for the Okeechobee airport earlier. The flight I'd booked under an alias was the last string holding me to the States. When I'd noticed the big black Caddy following me, I panicked and turned down another road—the one that led to Rambler's house. If I could have kept from panicking and crashing, I might now be on a flight and long gone from danger.

I needed the damn FBI to swoop in and protect me, protect us all. If they could capture and prosecute Niko, I could stop looking over my shoulder, and Rambler and Doc wouldn't be in imminent danger. Sure, they and their biker friends were rough and street-smart, but they were nice guys—definitely no match against Niko and his Russian mob connections.

"And here I thought I'd been so clever," I whispered on a sad sigh.

Instead of continuing to rehash the whole mess over and over, I rolled out of bed and tiptoed to the bathroom. Staying upright was harder than I'd imagined. My head swam. My stomach protested.

Too bad. If I wanted the man I loved to live, I had to leave. Unfortunately, I was in no condition to walk, run, or drive anywhere, especially since I didn't even have a damn car. I had no clothes except the bra and panties I was wearing. My stash of cash was...somewhere, probably being guarded by Rambler and Doc.

I wanted to scream in frustration.

As I headed out of the bathroom, feeling defeated and lost, the bedroom door suddenly opened. Rambler, Doc, Sparks, and Dozer strolled in.

"Hold up a fucking goddamn minute," Rambler bellowed as he turned and tried to shove the men back out the door. "All of you, get lost. Ella's not dressed."

Dozer gave a snort. "Too late. I've already filed all that...mmm, yeah to memory. Ms. Ella, you are one fine-looking woman."

My cheeks blazed.

Rambler scowled and slapped Dozer upside the head, then turned to face me. "We have news."

About what?

Dozer and Sparks stood gaping at me like a couple of hungry wolves.

Doc rolled his eyes, pushed past a snarling Rambler, and helped me back into bed. "There, Ella. Just ignore them. I do. Oh, and don't pay any attention to Rambler, either. He's gone a bit screwy. Damn knucklehead seems to have gone a bit daft since buying a Knucklehead."

"What are you talking about?" I'd been so focused on Rambler's possessive mien that I hadn't been paying attention to anything else.

"He's snarling about us seeing you all but naked. He forgets I'm a medical Corpsman and that all of us have seen plenty of female soldiers in their skivvies before."

My eyes went wide. "You're in the military?"

"We're all combat vets, active and retired from various branches. Me, I was a combat medic for the Marine Corps. It was my job to keep those Leathernecks alive."

"But...aren't you a biker?" The question sounded lame, even to my ears.

"We enjoy the freedom of riding. In fact, we've fought hard to preserve all our freedoms," Doc assured. "But we're much more than just bikers. Trust me."

I stared at all of them one by one. Like most people, I'd only seen what I wanted to.

Dozer sent me a wide smile. "Army grunt here, ma'am. I kick in doors and knock down walls. Hence the handle."

"The what?"

"The handle. Nickname. Like bulldozer. You didn't think Dozer was my real name, did you?"

Actually I had. "What is it then?"

"Maurice. I prefer Dozer."

I could see why. He did not look like a Maurice. "Of course."

Rambler still stood, silently watching me as if wanting to pounce.

I looked directly at him. "And what about you?"

When he didn't reply right away, Sparks edged closer to the bed. "He's a recon Marine. Attached to MARSOC. Very elite, very deadly, and very secret."

"Recon Marine?"

"He's a Marine, one of the Leathernecks that Doc was referring to, except he was into some next-level shit—"

Rambler cleared his throat loudly. "That's enough, Sparks."

It wasn't at all. I wanted to know more about Rambler, especially his past. Or maybe I didn't. What good would it do me?

"What about you?" I asked the guy Rambler had tried to silence.

"I'm an electronics geek—a glorified hacker. I was a spark chaser for the Navy. My official title was electronic warfare tech. Now I'm just Sparks. It's shorter and fits better on my vest."

"Wow..." There was so much more to them all than met the eye.

"Which brings us to these, Ella." Sparks held up something small in one hand. It looked like something metal. In his other was a flash drive. "This is the news Rambler mentioned."

"What are those?"

Rambler squeezed past Sparks and dropped a solemn expression my way. "The first one is a tracking device. We found it in the lining of your backpack."

"Oh, my god." I felt the blood drain from my face. All this time, my freedom from Niko had been nothing but an illusion. Fuck. Fuck. Fuck.

Sparks reached down and gently patted my hand. "I take it the backpack wasn't yours?"

"No, my ex-boyfriend's. I didn't know it had a bug. I didn't even stop to think... How could I have been so stupid?"

Sparks held up the drive. "You're not. Luckily, you inadvertently snagged something rather special. Let's just say this little baby here contains enough intel to put your ex and his buddies away for a long, long time. We're talking extortion, weapons, drugs, sex trafficking, and the list goes on and on."

"Oh..." Horror spread through me. Niko had been guilty of all that? "I had no idea."

"Which is probably the only reason you're still alive," Rambler added dryly.

"If you want your ex to go away, you have to call him, Ella," Sparks chimed back in.

"What?" Just the thought of speaking to Niko again had me trembling. "Why would I do that?"

Rambler took my hand. "Don't be afraid. We'll end this on our terms, not Nikolai Rusanov's." He spat the name with fury. "You're going to call and invite him here to collect his property."

I could feel the terror rising.

"But he thinks I-I'm his p-property," I said, pleading with Rambler. "He won't leave without me."

His stare was fierce. "I'll show him how wrong he is. I'll deal with that asshole."

"But Niko's with the mob. The Russian mob. He's too powerful for you to fight."

Rambler darted a look to his friends before they all began to chuckle. "Baby, you have no idea what we're capable of."

The confidence on his face was mirrored by the other men in the room. It filled me with something that I hadn't experienced in years—hope. Butterflies swirled in my belly as I pulled him down and into a tight hug.

After a minute, he eased away and looked at me solemnly. "It's time to clear the air. You ran out on me without so much as a good-bye, Ella. What guarantee do I have that you won't do it again?"

Out of the corner of my eye, I watched Doc, Dozer, and Sparks discreetly leave the room. Alone with Rambler, I had nowhere to look but at him.

I swallowed. "I—I thought… I mean, I found out I was being followed that night at the theater. I worried they would kill us both. So I left. They watched me go. And it hurt so bad. My only consolation was that they didn't know about you, about us."

"Why didn't you tell me someone was after you? I would have kept you safe."

I lowered my head and sighed. "I didn't believe anyone could help me. This mess is huge. I couldn't turn to you without putting your life in danger. But I did, anyway. I'm so sorry. I was trying to protect you. I thought if I was gone, they'd leave you alone."

"I can handle myself and take care of you. Did you think all the time we spent together was just for fun, some kind of game?"

"You never said how you felt. I just assumed it was a fling and—"

"That's where you assumed wrong, dammit. It wasn't a fling. It wasn't just sex, not for me."

My mouth went dry. I swallowed down the lump of emotion lodged in my throat. "I thought I-I was the only one."

He caressed my cheek with those rough fingertips. "Only one what?"

"The only one falling in love."

His face both softened and turned fiercer. "Kiss me, Ella, and I'll prove you're not alone."

My heart was ready to burst with happiness again. "Oh, Rambler…"

He clasped my hair in his fists as fire blazed in his eyes. "Fuck, I've missed you."

"You have no idea how much I've missed you, too."

"Then show me."

He stripped off what little I wore and picked me up as though I weighed no more than a feather. I wrapped my legs about his waist and found his sinful mouth with mine. His tongue traced the crease of my lips. The soft hairs of his beard tickled my chin. I instinctively opened, inviting his hungry sweep inside. I clung to him. My body was aching, throbbing, and wet as he rubbed and prodded my soft belly with his hard cock covered in stifling jeans.

"Please," I whispered.

"Mmm... I want you, baby. I've missed everything about you."

3

RAMBLER

My chest squeezed like a vise. I still couldn't believe she was in my arms again. My Ella. I also couldn't believe all she'd endured.

"After everything we've been through, this isn't going to be soft and sweet, baby."

"I know."

She smiled up at me with trust twinkling in her eyes. It warmed the beast within me. Was she not listening or understanding what I was saying? I tried again.

"It's going to be hard and fast, baby girl. I'm too wound up for gentle. We don't have time for finesse."

"Yes," she said simply. "I need you, Rambler."

"We can wait until you feel better."

"What? No!"

"Is your head okay? Do you feel faint again?"

"I feel fine. Will you fuck me now?"

With her legs still around my hips, she squirmed and reached down, trying to unfasten my jeans. Unable to brush them away, Ella mewled in frustration. I could definitely relate. With one strong arm, I gripped her around the middle and lifted her higher. With the other hand, I shoved my jeans down.

"If you feel sick at any time, you tell me and we'll stop."

"Like hell we will. You started this damn fire. I need you to put these flames out," she growled. "I'm getting stronger every minute. I'll be fine. Now, can you pretty please stop talking and get inside me? I'm burning alive here."

"Thank fuck," I muttered.

The time for talking was through.

I cupped her ass with one hand and held her just above my straining, aching thickness. Splaying my fingers open, I dipped along the valley before deftly sliding between her cheeks. Pausing, I rubbed and teased her crinkled, sensitive rosette. Slick, wet heat poured from the swollen lips of her sex. I cupped her sweltering cunt completely with my palm and gently squeezed.

"This is mine. You're so beautiful, but you don't give the orders, Ella."

She let out a long moan that had my cock swelling and lengthening even more.

"I'm sorry. But I need you so much. I need to feel you inside me again. Please."

"Then look at me, Ella. Keep your eyes on mine. I want to watch you come for me."

In two wide strides, I braced her back against the wall. My cock pressed against her sex. Her nails dug into my skin, making me buck hard against her. She was so fucking gorgeous, and I couldn't wait a second more, even if my life depended on it.

Urgent need beat at me. I reached down and guided my cock to her greedy cunt, as I let her slip down the wall a little at a time until she fully enveloped me.

Her soft baby blues, framed with her thick, dark lashes, were wide open and staring straight at me. Her pink mouth formed an O of surprise. Her breath spilled over my lips as her narrow tunnel softened to accommodate me.

With a slow slide, I deliberately retreated until just the head of my cock remained inside her. I paused, then leaned in to kiss her silken lips. She opened to me instantly, her tongue dancing against mine. I held her tightly and thrust hard and deep once more, all the way inside her snug sheath. We both groaned loudly, so fucking thankful and happy to be holding one another again. Then she squeezed around me tight and milked me as I set a hard rhythm, shoving and pushing my way in and out of her.

"Fuck, you feel good, baby." My voice sounded guttural and desperate even to my own ears. I felt like a conquering caveman with a very short fuse.

"Oh, Rambler. More, please. I need more."

I thanked all the fucking stars above. Like a too tight vest, I cast off the last of my restraint and gripped her hips before setting a blistering pace.

She kept up with me by locking those stunning long legs tighter about my hips. Clinging to my body, she rocked back, hard and fast, meeting me stroke for stroke. Her face was flushed, her eyes soft. Another splash of color stained her cheeks and flared in rosy tones down the elegant column of her neck. The redness spread across her collarbones and kissed the swells of her breasts. God, I loved her beautiful tits as they bounced unfettered. Her nipples were a deep, dark apricot now. The stems, thick and hard, all but taunting and begging for my mouth. But all I could do was hang on to her and stare hungrily.

I drew my gaze up to her huge, sparkling eyes, and they pulled me in deeper as I watched the irises shift, warming as her arousal flared. Her pupils grew larger the closer I drove her to climax. I was drowning in rapturous bliss, my breath sawing in and out of my chest as I struggled to hold back the explosion that would decimate us both.

"Come for me, baby," I demanded with a growl.

Obeying my command, Ella tossed her head back. She began to spasm and twitch, clutching around my cock so hard I could barely move as she screamed, then wailed my name.

Neither of us gave two shits about the others in the next room. We were lost in our own private oasis where only the two of us existed, joined together in bliss and love, where terror and what-ifs couldn't hurt us.

Then I was coming, too, pouring myself into her. She observed me, watched what she did to me—with her mouth open in awe—as I roared out the sweet agony of my ecstasy.

"My beautiful girl, I fucking missed you."

She mewled and melted in my arms as we slowly floated back to earth.

Then an unwelcome banging shook the door.

"What the fuck do you want?" I thundered.

"Sorry, man," Sparks said without an ounce of remorse. "Now that you're done, it's time to get down to business. She needs to make the damn call. We want to see them on our terms, not dance to theirs."

Fucker. But he was right.

As I released her, Ella's body stiffened. Fear flashed across her face.

"Easy, baby. That cocksucker won't get the chance to touch one pretty hair on your gorgeous head again."

She didn't look convinced.

"Trust me."

"I do. More than you'll ever know, but—"

"No buts. Come on."

Five minutes and a few lingering kisses later, we were dressed and standing in my living room, surrounded by Doc, Sparks, and Dozer. We'd all paid our dues to Uncle Sam and survived. We were all ready and willing to put our diverse set of skills to work to protect Ella. Each of us had been honed in various aspects of warfare—deadly force, weapons, demolition, intelligence gathering, hand-to-hand combat, computer skills, electronic surveillance, and more. Nikolai Rusanov didn't stand a chance.

I stood beside Ella as she engaged the speakerphone on her cell and dialed Niko's number. She trembled as she held the device in her hands.

The prick answered on the second ring. "I grow impatient, waiting for your call, malyshka. Do you not know how I have missed you? How I have worried?"

"Call your goons off, Niko. It's over. We're through."

The quiver in her voice made me want to punch the wall. The Russian prick had no right to fill her with such fear.

"Oh, but you are wrong. I say when we are through, and I assure you we are not. You belong to me. I will never let such beautiful treasure go."

The blood drained from her face, and she shrank in on herself. This was not the confident, vibrant woman who had been screaming my name moments ago. Forget beating the shit out of the wall; I wanted to rip the fucker's heart from his chest.

Doc set a reassuring hand on my arm. He softly shook his head and silently reminded me what was at stake: Ella's freedom. Ella's life.

"Fine. I'll meet you at the end of the driveway, but only if I have your word that you won't hurt my friends."

Anger blasted its way through my body. What the hell was she doing? I narrowed my eyes at her, shaking my head. No way would I allow her to trade her freedom for the safety of my brothers and me.

"Ah, you have come to your senses, malyshka. Good. But I cannot keep this promise unless you bring my backpack and everything inside it."

Obviously, he valued the information on the flash drive at least as much as Ella, maybe more. That fucker had to die.

"I'll bring the backpack, too." Ella's voice shook with fear. "If I have your promise."

"Of course. I am not monster. I pick you up in twenty minutes. Do not make me wait."

When she hung up, I tugged her into my arms and held her while she trembled.

Funny what you think of when the shit's about to hit the fan. I was thirty-eight and I'd served twenty years as a Marine. I had no wife, no home—nothing but myself when I'd retired. It had been a bit of a shock to discover that civilian life did not suit me. So, I found a new home and took a job with a private military contractor. It allowed me to continue practicing the skill sets I'd developed in covert operations that felt comfortable, familiar. I'd made a shitload of money in the process, which allowed me to indulge in my love of the three B's:

Bullets.

Bikes.

And babes.

Until now. Ella had changed everything. Somehow, she'd even changed me.

She was a target, and all my priorities had shifted. She was what I wanted most, valued above everything else. My brothers in arms and I were all that stood between her and the prick who'd made her life hell. In order to get to her, Nikolai Rusanov would have to go through us—through me—and that wasn't happening. I would move heaven and earth to keep her safe. I would protect her or die trying.

This bully of a Russian was about to find out my buddies and I were bigger, badder, and deadlier than anyone or anything the two-bit mobster had dealt with before.

Dozer was five ten and weighed 220 pounds. He'd been an Army infantryman and had seen more than his fair share of action in Mosul. Built like a brick shithouse, and nicknamed appropriately because he'd never encountered a door he couldn't kick off its hinges on the first try. He was an absolute gun fanatic, and there wasn't a firearm made he didn't know how to dismantle, put back together, and use with deadly, accurate force.

"Time to break open the safe and bring out the toys," I called to Dozer.

Junior Samples, our Army supply sergeant with a knack for acquisitions, owned a towing company, mechanics shop, and a small used car lot just outside of town. Junior made himself virtually invisible to the average citizen—until he was needed. The rich fucker's mother had obviously been a fan of Hee Haw and possessed a sense of humor. Junior had played along, embracing the joke. His personalized license plate read BR549. But he also had a screaming skull and wrenches for crossbones tattooed on the back of his hand and was a badass motherfucker.

Dozer gave me a thumbs-up. "The balloon is up."

Excellent. The final act had been staged. The bad guys were on the way. It was time to take out the trash. And poetically, they'd have it out right where Ella had crashed into the ditch.

4

ELLA

I HAD BEEN RELEGATED TO WATCHING THE PROCEEDINGS WITH DOC AND the dogs from behind the barricade of his truck that now blocked Rambler's driveway. Niko wouldn't be happy with that, but I didn't care. More bikers had arrived—big, burly men, some I hadn't met before. But I could easily recognize the swagger of fellow veterans. They had come to support their brothers, as apparently the balloon going up was some sort of code for shit is going down.

All hands were on deck, and all of them had come with everything they needed to blow said shit away.

Rambler stood alone in the road, his broad back to the rest of us as we waited.

Breath held, I watched the big black Caddy barrel down the road and skid to a halt in front of Rambler. Another nearly identical vehicle pulled up behind it, and a dozen Russians rushed out, including Nikolai Rusanov himself.

I struggled to keep myself composed. It hadn't been that long since I'd last seen him. Definitely not long enough for me to forget how dangerous and ruthless he could be. Niko still looked as handsome and polished as ever, but I knew what kind of demon crawled beneath his aristocratic façade. I was quaking in fear, not just for me but for Rambler and his friends, too.

Doc gave me a comforting pat on the shoulder.

"There's no fat lady singing yet, Ella. We've got this."

"I hope so," I whispered. "I don't want to see any of you hurt or killed because of me."

He would have answered, except Niko stepped up to Rambler. With a laugh, he spread his arms arrogantly wide and turned in a circle, taking in the men gathered on opposing sides. The tension pinging off me and hanging in the air was thick enough to cut.

"So I see we have boys on little bikes, thinking they have the balls to interfere in my business." The condescending tone I'd grown to loathe rolled off Niko's tongue. How had I ever found such a menacing and cruel man attractive? I'd walked away from my family and my career seven years ago for that bastard. I'd regretted it nearly every day since. "I am not seeing what is mine. Where are you, Ella?"

Rambler stood like a tree, firmly planted in the road. His thick arms were banded across his chest as he faced my nemesis. "Here's the thing, asshole. I will fight for a woman, but I learned a long time ago never to fight over one. And just so we're clear, I'm not fighting over Ella. She's already mine."

Rusanov threw back his head and laughed. Turning to face his men, he shook his head in disbelief. "You American fools think you can take what is not yours. Enough of this nonsense! Give me what I want or I will kill you all."

My heart skipped a beat. I wanted to dash out from my designated safe spot and put myself between Niko and Rambler. Doc gripped my shoulder and stared me down with a dark warning. "Don't you even think about it. If you truly love him, then believe in him."

I blinked back at Doc. I wanted to believe in Rambler—in all of them—but could they really protect me from Niko?

"That's funny, you commie cocksucker. Better men than you have tried. And all have failed."

Terror gripped me. Rambler was baiting the bear. Why on earth would he deliberately piss Niko off? Didn't he realize the danger he was in?

Apparently not.

He reached back and grabbed his T-shirt by the neck, pulling it over his head before throwing it to the ground between them. "You wanna dance, fucker? Bring it on. You and me. When I'm through with you, your face will look like a bowl of borsht. I'll use my shirt down there to mop up your blood."

Nikolai removed his jacket with slow, exacting precision and passed it to one of his associates. Then, he made a great show of removing his tie and shirt, one button at a time.

It was Rambler's turn to laugh, "Good idea. You'll need to save your clothes so they'll look good when the mortician lays you out in your coffin."

The glint in Niko's eyes, along with the sneer on his lips, told me he'd reached his breaking point. While his men stood by, tense, stoic, and silent through the heated exchange, Rambler's men had laughed and taunted Niko with slurs and insults.

The laughter died when my ex pulled out a heavy set of brass knuckles and slid them onto his fingers. Rambler didn't look impressed or concerned. He simply reached into his back pocket and pulled out his Karambit. His fingers fit right into the holes, the wicked blade curving out from his fist.

Anxiousness gripped my stomach as the fighters faced off. The Russians lined one side of the road. The Americans stood nearly shoulder to shoulder on the other.

When the rumble began, it happened so fast.

A practiced fighter, Nikolai was quick. He enjoyed getting his hands dirty from time to time. His movements were a blur as he brought his fists up in a rapid one-two combo toward Rambler's face, meaning to drop my big Marine where he stood.

But Rambler was quicker, more agile. More practiced. He dodged Niko's strikes effortlessly as he brought the wicked curved blade of his knife up, slashing through the back of Niko's hand.

A shocking, blood-curdling howl tore from Niko's mouth as he grabbed his damaged hand and backed away, his eyes pinpoints of hate. The minute his blood spilled, all hell broke loose. Doc's dog Sadie ripped off her leash and escaped the truck. When Doc raced after her, I didn't think, I simply reacted.

Rambler caught sight of me leaving the relative safety of the truck. He turned a scowl toward me. "Get back now, Ella."

By the time I realized I'd distracted him, it was too late. In my foolish attempt to help the man I loved, I'd given Niko his golden opportunity.

In horror, I watched my former lover draw a small pistol from his holster and aim it between Rambler's shoulder blades with an evil smile.

He intended to enjoy this.

I had to do something.

"Rambler!" I screamed as I raced toward him.

When my Marine turned to assess the situation, the .45 tucked in the back of his pants glimmered in the sunlight.

Without thinking twice, I yanked the weapon free, aimed as much as I could with trembling hands, and fired.

The sound of my shot rent the air. Blood splattered. Niko's eyes grew wide as he clutched the wound gaping in his chest. I don't know who was more surprised—him, Rambler, or me. The men on both sides of the road stood in stunned silence as Rambler marched to where the fallen Russian lay, the useless gun still clutched in his hand.

"Dead. I told you you'd need the suit, fucker! Not that the gators will leave much." Rambler sent me a concerned glance before turning back to Niko's henchmen. "She is far more than any of you gave her credit for."

The collective sound of the vets drawing and readying their weapons was deafening in the silence. We all watched Rambler drag Nikolai to the ditch and unceremoniously dump him over the edge.

Dozer stepped into the road, his weapon aimed at the Russians. "This might be a good time for you boys to leave. Nobody else needs to die today. But if you ever come back, we'll slaughter you."

With the head of their snake gone and the promise of death from

Every Mother's Son MC, the Russians nodded and eased back to their cars, leaving their slain boss where Rambler had tossed him.

EPILOGUE

A MONTH LATER

I SAT ON THE BACK OF THE KNUCKLEHEAD BOBBER, MY THIGHS WRAPPED around Rambler's back, while his hands idly rubbed my leg. We were parked out at the inlet at Fort Pierce, overlooking the beach, watching the full moon rise.

Since Niko's death, I'd been surprised we hadn't experienced any fallout, thanks to Sparks. The brilliant computer geek had forwarded the contents of the flash drive to one of his old shipmates, currently working for the FBI. A RICO investigation had immediately been launched into the Rusanov family's activities. Nikolai was presumed to have fled the country. Every day, he became a more distant nightmare for me.

That suited us just fine.

I wrapped myself around Rambler while I kissed and nipped at his throat. "Can we go home now? I need you."

His smile said it all. "You know I'll do anything you want, baby. Always. Let's go."

ABOUT ISABELLA LAPEARL

Isabella LaPearl is a USA Today bestselling author known for her collaboration with Shayla Black & Jenna Jacob for the Doms of Her Life Series. She enjoys writing sexy, erotic romance. A wife, mother, writer, reader and a love for riding motorcycles.

To say it's been an extraordinary journey thus far would be an understatement... what a rush! What a thrill to realize dreams and see them go from a seed to fruition. So for all you aspiring Authors, who like me, have a fire inside that burns brightly and demands to be sated by writing... Never give up.

To be notified of new releases or sales,
join Isabella's Mailing List: www.eepurl.com/D_Wrb
Connect with Isabella online
Facebook: www.facebook.com/IsabellaLaPearlPage
Instagram: www.instagram.com/IsabellaLaPearl
Visit Isabella at IsabellaLaPearl.com!

EXECUTIVE *Ink*

A MONTGOMERY INK SHORT STORY

CARRIE ANN RYAN

1

Exhaustion crept over Ashlynn Kelly's body, but she ignored it, pushing it deep down where she knew it would stay until she found time to actually take care of it. Much like she ignored the fact that her feet had gone numb about two hours ago in her red-soled stilettos, and how her back ached enough that she knew it would take at least three hour-long massages to get out the kinks. Of course, by the time she arranged appointments with her massage therapist, she'd need even more hours with him, and she'd be down another pair of shoes.

But she'd closed the damn deal.

Nothing could take that away from her.

Not even blisters on her feet and a throbbing temple or two or even the muggy Atlanta air.

She'd spent her life working countless hours and barely sleeping while dealing with condescending men in business suits. Guys who traveled on Mondays to get to out-of-town business meetings while laughing far too loudly and looking at her legs rather than her face before flying back home Friday evenings with even more leers. She'd dealt with them during her meetings as they called her "honey," and flashed them her patented icy glare when they gave her their coffee orders before every conference or panel instead of treating her like an equal. She'd gotten her MBA while working two jobs and dealt with men who only looked at her for her tits and pins—their words, not hers—not her brain.

Now, she was the CFO of a Forbes 500 company and kicking genuine ass.

At least, this week.

So, yes, her feet hurt, and she had a headache from hell, but there were no mediocre men with fat egos around to piss her off. Only, she had a feeling as soon as she walked back into the hotel lobby, she'd be surrounded by those blowhards in suits and loosened ties. She'd been in the conference center across the street most of the day, and rather than walk the extra mile to use the covered bridge that connected the two buildings, she'd opted to go outside and breathe some fresh air for what felt like the first time in weeks.

Between meetings, panels, lunches on the premises, and dinners that had, for some reason, only occurred in the revolving restaurant on-site, she'd spent her entire week breathing hotel and conference room air.

As soon as her crosswalk light turned green, Ashlynn inhaled a deep breath and almost choked. It was a little too humid and damp at the moment for that kind of breathing, and she knew the underneath layers of her hair were starting to curl. That was why she'd spent the days inside rather than out. Her throat might be dry and her skin in need of some serious lotion time thanks to the acrid air of the hotel, but her hair and makeup had stayed in place for the ten hours she'd needed it to throughout the day.

At the moment, however, she didn't give a damn how she looked. She'd made the deal, gotten her company's name in the hands of the few people at the event who didn't know about them and had even impressed the good ol' boys who thought her a stripper rather than their potential rival.

Silly men and their tiny dicks in this business, she thought. They never saw her coming until it was far too late and she'd walked all over them, wrapping them around her finger at the same time for good measure.

Ashlynn was damn good at what she did, and when she got home, she'd open a bottle of wine to celebrate.

By herself.

Because it wasn't as if she had time these days to actually go out and meet someone, let alone get to know them enough to bring them into her life like that. She hadn't had sex with another person in months, but that was fine. She had her hand, and a nice selection of vibrators—even one that blew little puffs of air right on her clit and made her come in five seconds flat—she didn't need a man.

Though a hot night of sex with no commitments might be nice one day. Just meaningless, against-the-door sex with a man who loved going down on her until she came over and over again before fucking her hard into the mattress until he released himself all over her. Just downright dirty, unhinged, no-holds-barred sex.

Ashlynn swallowed hard. Yes, that would be nice.

Not that she'd actually get that in her hotel at the moment since she knew probably half the men down in the bar area. That meant she needed to remain her professional, icy self and make use of the showerhead in her hotel bathroom when she got back up to her room. There was no way she'd sleep with someone in her profession—not when that would rebound on her. God forbid a woman want a night of hot sex without being labeled a slut. The rest of her coworkers could get away with that because they were men, but not her. She had to remain aboveboard because double standards were still a thing, no matter how many marches she attended or how hard she tapped that glass ceiling—at least for now, damn it.

It wasn't as if she were the only woman in this position either. Her company had more women than it had before—thanks to her—but she was the only one at this particular conference since it was her project on the line. Ashlynn didn't know the other women attending this week that well since they hadn't been in her panels as they each had their own jobs to do, so she was pretty much on her own. And while that suited her most days, tonight, she was a bit lonely.

Ashlynn shook her head as she stepped onto the pavement that separated the two large streets she had to cross in order to get back to her hotel. The pedestrian crossing lights were so short that it took two cycles to get from one side to the other—even with her power walk in heels.

Tapping her foot, she looked around at the traffic surrounding her and tried not to sway from foot to foot. Her feet hurt. Maybe she didn't need hot sex; a foot massage might be enough. Sadly, she knew from experience that doing it herself wasn't quite the same—much like an orgasm, but that was something she wasn't going to think about.

The red hand went away, and the little man lit up, so she looked both ways—as people were idiots when it came to driving no matter what state you were in—and stepped into the crosswalk. She'd almost made it to the other side when bright lights came at her, and she did the one thing she'd sworn never to do in an intense situation—something she'd never done before.

She froze.

Strong hands wrapped around her middle and tugged her to the side of the road, and her toe caught on the curb. With an oof, she found herself lying on a hard, male chest, a large hand on her waist, the other on her head as if protecting her, even though she'd been the one to land on him.

"You okay, princess?" the man rumbled. Yes, rumbled—she could feel the sound of his growl of a voice under her hands. She blinked down at him, the adrenaline pounding in her system and making it hard for her to catch her breath. The man beneath her wore a T-shirt with some logo on the front, and from what she could feel beneath her legs, he also wore jeans. His hair was a tad too long, and his beard was scruffy yet oddly sexy. And the ink she caught a glimpse of? Oh, my.

Maybe she'd hit her head when she'd fallen.

"Princess?"

"Don't call me princess." Not the thank you she'd planned on saying, but clearly, she wasn't thinking straight.

He smirked at her, but it wasn't like the ones the men in suits usually gave her. Instead, this one heated her inner thighs, and she really hated him for it.

"If you can snap at me like that, you should be okay. Want me to let you up, or would you rather lie sprawled like this outside? I don't mind it much since having a sexy woman on top of me is never a hardship, but I'm pretty sure there's a rock underneath my back digging into my spine that'll probably hurt in the morning."

Ashlynn scrambled off him, aware that she never scrambled. She was far too put-together for that, but she supposed nearly being run over by a car would do that to any woman. The man put a hand on her hip as she stood with him, and she took a step to the side, needing her space. He might have saved her life, but she didn't know this man, and for some reason, he screamed danger to her instincts. Not his looks since menace could wear suits just as well as ink, but she could still sense something that told her to walk away and never look back.

"Thank you for getting me out of the way," she said stiffly. "I shouldn't have frozen like that." She was so pissed at herself for not reacting quickly enough.

The man in front of her frowned. "No need to thank me, princess. And you didn't freeze. Not really. Everything happened so quickly that I'm pretty sure you could have saved yourself. I just helped it along since that asshole didn't even stop after running that red." He shrugged and stuffed his hands into his pockets. "Anyway, I'd still be sure to check for any bruises." He blinked when she narrowed her eyes at him. "Not meaning me, though I wouldn't say no since you're damn sexy right now with that glare of yours. I meant you, or your doctor or something. You want me to walk you to your hotel just to be sure?"

She shook her head. "I'm fine, but thank you again."

"No problem. Just keep a lookout for rogue cars." He nodded and started back to the hotel behind them. Her hotel.

That was a little too coincidental for her to keep up the icy act she'd perfected. "Are you staying here?" she asked his back.

He turned and raised a sexy brow. Who knew brows could be sexy? "Yeah. You?"

She nodded and licked her lips. It had to be the adrenaline making her want to say what she was about to say. But a girl didn't land on a sexy-as-hell man in the middle of a sidewalk every day.

"Can I buy you a drink?" Her nipples tightened. Adrenaline. Had to be the adrenaline. "To say thank you."

His gaze met hers before he smiled widely—not that smirk he'd given her before, but a bright grin surrounded by a big beard. A smile that once again went straight to the center of her thighs and made her knees weak.

"I'm Jax, princess, and I think a drink sounds perfect."

"Ashlynn. I'm Ashlynn." *And I'm about to do the most reckless thing I've ever done in my life.*

∼

JAX PRESSED HER BACK AGAINST THE HOTEL DOOR, AND SHE MOANED INTO his mouth, not able to get enough of him. He tasted of the beer he'd had when she bought him that drink in the hotel bar, though she couldn't remember what she'd ordered. She'd ignored the blatant stares from those she knew in the bar and would ignore them from here on out if they gave her any shit.

The man currently licking her ear and biting down on the lobe wasn't any of those men. He was hers. Just for this night—and that's exactly how she wanted it.

His beard wasn't as scruffy as she'd thought it would be. Instead, it was soft and slid against her skin in a delicious way that had her thinking about what it would feel like when he ate her out.

Not if. When.

Because she'd damn well get that talented tongue of his between her thighs tonight. That was a given.

"Damn, princess, you can kiss," Jax breathed as he licked up her neck.

Seriously, the man had a talented tongue.

"Call me Ashlynn," she panted, sliding her hands under his shirt so she could feel the heat of his skin beneath her fingertips. "I'm no princess."

He moved to cup her face and kiss her hard, his tongue sliding across hers in an erotic caress. "But you look like a dark-haired version of that icy one from the movie with that song that I'm not going to sing or we'll end up having it stuck in our heads for the next six months."

And now she would be singing it for at least that long. Thank you, Jax.

She raised a brow even as her eyes rolled to the back of her head when he sucked on the place where her shoulder met her neck. "She was a queen, and animated. I don't look like her."

He kissed her hard again on the lips. "You have her eyes. And that attitude."

"Call me Ashlynn if you want to finish what we started here. Because I won't just be a random woman for the evening. Tomorrow, when we part ways and never see each other again, you can think of me as princess all you want. Tonight? Tonight, I'm Ashlynn. Got me?"

Jax grinned this time, and it was a new smile to her. He had so many expressions, and she'd only just met the man. "I can do that, Ashlynn. As long as I get to suck on these tits of yours that have been talking to me since they were pressed against my chest, and as long as I can taste that pussy of yours that has pretty much drenched my thigh since you straddled me. Does that sound like a plan?"

She swallowed hard, her clit throbbing in response to his words. No need to be embarrassed when she could see his arousal just as well as he could feel hers. "As long as you fuck me, too. Because I'm going to need this cock of yours inside me." She reached between them and gripped the long line of him through his jeans. "Does that sound like a plan?"

He growled low in his throat, and she barely kept from pressing her legs together to relieve the ache. "We're wearing too many clothes for this." Then he gripped the back of her hair and tugged, pulling her head back so he could devour her mouth with his.

They pulled on each other's clothes, practically tearing them from their bodies. There was no finesse here, no tease of temptation. This was all need pounding through them as they learned one another.

Ashlynn reached between them, wrapping her fingers around his hard length. Of course, since this had to all be a dream, her fingers couldn't quite touch each other around the base.

Best. Fantasy. Ever.

"Jesus, Ash," Jax growled out. "You're gonna make me blow my load before I even get to taste your cunt. And believe me, I need to get a taste of you." He squeezed his hand over hers with a groan before pulling away. "On your back, Ash. I need you."

"Ashlynn. I'm Ashlynn." She never shortened her name, never wanted to be a pile of burned embers, the remnants of the woman she'd once been.

He kissed her again, and she almost forgot her name entirely. "You're my Ash. My Ashlynn. Just for tonight, remember." He winked at her. "I promise to respect you in the morning."

She laughed at the joke before letting out a little gasp when he tossed her onto the bed behind them. Before she could scold him for throwing her around like a sack of potatoes, she screamed his name as he buried his face between her thighs.

"Jesus," she panted when he lapped at her clit, his beard scraping her skin in such a way that it nearly sent her over the edge of bliss. He sucked and licked until she arched against him, coming so hard that she didn't have the air in her lungs to even call out his name.

Her nipples ached, and her breasts were heavy, so she lazily pinched the nubs between her fingers, still needing relief even while Jax licked up her orgasm.

"Those are mine for the night, Ash."

She blinked up at him in a haze as he leaned down and sucked a nipple into his mouth. "Damn," she breathed.

He chuckled against her, his beard scraping her overly sensitive skin. "You taste fucking sweet. I'm going to enjoy fucking that tight pussy of yours tonight. You still okay with this?" He kissed her breasts, then met her eyes. "Because we can stop if you want to. Just say the word, and I'll walk out of here without another word if this is too much for you."

For some reason, the care in his words made her choke up, and she hated herself for that. This was just meaningless sex, and it would do her well to remember that.

"Thanks for your concern, but I see a very thick and hard cock in front of me that needs to be inside me. So, if you aren't going to get the job done, then I'll just use my fingers on myself and leave you hurting. How does that sound?" Knowing she sounded like a bitch, she added, "Plus, I need to repay the favor, Jax. I want you. Right now. Just you and me for one night, remember?"

He leaned down and kissed her so softly it was just a bare brush of lips. "I remember. Just checking, Ashlynn. Don't want to hurt you."

"You can't hurt me." A lie. It was always a lie, but one she'd perfected.

He met her gaze. "Okay, then. Let me wrap up because I want you safe." He shuffled to his jeans and pulled out his wallet and a condom before locking eyes with her as he rolled the latex down his length. "Ready for me?"

In answer, she cupped her breast and slid her other hand between her legs. "Hurry."

He was on her in a flash, sliding into her in one deep thrust. They both let out a gasp, but he didn't pause. Instead, he pounded into her, edging her closer and closer until all she could feel was him inside and the heat of her need. Then she came with a groan, her inner walls clamping around him, hard.

Jax kissed her fiercely again as he came, his hips moving at such a vigorous pace that she had a feeling they'd both be sore in the morning. She clung to him, her orgasm slowly fading but her need for him anything but.

Yet this was only one night. And when she left in the morning, she'd never look back. She couldn't afford to.

There would be no last names. No numbers exchanged. No promises.

This was all she needed.

At least that's what she told herself.

2

Jax Reagan shouldn't have been surprised when he'd woken up the previous morning to an empty bed, but damned if he wasn't disappointed. He'd had the best sex of his life, and Ashlynn had left him while he slept without a backwards glance. Yeah, what they'd done was spontaneous, and they'd made no promises, but he still thought he'd have been the one to leave.

He'd never had a woman leave him sleeping in bed before, and while he wasn't sure how he felt about that, he knew there was nothing he could do. He didn't live in Atlanta anymore and wasn't going back anytime soon. He'd only been there to finish up a final job for a previous client he hadn't wanted to deal with in the first place. But his old boss still held a few strings Jax hadn't been able to sever until last night. So, Jax had flown from his new home in Denver to Atlanta to finish a tattoo he'd started the year before and hadn't wanted to fly back that night. Instead, he'd used his buddy's points and stayed at a hotel he normally wouldn't have paid for, but his friend had insisted. Jax had figured he'd spend the night watching a movie and sinking into decent sheets.

Instead, he'd sunk into something way more than decent.

Ashlynn. Ash. Princess.

The executive to his ink.

And he'd never see her again.

And what a damn shame that was—and not just because they'd fucked until the wee hours of the morning and he still hadn't gotten enough. No, he liked her. He'd only gotten to know her a little bit, but he liked what he'd seen. And he had to be honest that pulling her out of harm's way the first time he saw her had sent him over the edge just a little bit.

But now he'd have to put her out of his mind because he was back in Denver and working a half shift for the day at his new place of business. Montgomery Ink was a fantastic and popular tattoo shop in the heart of downtown Denver. A brother and sister who seemed to have around forty other family members coming and going from the black and hot pink doors at all hours of the day ran the place.

Austin and Maya treated him right, gave him the hours he needed, and actually cared about the ink they were hired to create.

That meant it was only about a thousand times better than his previous job.

Jax held back a shudder as he opened his sketchbook to work on his next project. Hell, his last place had been a dump where he'd been the best artist there, though that wasn't saying much. He'd made practically no money since his boss, Sammy, took a large cut for himself for one reason or another. Jax figured Sammy was in so deep with the mob and in so much debt that he needed Jax's ink money day in and day out.

And now that Jax wasn't there, Sammy wasn't making the kind of money he used to, and Jax had to deal with the endless texts and phone calls from his old boss.

Sammy wanted him back, and what Sammy wanted, Sammy got.

Only Jax didn't want to go back. He liked Montgomery Ink and enjoyed being out from under the mob's thumb. Luckily, he'd never dealt with them personally, but he'd been close enough to know fear when he scented it on the air.

In fact, he'd had a run-in with Sammy and a few men that Jax didn't really want to identify before he ran into Ashlynn—literally—on the sidewalk. The guys had found him a few blocks down, and Jax had just escaped with a few short words when he'd seen the car coming at Ash down the street. It had scared him shitless to see her in harm's way, and he had reacted without thinking by pulling her toward him. It was something he hoped anyone would have done, but he wasn't so sure these days. Not with the hell he'd been through recently.

He blew out a breath and ran his hands over his beard. But now he was home, and hopefully done with Sammy's Ink and his crew. The only thing he regretted about any of that was that he'd never see Ashlynn again. He didn't know where she lived, but he had a feeling it wasn't in Atlanta since it looked as if she was in the hotel for a conference.

Jax guessed one night of hot sex and unforgettable tastes and touches would have to do him for a while.

It was a damn shame.

"You good over there, or do you need a minute to yourself?" Austin Montgomery teased from over in his booth. The Montgomery Ink setup was similar to the other shops Jax had worked in. There were booths lined up on two sides of the large room, and each artist had his own workspace that he or she could make their own depending on what they needed. A couple of new rooms had been added recently—the privacy room with curtains they used for those who needed it, and a piercing room. There were also three booths in the back for rotating and visiting artists; Jax had one of those spots now. He was still new enough that he worked full-time hours but wasn't a full member of Montgomery Ink yet. He'd have to work up to that like everyone else who worked for the Montgomerys, and if he was lucky, he'd stay for longer than a month or two like some of the people who came and went.

"Jax?" Derek asked from the booth next to him. "You good? You didn't even rise to the bait with Austin's joke."

Jax shook his head and gave Austin a look. "Oh, I heard it. I was just 'taking a minute to myself.'"

His boss rolled his eyes and grinned. "Just don't jerk off in your booth. That'd be hell to clean up. For you. Because there are things friends and co-workers don't need to see or think about. And especially not do."

Jax flipped him off before turning to a blank page in his sketchbook. He had a client coming in who wanted a small dragon on his ribs. The client had been adamant about the size and placement, and Jax hadn't been able to dissuade him. The problem with the level of detail a dragon required was that it looked like crap on a smaller scale—and the rib cage was the worst for things like that. So, Jax would have to figure out a compromise because there was no way he'd give this guy a crappy tattoo.

Finding the balance between a client's needs and what could actually be done was the main part of his job. At least, it was supposed to be a big component. It hadn't always been like that when he worked for Sammy, and he'd hated it. He'd been bogged down by the drama of the shop and everything that came with that. It wasn't until he'd finally gotten his mom and sister out of the city and into Denver that he'd been able to get out from under Sammy's thumb.

Someone nudged his shoulder, and Jax looked up to see Austin frowning at him. "What?" he asked, his voice hoarse. He hadn't slept that well the night before since he was thinking of his time with Ashlynn and he was starting to feel it.

"You look like shit, man," Austin said with a frown. "Go catch a power nap on the couch Maya keeps in the office. It's still early enough that you won't have a walk-in, and you're clear on the books until this afternoon anyway since you planned to take your sister out to lunch."

Jax shook his head, feeling like an idiot for disappointing his new boss. He liked the Montgomerys and didn't want to screw things up because he wasn't sleeping. "I'm good."

Austin sighed. "No, you aren't. Just take a nap. We've all been there. Either that or chug some coffee. Hailey next door knows your order by now, and since that woman seems to have a sixth sense with these things, she's probably already making it."

Sloane, the other tattoo artist in the room, grinned. "My woman knows what she's doing." Hailey and Sloane were married, though Jax didn't know the details of how the sweet woman who owned the café next door had gotten together with the big and brash inked man who worked with Jax, but he figured it was a good story.

"She does make damn fantastic brownies," Jax said, his stomach rumbling. "Think she'd let me have one for breakfast?" He was already up, feeling a little peppier at the thought.

Sloane snorted. "For you? Sure. For me? Not so much. Apparently, at my 'old age' I need to start thinking about my sugar intake."

Austin flipped them both off. "I'm older than both of you, so screw you. But, really, if you don't want the nap, go get some caffeine and maybe get us some, too." He winked. "Hailey will know our orders."

Jax laughed and made his way to the door that connected the two shops. "You really just wanted me to get up and get your coffees."

Austin gave him a mock salute that didn't look out of place with his big beard—the thing rivaled Jax's for sure. "Now you're getting it, young one."

"I'm not that much younger than you," Jax put in. He was in his thirties, just like Austin, and had lived through hell. Then again, he figured the Montgomerys had probably gone through some stuff of their own.

"True, but you're still the newbie in the shop," Austin joked, and Jax flipped the crew off before heading into the café. He couldn't help but smile as he did so, feeling more at home at Montgomery Ink in the few short weeks he'd worked there than the years he'd worked at Sammy's.

A change of scenery was good for me, he thought, just like the move had been needed for the rest of his family.

Now, he just had to make sure he didn't screw it all up.

JAX LOOKED DOWN AT HIS UNTUCKED BLACK BUTTON-DOWN SHIRT OVER jeans and winced. He probably should have changed into slacks or something to pick up his sister, Jessica, from her job so they could grab lunch. She was on her second week of being a paid intern at a major company, and was just now letting him pick her up for lunch. She didn't have much time off and was working crazier hours than he was, but he was so damned proud of her.

She was over ten years his junior and his perfect baby sister. She'd worked her butt off during college and had graduated with not only honors but also a position at a prestigious company in downtown Denver. Considering the state of the economy and the debt people her age were in these days, he knew she was not only talented but also lucky.

How his tattoo artist self had ended up with a corporate-ladder-climbing baby sister, he didn't know, but he figured it hadn't been all him helping her get where she was. Their mother had worked her tail off at two jobs to keep a roof over their heads when he was a kid, so raising Jessica had been a group effort.

At least, that's what his mother said. If you asked him, Jessica had done pretty well on her own with his hovering and glares at anyone who dared come near her. She'd been the first in his family to finish college, and one of the few to even attempt it. No one was going to ruin this for her. Not even him.

But maybe he should have worn something other than jeans. At least there weren't any holes in them, and he was wearing a shirt that covered most of his ink. He'd thought about rolling down his sleeves to cover the tattoos on his forearms, but he figured that would be pushing it.

He looked up at the high-rise building that was one of the many that dotted the Denver skyline and couldn't help but grin. He'd always thought the tall buildings looked so tiny compared to the dramatic backdrop of the Rockies behind them, but standing next to one and knowing Jessica worked inside just made him realize how far she'd come. He couldn't wait to see where she went next.

Still grinning, he walked into the building and ignored the curious looks from people in stuffy suits and ties. He couldn't help but think of Ashlynn at that moment and how out of place he'd looked next to her, but damn if they hadn't burned up the sheets once they stripped off the clothes that set them apart.

Jessica had promised to meet him in the lobby so he didn't have to go up to her floor. Most likely so he wouldn't embarrass her—not because of how he looked, but because, hey, he was her big brother, and it was sort of his job. He stuffed his hands into his pockets and waited until he heard the sound of stilettos on tile.

Only he knew that sound, and it wasn't from his little sister.

Hair rising on the back of his neck, he turned, his smirk in place. Well, hell, it seemed today might just be his lucky day.

"Ashlynn."

3

Ashlynn had to be seeing things because there was no way her one-night stand could be standing in the middle of her company's front lobby. She'd left Jax sleeping in his Atlanta hotel room bed, all naked and roughed up from their sexcapades the night before, and she hadn't looked back.

Okay, that was a total lie since he'd been the primary focus of her thoughts and dreams since she walked out of that room, but she'd been doing a pretty darn good job of lying to herself since then.

Now that was all out the window because, dear God, the man was sex on a stick.

Inked and bearded sex on a stick.

And right in front of her.

"Did you follow me?" The words came out as a whispered snap, and she held back a wince. She hadn't known what she planned to say if she ever saw him again, but those particular words weren't the right ones. Not when Jax's smirk fell off his face, and his eyes narrowed at her.

"I was going to say it was damn good to see you, but maybe I should have asked if you were following me." He ran a hand over his beard, and Ashlynn wanted to cover her face with her hands.

She wasn't handling this right and was beyond flustered. Ashlynn

Kelly did not get flustered. She was the one who made others quake in their boots. She was always the one in control.

That's what made Jax so dangerous.

And she didn't even know his last name.

She raised her chin and did her best to keep from drawing attention to herself. She didn't need gossip within her company about her, not if she wanted to keep doing what she was.

"I didn't follow you," she said softly. "I work here, Jax. I was just surprised to see you. What are you doing here?"

"Here as in Denver? I live here. Here as in this building? My little sister is an intern, and I'm taking her to lunch." He frowned at her. "Small world," he whispered.

She swallowed hard, remembering the way the heat of his whispered words felt against her skin. She couldn't let him do this to her, not here. Not now. Maybe not ever. He was supposed to be her one-night stand. Then something he'd said clicked.

"Your sister works here? She's an intern?" Ashlynn tried to remember every face that was hired, but they'd just gone through a few new interns, and she hadn't met everyone yet. Not all the new hires worked under her, but many did, and if one was related to Jax…well, it might not be the best idea to keep talking with him.

Jax's smile went soft as he spoke of his sister. "Yeah, just started a couple of weeks ago. We're proud."

"We?" she blurted and could have slapped herself.

Jax snorted. "Our mom. And me. Jessica's a bit younger than I am, so I feel like I helped raise her, even though she pretty much did most things on her own. She's a go-getter that way."

Ashlynn tried to keep her brain on the conversation, but she kept flashing back to her night with Jax. It had been the single most impulsive thing she'd ever done in her life, and now he was here, right in front of her, as if fate were taunting her decisions.

"Jax?"

Ashlynn turned to see a young brunette with a cautious smile walk up to them. She wore a nice suit with a skirt and sensible heels that still had a bit of fashion to them. Her hair was up in a cute bun at the base of her neck, and Ashlynn didn't see a hint of ink or piercings anywhere except her small hoop earrings. If it weren't for the eyes, Ashlynn wouldn't have known that Jessica and Jax were siblings, but the eyes spoke volumes.

She turned as Jax smiled widely at his sister. "There you are, runt," he said with that typical big brother attitude as he held out his arms.

Jessica glanced at Ashlynn before rolling her eyes and going in for a hug. Jax kissed his little sister's forehead, giving her a tight squeeze before he pulled back and shook his head.

"You grew up."

Jessica sighed. "You saw me four days ago." She turned and held out her hand. "Hi, I'm Jessica Reagan."

Ashlynn took the younger woman's hand and gave it a quick shake. "Nice to meet you. I'm Ashlynn Kelly. I don't think we've met, correct?"

Jessica shook her head. "No, I'm in another department, but I've seen you on my floor. I think you were out of town at a conference this past week when introductions were made."

That made sense, and Ashlynn nodded. Of course, she'd met Jax while at that conference and then had sweaty, filthy sex with the man, so things were just a tad more complicated than the other woman knew.

Jessica looked between Jax and Ashlynn with a weird look on her face, as if she was dying to ask how they knew each other but was holding back by only the barest of threads.

Ashlynn cleared her throat, needing to get out of this situation quickly before she couldn't look at herself in the morning. "Have fun at your lunch. I have a meeting." She gave Jessica a nod before barely glancing at Jax—she wasn't sure what she would do if she stared at him for too long.

Jax just gave her a knowing smile before nodding. "Enjoy your day," he whispered, and Ashlynn took off. She didn't run toward the elevator, but it was damn close. She heard Jessica whisper quickly to her brother and had a feeling it was about her, so she kept her chin up and did her best to ignore it.

Ashlynn would not see Jax again. There was just no way it could work, and she'd already told herself she didn't have time for men. Today was just a coincidence. Nothing more.

And if she kept telling herself that, she just might believe it.

A few hours later, most of the rest of the company had gone home, and Ashlynn had just watched a spectacular sunset from her corner office. Of course, she'd merely glanced at it since she had around four hundred things left to do on her checklist, but she'd noticed it, which was far better than most days.

Yes, she was a workaholic, but at least she was aware of it—something that couldn't be said for most of her friends and coworkers.

And though, yes, her mind was on work and finalizing the deal she'd made in Atlanta, that wasn't the only thing she was thinking about. No, it was the other event that had happened in Georgia that occupied far more of her thoughts than was healthy.

Jax.

He lived in Denver.

He'd been in her building that afternoon.

His sister worked with her.

And though she'd left him in the lobby without a look back, she had a feeling that wasn't the end—no matter how much trouble doing anything more would be.

With a sigh, she rubbed the back of her neck and frowned at the numbers in front of her. If they were starting to blur this early in her evening of work, she should probably go home and eat something so she could work some more. She'd been smart that morning since she hadn't been able to sleep the night before—thanks to naked dreams of Jax and that beard of his—and had put some food in her Crock-Pot. When she got home, she'd have a perfect chicken, potato, and veggie medley waiting for her.

At that thought, her stomach grumbled, and she saved her file before closing out of her programs. Screw it. Between thoughts of food and Jax, she couldn't focus.

She might as well get one of those things since she wouldn't be having Jax tonight.

Or ever, she reminded herself. She wouldn't be having Jax ever.

"Knock, knock, princess."

Her head shot up so quickly she almost fell back in her chair. "Jax?" she breathed, then cleared her throat. "What are you doing here? How did you get into my office?" And why did she keep accusing him of things when he flustered her?

Jax tilted his head, and his hair fell over his eyes. "It's late, and there aren't that many people in the building. Your assistant, Neil, let me in when I told him who I was." He raised a brow. "The guy seemed to grin at the introduction before letting me back on his way out."

She was going to kill her assistant—well, not really because he saved her life daily, but still. She'd deny him his favorite creamer or something. She hadn't meant to blurt out what she'd done with Jax in Atlanta, but she could never hide things from Neil—not when it mattered. The man seemed to be a matchmaking fiend, and it would annoy her, except he was happy with not one but two people—a man and a woman—in his triad. He had his happily ever after and wanted Ashlynn to have one, too.

Only she didn't have time for that.

"Neil is fired," she said simply and held back a laugh at Jax's eye roll. His sister had done the same thing earlier, and she couldn't help but think how alike they looked with that action.

"Sure, Ash, sure."

She swallowed hard and finished packing up her purse to give herself something to do with her hands. "Why are you here, Jax?"

He moved closer, and she held back a shiver as she looked down at his hands. Those hands had touched her, caressed her, had made her come with just a brush of calloused fingertips on her skin.

And she still didn't know his last name. Or his profession. She knew nothing about him, and yet here he was, in her office, in her hometown...and she didn't know what came next.

"I'm here because you are; because no matter what we said back in Atlanta, there was something between us. And I've got to think, an opportunity like this? Where we're together again out of all the places we could be? We can't let this chance pass us by."

She licked her lips, her breath shaky. "Why are you here, Jax?" she repeated. "What do you want from me?"

He was closer now, so close she could feel the heat of him on her skin. He should have looked so out of place in her high-rise office, yet for some reason, he seemed like he belonged. She wasn't sure what to think about that.

"I want you," he said simply. "I didn't have enough of you that night, and I want more of you now. Anything you can give, Ash. Anything."

She swallowed hard and tried to get her emotions under control. "You didn't know who I was when you saw me on the street," she whispered. "Didn't know I'd be here today."

He kissed her softly, just a brush of lips. "I want to get to know you, Ash. Let me take you out to dinner, let me see who the real Ash is. You can see who I am, too."

She shook her head. "I..."

"Ash...don't say no. I'll listen if you do, but I don't want you to say no."

"I meant to say no because I don't want to go out. I have food in my Crock-Pot at home." She winced at that, and he grinned.

"My executive cooking in a Crock-Pot? That's perfect. Just tells me you know your time is valuable. So...is there enough for two?"

She let out a soft laugh. "Yeah, Jax, there should be enough food for you. I have no idea what I'm doing, but I just hope it's the right thing."

He kissed her. "I hope it's right, too, because it feels right. But if we're wrong? Then we'll be wrong together. Okay?"

She leaned forward and ran her hand through his beard. "Okay."

"So, do you like working at Montgomery Ink?" she asked as they did dishes together. It was weird having a man in her space and sharing chores with him, but not as weird as it could have been if it were anyone other than Jax. For some reason, he just fit. That probably should have worried her more than it did, but at the moment, she'd just go with the flow—something she didn't normally do.

Jax leaned against the front of the sink and nodded. "It's a good fit, I think. I like my co-workers and the clients. Sure, there are still some people who come in and annoy me, but that's any job."

Ashlynn nodded. "Tell me about it."

"And you like being a CFO? I don't know your business day in and out, but I know enough to understand you're a big deal." He winked. "A sexy big deal, but I'll refrain from saying that in front of others if you want."

She laughed then, wondering how she could be so at ease with someone she barely knew. Yes, she knew Jax intimately, but she was only starting to know the man beneath the ink—and she liked him.

"I love my job," she answered once she stopped laughing, though she still had a smile on her face. "I work too hard, and I know that I should scale back and delegate, but I love what I do so much that it's sometimes hard."

"If you hated it, it would be another matter, no? Working at a place you hate drains you, makes you regret the decisions you make, even if they were the only ones you could."

There was something in his voice that made her pause, and she set her towel down on the counter. "Jax?"

He shook his head. "I worked for some bad people in Atlanta. Didn't mean to, but my old boss was a crook who had the worst kinds of connections. Once I could get out, though, I did. I was a stupid kid who needed a job and had to stay because I thought I owed him." He turned to her then, and they stood face to face. "I was an idiot, but I'm not now. I work with great people and love my job. I'm staying in Denver long-term and don't plan on going back to any place that treats me like shit or to people who think they own me." He shrugged, and she knew there was more to his story.

"You can tell me more if you want," she said softly. "You're a good man, Jax. You saved my life when you could have just stood back and protected yours. Plus, any man who makes sure his partner comes at least twice before he does is a good guy in my book." She winked as she said it, and Jax chuckled.

"Any man who doesn't make his partner come like that isn't a man I want to know." He reached forward and brushed his knuckle along her jaw. "I'm glad we found each other again, Ash."

She swallowed hard, forcing herself not to move into his touch. "Me, too."

"Now I can leave after I kiss you if you want, and we can take this slow. But, Ash? I want to taste you again. And if you want me, I'll make sure you come at least twice before I sink into you again."

She chuckled with him and let herself lean closer. "I don't want you to leave. I don't know what we're doing, but I don't want it to end."

He brushed his lips over hers, his beard softly scratching her chin in the best way possible—hell, she could get used to that. "Let me take you to the bedroom, princess."

She knew she was probably making a mistake, but she did the only thing she could at that moment. She went up on her tiptoes since she'd taken off her heels when they walked in and kissed him hard in answer.

He groaned and hoisted her, rucking up her skirt around her thighs so she could wrap her legs around his waist. She knew she'd probably torn a seam, but damn if she cared right then. She'd have thought being with him in her home would be different, that it wouldn't feel quite the same as when she'd been playing with fire and the unknown in Atlanta.

She would have been wrong.

Since the layout of her place wasn't that hard to figure out, Jax found her bedroom in no time. He sucked on her neck as he lowered her to the bed, her body arching into him, craving him. Somehow, they'd twisted so she was on her back and they kept their mouths on each other even as they stripped off their clothes, leaving them naked and twined together, his rigid cock pressed hard against her belly.

"I need you," she panted. She'd never needed anyone before, but right then, she had to have Jax inside her, over her, with her.

He smiled sleepily even as his eyes burned with desire. "Then you can have me." His fingers trailed over her spine before resting on her butt to give it a squeeze. "You're fucking beautiful, Ash. Inside and out."

She ducked her head, a blush heating her skin. "Jax."

He rolled them over once more and reached between them, sliding his fingers over her folds. "You're wet for me."

"That seems to be a perpetual problem when I'm around you," she teased, her breath going choppy when he circled her clit with his thumb.

"That's good to hear," he growled before sliding down her body and pressing his mouth against her.

She let out a gasp as he licked and sucked, using his fingers in unison with that tongue of his. And when he curved his fingers in just the right way, she came, her body shaking as she called out his name. Her eyes were still closed as she came down from her orgasm when he turned her over onto her belly, and she heard the sound of a condom wrapper.

"I'm going to fuck you just like this, princess. With your legs close together and your ass sticking up just so. You ready for me?"

In answer, she wiggled her hips, and he groaned before giving her a quick slap. "Jax."

"Ash," he panted before slowly sliding into her. He stretched her just right, the angle just different enough that he went deeper than he had before and yet, because her legs were squeezed together, she knew her inner walls were tightening even more.

"Perfection," he growled, his hand on her hip as he thrust in and out of her. "I could stay inside you forever."

Forever.

That should have scared her since she'd only just met the man, but for some reason, she didn't want to run away in fear. Forever was just a word, after all. They were only having fun. Then she came around him, and he shouted her name, and all thoughts of whatever they were, of what they could be, fled her mind in a rush of sweet ecstasy.

Soon, she found herself wrapped around him, her body shaking against his. "Wow."

He chuckled against her temple. "Wow, indeed." His hands ran over her body lazily, as if he couldn't help but touch her. She liked it—maybe a little too much.

She was about to say something when his phone beeped from the floor, and he cursed. "What is it?"

He shook his head. "I know that tone. Give me a sec." He kissed her hard before moving to get off the bed. He walked naked around the edge of the mattress and bent over to pick up his cell from where he'd dropped it. His brows furrowed as he read the screen, and she sat up, pulling the throw that had been on top of the bed over her body so she wouldn't end up sitting there naked and confused.

"What is it?" she asked, not sure what to feel, what to think. They'd just had sex again, and yet she knew it hadn't been just sex—not when she'd started to feel something she probably shouldn't. But she had no idea what he was feeling, and now she wasn't sure she would get to find out.

"I need to go," he said gruffly as he stuffed his legs into his boxer briefs and then jeans. "I'm sorry, princess."

She could practically feel the icy exterior she wore like a shield slide over her at that moment. "I understand."

He cursed under his breath and walked to her, cupping her face with his hand before kissing her hard. "No, you don't, and I'm sorry for that. I'm going to write my number on that whiteboard I saw on your fridge, but then I need to head out and deal with something. But I don't want to end things. I'm not leaving for good. Got me, Ash?"

"If you need to go, then go. It's not like we're serious." She knew she was just saying these things because she was scared, but she still hated the words that came out of her mouth. "It's no big deal."

He kissed her again, running his hand over her jaw. "Yeah, it is. And I'm sorry I have to leave. But I want to see you again."

"We'll see," she said honestly. Because she wasn't sure. She'd told herself she didn't have time for a man, and she didn't. She'd had work that needed to be done when she came home but hadn't done it because she was spending time with Jax. He had his own complications and life, and she wasn't sure how she fit into it all. A relationship wasn't a good idea, and if she were smart, she wouldn't look at his phone number when he left, and she'd push Jax from her thoughts altogether.

And though she was an intelligent woman, she wasn't sure she could be smart in this.

"Goodbye, Ash," he whispered. "But not forever."

She pressed her lips together and nodded, confused and unsure about what to do. Jax sighed and picked up the rest of his things before leaving her in her bedroom, naked, sated, and alone.

It didn't make sense that she was so confused by this man. She barely knew him. The problem was, she liked the things she did know. A lot. The safe thing to do would be to stay away from Jax and any complications that came from a relationship with him.

So why did Ashlynn want to dance with danger instead?

4

Jax wanted to throw his phone at the wall and watch it shatter, but not only did he not have the money for that, he knew it wouldn't solve anything. Sammy had been texting him threats since the night before when Jax was with Ashlynn and hadn't stopped. He'd thought he left all that behind in Atlanta, but he should have known Sammy would never let go.

Jax was well and truly fucked.

Sammy was still in Atlanta, thankfully, but he was hurting for money and threatening to hurt Jessica if Jax didn't come back to the shop and work. It didn't make any fucking sense; there were other tattoo artists in the damn city, but no one was stupid enough to work for Sammy anymore, and that meant Jax's old boss was in deep shit with the mob.

The damn mob.

Jax didn't know how his life had come to this, but he was done with it. He'd left his old home behind and had thought he'd start a new life out here, but the past kept coming back for him. It had even interrupted his time with Ashlynn, and he hated himself for it. He'd never forget the insecurity he saw on her face when he left. They hadn't made any real promises to each other, but damn if he didn't want to make them to her. He liked her, wanted her, and saw himself with her beyond a few short hours in bed.

He just hoped she saw the same in him. Yet with all the things he had going on in his life right now, he wasn't sure he'd be good for her. He was just a tattoo artist with a crap past, and she was the brilliance behind a multimillion-dollar company with a future so bright it was almost startling.

They weren't compatible on paper, yet Jax had felt something different when he was with her.

He just hoped she would call.

She had to call, damn it.

"Jax, do you have that other notebook you were using?" Austin asked from his station. "You wanted to show me that dragon, right?" The other man looked tired, but considering he'd had his own kids plus a few of his nieces and nephews over for the night so the rest of the adults could have a night out, Jax didn't blame the guy for looking like he needed four cups of coffee.

Jax rolled his shoulders and looked down at the stack of books in front of him before cursing. "Must have left it in my car. I'll go out and get it." Austin didn't need to double-check his work, but Jax had wanted the advice anyway since it wasn't the easiest design.

"You doing okay today?" Sloane asked.

"Yeah, you've seemed in your own world this morning," Derek added from Sloane's side.

Jax shook his head. "Some shit from my old shop keeps coming back, but I'm ignoring it. Hopefully, it will go away."

Austin raised a brow. "Think that'll actually work?"

Jax shrugged. "Not sure what else to do so, yeah, it better work." He grabbed his keys and lifted his chin towards the other guys. "I'll be right back with that notebook." Yeah, he was changing the subject, sue him. He didn't know what to say anyway.

He'd just made it out of the back door and into the private parking lot for Montgomery Ink employees and family when large hands gripped his shoulders and slammed him into the brick wall of the tattoo shop.

"Shit," he grunted, trying to fight off his attackers. His keys fell from his hands, and he kicked out, but he was no match for three large men who looked to be bruisers rather than mere muggers. "What the hell?"

"Sammy owes the boss money, asshole, and since he's not paying, you will," the biggest one growled. Though biggest was a bit of a misnomer since they were each huge. It wasn't until Jax saw the glint of a knife in one of the man's hands that he froze.

Jesus Christ, this couldn't be happening.

"I don't work for Sammy anymore," Jax said calmly—or at least as calmly as he could considering he was being held at knifepoint by three goons.

"He says differently. He tells us that you're moonlighting and not paying him so we can't get our cut."

That goddamn bastard. Jax didn't say that aloud, but he screamed it in his head. He just prayed that these guys were only focusing on him, though, and not his family. Icy dread snaked down his spine at the thought of his mother or Jessica or Ash getting hurt because of his old boss.

"I don't work for him anymore. If you want your money, then get it from him. He's the one who works with y'all." Jax never had, and never would.

"Maybe we should make an example of you anyway," one of the guys whispered. "Teach Sammy a lesson."

Jax swallowed hard, trying to keep cool. "Sammy doesn't give a shit about me. You won't be getting your money at all if you hurt me. Find Sammy and get what you're owed. I'm not that man." He'd never been, no matter how hard his old life had tried to make him be.

The main goon tilted his head and studied him. "You know... Sammy has been flapping his gums for a while now. Maybe we should pay him another visit."

Shit.

"Is there a problem out here?" Austin asked from right outside the door, Sloane and Derek right beside him.

The goons dropped Jax quickly, the knife sliding back into whatever pocket it had come out of. One day, the adrenaline might dissipate from his system, but Jax didn't think that day would be anytime soon.

"We're just talking to our old friend out here," the main goon said smoothly.

"Seems like he doesn't want to be talked to," Sloane said just as simply. Jax's three friends didn't move, but they looked damn intimidating with all their ink and muscle. Things couldn't escalate, though. Jax couldn't let it because his friends weren't armed, but he had a feeling all the guys from Atlanta were.

The main guy held up his hands. "We were just heading out." He looked over at Jax. "Stay out of trouble."

Jax gave them a tight nod, his body as tense as ever, but as the guys from his past walked away, he had an odd feeling that they might be leaving for good. They'd threatened him, sure, but they hadn't actually hurt him like they could have. And, hell, they had to know by now that he didn't have a damn thing for them. He'd never been part of that business and had made damn sure that everyone knew that. He just hoped that would be enough. As for Sammy? Well, Sammy had made his own mess and would have to deal with the consequences.

Jax was done. He held back a wince as he turned to Sloane, Austin, and Derek. Well, he hoped he wasn't done completely because he hadn't meant for anyone to know exactly what he'd gone through before he came to Denver.

"I have a friend I'm going to call to make sure they don't come back," Sloane said softly before heading back into the shop, and Jax's eyes widened.

Austin shrugged. "We have friends in good places sometimes. Now get that damn notebook and come back inside. We'll talk about what happened later with Maya because if she hears about this from anyone else, there'll be hell to pay."

Jax would have laughed, but he didn't have it in him at the moment. Maya was a force to be reckoned with, and you did not mess with Austin's sister. That was probably why Jax liked her so much.

"Okay."

"We'll stay out here with you," Derek added. "Just in case."

Jax blew out a breath. "Okay." He cleared his throat. "Thank you."

In answer, Austin raised his chin, and Jax moved quickly to his car, picking up his keys from the gravel on the way. He wasn't shaking, but he was damned close. He could have died just then, and it wouldn't have been his fault. Yet, in the end, it wouldn't have mattered—not when it came to Sammy's problems.

By the time he made it back inside the shop, he was ready to sit down and find something cool to drink to help his parched tongue. What he hadn't been expecting to see was anyone in his booth.

He damn sure wasn't expecting Ashlynn in her sexy-as-hell high heels and stone grey skirt and jacket.

"Ash?"

She turned at the sound of his voice and widened her eyes. "Jax. Are you okay?" She rushed to him and cupped his face. "You have a cut here." Her other hand hovered over his jaw, and he winced. He hadn't felt it until she pointed it out and now it stung, but he ignored it since she was here and touching him.

"I'll be okay," he whispered, aware that the others were staring at him, but Jax didn't want to go outside to talk to her privately, not with what had just happened.

She bit her lip, looking unsure. "If you say so."

"What are you doing here, Ash?" he asked softly. "Not that I don't love seeing you."

"I wanted to see you," she whispered. "I didn't like how we left things last night. I was a little confused, and heck, I'm still a little confused, but I shouldn't have been so cold when you said you had to go."

He cupped her face then, loving the softness of her skin under his touch. "You weren't cold." She'd been scared, probably because they were moving so fast, and he'd understood. "I'm glad you're here."

She smiled then. "I could have called, but I wanted to see you." She cleared her throat. "So...want to go get lunch?"

He laughed then. "Lunch I can do."

"And I want to get to know you more. Not just...you know." She blushed, and Jax fell a little for her then. He wasn't ready to fall completely, but with this woman, he knew he eventually could. They needed time together, and then...well, then they'd learn each other even more.

"That sounds like a plan, princess." He kissed her softly. "You okay with the fact that I'm a tattoo artist with no degree or fancy car?" He winked. "I have a bike that you'd look fucking sexy on, though."

She rolled her eyes. "You okay that I'm kind of icy sometimes and work long hours?"

"I can work with that," he whispered before kissing her hard, pulling her so close that he knew his dick pressed into her even through all their layers of clothing. Ashlynn did that to him with a mere glance, and he loved it.

"Awww."

Jax didn't know which man had said it or if it was more than one of them, so he just flipped off the room even as he kept his lips on Ash.

Ashlynn pushed away and ducked under his chin. "I forgot we weren't alone."

He kissed the top of her head. "I like that you forgot."

She pulled away and frowned. "You're going to tell me why you're cut, though."

It wasn't a question, and he didn't mind. "Tonight. I promise. I'll tell you everything."

"Good," she said with a smile, and he kissed her again.

"I could get used to this," she murmured against his lips.

"Yeah? Me, too."

He kissed her once more.

He hadn't planned on Ashlynn in his life. Hell, he hadn't intended anything but freedom. But now that he had his woman, his executive in his arms, he knew he didn't mind the surprise.

Ashlynn was the best shock of his life.

And he couldn't wait to find out more.

ABOUT CARRIE ANN RYAN

Carrie Ann Ryan is the New York Times and USA Today bestselling author of contemporary and paranormal romance. Her works include the Montgomery Ink, Redwood Pack, Talon Pack, and Gallagher Brothers series, which have sold over 2.0 million books worldwide. She started writing while in graduate school for her advanced degree in chemistry and hasn't stopped since. Carrie Ann has written over fifty novels and novellas with more in the works. When she's not writing about bearded tattooed men or alpha wolves that need to find their mates, she's reading as much as she can and exploring the world of baking and gourmet cooking.

To be notified of new releases or sales,
join Carrie Ann Ryan's Mailing List: www.bit.ly/CARyanNewsletter
Connect with Carrie Ann online
Facebook: www.facebook.com/CarrieAnnRyanAuthor
Instagram: www.instagram.com/CarrieAnnRyanAuthor
Visit Carrie Ann at www.CarrieAnnRyan.com!